Light Bird's Song

a novel of fear, love, and longing

Tim,
You have always been dear to me.
Sydney Tooman Betts

Sydney Tooman Betts

Copyright © 2013 by Sydney Tooman Betts. All rights reserved.

No part of this book may be reproduced, stored in a retrieval system or transmitted by any means without the written permission of the author.

ISBN 13: 978-1-7329079-1-1 Softback

Cover Sketch of Light Bird by Anita Thubakabra Mihalyi
Oak Tree by the Columbia River cover photo by Don Paulson

To Jesus,

my savior and friend,

&

to my loving daughter,

who inspired this heroine

The People of the Book
By Sydney Tooman Betts

A River Too Deep
A novel of loss, love, and faithfulness

Light Bird's Song
A novel of fear, love, and longing

Straight Flies the Arrow
A novel of love, loyalty, and wonder

Chapter 1

Near the end of the Moon of Opening Buds

1839

PACING WOLF RESTLESSLY shifted atop a small rise, just beyond the range of a dozing sentinel's arrows. Hidden in the tall, coarse grass beneath the canopy of an ancient crabapple tree, he took in the size and number of his enemies' lodges. He was eager to exact his vengeance. The grass felt prickly and cold, even through his deerskin shirt; and his breath, swirling up as he warmed his fingers, clung damply to his high cheekbones.

Wiping them irritably, he spied a faint pale wisp drifting aloft above a smoke-hole and tilted up the edges of his mouth. He would not need to wait much longer. Hidden within the layers of a lodge-cover, a woman was coaxing her dying embers to flame. Her dwelling awoke like a living thing, glowing welcomingly against the chilly night sky.

The earth had been like her this year: stirring early to arouse all that depended on her care. Her unseasonable warmth had helped him cover twice the ground he could have in snow and kept the moccasin impressions he followed fresh. All the while he tracked them along the riverbank, he had thought their wearer's carelessness odd; and when they met the hoof prints of a small war party, also undisguised, he began to grow suspicious.

They led me to this village too easily, Pacing Wolf concluded. *This warrior is overconfident or he intends to incite us.*

The surrounding lodges looked flat, like black peaked mountains painted across an unbleached buffalo hide, but as the first shoots of light streaked purple across the horizon, they began to take on a conical shape. A nearby bird greeted the morning, and a sniffing dog poked its nose through cold ashes from last evening's cook-fire. Mothers would soon search their larders for food, and daughters would scavenge firewood below trees that sprang, like the one that hid him, from the bottom of the hill on which he lay.

Before finishing the thought, Pacing Wolf's patience was rewarded. Young women streamed from their nests like geese eager for a morning swim, their dark, bobbing heads disproportionately small above their bulky buffalo robes. As the first crossed the meadow and commenced her chore, he supposed she was the village beauty. The scant light obscured her features but did nothing to disguise the pride in her bearing. Greedily grabbing the most useful branches, she bundled them on her back before the next girl reached the tree line. He suspected she did the same with the choicest ganders, securing their desire before others gained a glance. His dead woman had been like her—arousing the ardor of all who confused soft, well-placed flesh with a tender heart.

I will snatch this haughty goose, he sneered, *and enjoy humbling her.*

As a light peal of laughter interrupted his thoughts, he shifted to a thinner spot between the sprouting branches. Beside a lodge on the village-edge, a newly lit cook-fire cast light on a latecomer. His glance passed over her quickly, doubting such a pleasant sound had arisen from a silver-haired grandmother's throat, but as he followed the old woman's lively gestures, an attentive young companion stepped into the fire's glow. She reminded him of a doe, her neck slender and long, and as she laughed at the old woman's tale, her features shone with affection.

While he watched her crossing the meadow, her graceful form stirred his senses, but as she rummaged among the trees, he began to question her intelligence. She wove in and out of them slowly, brushing pink buds from the thickest branches and then passing them over for shorter, thinner twigs.

The old one's sight has dimmed, he concluded, noting the doe's frequent backward glances. *She leaves the better kindling for the grandmother. I will snatch her instead.*

Glancing toward the lodges, he realized he must act swiftly. Taller, more menacing shadows had begun stirring beneath the large, softly illumined hides; but as he imagined the terror that would fill the graceful doe's eyes, his gut twisted sharply. He turned to reconsider the haughty goose, but a change in her posture guided his gaze back across the field. Outlined by another cook-fire, three warriors stood staring hard in his direction.

Pacing Wolf unsheathed his knife and inched back beneath the plentifully budding branches, but though the warriors sauntered directly toward his tree, the gaggle held their attention. Glancing quickly at the haughty goose, he watched her tilt her chin away as if she thought herself above these ganders' notice. The change in her hips declared otherwise. He followed their generous sway until a sudden, nearby movement diverted his attention.

The silver-headed storyteller had stumbled over the roots of his tree and was rocking back and forth amidst her scattered sticks. Tossing down her bundle, the doe rushed to the old woman's side—a mere leap from Pacing Wolf's hiding place—and her smooth face, awash with tender concern, decided his course. She looked markedly younger than he had previously thought, and while he admired the self-possession that lent her several summers, he resolved to leave her as she was.

While the doe was gently probing the grandmother's swelling ankle, the silly geese fluttered after every insignificant twig that placed them in the three ganders' paths. The youngest man responded like a woman sowing kernels, randomly tossing smiles in hope that one might land on fertile ground. His stockier friend showed more discrimination: he aimed only for the haughty goose, though she never looked in his direction. Her eyes were fixed on their handsome companion, as tall as one of Pacing Wolf's own people.

As she offered him a beguiling smile his lips responded smugly, but he swaggered past her to the storyteller and the doe. Towering above them, he blocked the faint light; and when the doe refused to look up, he gouged her with his toe.

Pacing Wolf hardened his mouth into a rigid line. *What right does this man have to her? He would crush her like a buffalo trampling flowers in the grass! Let him pursue the haughty goose—her affection will prove shallow, stingily bestowed and paid for unendingly.*

As he watched the doe's reaction, his lips softened. She continued to examine the ankle, as though bumped by a mere fly, then hoisted the old woman onto her feet and helped her hobble toward the lodges. The tall gander glowered sullenly after them, but the doe never cast him the slightest glance.

The two other ganders lay back against the hillside, unaware the tree above them hid an enemy; and, while they evaluated the lingering geese, Pacing Wolf inspected their regalia. He would not take a life without just cause, but knowing their strengths would provide an advantage if they discovered his presence.

The youngest wore nothing to denote a single act of bravery; he was of no consequence. Pacing Wolf would make sport by touching him lightly with a bare hand. The stocky warrior's crown boasted several feathers angled to proclaim different feats. Pacing Wolf decided to tap him with his coup-stick. He would not be satisfied, however, to gain an unacknowledged victory against the tall gander. In addition to feathers, the man's leggings boasted red painted stripes—awarded only for drawing enemy blood.

I will cut the quiver from his back.

While perusing its feathered contents, he felt an unexpected ripple of excitement. The quiver's arrows matched the two he had broken from his dead woman's throat. Pulling the jagged, blood-soaked shafts from his pouch, he methodically turned them over. His uncles had taught him the subtle differences between each enemy's arrows as soon as he could run. These were yellow on one side and blue on the other, characteristic of this tribe. They also bore distinctive marks to distinguish them from those of his clansmen. If the tall gander had wished to hide his identity, he would have used a knife.

As the youngest man watched the haughty goose retreat, he let out a deep sigh. "I would give many horses to have that one warm my robes at night."

"You are a fool," scoffed his tall companion. "Wait until the Allies assemble this summer. I will pull her from the Dance of Untouched Women, and her father will pay you to take her."

The young man spat, though whether he was offended for the haughty goose or himself, Pacing Wolf could not tell. "You hunger after Light Bird like a vulture for a wolf pack's scraps. Unless you go down into the water, Preying Eagle will never yield her."

Light Bird. Pacing Wolf rolled her name over in his mind. *It does not suit her. She does not chirp or flit about.*

What her father had required of the tall gander was unclear. The man looked as if he bathed, but though Pacing Wolf's language and the one spoken by this enemy had sprouted from a common root, time had altered many words. It did not matter; his thoughts had already left the doe and turned from sport to vengeance. Arrows would suffice for the shorter two ganders. He killed them only out of necessity; but he convulsively gripped his ax handle, eager to split the murderer's chest.

"When the sun reaches the lower branches," the tall man continued, "we leave for our own village and take Light Bird with us.

"No," scowled his stocky cousin. "Her father and uncles are too strong, and what of Straight Arrows and her other brothers?"

Ignoring his protest, the tall man rose to his feet. "I go to warn Old Many Feathers that the Raven-Enemy are heading this way. While the elders make their war council, I will slip away to get her. Ready the horses and bring them here."

"Do not discount her women-folk," the stocky warrior cautioned. "They will beset you like a pecking flock of blue jays."

"What can a lame, half-sighted old woman do?"

"Turn aside," pleaded the youngest. "Would you break the alliance between our bands?"

The tall suitor only set his handsome jaw, but the stocky one grimly shook his head. "Walks-Behind-Them is right. This band is large and the Creator favors them."

"Pah!" spat the suitor. "The Creator does not live in a book. The Raven-Enemy possess many lodges—too many to count. When the sun next awakens, they will turn this village to ash and smoke."

"And if they do not?" asked the stocky one, getting up on his feet.

"Preying Eagle will accept my horses or I will pull his daughter also from the untouched dancers and proclaim her impure before the assembly."

"No one will believe you," replied the one they called Walks-Behind-Them, rising also from the grassy hill.

"They will when her waist begins to thicken."

Walks-Behind-Them frowned. "Take the other woman. Her face is more pleasing and she will come with us gladly."

"You know nothing," replied the handsome man, twisting his face into an ugly sneer. "Her mother is like that pony you ride: she casts only daughters. Light Bird's women-folk yield sons—many, and all hearty—and revere their husbands like they do their white man's god."

"Preying Eagle will not rest until he deals with you justly," warned his thickset cousin, "and we also will be caught in his wrath."

"You heard what they read in their book last night. 'If a warrior steals your hunting shirt, give him your buffalo robe also.'[1] Too bad she lacks a pretty sister!"

"If you want her so badly," asked the youngest, "why not do as her father requires?"

The tall suitor turned on him and snarled, "I am Wild Dog. I do my own bidding! Three summers I have waited like a whelp near her cook-pot. I will wait no longer!"

"Wild Dog." The syllables slid distastefully off Pacing Wolf's tongue as he allowed all three to stride away. *They have named you well. My ax craves justice, but I will be patient—and bait my trap with a doe's tender flesh.*

Stowing his weapons, Pacing Wolf scanned the illumined dwellings and found two side-by-side without morning fires. He studied them closely to determine which, if either, held his prey. Once he had slit a lodge cover, he could not turn back; he would have to snatch or kill whatever woman he found inside. He hated to harm the storyteller, not only because he respected her age, but he also because he might need to slay her before the gentle doe's eyes.

Brushing the image from his mind, he caught sight of a slender, dress-clad form ducking through the first door-flap. His lips curled into a satisfied grin. He knew her instantly. While he watched her wend past cook-fires toward the dusky meadow, he reached into his pouch for a small offering to give his spirit guide, hung it among the newly forming buds, and crept down the hill into the crabapple's deep shadows.

Light Bird paused at the village edge, peering cautiously at the spot where her grandmother had fallen. Seeing neither Wild Dog nor his cousins, she hurried across the field. Without wood, she could not prepare her family's early meal. She did not know where her two older brothers had gone, perhaps to the council along with her father, but the two younger ones were already complaining of hunger.

Every step that brought her closer to Pacing Wolf increased his heartbeat until he inwardly trotted to and fro like the restless animal whose name he possessed. Conforming each muscle to the twisting lines of the thick, gray trunk, he drank in the cold air slowly, evenly, tamping down the urge to hastily rush out.

Within feet of her abandoned bundle, something—Light Bird could not say what—pulled her to an abrupt halt. She stood perfectly still, as if sniffing for a predator's scent, but could detect nothing amiss. Concluding her imagination was playing tricks, she scooped up her firewood and flung it over her shoulder, intending to return later for her grandmother's, but it felt so light she reconsidered. Its thin, short twigs, divided between two households, might burn too quickly.

Laying aside her bundle, she slipped to her knees to gather the scattered sticks, but as she was crawling among the crabapple's roots, the skin on her arms began to prickle. She froze, listening intensely while her eyes darted this way and that, but she heard only the wind rustling branches overhead.

Suddenly, a dark shadow knocked her over with such force she could not scream. Hard-muscled arms pinned her own against her ribcage and rolled her within her buffalo robe before she could draw a breath. Twisting and turning frantically, she tried to squirm out of its dark folds; but her unseen assailant hoisted her off the ground, slung her over his shoulder and bounded effortlessly up the hill.

"Put me down, Pretty Face, put me down!"

Three years her senior, her brother had abducted her so often that her boredom usually spoiled his fun, but this morning was different. In addition to preparing her family's early meal, she needed to complete the chores her grandmother could not perform with a twisted ankle. Besides all this, Pretty Face had grown considerably rougher over the past winter. He tossed her across his mount as if she were dead prey. As she pictured their cousins breaking into boisterous laughter when he finally set her free, she renewed her wriggling; but she instantly stopped when a large, firm hand clamped her rump.

He does not know where he touches me, she reasoned. *The robe is too thick,* but when she felt his hand slide down her bare leg, the hair on her nape stood up.

As he tied her ankles together, a wide grin split Pacing Wolf's face. She had fought harder and longer than he had expected, heightening his excitement and increasing his admiration. Stringing the rope beneath his sorrel's belly, he tethered its other end around her wrists. He was not about to lose her.

Leaping down the hillock, he secured one of Wild Dog's bloodstained shafts to his own distinctly marked arrow and fastened both to the doe's full bundle. Her clansmen could not miss the implication: he had intentionally chosen her and the bound arrows told them why. Springing back over the rise, he leaped atop his mount and galloped toward the great Muddy River, leaving only forest creatures to lift their heads when they heard her muffled cries.

Rescue me, Lord, from the evildoers; protect me from the violent, who devise evil plans in their hearts and stir up wars every day.
Psalm 140:1-2

Chapter 2

"STRAIGHT ARROWS, Pretty Face!" called the silver-haired storyteller when she heard her grandsons' voices on the other side of her lodge-cover. As they ducked inside, their perturbed faces announced that something was wrong.

"Where is Light Bird?" asked Two Doves. "She set out for her bundle before the sun arose from sleep."

At a loss, Pretty Face looked to his older brother, but he saw from Straight Arrows' expression that he had not seen their sister either. "We have been with the elders since sunrise. Wild Dog and his cousins arrived last night."

"Yes," the silver head nodded. "I saw them in the meadow."

"They came to warn Old Many Feathers," offered Straight Arrows. "The Raven-Enemy have crossed the grasslands and are heading toward us."

His handsome, earnest face reminded Two Doves of his father, Preying Eagle, and of her husband, Running Deer; but as the younger grandson squatted over her outstretched leg, she thought how very much he looked like Light Bird. Both he and his sister had inherited the finer-boned features characteristic of their mother's people, lending Pretty Face his unusual name, but neither possessed her odd eye color.

"What happened, Grandmother?" he asked, lightly touching her puffy, purple skin.

"While gathering wood with your sister, I stumbled over a tree root. Is Running Deer still with the council?"

Straight Arrows nodded.

"Ask your mother to come here and tell Small Deer to look for Light Bird. It is not like her to dawdle. I grow hungry, and she knows I cannot keep warm without wood."

Moments after they ducked out of her dwelling, Brought-Us-the-Book slipped inside with a bowl of hot porridge. "This will keep you warm until Light Bird returns." Seeing her mother-in-law's far-off expression, she asked, "Is it pain or your thoughts that carry you away?"

Two Doves' silver braids bobbed as she nodded. "Both," she acknowledged, smiling up at her companion's affectionate blue-green eyes. "I was remembering you, so thin and pale when you first wintered among us. How long has it been—twenty-two summers?"

"In two moons I will have lived thirty-nine altogether," answered Brought-Us-the-Book. "So yes, I have been with you nearly twenty-two of them."

"They have brought you good health and rounded you nicely. I was thinking about Light Bird also. It seems a short time since you bore her, but she is nearly as old as you were when you married my son. Soon, she too will want to marry and bear little potbellies of her own. I hate the thought of parting with her."

"Unless the Lord clearly tells him otherwise, Preying Eagle will likely keep her in our band."

"Even if he does, she will belong to her husband's family and do her chores with his women-folk."

"She will still spend afternoons weaving with our guild in Quiet Woman's dwelling."

"Yes," nodded Two Doves, quitting the melancholy trail of her thoughts and craning her neck to see the cradleboard hanging on her daughter-in-law's back. "How is my new little granddaughter?"

"Growing heavier by the day." Brought-Us-the-Book turned so that Two Doves could better see the babe nestled snuggly between her long, thick braids. Against the little one's coal-black hair, they looked like deep mahogany. "If she does not quit eating so greedily, my back will bend to the ground. Do you remember when I wanted a full quiver of potbellies?" she chuckled. "Half of one is plenty!"

As Two Doves stroked the tiny, soft cheek, the babe offered her a toothless grin. "She reminds me much of Light Bird. Where is the girl?"

"I do not know," admitted Brought-Us-the-Book, frowning as she turned again to examine her mother-in-law's discolored ankle. "Does it hurt to walk?"

The silver head nodded.

"It is not like her to leave you so thoughtlessly."

Two Doves shrugged. "She probably met up with a cousin. Talks-to-Birds and Smiling Girl ran past us earlier, chattering away about Swallow Woman's handsome pup."

"Wild Dog?"

"Yes. I do not like him. He is far too bold. This morning he made straight for your daughter, and when she refused him notice, what do you think he did?"

Furrowing her brow, her daughter-in-law shrugged.

"He gouged her—hard!"

"He hurt her?"

"She pressed her lips together in pain, but he was too dull to see."

"I am surprised he took time to pester her before warning us of this troubling threat. He asked your brother to call a council."

"Yes, your two eldest told me. I have not heard of this Raven-Enemy."

"Neither had I before this day. They roost high in the mountains toward the sleeping sun and are angry because some of the Allies are encroaching on their territory."

"We encroach on no one, though the white settlers creep closer every day. I am afraid what Running Deer has always feared for you will come. I hope Spotted-Long-Knife can work out an agreement with your white fathers."

"I hope so, too. It has been long since I have lived among them, but there were many fine and godly men at that time—and as many scoundrels as there are among our people. Elk-Dog confirmed much of what Wild Dog said. He told Preying Eagle the Raven-Enemy are like a wolf pack, attacking each of their neighbors."

"The Lord has delivered us from the mouth of the lion; he can deliver us from the mouth of the wolf also."

Brought-Us-the-Book smiled, admiring Two Doves' faith, as she had so often over the past twenty-two years. "I remember when Little Turtle first joined the warriors. It was against the Horned People and my first taste of battle. Only with Cuts-His-Face have I been so scared."

"What a celebration we enjoyed when our men-folk came home!"

"Pretty Face wants to join our warriors, but he is so young."

Two Doves shook her silver head slowly. "Little Turtle possessed fewer summers than Pretty Face does now, but you were also very young. Age has given you a different vantage point. The Creator confused our enemy then and He will confuse them again. 'Do not fret,' my daughter. 'It tends only to evil.'[2]"

Harsh shouts from outside disrupted their conversation as Two Doves' door flap was abruptly flung back. "An enemy!" spat Straight Arrows, poking in his head. "He has stolen her!"

Too stunned to reply, his mother and grandmother stared blankly before peppering him with questions.

"Light Bird?"

"How?"

"We found her bundle and yours, Grandmother, half scattered under the largest tree. He tied two arrows to hers, joined together—his own and Wild Dog's, dyed brown with dried blood."

"No," groaned Brought-Us-the-Book, covering her mouth with her hands. "The Creator would surely not allow it!"

As tears streamed down her face, Two Doves pulled her into her arms.

"Of what people was he?"

"The one Wild Dog warned the council about," answered Straight Arrows. "The Raven-Enemy."

"So!" snapped his grandmother. "He had reason to suspect an attack—Wild Dog has killed the man's woman or sister."

"Father and our uncles are already mounted, and grandfather and I follow. Pretty Face is getting our horses and will come with us."

"Pray it was only a sister—if so, you may be able to get Light Bird back. What of Wild Dog?"

"We have driven him from the village. Father is black with rage."

"And his cousins?"

"They fled also."

"Go!" urged his grandmother, "—and God go with you."

His mother only nodded, too upset to speak, while they listened to hard-driven horses pounding the turf outside. A single mount halted close by.

"Brought-Us-the-Book! Two Doves!" Preying Eagle shouted.

Straight Arrows helped his grandmother hobble out as his mother fought to compose herself. She knew her husband must keep his head and refused to add to his struggle.

"Go!" he ordered their son. "Your brother is bringing your mount. We follow the trail from the meadow."

Preying Eagle leaned down, pulling Brought-Us-the-Book so close that his lips brushed her hair while they whispered a prayer to the Almighty. As she pulled away, he lifted her chin and promised, "If she can be found, I will bring her back."

"Straight Arrows told us of one warrior," his mother told him. "Are there many?"

"We will soon know," he answered, wheeling his mount as his three brothers joined him.

Kicking their heels into their horses' bellies, they tore over the meadow and up the hillock, ripping Pacing Wolf's offering from the old crabapple and hurling it to the ground.

LIGHT BIRD STRUGGLED to arch her ribs off the horse's sharp withers but encumbered by her heavy buffalo robe she soon fell exhausted. Each hoof beat pummeled her courage until she could no longer fend off the alarm that gripped her heart. This was not a prank. Her captor had traveled too far and fast. As her thoughts trailed back to Wild Dog's disrespectful behavior, she grew surer he owned the hand she felt. She had often thought him reckless but not wicked. Still, she could think of no else.

How she had attracted him, she did not know. Almost three summers past, when the Allies were assembled, she and her other cousins who had just entered womanhood took part in the Dance of Untouched Women. She missed a step when she happened to look up to into the eyes of a fine young warrior, handsome and strong, holding a lance already boasting enemy tokens. While she wended through the other dancers, he watched her with open admiration, but the shriveling glares of her older rivals drove her own eyes downward. Once she found the temerity to raise them again, he had passed to another place in the crowd, but as she returned to kneel beside her mother, she saw he had seated himself directly in her view.

Within days, his uncle spoke on his behalf to her father, but though Preying Eagle did not want to offend a valued ally, he told them she was too young to court. Light Bird felt relieved as much as disappointed, but when she saw him ride into their village with his two cousins a few moons later, she could not entirely quell her excitement.

Assuming they had come to hear God's Word, Straight Arrows encouraged them to visit often, and Pretty Face, in awe of Wild Dog's achievements, frequently invited them to eat meals in their mother's dwelling. Light Bird soon found these occasions torturous. Like a lone buffalo on the open prairie, the eyes of the hunter never left her; and afterward, her little brother, Small Deer, teased her mercilessly.

Wild Dog's uncle had traveled to their village just before the last snows. "Light Bird will soon possess sixteen summers," he told her father. "Many girls her age are betrothed. Wild Dog has lived through twenty-one and amply proven he can provide for her. His skill as a warrior is beyond doubt. Our two bands have long exchanged daughters to keep our alliance strong.

Swallow Woman, Wild Dog's mother, was born in this village and her sisters still live among you. He has demonstrated great patience—give him his reward."

Preying Eagle acknowledged the uncle's statements but answered with his usual practicality. "How can a husband and wife walk together if they travel separate paths? Light Bird has chosen the Creator's way. Whose way has Wild Dog chosen, and whose trail will their children follow? 'A family divided against itself cannot stand.'"[3]

A clatter of hooves pulled Light Bird from her memories and offered her hope: they were traveling over rock. If Wild Dog were her captor, they were probably ascending to his village. She had never visited it, but all knew his band camped in the high and rocky hills. He would surely take her to his mother, Swallow Woman, with whom she could reason. In turn, Light Bird would assure her father that Wild Dog had harmed nothing deeper than her dignity, and no one need suffer severe consequences. Rather than climb higher, however, the horse lowered its neck, and through the robe's open end, she caught a glimpse of swiftly rushing water. Severely disappointed, she began pleading with him to turn around before the damage was irreparable.

Pacing Wolf urged his sorrel down the slope, glad the Muddy River was not yet flooding. He thought his captive's voice pleasant, even while raised, like a meadowlark in the grassland.

Perhaps they called her Light Bird for the sweetness of her song. I will call her Small Doe.

Resolving to treat her gently, he congratulated himself for the ease with which his plans had fallen into place. Not only had he thwarted his enemy's cravings, but he had gained their object in his stead. He imagined Wild Dog alarmed and angry when he learned that a wolf had carried off his desired woman and her clansmen's violent fury when they discovered why he had snatched her.

Before my ax meets his chest, I will prance her rounding form before his hungry eyes; and when my son grows old enough to grasp a bow, I will teach him to devour that wild dog's people. As he finished the thought, the corners of his mouth drooped, and victory, sweet on his tongue just moments before, tasted like grit between his teeth. *They are also her people. When she asks her spirit-guide to protect our children, she will invite the deaths of her father and brothers, her uncles and cousins. I should have stolen the haughty goose. I could use her to ease my grief without a trickle of remorse.*

As he remembered his dead woman's ravaged flesh, he spat in disgust. *They named her murderer well. He tears what he pleases, but the little doe will think I am no better. Her laughter will melt away like snow that has come too early and her eyes will...*

When the deepening water interrupted his thoughts, he slipped a hand beneath the pelt to cradle her head. *I should take her life instead—quickly—before terror has a chance to crawl into her heart, but drowning is cruel death. I do not want her to suffer.*

As Light Bird felt him lift her head, she welcomed the respite. It throbbed from hanging lower than her torso, and though the crossing diminished her hope for quick release, the horse's smooth, buoyant motion offered her ribs relief. The river surged over her calves, chilly and strong, jostling the horse so hard she feared her captor might lose his hold. While they strained against the current, swimming farther and farther from the bank, she began to realize this could be only one river: the great one that marked the boundary of her people's hunting lands—one she was never likely to see unless captured by an enemy.

Fear ran up her spine until it felt colder than her feet. Women were the rightful spoils of war, and warriors often stole them to replace their dead, but she had never expected to be either. Since embracing Jesus, her band had neither raided nor attacked other villages, and the Lord had given them peace on every side. While possible enemies galloped through her mind, most of whom she had never seen, she felt she could no longer breathe.

The Puckered Toes live toward the cold wind, but the Horned Enemy...

Shivering, she pushed the thought away. They were too horrible to consider. To quell her distress, she rehearsed the many times the Almighty had rescued His people—particularly when they were too weak to defend themselves. He parted the Red Sea[4], prompted Sennacherib to abandon his siege of Jerusalem[5], told an angel to release Peter from prison[6], and saved the Jews from extermination through Queen Esther.[7] Rather than bolster her confidence, though, the last undermined it. A strange man had also snatched Esther. *O Lord, save me as you did my mother.*

After a time, the horse lunged upward onto firm ground, and her captor lowered the end of the robe that surrounded her head, but instead of emerging on the opposite bank, he urged his mount forward within the river. With a sinking heart, she recognized the cleverness of his strategy: their tracks would be impossible to follow. The mud might be deep enough to hold their impressions, but the current would smooth them away.

Feeling sick, she considered her old aunt Quiet Woman, the wife of Many Feathers, her grandmother's esteemed brother. Their people so loved her that few remembered she was not born an Ally. On the eve of an attack last spring, her mother had sent her to this aunt's dwelling.

"With every passing summer, you look more like Brought-Us-the-Book," Quiet Woman told her. "When she was a little older than you are now, your father sent her to me. I told her then what I tell you tonight: Your wits must guide you tomorrow. Women have few choices in life and a just warrior remembers this. If the Puckered Toes enter the village, they will take our pleasing women for wives or slaves. Choose your hiding place well, little bird; but if an enemy finds you, welcome him. He will take you anyway. A warrior's vanity is a formidable weapon, so use it to your advantage. Smile. He will think you clever to recognize his worth but may become spiteful if insulted. You also carry stolen blood. Two Doves' grandmother was captured from a fierce people living in the lands your mother traveled with her white father. Each of us possesses an aunt, a grandmother, or a sister-in-law from another tribe, and the same is true in theirs. It is the way of war."

Reading the revulsion in Light Bird's eyes, Quiet Woman had reassured her, "The Creator knows the lot of women and holds your future in His hands. Had He not brought me to this people, I would still be enslaved to sin. Trust Him."

Light Bird had trusted Him, and He faithfully delivered her. Not only did He give the Puckered Toes into her men-folks' hands but also much booty to enrich them all. The occasion had been particularly joyous for her family: Straight Arrows had won weapons and horses, demonstrating his prowess in battle and clearing the way for him to marry Corn-Tassels when she returned from the white men.

"The Lord is faithful in all His ways,"[8] she reminded herself. *Nothing is impossible for Him.*

I called to the Lord, who is worthy of praise, and He rescued me from my enemies.

Psalm 18:3

Chapter 3

AS VIOLET GRAY clouds drifted across the pink horizon, Pacing Wolf searched the black formations looming above. He must kill the doe now, before he headed up the bank and into the hills, so the current would carry her downstream to the land of the Earth Lodges.

Her gentle care for the old storyteller warred with his resolve. It had drawn him as powerfully as her more obvious charms. Since his sister had remarried, concern for their grandmother had been weighing on his mind. Still, he cringed while recalling his mother-in-law's tongue, honed sharply through many summers of use.

Jackrabbit will make her suffer as long as she draws breath. A quick thrust of my knife could spare her much pain...

Unsheathing the weapon, Pacing Wolf felt for the valley between the doe's shoulder blades. If he placed his blade well, its tip would penetrate her heart before she felt it enter. He breathed deeply as he grasped the hilt and then capped the end with his other hand to strengthen the blow, but as he was about to shove the point downward, a startled blackbird darted angrily from the grass. Shying and snorting, his horse pitched him sidewise, nearly flinging him into the river.

As Light Bird felt him right himself, a new clatter of hooves deepened her conviction that God alone could save her. The rocks over which they climbed from the river would tell her men-folk nothing. She knew they were ascending higher when her body pitched slightly backward toward her captor, but the scant glimpse she gained of the rough terrain was not useful. The weary sun washed everything an indistinct color.

Dismounting atop a flat expanse of rock, Pacing Wolf loosened the ropes that bound her limbs. Her legs, numb after many hours in the same position, buckled beneath her when he set her on her feet, and, still trapped within her robe's stifling confines, she fell, striking the hard surface. Thankful the robe had provided some cushioning, she lay still, unable to do anything, torn between hope he might soon release her and dread of what might happen if he did. She soon found out.

He unbound the buffalo hide, first loosening the folds about her face and then slipping his hand down her back to seize the knife she kept in her belt. Free of the clinging damp fur, she attempted to push up to a sitting position but found that her arms were as useless as her legs. Pacing Wolf came to her aid, setting her in a more dignified pose.

When he slipped off her wet rabbit-fur boots, Light Bird felt too petrified to protest. She sat perfectly still, unable to will away the calloused hands that briskly rubbed her limbs to restore their blood-flow or even to raise her eyes. To look at his face was to gaze into her fate.

As Pacing Wolf cupped her frigid feet, her composure unnerved him more than a battle cry. He had expected curses and well-placed kicks, not this silent trailing of his hands with her eyes. Thanking his spirit guide for the blackbird, he tried to push aside his earlier misgivings, but they returned like a pack of coyotes, creeping up to steal each sweet morsel of triumph.

I have spoiled Wild Dog's plan and made him a stench in their village. I can return her, he decided, but the smooth skin beneath his palms guided his mind to a fresh concern. *Her clansmen may consider her ruined, leaving her to beg when her brothers join the dead. Her soft flesh should not wither unnourished and untouched—and what of my son? Can I rest without also avenging him? No, I will take her as planned, and if she possesses intelligence she will soon accept her fate.*

Relieved when his hands went no further, Light Bird braved a quick, upward glance. His head, bent over his task, was lost in the dark silhouette created by his wide shoulders; but as he lifted it, her eyes grew wide. Standing erect like a stiff clump of reeds was the short-cropped thatch of a Horned Warrior! They abducted untouched women, treated them well, and then burned them in fire for their earth-god. An aunt had told her they had stopped this custom, but it readily explained his unexpected care.

When she began scrambling backward, Pacing Wolf tightly gripped her ankle. Her manner had changed so abruptly that he looked over his shoulder, half-expecting to see an evil spirit. He wanted his enemies to shrink in fear, but not this young doe. Even before he snatched her, he had dreaded her horror, but he had not anticipated how deeply it would cut.

Who did she suspect had stolen… He cut the question short, newly aware he had overlooked something in the meadow. *Her tribesmen said nothing of her heart—they spoke only of her father's. No warrior trails prey he knows he cannot catch. She feigned indifference for the grandmother!*

As Pacing Wolf considered how skillfully she had done so, his stomach began to churn. He had been pleased with his success, not only because he had avenged his dead woman but also because he had saved the doe from a vile fate. Now he felt a fool and loathed the tender feelings she had aroused. *Let her fear me!* he sneered. *She can cower every night!*

Pulling her upright, he thrust his water pouch and a piece of dried buffalo in her direction, but though she had not eaten all day and her throat felt parched, she could not bring herself to take either.

"Drink!" he commanded. To exact his full measure of vengeance, he needed to keep her alive.

Recalling Quiet Woman's story, she sipped the water but shook her head at the meat.

"Eat!"

His voice sounded hard, confirming the impression the cut of his muscles suggested—whether from advanced years or a malicious temper, she lacked light enough to tell. Aware she had best obey him, she tore off a piece and slowly chewed it while he slipped the looped rope over her head, tightening the knot until it sat like a collar surrounding her throat. Winding the other end around his forearm, he held it in full view against the clear night sky, mounted his horse, and pulled her up behind him. He assumed she could both jump and land without injury, but not even the most desperate woman wanted to be dragged by the neck.

Although Light Bird's stomach contracted with hunger, the morsel she had eaten felt like a stone. She struggled to keep up her courage as the sorrel picked its way up a narrow stone ledge that twisted back above the river. Every part of this journey had grown more frightening than the last, and if her father did not come for her soon, she knew it would prove far worse.

Why had she taken such care to ensure the meadow was empty? She regretted it deeply. Wild Dog embarrassed and annoyed her, but even if he could not have kept this thatch-haired enemy from snatching her, he would have raised the alarm. Who knew how long it had taken her women-folk to realize she was missing?

Looking down at the black riverbank, she searched for someone who might have followed their trail. Her mother had once been abducted, and all the while she had thought herself alone, her youngest brother had been hidden nearby. *Even now, Straight Arrows or Pretty Face may be in the shadows,* Light Bird told herself, but the hope was too slim to sustain. *No warrior can track over rock, much less while the sun deeply sleeps. He has made me impossible...*

The very word, as she thought it, offered her courage, for it brought to mind her first memory verse: "Nothing is impossible for God."[9] *Lord, "even darkness is not dark to You, and a starless night is bright as the day"...and*

"You wrote each of the days You formed for me before there were any!"[10] *I know my father will waste no time…but Lord, please show him where we are!*

Pacing Wolf welcomed the clump of soft-needled pines growing up the cliff-face that marked the end of this day's journey. He hated the violence his clansmen bound him to commit and was eager to get it behind him. Dropping his captive to the ground, he dismounted, parted the woven pines, and stepped into a hidden cavity. The rope gave Light Bird no choice but to follow; however, when a startled creature brushed its wingtip against her temple, she sharply jerked backward.

"Bats, not owls," the warrior firmly assured her, but its sudden flight had caused her alarm, not the creature's identity. Since her people embraced the Creator, they had stopped regarding owls as omens of death or harm.

Pulling her robe more closely about her neck, she wondered what sort of world they entered. It seemed devoid of all light. Her captor did not give her long to speculate. He plunged them hurriedly down a passageway so narrow her shoulders occasionally bumped into walls. The air, cool and clammy, moved noiselessly against her face and smelled of a mixture of dirt and dampness.

Unsure of the way, she dropped a pace or two behind until a tug on her leash urged her to keep up. She was scared to do otherwise, but as she quickened her pace, her feet unexpectedly slid out from under her. Flinging out her hands, she scraped them against the stone walls in a vain effort to thwart a fall, dropping her robe and roughly twisting the rope about her neck. Her captor let out a startled grunt as she thudded into his legs, but instead of tumbling backward on top of her, he managed to recover his footing.

As he hauled her up against his hard chest, she could smell the scent of sweet tobacco that clung to his shirt, and his breath, shallow and rapid, mingled warmly with her hair. Every part of her screamed to turn and flee, but she swallowed the instinct. If she ran, he might drag her by the neck to the frightening place they were going.

Once Pacing Wolf was certain that her feet were steady, he slid his hands down her arms, found her slim fingers, and guided them to his belt. "Hold on here," he advised. "The way has more slopes and bends."

When he turned his back, Light Bird hesitantly complied, gingerly slipping her fingers inside the leather band about his hips. She was thankful he slowed his pace to allow for her close proximity, but she felt ashamed that the contact provided her comfort. He wound along curving corridors and down several more grades less steep than the first; then at last he stopped, withdrew her hands, and turned to face her. Unable to anticipate what he intended, she held her breath, but as she felt her leash jostled slightly, he simply slipped away.

Pride alone kept Light Bird from crying out while she listened to his soft treads fading. The place was so dark that she could not see the hand she held up directly in front of her eyes. Whatever he planned, she was determined not to panic again, or if she did, to hide it better. She stood quite still, straining to hear his footfalls or any sound that might betray his location, but all she heard was the hollow echo of trickling water.

When he did not soon return, she began to fear that he was not coming back. He had shrugged off the winged creature as a bat, but childhood images of the dragon sealed in the abyss[11] and Molech, the many-winged Ammonite god, began stirring within her imagination. The heinous rites[12] of the latter sounded so similar to the Horned-Enemy's, that her cousin Chirping Bird had concluded the two were the same. Perhaps they were, in spite of her mother's reassurances.

Looking up, she noticed a few small stars, but even these seemed peculiar. They provided no light and were unnaturally confined within a narrow line about the length of her forearm. As her eyes began to adjust, they drifted to vague forms lurking stiffly in the darkness over her head, raising beads of perspiration across her brow.

She did not move, supposing they were the flying thing's companions, but some were as tall as or taller than her captor. How they stayed aloft, she could not fathom. They kept their wings pulled in tightly, and she detected nothing on which they perched.

Afraid they would swarm her, she eyed them uneasily, and her stomach grew weak when she happened to glance down. Others stood close by, one so near he might easily grab her. Indeed, as her eyes further adjusted to the dark, she thought the creature held her rope. Rummaging through the storehouse of her memory, she searched for descriptions of demons but found none that feasted on human flesh.

Fear is dragging me like a wild pony. Surely such a number of creatures could not keep so still.

Surmising they were part of the strange place, she began again to speculate about the Horned-Enemy's earth-god ceremony; but after a good while had passed, curiosity compelled her to gently tug the rope. It resisted, as she suspected it would, but neither pulled her back into place nor attacked her. Testing it further, she yanked harder, chafing her neck where the rope twisted, but whatever held its end did not move. Light Bird exhaled deeply, embarrassed by her own anxious fancies, but she could explore no further. A drifting cloud had extinguished the stars, provoking less ethereal horrors.

As Pacing Wolf stood between the pines that hid the cavern's mouth, he took in the pleasant scent of the buffalo robe he had stumbled over in the passage. It smelled of grass from the meadow, cooking smoke, and the spiced herbs she used in her hair. He waited for a few moments, listening for changes in the usual night sounds before venturing out to obscure any tracks they had left on the narrow incline.

They are sure to search, and her father's no fool—he kept her from the murderer.

Piling several fallen limbs against the cave's opening, he led his sorrel around the far side of the cliff to a hidden path leading into a valley below.

Bereft of her warm robe, Light Bird's teeth began to chatter. She felt so awake, she guessed it was still evening, but her feet were growing weary. When she tried to sit down, the tether pulled tautly, lacking enough slack to allow much movement, so she fingered it upward as far as she could. Her captor had secured it exactly as she expected: too high above her head for her to reach.

Perhaps I should feel thankful. If I sit or lay down, I might fall asleep and awaken in the jaws of a bear.

She had never encountered one herself, but her uncle, who had killed two, said they were the fiercest of all creatures. He wore two strands of their huge yellow teeth dangling from his neck, and she remembered the hard, cool feel of them well. As a little girl, she often crawled into his lap, tracing them with her fingers or squeezing them in her palms while the elders read the Scriptures. They could easily shred her flesh as she hung helplessly from the rope, making her wonder if this were her captor's intention. He had not promised to return and had taken her knife, though it could offer little protection. Alert or asleep, bound or unbound, she was no match for a hungry bear awaking from its long winter sleep.

All at once, her skin began to creep. Something was stirring the air nearby, and when it brushed the hem of her doeskin dress, her ability to control her limbs began melting away. Feeling herself going limp, she feared she might faint until a quick, familiar scrape skipped sparks near her feet.

Flickers danced below a tripod of sticks, swirling up wisps of smoke as they consumed dry grass. As they leaped to thicker twigs, she grew sick with relief. Stone icicles, not creatures, hung above her head and jutted up from the ground near her feet; and the warrior squatting in the fire's glow was clearly not a Horned-Enemy. He stiffened the hair atop his pate, but rather than shear it off the sides and back of his head, he wore the longest braids she had ever seen. They dragged dangerously close to the fire and when he arose swung almost to his breechcloth.

As he casually tossed her robe onto a pile of others, she searched his moccasins for the distinct puckered toes of the northern enemy. She found none, but his bearing confirmed what she had earlier suspected: he was a well-seasoned warrior of twenty-five or possibly thirty summers.

When he approached her side of the fire, it cast his shadow upward, larger than the horrid specters she had envisioned; but as he leaned in close, his eyes flickered with all the keen intelligence his actions had foretold. He was not handsome like her father and brothers, but he radiated strength, fascinating and frightening her together.

"Wh..who are your people?" she asked, struggling to keep her voice from quavering.

"I am a Sparrow-Hawk."

She detected pride in his restrained tone, though she had not heard of them, but many people called themselves by names their foes did not. "Why have you stolen me?"

Pacing Wolf's gut tightened and he hardened the line of his mouth. Her voice held respect, but her question, though natural, felt like an accusation. "Ask the tall warrior whose lodge you desire."

Light Bird could not answer, perplexed as much by his change in tone as she was by his reply. After a few moments, she timorously admitted, "I do not understand."

"The one your clansmen call Wild Dog."

"Wild Dog?" Light Bird cocked her head. "Did his band attack your village?" She considered it unlikely. War parties waited until spring or summer, yet nothing else she could think of made sense.

Her plain incredulity sorely pricked Pacing Wolf's patience, casting him as he expected in the same cruel role as his woman's murderer. He did not like to speak of the dead, but he wanted her to feel all the horror of Wild Dog's crime so she that could see his own conduct was unmistakably just. Withdrawing her suitor's other arrow from his pouch, he held it so she could clearly see the markings.

"I found my woman, her clothing torn, lying in the deep grass—this arrow stuck in her throat!" He jabbed it toward his own, savoring the revulsion washing over Light Bird's face. "But killing her was not enough. After he had shamed her, he sliced her belly open, snatched out my son—like so—and smashed his head against a jagged rock!"

Punctuating each part with vivid gestures, he gained the result he desired. Light Bird unsteadily staggered backward, one hand clutching her mouth and the other her stomach.

"He has robbed me of my woman and son—so I have taken his."

Light Bird was unable to utter a sound. Casting her eyes to the ground, she slowly shook her head. "I...I am sorry," she whispered, once she had regained her voice. "His attentions made my skin crawl, but I never grasped the evil that dwells in his heart."

Pacing Wolf fell silent, disarmed by her obvious grief,[2] but before he found a way to lessen the sting he had inflicted, she crumpled up her brow and began again to speak.

"I am untouched," she murmured faintly. "I carry no son."

He did not need her to tell him this, he had learned as much from Wild Dog and his cousins, but he found her regret bewildering. *How do I degrade such a woman?*

Lifting her chin, he studied her closely. Her eyes were round, like pools of obsidian, as gentle and wary as the graceful creature she had brought to his mind all day. His dead woman's had looked like hard almonds pushed deeply into a pleasantly shaped apple. Running his thumb over her angular cheekbone, he hoped their characters were as different as their appearances.

"I wish to free you of this," he mumbled, fingering the noose that bound her to the pillar. "But you must not wander. The cavern has many twists—some lead far, some to nothing. I have eluded enemies here during many summers and know where each step will lead. You will become lost—or worse—if you stray."

Casting her eyes toward a dark tunnel, she wondered what dangers it held. She wished he would keep his fingers still. Their tips slid softly across the area the rope chafed and then along the dip of her collarbone, ruining her ability to think.

"You will not flee?"

She nodded her head, almost imperceptibly, too overawed to speak, and stopped breathing altogether as he slipped his other hand around her back. Drawing her closer, he guided the rope over her head, flung it into the dirt, and then he slipped through a narrow opening she had not before noticed.

Free from his intense scrutiny, Light Bird sank down against the nearest wall and curled her knees up under her chin. Aside from the unusual stone formations, the cave looked much like a dimly lit dwelling with a smoke hole darkened by years of use.

Someone, she supposed the warrior, had piled branches within easy reach of the fire and under her own robe lay a generous pile of pelts. She was no longer cold, but they drew her eyes with ghastly fascination, forcing her to admit what she tried hard to avoid.

He has prepared well for his vengeance. I will not leave this place the same as I have come.

I watch in hope for the Lord. I wait for God my savior. He will hear me. Do not gloat over me, my enemy. Though I have fallen, I will rise. Though I sit in darkness, the Lord will be my light.

Micah 7:7-8

Chapter 4

LIGHT BIRD HAD promised to remain where she was, but her eyes often wandered to the dark passageways, wondering which of them led outside. She had been standing in the middle of the room when her captor lit the fire, and her captor's footprints betrayed nothing. They traveled to and from all three corridors, and she could not distinguish any of her own among them. By the fire's light, she clearly saw the one he had just taken—she would not take that—but it was so close to another, she feared they might meet.

Clearly, his reasons for revenge were just—her own men-folk would have acted the same had Jesus not shown them a different way. She had recognized Wild Dog's arrow immediately, and no warrior, not even an enemy, would craft such a tale. Over and over, she turned the vivid images in her mind, and they lost none of their power to shock and sicken. All people knew the risks of war, but his woman had been alone.

Lord, I never wanted Wild Dog's attention. Why must I pay for the evil he has done?

As if in answer, the most recent verses she had committed to memory stepped forward:

> It is commendable to bear up under the pain of unjust suffering because you are conscious of God. How is it to your credit if you receive a beating for doing wrong and endure it? But if you do what is right and suffer patiently, this is commendable before God.[14]

Their implication was clear but horrid. Unable to recall the rest of the passage, she clasped her head between her hands. *No, Lord—You surely cannot mean...* With unsettling suddenness, she saw something she had missed when Quiet Woman and she had spoken before that last battle. *She did not mean You would deliver us from the Puckered Toes, but that You would be faithful no matter the outcome!*

Lifting her head, she saw her captor returning through one of the openings. He walked directly to her, carrying a freshly filled water skin, and squatted down while she satiated her thirst.

"I do not blame you for my woman's murder."

Then why must I pay for it? she thought, but she knew such a reply would not help. Seeing his skin and hair looked damp, she thought of a way she might postpone what she could not thwart, allowing her father and uncles more time.

"I am unclean from the day and the long ride. May I also wash?"

Pacing Wolf nodded, thinking, *she shows much sense for one so young.*

"How many summers do you possess?"

"When the new one comes, I will have sixteen."

"Good." He wished she was older but had feared she had only fourteen or fifteen. "Come."

Sticking a dried bough into the fire, Pacing Wolf led her to an underground spring; but when he did not turn to leave, Light Bird grasped the unforeseen awkwardness of her request. To bathe in front of him was unthinkable, but how would she find her way without light?

"Will you leave the torch?"

"No," he shook his head. "It will burn out shortly."

The fire had already consumed a large portion of the branch, confirming his claim, but caught in her own humiliating snare, she could not think what she should do.

"You will leave me?" Even while she asked it, she realized her tone sounded like a plea for him to stay as much as a request for him to go.

"No—the spring makes the slope slick." He swung the torch toward the incline. "It narrows and descends far into the mountain's belly. If it swallows you, I will not be able to pull you out."

The graphic portrayal robbed Light Bird of protest. *What can it matter if he stays? If I cannot escape him, he will do with me as he pleases. Lord, where is my father?*

Eager to rid herself of the day's sweat, she turned her back, removing nothing more than the leather strips securing the ends of her braids. She combed her fingers through her hair, sticking it under the cold stream that spilled from the cavern wall until a change in the light announced he had moved closer. All but her pounding heart froze in place while she waited to see what he intended. Out of the corner of her eye, she watched him wedge his torch into a high crevice, then he came up behind her to lift a handful of her unbound tresses.

"Our women have hair like the placid brooks that slide through the grasslands. Yours is like the water of the Echata, twisting over rocks in all directions. Do all your people possess such hair?"

Glancing cautiously over her shoulder, she shook her head. "My mother was born a white woman. My grandmother says I am like her."

That explains her unusual features, he reckoned, *though the few white women I have seen were very ugly.*

As the torch sizzled out, she grew acutely aware of his warm fingers. "I am not finished," she muttered, hoping he might step away.

He did, forcing his thoughts down a less engrossing path. "Your clansmen called you Light Bird."

"Yes," she nodded, wondering how he could know this. "My skin was pale at birth."

Though she could not see, his lips turned down. She had unwittingly invited him back onto the trail he was struggling to avoid. "I am called Pacing Wolf," he answered, more tersely than he had intended, "for my eagerness to attack my enemies."

Even his name is fierce! she decided, as her limbs began shaking.

When silence announced that her task was complete, he gripped her arm in the blackness and led her back into the dwelling room. He paused before the dying embers, considering how he might conquer her defenses. Through patience, he had gained many victories and most often found restraint less costly than a sudden onslaught. He resolved to wait, to allow her to grow used to him, but her frequent glances at the passage made him dismiss the notion.

The end will be the same. If I do not complete my vengeance now, she will plague me with attempts to run; but I will waste no time with pretty words. She will not want them, and they do not roll easily from my tongue

Grasping her chin, he tilted it upward, insisting she looked him in the eye. Light Bird felt like a partridge caught in a trap, incapable of moving. While his fingertips explored the column of her throat and found her pulse wildly beating, she wondered if fear might burst her heart.

"You are now my woman," he announced. "My lodge is warm. I will hunt when you hunger and supply skins for your dresses. The small-things you bear me will lessen your sorrow and help you forget the people of your birth."

While she listened, a whirling wind began twisting inside her. She did not want to forget her people, and though she knew what she must say, her lips refused to form the words. His grip on her arm decreed she had no choice.

Though Pacing Wolf did not expect her to reply, her frightened glances felt like jabs with a sharp weapon. He, too, had experienced heartache and anguish, but he knew she must confront them like a warrior confronts a foe. She would not awaken from this night terror, nor could she brush it away.

As he crushed the dying embers, he heard her stammer, "I...I am yours...altogether." She spoke the vow so softly, he doubted his ears—she might only have breathed a sweet sigh—but he was grateful for the darkness. Her yielding aroused such tenderness, he doubted he could keep it from his face. Resolving to be patient, he backed her toward the pile of robes and gently stripped her of childhood dreams.

LIGHT BIRD CURLED into a tight ball, sobbing so violently she feared her soul might rend. She felt like a ransacked village with everything in it overturned. Her captor had left no part of her untouched, no inch that she might say was hers alone. The scent of his braids so clung to her that she could no longer distinguish it from the sweet herbed oil her mother had last combed through her hair. Worse than all, her favorite Scripture, "I will never fail or forsake you," made her feel only mocked and confused. Afraid her sleeping enemy might pillage her again if he awakened, she inhaled deeply to calm herself, but as the silence magnified his breathing, she began sobbing anew.

Lord, I want to die! Please—I beg You—take me now!

She hoped He might make the earth swallow her up or cause the roof to fall in. Recalling Pacing Wolf had warned her about the spring's run-off, she fleetingly wondered if she could find it in the dark.

Anything would be better than...than....

The thought was too horrid to complete. She wished she could crawl into her father's lap, to feel his protective arms around her, hear him tell her everything would be all right.

But it is not all right—nothing will ever be right again!

She wished she could forget all that had happened—forget how she had been raided; forget she would never see her mother or brothers again; forget that Jesus, whom she had loved and trusted as long as she could remember, had done nothing to intervene. Instinctively feeling for the small cross that Pretty Face had whittled for her last Christmas, she found that this, too, was gone. Distraught and irrational, her deepest anguish yet came flooding through her sobs.

The Creator has abandoned me!

Pacing Wolf woke from a satisfying slumber. *She is trembling*, he thought, regretting that he had not relit their fire. Curling around her back, he deeply inhaled the scent of her hair, as pleasant as her voice and graceful ways, but when he slipped his arm around her chest, he found the robe was damp. Fingering her cheeks, he discovered the reason.

"You own pain?" he murmured, his voice thick with sleep.

Light Bird shook her head, not trusting herself to speak. *Not the way you mean.*

Awaking more fully, he grasped why she was crying and that he was the cause. He had found her pleasing, and his inability to comfort her sorely pricked his already accusing conscience; but as he pulled her tightly against his chest, she became rigid.

Is he dull, she wondered, *or just conceited, that he thinks I desire his caresses?*

Nuzzling against her plentiful locks, cool and soft beneath his cheek, he smoothed away the damp hair clinging to her face and remembered an earlier statement that aroused his curiosity. "How did a white woman come to give you birth?"

"My father kept a cruel enemy from shaming her," retorted Light Bird, not caring if her words offended or made him angry. *He has already done his worst!*

"Humph," he grunted, sounding neither injured nor deterred. "'Mother and daughter are alike.'"

Though she had often heard the old saying he quoted, she was unsure what he meant. No one had kept *her* from shame. "I do not understand."

"The evil warrior—your suitor."

"My father and uncles would not have let him have me."

"While they were with your council, he planned to snatch you from the silver-haired storyteller's lodge."

Pacing Wolf felt rather than heard her gasp. "How can you know this?"

"After you helped the old one hobble away, he told his companions what he intended."

"You were in the meadow?"

As he nodded against her hair, its silky texture disrupted his concentration. "He intended to shame you so your father would no longer withhold his consent."

Light Bird lay very still, too appalled to speak, and a needle-prick of hope began lessening her despair. *If what he says is true, the Creator did not forsake me, He kept me from...*

Her stomach turned as she imagined Wild Dog. Though she longed to forget the Sparrow Hawk's invasion, she saw a sharp contrast between the two. Her captor had been gentle, though his vengeance quest was just. Wild Dog had been brutal, though he sought only sport. *He, not this Sparrow Hawk, has caused my sorrow.*

"Thank you," she whispered. "What you have told me matters much."

Pacing Wolf was as mystified by her thanks as he was pleased. More at home with actions than words, he responded the only way he knew. He curved himself around her to keep her warm and felt relieved when she relaxed into an exhausted sleep.

There are three things that surprise me; four I do not understand: how an eagle keeps aloft in the sky; the thoughts of a snake on a rock; why a canoe stays atop the water; and the way of a warrior with an untouched woman.

Proverbs 30:18-19

Chapter 5

EARLY MORNING RAYS streamed through the ceiling's gap, dragging Light Bird from the deepest portion of a fitful slumber. She resisted waking, oppressed by a strong sense of dread, but she knew she must. Her mother and grandmother would soon need firewood and she had not yet dressed her younger brothers. More compelling was her buffalo robe: it had grown inexplicably heavy and uncomfortably warm as if the unwieldy beast still occupied it.

As she pried her eyes open, she sprang alarmingly alert. Instead of resting on the soft, pale hides of her mother's dwelling, they flitted across darkly variegated stone. She could not at first place her surroundings; but dropping her gaze toward the heavy hide, she found stark proof of yesterday's terrors. Just below her chin lay the Sparrow Hawk's cropped pate. His stiffened hair tickled her neck when he shifted, and her arm prickled from his weight.

Only by recounting her old aunt's cautions could she squelch the urge to shove him away. She searched for something, anything, to keep from kicking up the past night's memories and settled on the features she had seen only by the firelight. Below his upright thatch lay a broad forehead, creased deeply between his brows. A strong, slightly crooked nose jutted from these furrows, and peeking out beneath it was an equally determined chin. Lying between the two was a hint of his lips, full and sensitive in repose, but they had twisted too pliantly last evening to trust anything they hinted of his character. As she wondered which expression they would hold when he awoke, the walls of the cave seemed to close in.

He has paid his debt to his dead woman. Will he follow if I slip away? As her heart grew eager for her family's embrace, she tried cautiously to edge out from below him, but he slipped his hand into the hollow of her back. She held her breath, afraid he was waking until he pulled her against him and nestled his weathered cheek into softer territory.

Unable to budge, she lay staring at the smoke-stained crack high above their heads. *It is no use. I am as trapped by my pledge as I am by his arms…and even if I could escape, nothing would be the same. He has made us one flesh.*[15] *I am…*

A distant shout pulled her from her quandary and set her wondering if she should wake him. Perfectly still, she listened for words or a tone that might announce the shouter's allegiance, but the answering voices were indistinct. *I cannot tell if they are friend or foe,* but the thought, once voiced, seized her with the urge to laugh. *If they are one to him, they are the other to me!*

As Pacing Wolf turned his head, his heart began pounding wildly. He was running through grass so tall it caught at his long braids, but his legs felt as heavy as tree trunks. Without warning, the grass parted, catapulting his stomach into his throat. His captive doe lay at his feet, an arrow sticking out of her neck and her waves spilling into a creek. Gathering her limp form into his arms, deep, inconsolable wails racked his chest.

Light Bird glanced down as she heard him moaning, doubtful she could lie still much longer. He was clutching her so tightly that she feared her ribs might crack. Just when she thought she could no longer endure the pressure, a triumphant cry, very close above them, jolted him onto all fours.

Quicker than thought, he clamped his hand over her mouth. *It was a dream!* he panted, staring down into large round eyes that were startlingly alive. He fleetingly wondered if he had imagined the shout until a second warrior answered.

"Here!"

Lord, cried Light Bird, *You rescue me now?* As dismaying as the timing were her contending emotions. She ardently wished to return to those she loved, but they would need to kill the Sparrow Hawk to free her.

Pacing Wolf dared not take his hand from her mouth. Each muscle alert, he listened for other warriors, certain she had also recognized the accent, but he could not read the thoughts leaping through her liquid eyes.

"I see nothing!" called a younger voice a short distance away.

"Three," Pacing Wolf murmured, looking up at the ceiling. "My ax grows eager to greet that wild dog's chest." Glancing down at the young doe beneath him, he watched her brows crease. *She fears for his life.*

As his lips twisted grimly, Light Bird felt bewildered. His face held contempt, even loathing; and when he pressed a knife-blade against her throat, she began desperately pleading with her eyes. Shifting his hand so that only his fingers covered her lips, he felt her whisper against their tips.

"Do not leave me!"

The unexpected plea sent his thoughts hurtling back over all that had transpired since he had awakened. *My blood is churning for his death, but the dream…*

"Look!" yelled Large Man, Wild Dog's stocky cousin. "Light Bird's cross!"

Pacing Wolf sprang to his feet. Slinging his quiver across his shoulder, he tucked his knife and ax into his belt while Light Bird hastily slipped into her doeskin. He grasped her arm, pulling her through one of the openings and up a curving passageway that plunged them into darkness. Sliding silently along the rock wall, he came to a recess and shoved her in.

"Stay here," he ordered. "The incline ends there."

Unable to see where he indicated, she pressed herself as far as she could into the black alcove. She was surprised he had rushed toward the voices, but she soon worked out his strategy. *The morning is bright—before their eyes can adjust to the darkness, they will lose their footing like I did yesterday.*

"Tie the rope to that tree," she heard Large Man calling, unaware his quarry lurked close by. "I will test the cave's depth."

Strong eastern sun, filtering through parted pines, silhouetted Pacing Wolf briefly; but he sprang from view when her startled kinsman scuttled down the slope.

Light Bird heard a sickening thud and then only eerie silence. *What have I done?* She picked through the conversation her captor had repeated, aware his word alone cast these Allies as enemies. Feeling warmth close by, she realized he had silently melted into the black recess.

"It has been too long," he whispered. "The others do not follow."

As if it meant to contradict him, light streamed into the tunnel, and Walks-Behind-Them, Large Man's younger brother began fretting, "He should have climbed out by now."

"Yank harder," Wild Dog ordered. "He may have found something."

The younger obeyed the elder but felt only dead weight. "Something is wrong. Large Man does not answer."

"Haul him out."

Straining to comply, Walks-Behind-Them admitted, "I cannot. He is too heavy."

Only the sound of dragging and occasional grunts disturbed the silence until another stream of light announced that Light Bird's tribesmen had parted the pines a third time. As she listened for their footfalls coming down the slope, she heard a sickened yowl and instantly grasped the reason. Pacing Wolf had cut away the thick-haired skin covering the back of Large Man's head, exposing his skull to the crisp morning air.

"Get up—you are a warrior," Wild Dog bit out, after which she heard a hard thump and a sharp groan. "Bring up the horses. The Raven-Enemy possesses the darkness, but we will turn this cave to our advantage. Haul up those rocks. We will close its mouth."

"But Light Bird may be in there," Walks-Behind-Them protested.

"This Raven Enemy is shrewd—he will have shamed her lest she try to run. Better for her to die than bear his vermin."

"But Preying Eagle will be grateful if you rescue her. He will give her to you."

"Pah!" Wild Dog spat. "A raven's picked-over prey? Her belly is fit only for my knife."

Pacing Wolf, reaching through the blackness, found the young doe's arm, followed it to the base of her stomach, and guessed what she was thinking. "What is done cannot be undone," he stated firmly. "You have become the woman of a Sparrow Hawk and will live and die as one."

I am nothing—a bird without feet.

When she did not answer, Pacing Wolf began to consider what he next needed to do. "Do not move from here—you are safe," he told her, and then quietly padded away.

Sealing up the cave would keep her kinsmen too busy to search for another entrance, but having underestimated Wild Dog's ability to track them there, he would not take chances. Weaving back through the long passage into the dwelling room and past the spring, he descended a winding slope through the belly of the cavern to the valley below.

As Light Bird's kinsmen clunked stone upon stone, her mind wandered to Standing Elk, the one warrior who, though much older than she, had awakened her admiration. Sighing deeply, she remembered how persistently he teased her…*and then when I could hold in my laughter no longer, he would scold me, saying he refused to take a silly wife.*

She had run sobbing to her grandmother when he married during the summer before she came into womanhood. "Why did he not wait for me? He was supposed to wait for me!"

"He has already lived through twenty-two summers, little one," answered Two Doves. "How long did you expect him to wait? A man wants sons. The Creator has already chosen your warrior, but you need a woman's body before you can be of any use to him."

I have a woman's body now, but how will the warrior God has chosen find me? And if he does…

Silence interrupted her thoughts. The dragging and clunking had seemed like they would never stop, but now that they had, she heard her growling stomach. She had eaten nothing yesterday, save the few bites of dried meat she had choked down; but without light, she knew neither the time nor the way to the sunlit room.

Perhaps I can feel my way back. No—he told me to stay here, and if I go down the wrong alley, I may get lost or fall into a hole. As she remembered last night's wish for that very event, she felt astounded the idea was now wholly abhorrent.

"'Weeping may last while the sun sleeps'," she recited, "'but the sun fetches fresh joy when it awakes.'"[16]

Joy? She was seized by another urge to break into laughter. Mostly, she felt numb—numb or too weary to think much at all. As she laid her head atop her knees, she remembered Wild Dog's vile pronouncement and a cold tremor shook her from head to toe. She certainly would have fought him, supposing her old aunt's advice did not apply.

Leaning her head back against the hard stone, she asked God to forgive her unbelief. *"We know that God causes all things to work together for the good of those who love Him and are called according to His purpose"*[17]—*'even those that seem horrible.'"* Her mother had frequently repeated the verse, so often adding the last, the two had become inextricably linked in Light Bird's memory. As her captor's keen eyes crept into her musings, she began to feel genuinely grateful, not only to God but also to him.

"Lord, what the Sparrow Hawk said is true. 'What is done cannot be undone.' It is useless for me to long for yesterday."

PACING WOLF HURRIED down a long tunnel snaking through the cavern's belly and cautiously pushed aside a curtain of vines. They were hanging as he had left them, undisturbed and unbroken, and as he squatted to inspect the rocky soil below, he did not find a single displaced pebble. Stepping into the bright morning light, he spotted some leaves that had been damaged by a badger digging for grubs, but none of the surrounding vegetation showed the presence of a man.

Much of the morning is already spent, he concluded from the height of the sun. *Better to stay in the cavern tonight.*

Trotting the short distance to his sorrel, he led the animal across a small creek far enough away from the cave that the discovery of one would not lead to the other. He considered climbing up the hidden path around the other side of the cliff where he might end their threat at once. Even if Wild Dog had already finished his task, mounted, and was picking his way down toward the river, Pacing Wolf's arrows might reach them.

Waugh! He is a coward, afraid to enter the cavern himself and face my ax.

As he thought of the young doe, he decided against it. He needed to hasten back to the lower entrance lest the shamer find it. How Wild Dog had followed yesterday's tracks, he did not know. He had chosen the way with exceeding care.

They were the intruders, he concluded, *who lit a fire on the great rock. They were as careless with their ashes as they were their trail. No Sparrow Hawk would have been so foolish.*

Gathering several armloads of dead branches and pine boughs, he swept away all traces of his footprints and then piled the rest behind the vines. He wondered what he might find as he bounded back up the passageway. Wild Dog's denunciation had been savage, but it might also prove useful, cutting away false hope that might keep the doe's heart from healing.

Coming to the spring, he drank plentifully before filling his pouch. The dimly lit dwelling room lay undisturbed, but as he treaded past the bed of pelts, his waking nightmare and relief, panic and anger, all raced like spooked horses through his memory. They pulled to a halt when he spotted a small dry stain, verifying her purity as plainly as her pleas had shown her preference for him over her tribesman. She had proven sensible, both in yielding last evening and placing her life in his hands at dawn. What might her eyes hold now that he had saved her? As his thoughts drifted to the feel of her smooth skin, he realized he yearned for more than compliance. He wanted her to...

Wagh! Women are snares, and she is the softest. I am a warrior—I will do what I want! She will serve me and learn to be grateful.

Nearing her hiding place, his senses leaped alert. She was talking to someone. While waiting for an answer, his mind rushed through each dark passage to discover how another warrior could have entered. He had seen no sign of intruders below, and if Wild Dog had not closed off the upper entry, sunlight would be filtering down the slope ahead through the damage pines. Firmly gripping his ax, he inched silently along the cool rock until he could proceed no further.

"You are wonderful," he heard her saying, "strong and mighty in battle. I will do anything you ask of me. Help me to honor my...husband...as You have commanded[18] and to do him good, not harm, all the days of my life."[19]

Pacing Wolf slowed his breathing, but when at length no reply, he recalled something Wild Dog had mentioned in the meadow. *She is speaking to her white-men's spirit-guide!* Returning his ax to his belt, he tried to unknot her puzzling requests. They aroused unwanted tenderness within him, cracking the tough pouch that encased his heart. Thrusting the feeling away, he intended to slip around the wall to catch sight of the unfamiliar spirit, but she again began speaking.

"Give me the courage to face what lies ahead, trusting You will act on my behalf."

She will need much courage, he thought, approving the request, *but what does this mean, 'you will act'? Is asking this spirit to bewitch me?*

"You told us to love our enemies, to feed them when they hunger and bring them water when they thirst..."[20]

Bah! He-Who-First-Made-All-Things would show more sense!

"I am willing, but if it is good in Your sight, please soften his heart so he does not hate me."

Waugh—she turns things upside down! I do not hate...

Muffled voices overhead, becoming clear once a stone was pulled from its place, ended both his thought and her prayer.

"Why would he bury her?" they heard a young warrior ask.

"Lord, it is Straight Arrows!" Light Bird whispered, overcome with awe and relief.

"Who knows the mind of this enemy?" answered the voice of her old grandfather. "The tracks lead here and away, but these rocks are freshly piled."

"Look!" cried a second young warrior. "Her cross. I found it in the pine needles."

"Ride swiftly downriver," the old voice commanded. "Tell your father and uncles we have picked up the trail. Straight Arrows and I will pull away the stones."

Light Bird ran toward their voices, but her blood turned cold as she saw Pacing Wolf's outline. *He will cut them down!* Swiftly closing the small space between them, she frantically clutched hold of his arm.

"They are my grandfather and brother—they are no match for you."

Shaking her off, Pacing Wolf drew out his ax and knife.

"If I please you at all, I beg you not to do this. I will fulfill my vow and serve you faithfully—only do not raise your hand against them."

"You offer what I possess already," growled Pacing Wolf, appalled that her pleading, like her prayer, made his heart feel soft.

"I offer you willingness. I have nothing else."

Above them, they heard more forceful voices and rocks thudding furiously to the ground. Grasping Light Bird's wrist, Pacing Wolf hurriedly retraced their steps to the sunlit room and then turned down the damp corridor that led past the spring. It descended and narrowed so rapidly she was certain they could continue no farther when he abruptly pressed her through a small opening into a blind cavity. Surprised he could follow, even by stooping and twisting, she hoped her quick compliance had lent her petition force.

"The new voices belong to my oldest brother, my father and three uncles—all skilled warriors. What can you do against seven?"

She speaks sense, Pacing Wolf thought, *but what does she want from me?*

When he did not reply, Light Bird thought he might have left already; but as he turned, she felt his breath on her hair.

Lord, do not let them die for what is lost already! Tell me how to sway him.

The pit of her stomach contracted, bringing to mind his earlier gesture. Finding his hand, she pulled it to her abdomen. "Your son may be growing within me. If they kill you, they will raise him to make war against his own blood."

Waugh—she has found the one spot she can work upon! My dead woman so quickly began to round, I doubted her purity. Handing her his water sack, he calculated how much time might pass before her kin broke through the pile of stones. "Drink."

When she had drained a good portion, he cut a small pouch from his belt, gripped the back of her loose hair, and tilted her head sharply upward. "Open your mouth." His fingers felt it. "Wider!"

Without hesitation, she did as he demanded, aware that her obedience would influence him far better than protests; and he stuffed her mouth so fully she could make nothing but the faintest sound.

Lord, please do not let him harm them! she prayed, standing perfectly still while he bound her ankles, tied her wrists behind her back, and then ducked out into the black passage.

The Lord loves justice. He will not forsake his faithful ones. He will slaughter the wicked and cut off their offspring.

Psalm 37:28

Chapter 6

PACING WOLF EDGED cautiously toward the sunlit room. Snatching up Light Bird's robe and his hunting shirt, he covered his tracks from the lower entry and then backed his way toward the spring. There, he filled his water pouch to bursting and emptied it over the smoothly worn conduit. Her father and uncles would avoid the narrow run-off, knowing the danger posed by a constricted opening; and if her brothers were foolish enough to follow its course, he would assist their descent into the mountain's belly.

Once Light Bird's men-folk had cleared away the largest stones, Little Turtle, the best tracker of the party, tied his rope to Preying Eagle, who in turn tied his to Two Bears, then Elk Dog Man, Straight Arrows, and finally to Running Deer. The last knotted his to the same sturdy pine Large Man had used.

"Build a small fire," Preying Eagle charged Pretty Face, the younger of his two sons present. "And have cut branches to pass forward so we can light our way. This cave may be deep."

As Little Turtle cautiously entered the tunnel, he prayed they would find his niece before it was too late. Squatting to examine the baffling pattern of prints and markings, he saw that a heavy weight had been dragged through the loose dirt and spotted half of one—no two—imprints of a warrior's large moccasin. He thrust a lit bough as far before him as he could reach, illumining the steep slope, and descended it without mishap. Signaling for another, he stuck it in the alcove, where he spotted several undisguised but confusing tracks and followed them eagerly until the rope ran out of slack.

While Little Turtle waited for his brothers to navigate the slope, he studied the size and composition of the rock, until a mark, smaller and differently shaped than the others, caught his attention. He held his torch close to the stone floor, touching the mark to determine it was fresh, and then searched intently for any sign of another. Proceeding forward until a third and then a fourth branch burned out, he spied sun filtering through the ceiling, untied the restraining cord, stretched it over the floor to guide the others, and walked toward the light.

The pile of hides in the dwelling room ignited Little Turtle's imagination and laid kindling to his fury. Determinedly shaking off the repellent images, he signaled for a new torch before crossing to find the source of trickling water. The summers seemed very few since Light Bird had nestled in his lap while listening to Spotted Long-Knife read The Book. He remembered her shy and happy smile when he had carved her first doll and could almost feel her tiny arms as they warmly squeezed his neck. As quiet and serious-minded as he, she had secretly been his favorite.

Tucked behind a bend in the lightless passage, his niece's captor watched him approaching. He considered Little Turtle's build—it lacked both Wild Dog's height and Large Man's girth—but Pacing Wolf, of similar wiry stature, knew better than to discount this warrior's strength. His own scalp shirt bore testimony against several enemies foolish enough to make such a mistake. Flattening his chest against the rough stone, he concluded Little Turtle possessed more cunning than his thickset tribesman and thought he might be the doe's father.

The wiry warrior squatted beside the spring to examine the moist run-off, rubbing the water between his thumb and fingers before touching it to his tongue. Thrusting the torch down the narrowing channel, he continued several paces.

Pacing Wolf held his breath, afraid the slightest exhalation might make the flame quaver. As it grew painfully hot against his shoulder, he struggled to suppress a desire to startle and hurl the man headlong down the shaft. He might well need to do so. If the warrior pressed one step deeper, he could not miss the cavity's small opening, but to prevail against so many at once, Pacing Wolf needed to retain the advantage of surprise.

Noting the channel sharply narrowed, Little Turtle scooped up a handful of the water and padded back around the corner as his light sizzled out. Pacing Wolf stepped forward through the darkness to see him take a new, freshly lit bough from a warrior standing over the hides. This second man was striking in appearance and both taller and older than the first. A third warrior, taller still and in his prime, and a fourth, wearing a double strand of bear claws, followed the wiry tracker down an unexplored passage and out of view.

As the striking warrior crouched over the stained buffalo robe, he rubbed a hand through its thick brown fur and raised it toward the sunlight. At once, agony twisted his features. Caught between his fingers were several spiraling strands that could only have fallen from his daughter's head. Gathering the pelt as though it still wrapped her, he rocked back and forth, splitting the silence with cadent wailing.

Light Bird had felt miserable when the glow of a torch stopped just short of her enclosure and she could do nothing to encourage it on; but when she heard her father's anguish echoing through the cavern, she could not contain her sorrow. Tears ran down her cheeks, her neck, and over her dress until she felt cold and damp. Still, she was oddly grateful for the precautions her captor had taken. Had he not stuffed her mouth with his leather pouch, she doubted she could have kept herself from yelling out, and he would surely have struck her father down.

"*Lord, please pour mercy into his heart or send your angel to restrain his arms.*"

As Pacing Wolf watched her father grieving, he grew so uncomfortable, he resolved to quickly end it. Swinging an arrow into place, he pulled back sharply, but he could not bring himself to release the string.

The doe has *bewitched me! Her father would dispatch my spirit without hesitation—and then what would become of her? Her tongue would swell from thirst, choking her even as she listens to the trickling water.* Deciding to wait until he could slay them all at once, he lowered the bow. His arrows were swift and he knew the cavern well. They would lie dead before discovering his hiding place.

Hearing a pebble roll, he found a grandfather and a fit young warrior treading toward the sunlit room as the uncles slipped through the passages opposite. Pacing Wolf grinned, thanking his spirit guide when the old one waved them toward the spring to speak beyond her father's hearing.

As he raised his bow, memories of his mother surged painfully from the place he had tightly bound them. He remembered her weeping after a Blackfoot war party had killed his father, slashing her smooth, soft arms in despair and allowing her life to drain out with her tears. Never again had he gazed over the early red prairie grass without recalling the meadow soaked with her blood.

"They are gone," the wiry tracker told the grandfather. "There are long tunnels that way, breaking off in several directions, but none hold footprints. They have only traveled these." He nodded toward the spring and then back to the cave's upper entrance. "We will search for a trail that leads down from this mountain."

The old man shook his head. "We have done this. The only tracks lead to the river—three horses. Did you find nothing coming up from the south?"

"No."

"What of the stones?" asked a handsome younger warrior. Pacing Wolf guessed he was the doe's brother. "Why pile them?"

The man who wore bear claws sadly shrugged. "I do not know. We are not familiar with this enemy's ways. Go—tell Pretty Face your sister is beyond our help."

"No," the grandfather countermanded. "Bring him down here."

When the handsome brother returned with another, more youthful in appearance, Pacing Wolf immediately recognized his features. They were very like the ones he had studied by last night's fire and had briefly looked into this morning.

"Come," directed the old man. "We will thank the Creator and ask Him to care for her."

"Thank Him—why?" demanded the younger brother. "A Raven-Enemy has ruined her!"

The tallest uncle gestured for him to be quiet, though his face held understanding. "Do you wish to increase your father's sorrow? The Creator does not guarantee us life without trouble."

"Then why serve Him?"

"Because He is the Almighty," retorted the grandfather, "and did not create our short lives for our pleasure."

The young warrior's nostrils flared. "Do you not grieve?"

"My head is bowed down with such sorrow I can barely keep it above my shoulders, but I have known the Creator for many summers. The painful is often more useful than the pleasant to accomplish His plans."

"What about Light Bird's plans—or Father's?"

"You snarl like that mangy red dog you kept from the rattlesnake. He snapped at you to show his anger, but he is better off because you restrained him."

"I kept him from harm. The Creator has stood still while evil swallowed her!"

This one speaks sense, thought Pacing Wolf. *Their white-men's god possesses no power.*

"Ignorance enraged your mangy dog and it enrages you now," answered the old man. "The Almighty's heart is good, and He is worthy of our confidence."

Once the striking warrior joined them, each prayed for Light Bird in his own fashion. Her brothers asked the Creator to help them find and kill her abductor, releasing her from the bonds of a forced and unwanted marriage. The old grandfather prayed that her faith would not fail, but Pacing Wolf found her father's requests wholly bewildering.

"O Lord, my soul is brought down in sorrow. My sons have spoken my heart well, yet You tell us to pray for those who misuse us and leave vengeance to You.[21] How do I ask You to bless a man who has ruined my daughter, the joy of her mother and grandmother, the joy of all our hearts?

Yet, I know you were not sleeping while he took her. We all want Light Bird back; but if You have sent her to this unfamiliar people, go with her as You went with my woman when she came to us. Grow love for her in this Raven-Enemy's heart and grant her favor among his people. Help her to trust Your faithfulness, to take comfort in Your nature, and make her enemy-husband worthy of her love."

When his father finished speaking, the youngest broke from the others, striding angrily toward the mouth of the cave; but his little sister, savoring each of her father's words, found consolation for her soul.

"We can do no more here," observed the grandfather. "Let us leave this den of misery."

Once Pacing Wolf was certain her men-folk were gone, he ducked back into the lightless hole. He had little trouble finding her and cutting her ankles loose, but as his fingers traveled up the curve of her neck to her damp cheeks, memories of the past night awakened his senses. Hastily removing his pouch from her mouth, he slipped his hands behind her back and felt for the cord that bound her wrists; but before he could cut her free, she crumpled against him, sobbing like a miserable child. Her breath caught in convulsive jerks, so he sheathed his knife lest he nick her skin, but every place he laid his hands rekindled desires he already struggled to ignore. She had been through enough today; he would not add his unwelcome attentions. Knowing nothing else to do, he held her stiffly, afraid she might topple over if he set her on her feet.

As Light Bird had expended her sorrow, she became keenly aware of the Sparrow Hawk's rigid embrace and mistaking this for censure grew deeply embarrassed. *He thinks me a fool,* she imagined while he slid his knife carefully beneath the leather bindings; but as her hands brushed his hunting shirt, she wished the ground might open. It was sopping wet. Hurriedly, she tried to wipe her tears away.

"Do not do this," he snapped, seizing her hands and holding them slightly away from him.

"I am sorry," she sputtered, staggering backward. "I…I did not mean to offend."

He kept her wrists imprisoned while weighing his reply. He was glad that the darkness hid her expression; he knew he would find hurt in her eyes. *I do not know which is worse—my dead woman's heart, as tough as scrub oak, or this little doe's that bruises so easily!*

When he finally spoke, his voice was so low and gravely that she hardly recognized it. "I am a warrior."

Why does he tell me this? Light Bird wondered. *Does he think I doubt his skill?* At a loss, she blurted out the only thing she could think to say: "I meant no insult. I...I..."

Pacing Wolf impatiently cut her off, "Your touch invites my attention."

Light Bird grew deadly still for a moment, and then, as she tried again to pull away, he so abruptly released her wrists that they bounced against her chest. Gripping her arm, he steered her through the opening, stopping only to thrust their personal items into her hands, guided her past the spring into the sun-lit dwelling room, and he hastily trotted away.

On the steep pathway through the secret place, let me see your form. Let me hear your voice, for your voice is sweet and your form is lovely.

Song of Solomon 2:14

Chapter 7

LIGHT BIRD GATHERED UP the buffalo pelt, damp with her father's tears, and cradled it against her heart. "Lord, please comfort him and let my mother know that I am all right, that this Sparrow Hawk warrior is…is…."

Feeling bruised and bewildered, she could not think of a way to complete her sentence. Besides his unmistakable intelligence and ability to perplex, she found contradictions of each description that came to mind. In the few hours since the sun had awakened, he had threatened and then protected her, intended to kill her men-folk and then shown them mercy, held her as she wept and then rebuffed her touch.

Still, I owe him much. He could have killed any or all of them, yet he let them go.

Thanking the Almighty for answering her pleas, she set about tidying up as she had her mother's dwelling every evening for as long as she could remember. His scent, inhaled while folding his shirt, stirred her own contradictions. When he was present, she wished him gone; yet, she had never felt as alone as she had when trotted away. Even as she peeked into his necessities sack, she found conflict. *He freely touches everything I have called my own, but I feel like an intruder looking into his bag.*

Growing hungry once she had finished her few tasks, she began to ask herself where her captor had gone and why he had not returned. *Maybe the Lord has answered Pretty Face's prayer and the Sparrow Hawk has fallen from the cliff.*

Surprisingly, the thought alarmed rather than comforted her. *I am just uneasy in this place without him,* she decided, but she knew she was not being entirely honest. The sun had dispelled her fear of winged creatures, and now that her men-folk had torn the stones away, she was sure she could find her way outside. They would have left tracks she could follow, but how would she get across the river?

"Lord, I feel so many things that I cannot explain. When a warrior invades a woman, does he also capture something of her soul? I cannot go back but am afraid to go forward. My vow has bound me until he dies, but

I do not crave that death. Give me courage to face what is ahead and grace to serve him well and willingly."

Her growling stomach disrupted her prayer, compelling her thoughts to the cave's mouth. Anything seemed better than idly going over and over her present situation. Erring only once, she ascended the steep grade, pausing between the damaged pines to question what the Sparrow Hawk might do if he found her outside.

Stepping tentatively into the bright daylight, she scanned the nearby tree roots for a spot that might hide a squirrel's cache. However, as she was about to move forward, a new fear found its voice. *What if Wild Dog has come back?* This would easily explain why Pacing Wolf had not returned.

Eying the tops of the soft-needled pines, she tested the strength of the taller tree's branches and assessed the amount of cover it might provide. She could see a bit of the river through a gap in the rocks—it was closer than she expected—and began climbing higher to view its length.

From the uppermost branch that could support her weight, she searched each crevice for signs of Wild Dog, Walks-Behind-Them, or her Sparrow Hawk captor; but as she twisted precariously in the direction of the river, her heart leaped so suddenly, she nearly lost her balance. On the closest bank a small war party whom she instantly recognized watered their horses.

Hidden halfway up the crag, Pacing Wolf watched Light Bird's ascent. *This little doe is clever. She makes soft oaths to bend my will, then slithers out like a snake.* Turning his bow toward the swiftly churning water, he withdrew an arrow, fit it into place, and calculated the force necessary to reach her father's back.

A quick movement shifted his attention: the doe cupped her hands around her mouth to lend volume to her voice. Swiftly swinging his bow toward the soft, warm place he had pillowed his head that morning, he drew the string back tautly; but just before he let the arrow fly, she flattened her palms against her lips.

God help me! she prayed. *He did as I asked. I cannot break my promise.*

Pacing Wolf's ears pounded. *In half a breath, my arrow would have pierced her heart!* Remaining alert, lest she still betray him, he swung his bow back toward her men-folk, but he could not shake the image of her plummeting to the rocks below. Inhaling deeply to calm himself, he watched them urge their mounts down the bank.

Glancing back to the tree-top, he could tell she was weeping; but though he quickly quelled the guilt her trembling shoulders provoked, he could not squelch the intense satisfaction he gained from her faithfulness. It sprung up within him like a well-watered vine, yielding fresh fruit while it wound back over his prior observations.

From her perch in the pine, Light Bird watched her men-folk until they looked as small as ants. They headed north on the far side of the river and disappeared, along with her hope. Pulling apart every decision she had made since the Sparrow Hawk snatched her, she weighed each against the Scriptures. Step by step, she had tried to choose whatever her Savior or her reason prescribed, yet everything had turned out wrong.

If I had not returned his vows, I could have fled—shamed but not bound. He has already done his worst. No, this is not true. He could have robbed my mother and grandmother of husbands, sons, and brothers....What is done is done. I am his until death.

As pangs of hunger directed her eyes to some green shoots sticking up on the sunny slope, she abandoned her tall pine and cautiously wound around an outcropping. It could handily hide an enemy. Finding nothing of concern, she sidled down the slope and began plucking up new lance-shaped leaves. She had never liked this variety, but wilting them on a stone near the fire would lessen their bitter taste.

Gathering all she could see, she turned to the roots of several sheltering trees for her brothers' favorites: crinkly-topped whitish-brown thumbs poking up among the dead leaves. They would not make much of a dinner but were tastier than the greens, and with the addition of items from her captor's bag, they would suffice.

She sets upon the sprouts as if they are her enemy, mused Pacing Wolf, as one spot after another on the hillside turned browner because of her quick industry. Once she had reached the outcropping's farther side, he lost sight of all but the crown of her head. It bobbed along from tree to tree, disappearing and reappearing every few minutes, until she came across a nearly naked sumac. Bracing her feet between two sturdy lower branches, she stripped the few stubbornly clinging leaves she found remaining toward the crown.

These will make good dye for the skin Pretty Face gave me yester...

Engaged in her task, she had almost forgotten her life's grim alterations; now all at once, she felt vulnerable and alone. Carefully holding up the edges of her skirt, she looked for the pines that marked the sheltering cave.

How many times, she asked herself, *did David hide from Saul in caves such as this?* Her two little brothers loved these stories, begging her to read them so often that she had learned them by heart; and every time she repeated one, she discovered new marvels. Rounding the outcropping, she recalled Saul and his army chasing David around a mountain. Just before they caught him, a runner came to Saul from home. The Philistines, he told Saul, were attacking their village, and the whole army turned back from their pursuit.[22]

Rubbing the tense crease between her brows, she questioned why the Creator had waited until morning to bring her men-folk, and despair began creeping up like an enemy. *No! Grandfather and Father are right. The Creator was not asleep last night or today—and His heart is good!*

Starting with Genesis, she searched her inner store for accounts of the Almighty triumphing through dismal situations and found plentiful encouragement and relief. *'The Lord is my portion, says my soul. Therefore I have hope in him.'*[23] *Do with me whatever You will, Lord—only please help my faith not to fail.*

Turning to squeeze between the soft pines, she found the filtered daylight greatly dimmed. The sun had climbed above the cliff so that only the first few steps were easily navigable. With one hand she secured her bounty, and with an outstretched foot, she felt along the floor until she found the drop. Judging it safer to scoot down the decline, she sat; but when the pines parted and a large shadow replaced the momentary dusk, she pressed her back against the cool wall.

Light Bird breathed as shallowly as possible. She had not seen her captor for several hours. Before she could make out his distinguishing thatch, the boughs closed together and soft steps padded in her direction. A firm grasp pulled her to her feet and the scent of herbed oil, so offensive last night, filled her with relief. Wild Dog smelled only of horses.

While Pacing Wolf lit a fire, Light Bird busied herself with the foodstuffs she had gathered. She attended the simple chore with the industry and agility he had noted earlier; but as he drank in her quiet grace, he concluded there was nothing simple or ordinary about her.

He had never eaten the small crinkly things she had gathered. Raw, they were brown-white and reminded him of pitted snake heads attached to a man's thumb; cooked they turned limp and gray-brown. While handing him the larger portion, she raised her eyes briefly, offering him the first full, well-lit glimpse he had seen of them since morning. They looked like dark pools, forgotten by all walking creatures, but this neither surprised nor disheartened him. He had expected hate.

When his eyes were not on her, Light Bird examined him from behind lowered lashes. She had been uncertain he would approve her errand, but he had said nothing. Even to a chosen woman, a warrior rarely accounted for his time, so she had not expected him to tell her where he had been, but he had shown no surprise when he found her near the cave's entrance. Quickly looking down as their eyes met, she noticed they needed firewood.

"The evening grows cool," she ventured. "I will gather more sticks before the sun settles down for its rest."

Pacing Wolf shook his head: "You will not be cold tonight."

When Light Bird's caught his meaning, her eyes grew wide and flitted up to his, but the glint she found there was so disconcerting, she quickly glanced around for another occupation. She found it in sumac leaves, laying them to dry before embers that felt much cooler than her cheeks.

Swirling his finger toward the hole in the ceiling, he added, "Smoke may draw enemies. We have had enough tumult for one sun."

Heartily agreeing, Light Bird looked around for a task that might carry her away from his attention. "I will fill your water sack," she offered and felt relieved when he simply nodded rather than following her toward the spring. Shielded from his view, she availed herself of its plentiful flow, washing away tears and disconcerting questions with the soil of the turbulent day.

Pacing Wolf added intelligence to the collection of pleasing attributes his captive bride possessed. Asking for neither light nor guidance, she had walked directly down the correct passageway. Without her appealing presence to distract him, however, his mind wandered back to her silence in the pine tree.

What fawn stays in a wolf's den when she sees the way is open?

He was not inclined to credit such costly fidelity to a woman, but though he tried to ferret out a secret motive, he could find none. Becoming aware ample time had passed for her to return with fresh water, he lit a branch and went to see if she was lost.

As light flickered off the moist stone, Light Bird raised her head from the cascading water. Casting a frantic eye down the passage, she spotted his shadow rounding the corner.

One glance told Pacing Wolf she was frightened. She stood perfectly still, her slender fingers frozen within her long spirals. Supposing she had spied another bat, he ran the torch along the ceiling.

He is my...my...husband, she reasoned with herself, trying to tamp down her rising panic.

Finding nothing, Pacing Wolf wedged the branch into the wall, came up close behind her, and began gently winding his fingers through her dripping tresses.

Lord, he has a right to me, she prayed. *Help me yield willingly, as I promised.* Mustering all her courage, she murmured over her shoulder. "I...I am yours...altogether."

Engrossed in her waves, he was only half listening, but as he caught what she was saying, his gaze darted up to her round black eyes. His insides flinched. He had seen the exact look often and recognized it instantly: trapped prey, desperate to escape. Dropping her hair, he stepped away, waiting for her to brush past him or back further into the alcove, but she lowered her eyes and repeated the vow.

I will not take her like this; she has endured enough today! Striding from the spring, he hurried toward the lower entrance, not bothering to count the steps. Sweeping aside the pine boughs and vines, he crossed the creek to greet his sorrel, who had picked up his scent and was trotting excitedly back and forth.

Pacing Wolf patted the horse's warm neck. "Tomorrow we go home," he whispered, "and you will be lonely no more." As the prospect nudged his own heart, he brusquely shoved it away. It was not for home that he longed. "Waugh! Did I not tell you? Women are the softest snares. They weaken the strongest warrior."

Even the smooth muzzle nuzzling his shoulder called the doe back into his mind. "It is the strange god her people serve," he declared to his four-legged companion. "He uses her to weaken me toward her people, but I will show her differently. She is mine and I will do with her whatever I wish!"

Baffled by Pacing Wolf's departure, Light Bird wore a furrow between relief and worry. *I am safe—for now—but why did he go? Did I anger him? What does it matter as long as he is gone?* As she recalled how tightly he had gripped her while he was dreaming, she turned over several possibilities in her mind. *Did the sunlight reveal I am ugly? Perhaps he had been dreaming of his dead woman.* She imagined the distaste her father would feel if he awoke with a woman other than her mother. *Maybe he waits for the embers to die so that he can pretend it is her he caresses.*

Having nothing else to do, she sought warmth between the buffalo robes and reflected back over the day. Her insides tensed as she recalled his hand upon her stomach and also the reason she returned it there while they hid behind the spring.

I am an Allied guest-lodge stolen to shelter the Sparrow Hawk's children. Perhaps what he said is true: by loving them, I too will find comfort. Lord, let me conceive quickly.

Once Pacing Wolf emerged from the long underground tunnel, he easily found his way to their bed, but the new moon did not offer enough light to see if his captured bride was awake or sleeping. She was curled in a ball. As he lifted the edge of the pelt and slipped beneath it, he felt her shiver—whether from the rush of cold air or revulsion he did not know. Wrapping himself around her back as he had last night, he expected to feel her stiffen.

Instead, she twisted around to face him. He kept every muscle taut, lest a false move turn her away, waiting to learn what she might do or say.

"Thank you for sparing my men-folk," she whispered. "You possess much skill and your arm is strong. You could have killed them easily."

Pacing Wolf could not reply. His heart had so swelled it seemed to choke him, but when he felt her cool fingertips tentatively touch him, he enclosed them in his own and pressed them to his chest.

"I...I have asked the Creator of all life to allow me to bear you a son to lighten your sorrow."

Once spoken, the admission startled her as much as him, but though his tongue was still tightly knotted, the tough sheath he wrapped around his heart began threatening once more to slip away. He replied in the only way he knew, aiding her unknown spirit-guide in granting her petition.

Enfolded in the slumbering Sparrow Hawk's arms, Light Bird felt the first hint of peace, even security, since she had entered the meadow to retrieve her bundle. She could not explain why—maybe she had begun to accept her lot—yet she felt hope, not resignation. Looking up at the crack in the roof, she watched a thin, curved sliver of light emerge from a dark, billowing blanket.

"*Lord, please help me to follow the moon's example...shining in both happiness and sorrow. Help me honor You by treating this...my husband...as Your Word and my mother have taught me.*"

Let love and faithfulness never leave you; strap them around your neck, paint them on the lodge-cover of your heart.

Proverbs 3:3

Chapter 8

During the Moon When Buffaloes Drop Their Calves

PACING WOLF'S HEART contracted as his captive bride turned toward the place he stood dressing. She looked like a child peacefully sleeping between his buffalo pelts. As he pondered the resilience hidden beneath her delicate exterior, he thought of the blossoms that painted the prairie each spring. Sprouting exposed them to wind and heat, yet they refused to stay safely sleeping within earth's womb.

She is worthy of the fiercest warrior!

His dead woman had been like the showy crabapple blossoms: inviting every eye but falling to the ground at the slightest touch. As her sly glances at Speckled Horse slipped into his musings, Pacing Wolf gathered the time-toughened sheath back over his heart and began sharpening his knife so violently that Light Bird began to stir.

Engulfed in a haze of sleep, she reached toward his side of the pallet, hunting for the only benefit of marriage she readily welcomed—warmth. The sun offered little this morning, and she was growing too chilled to defend herself against its ever-brightening rays.

As Pacing Wolf watched her, he considered sliding between the hides. He wished he could delay their return home. Her willingness last night had sparked a flicker that he looked forward to coaxing into bright flames, but her kinsmen's discovery of the cavern yesterday made staying there impossible.

Reluctantly waking, Light Bird rose up on an elbow and looked about groggily for the source of repetitive grating. Her eyes danced over the room and found her captor sitting cross-legged a few feet away. From behind disheveled locks, she watched a small ring of porcupine quills swinging from his ear in rhythm to his chore. Two eagle feathers hung above it and several others peeked up from his crown, all proclaiming what she already knew: he was a well-skilled and accomplished warrior.

Deciding he looked almost handsome, one glance into his keen black eyes rushed blood to her cheeks. They stared into hers with satisfaction, declaring plainly that he had noticed her shy appraisal, and raised a hope so fragile that she hesitated to give it voice. A warrior normally wore a hunting shirt or only his breechcloth and possibly leggings. This morning Pacing

Wolf was dressed in full regalia, as a warrior did to impress a woman he desires, donning all the tokens that proved he was able to protect and provide. As she modestly dropped her eyes, however, her whole countenance fell. His readied gear and sharpened weapons lay beside the buffalo robes. He was preparing to go home.

He wears his finery for his people, to announce he has accomplished his vengeance.

As Pacing Wolf watched her rapidly changing expressions, he felt keenly disappointed. He had not missed her admiration, had enjoyed the shy blush he had raised on her angular cheeks, but the brow she now furrowed and lips she compressed strangled all his pleasure.

"Dress yourself quickly," he ordered. "We go."

Thrusting his ax into his belt, he was rolling up the pelts almost before she could step out of them, carelessly scattering her drying sumac leaves. Light Bird scurried after them, her loose hair cascading enchantingly about her hips.

Just like a woman, he inwardly scolded. *A hard journey lies before us, but she is concerned with frivolities.*

He was in no mood to admit he admired her careful conservation, but he added the pleasing trait to his secret store. Through the cliff's belly, he plunged them at a pace that offered Light Bird little time to marvel at its depth, braid her hair, or consider why her enemy-husband had turned stone cold.

When at last he brushed away the thick barrier of branches and pushed aside the vines, she was astounded by the change in the distant terrain. In place of the thick forest that covered her people's dark hills was a flat plain, as endless and bleak as the new life spread before her.

The sorrel began neighing, anticipating his release from the secluded pen and gladly accepting his beaded bridle. Following the horse's lead, Light Bird lowered her head to receive her master's rope, but her acquiescence decided the matter. Pacing Wolf swung her up behind him unbound, and then carefully picked through the remaining trees.

While they galloped relentlessly from all she loved, Light Bird tried vainly to suppress her fears. Her husband's people might scorn the enemy blood running through her veins and hate her because of her kinsman's crime.

Does he have other wives, she wondered, *besides the one that Wild Dog slaughtered?*

If so, she would likely find her lot much worse. Elder wives gave new ones the hardest chores and beat them severely if they faltered or complained. Even the gray-green bushes they passed seemed to mock her.

They are like his sporadic tenderness—offering a brief respite from the harsh wind but too puny to provide shelter. Why did he become angry this morning? I did nothing but look at him. Is my face so poorly formed that he finds it hateful?

Amnon, she recalled, despised Tamar once he had taken her.[24] *Perhaps this is the natural way of men.* The story had unsettled her faith as a child, and her mother's answer did nothing to ease her present distress. *'God gave men the freedom to love or reject Him. One person's sin often harms many others.*

Surely he found me a little pleasing—why else would he keep me from Wild Dog and show mercy to my family? With a sinking feeling, though, she recalled her own question: 'What is the strongest warrior against seven?' *My father and uncles are enough to frighten any man...and Grandfather, in his day, was just as strong...even Straight Arrows has won tokens in battle. Perhaps he simply showed good sense.*

When she considered her expressions of gratitude last night, her stomach gave way, and she was no longer sure how to feel. *If only he were cruel, I might turn my heart to stone...*

As if it happened yesterday, a childhood remark she had made about Swallow Woman, sprung vividly to mind. "Why do they call her after such a pretty bird?" she had asked her grandmother. "I would call her Stone-Heart-Woman." Two Doves had scolded, telling her to pray, not criticize, when she saw a flaw in someone's character; but Light Bird had secretly thought the woman was beyond hope. Now, she felt ashamed of her lack of mercy and wondered what sort of bitterness had spoiled the once beautiful face.

O Lord, I take my request back. I do not want to be made of stone. Please show me how to... Before she had completed her prayer, the verses she could not retrieve two days ago poured into her heart as if the Creator had spoken them aloud.

"If you do what is right and patiently endure suffering, this is commendable before God. To this you were called, because Christ suffered for you, leaving you an example to follow in His steps. He committed no sin, nor was any deceit found in his mouth. While being reviled, He did not revile in return. While suffering, He uttered no threats, but kept entrusting Himself to Him who judges righteously."[25]

Lord, this is different!' she protested, but, scouring her memory for the context, she realized it was not. Peter had written it to slaves whose masters treated them unfairly. *I am also property, punished for the deed of another...Lord, help me. I do not want to turn hateful and cold. How then could I reflect You to anyone? Your grace is enough for me. Make Your strength perfect in my weakness.'*[26]

Knowing Jesus' promise to grant anything she asked that was in keeping with His will, she lifted her face from Pacing Wolf's back. The view that greeted her took away her breath. Enormous peaks, more imposing than any she had ever seen, stretched determinedly toward the setting sun. Lined up, row after row, they looked as fearsome and magnificent as a huge party of Allied warriors arrayed for battle.

As darkness descended, Pacing Wolf pulled to a halt beside a small creek and indicated a clump of low trees that might offer Light Bird privacy. He watched her normally nimble legs wobble as she walked away and wondered if the long journey or dread made them unsteady.

She has much to fear, he concluded, dipping a finger into a bit of clay. *I have paid my debt of vengeance, but my dead woman's mother will not let her forget. Perhaps the Kicked-in-the-Bellies will summer with Those-Who-Live-Among-the-River-Banks.*

Light Bird's insides dropped as she glanced over her shoulder. Her captor had braided his sorrel's tail and was painting its rump for his triumphant ride through his village. Leaning back against the rough bark, she breathed deeply to calm her heart. It had taken off like a deer that smelled a wolf's distinct odor on the evening breeze.

"We go!" called Pacing Wolf, impatient to finish the impending unpleasantness.

"The Lord is my light and my salvation; who will make me afraid?" she recited. "The Lord is the war-shield that guards my life, who will fill my heart with dread?"[27]

Scurrying back to the place he stood waiting, Light Bird noticed the red stripes painted across his leggings, but the feathers dangling from the staff he held coaxed her eyes upward. They climbed token after token until her racing heart lurched to a painful halt. At the top hung Large Man's hair. She imagined it fluttering in the wind as Pacing Wolf dragged her through a jeering, hate-filled throng. While she ran to keep up, his rope would bite into her still-tender neck, cutting off her breath every time she stumbled.

Tottering backward, she glanced from the lance to her captor's face. It was replete pride and confidence. He displayed as many trophies as her father; but though she awed, she also felt a traitor to the Allied scalps that might one day join Large Man's, many that her heart might hold quite dear.

Pacing Wolf recognized her inward battle, but he fought another of his own. He had intended to impress her, but he detested the way her admiration swelled his heart. Only the weakest warriors handed such power to women. Closing the gap between them, he slipped a hand behind her skull and, with the thumb of the other, smeared a red line across each of her cheeks. He repeated the action again and again until she wore the distinct markings of a captured bride. Aware of the envy she would inspire, his heart swelled even more; but this, too, filled him with alarm.

Coveting trails envy's footprints. My Fox rivals will hand me trouble when the grass turns green.

"You are my woman," he declared gravely.

As she nodded in agreement, she wondered why he had said it. Was he offering her his protection or making certain she understood her place? Whichever he intended, she would soon find out; he directing her gaze toward the heights.

"We sleep tonight on the Cliffs-That-Have-No-Name."

Those who look to Him are radiant; their faces are never covered with shame.

Psalm 34:5

Chapter 9

TWO DOVES PUSHED a bowl of rabbit toward her daughter-in-law. "You must eat."

Brought-Us-the-Book's eyes looked intensely green as they wearily peered from their puffy, red surroundings. "Food lands like rocks in my belly."

"I know," replied Two Doves, patting the infant nested in the nearby cradleboard. "But do you want my new granddaughter to suffer as well?"

"No," murmured Brought-Us-the-Book, reluctantly accepting a handful of chokecherries. "But why Light Bird?"

"Do you wish he had snatched Red Fawn's daughter?"

"No! Yes! Anyone but Light Bird! I know I should not feel so, but of what use is pretending—I cannot hide my thoughts from the Creator. I just want her back. You waited far more summers than I for a girl-child—how can you take her loss so calmly?"

"Have you been with us so long and still do not understand our ways? Sorrow has tossed me off a cliff and I am still falling, but the Creator is either who He says He is or He is our vicious enemy. He cannot be both. I love all my grandchildren more than I have words to express, but Light Bird is closest to my heart."

Brought-Us-the-Book looked up in surprise. Not once had she seen Two Doves show Light Bird favoritism, and their people typically valued sons over daughters, as fighting and hunting kept the band alive.

"My grandsons are full of tracking and shooting, their fathers and their grandfather. Light Bird is yours, but she is also mine. I spend the largest portion of every day with her helping and learning by my side."

"You make me feel ashamed."

Two Doves held out her open arms. "Come."

Brought-Us-the-Book immediately responded, resting her head between the silver braids.

"If you did not feel as you do, I would wonder if you were carved from wood, but I know your heart as well as I know my own. You speak from your grief, but you would not wish this on anyone, even Swallow Woman."

"Swallow Woman!" spat Brought-Us-the-Book. "She was my torment when I was young and now her son…"

"Shhhh." The older woman stroked the younger's loose mahogany-colored waves. "Do not allow sorrow to choke your heart with bitterness. The Creator endured like pain, only His beloved child was murdered in the vilest manner. He has a plan for Light Bird, just as He did for you when He brought you to us."

"But I wanted to live here!"

"Did you? While safe and secure in your father's dwelling, did you one day decide, 'I will go up into the mountains and join a people I have never met?'"

"No," Brought-Us-the-Book mumbled. "But she is so young…"

"And you were so old?"

"No," she admitted.

"Barely seventeen, and Light Bird has advantages you did not."

Uncertain of what she meant, Brought-Us-the-Book twisted her head to gain a better view of Two Doves' eyes.

"All our daughters know they may one day meet this fate."

"But it was different with Preying Eagle—he treated me well. We know nothing of this man except he craves his enemies' pain."

"He wanted vengeance, yes, but…"

"They come! They come!" echoed frenzied voices outside the dwellings.

Joking Woman, a petite grandmother, stuck her graying head inside the door flap. "My daughter and her husband," she exclaimed, trying her best to temper her joy for love of her grieving friends. "They are back!"

"Valuable Woman and Spotted Long-knife? We had not expected them so soon."

"And Corn-Tassels is with them!" Joking Woman had not seen her honey-haired granddaughter during the past four summers or her daughter, grandson, and son-in-law since the leaves had last turned yellow and orange.

"Go ahead without us." Two Doves pointed to her ankle. "We come, but slowly."

Joking Woman ran to welcome them home while Brought-Us-the-Book helped her mother-in-law onto unsteady feet.

"Perhaps you, too, will welcome a grandchild before long," Two Doves teased. "Your eldest is sure to take Corn-Tassels quickly, and Wooden Legs is eager for him to have her. She already grows old. Most her age have a little potbellied thing crawling about their feet or hanging onto their dresses. Several grow round with a second."

Attempting to smile, Brought-Us-the-Book helped her out onto the path, and they hobbled toward the gathering swarm.

The fading sun glinted off Anna Mary Anderson's auburn curls as she stood with her daughter, Abigail, atop the wagon seat. Something, she sensed, was amiss. She had spotted her mother making her way toward them through the crowd, but she could see neither her father nor any of her brothers. She also wondered what was keeping her Aunt Two Doves and Brought-Us-the-Book. The latter had long been her closest friend. Indeed, because they shared the same heritage, everyone, even their own families, regarded them as sisters.

When she finally saw a set of dark brown braids, she waved her bonnet happily, but she dropped it to her side when noticed her friend's eyes. They looked red and swollen—even from a distance—and the smile she wore seemed forced. Climbing down, Anna Mary weaved past aunts and cousins to greet the gray-haired woman who had raised her so lovingly.

"Where is Father?" Her mother looked older than she remembered and her black eyes lacked their usual sparkle. "Has something happened?"

Before her mother could answer, Abigail threw herself into Joking Woman's copper-colored arms.

"Grandmother!" cooed Abigail, hugging the older woman fiercely. "How I have missed you!"

"Corn-Tassels!" Joking Woman scolded, hastily wiping a tear from her brown cheek. "Have the white men made you forget our ways? What will your cousins think?"

No one, least of all Corn-Tassels, believed her grandmother felt displeased, but the girl readjusted a moss-green bonnet and made an effort to show greater decorum.

"You must teach me all over again. I do not intend to leave your side for one moment!" She dimpled deeply and then slipped away from her grandmother to squeeze through the throng. "Two Doves, Brought-Us-the-Book!" Grabbing them both, she kissed their cheeks soundly before noticing the cradleboard strapped to her *aunt's* back. "And who is this?" she laughed, caressing the infant's black head, but rather than wait for a reply, she chirped, "Where are Straight Arrows and Light Bird? I cannot wait to see them!"

When Anna Mary caught up, her amber glance gently censured her daughter for such reckless effervescence. "All in good time. Your father and I also wish to greet them." Peering into her old friend's face, however, she felt torn between the conflicting strictures of their two shared cultures. She followed Brought-Us-the-Book's lead, showing proper restraint with all but her eyes; and in that instant, Anna Mary Anderson once more became Valuable Woman.

A tall man wearing a gold-braided dark blue coat slipped up behind them. Nathaniel Anderson's eyes were as amber as his wife's, but through the years, a smattering of white had lightened his auburn hair to the color of red clay mixed with sand. His face was so heavily freckled that the white parts looked like spots. That, coupled with his military saber, formed his name among the Allies: Spotted Long-knife.

Even Joking Woman did not at first glance recognize the ginger-haired youth that stood beside him, smiling from ear to ear. Samuel had grown taller than his father since she had seen him last fall.

As Two Doves answered questions about her ankle, Nathaniel wiped a dusty glove across his freckled forehead. He also wondered what was amiss. The village was in good form, and he had not noticed any burial platforms along their way, but he could not help noticing many warriors—all the ones he wanted most to see—were absent. This was not unusual. The forests were emerging from winter's grip, teeming with game to replenish their dwindling stores of meat, but some unspoken sorrow hung heavily in the air.

"Where are all the men-folk?" he asked, lacking his wife's delicacy.

Two Doves and Brought-Us-the-Book looked from Nathaniel to the blue-coated young man they had noticed standing a little apart. He held his round, broad-billed cap across his chest as if apologizing for the intrusion. Had Brought-Us-the-Book been less wretchedly occupied, she would have noticed how eagerly his eyes traced each contour of her face.

"Light Bird is gone," Two Doves muttered grimly.

Nathaniel thought he must have misheard. Knitting his brow together, he glanced at his wife and daughter, who looked equally stunned.

"What…what do you mean—gone?" stammered the honey-haired young woman. "Did she marry that handsome tall warrior from the northern band?"

"Slow, granddaughter, slow," replied Joking Woman. "We will tell you all, but one thing at a time. First," she addressed her son-in-law, "you will make this warrior of the Long-knives known to us."

Only then did Brought-Us-the-Book look directly into the young man's face. Whether grieving or joyful, she did not want to make a stranger feel unwelcome. His thick black eyebrows and lively dark eyes hailed something deep within her, like an old friend seeking entry at the door-flap of her memory, until clear recollections came suddenly charging in.

"Tommy?" she whispered. "It cannot be!"

A wide white smile broke beneath his black mustache and mischief danced through his darkly lashed eyes. "No, ma'am," he replied, "but I'm often told that I look like him. Joshua Wilson, and I believe you are my godmother."

"Joshua? Allison's son?" If his looks had not instantly convinced her, his rich resonant voice did. Forgetting all restraint, she hugged him hard. "But how…Oh, I cannot believe it."

Warmly returning her embrace, he felt glad to have brightened her eyes, if only for a moment. "I can see I've come at a difficult time, but I had to take the chance. Mother has told me so many stories—and Uncle Thom—I feel like I've known you all my life. Grandmother sends her love."

"Ah, Mama Pierantoni…" Why did she have trouble calling up the beloved features? Every time she thought of her, Quiet Woman's face came to mind. "How is she?"

"Just fine. A few aches and pains, but she turned sixty last December."

"She was so good to me when my mother went home to the Lord. I've missed her almost as much as I've missed Allison. Look at you—I just can't believe it—Allison's son, all grown up. You must be…" She remembered he'd been born the summer before she married.

"Twenty-two."

"Yes, twenty-two. And your mother, how…"

Pounding hooves shook the hard earth as warrior after warrior rode into the village, but instead of whooping triumphantly, they wore somber faces. Even Joking Woman's honey-haired granddaughter, fresh from several years of schooling in Boston, did not miss the significance. Connecting their dejection to her battery of unanswered questions, she murmured aloud what everyone else was thinking.

"She is not with them. They did not find her."

As one man, they ran to the center of the village, but one look at Preying Eagle confirmed Abigail's conclusion. He leaped from his mount, grasped Brought-Us-the-Book's wrist, and pulled her toward their family's dwelling. The rest of their men-folk ducked in after them, followed closely by their families and the newly arrived white cousins, but they were all too staggered by the unspoken tidings to ask any questions.

With one look into his wife's green eyes, Preying Eagle's lost his battle for self-control, and a cacophony of shrill wails echoed his lament. It rang in an undulating contagion throughout the village: hushed silence replacing exhausted cries in one sector as loud wails broke out afresh in another.

Joshua had been forgotten. As the only person who harbored no affection for the missing girl, he stood outside and listened to the disparate voices of their grief. He was not alone for long. Children too young to comprehend the trouble tugged at his soldier's clothing and stepped on his hard leather riding boots until the Andersons' red-headed son belatedly ushered him inside.

A strange mixture of scents, some agreeable, some less so, assaulted his nostrils as he ducked into the tall round tent. Unaccustomed to unfettered emotion—particularly displayed by men—he felt both revolted and awed by their open anguish. He found it shameful and womanly even while envying their freedom.

More often than not, he rested his eyes on his mother's childhood friend. He had long been intrigued by her youthful decision and was curious to know how she coped in such foreign environs. As several gray-haired women warmly offered her comfort, he saw clearly she had been well accepted.

A pleasant-faced matron standing near her confided, "I am glad Red Woman and Old Man did not live to see this day. I feared she would die from grief when the Horned-People took you, and when he learned of it, we needed several young warriors to restrain him."

Joshua, who could not help overhearing, felt taken aback. He had poured over each of his godmother's letters as his family received them. Indeed, they were the initial spark that had interested him in his current ambition, but none mentioned she had been captured. Perhaps she had not wanted his mother to fret or he may have misunderstood the pleasant-faced woman. He was not yet fluent in their language.

During their long journey, his commanding officer and family had set aside time each day to teach him, but he still felt confounded by the way they conveyed thoughts. An entire string of words was needed for a single object. Instead of saying east, for example, to describe the direction from which they had just traveled, Samuel had instructed him to say, "the wind from the mouth of the dwelling," and if he were to refer to a maple, he would need to describe "the tree with pale bark."

When Joshua was not observing his godmother, he watched the Major's pretty blonde daughter. She exchanged frequent glances with a handsome warrior on the opposite side of the tent. Some were filled with sorrow, others with longing, and all with offers of comfort. The warrior was a good deal taller than he, slightly taller even than his godmother's husband. In fact, as he compared their features, he came to an awkward conclusion: this was her son, a man he had looked forward to meeting and hoped to befriend. He disliked him immediately.

Everyone fell silent while Two Bears recounted all that had taken place since the morning his brothers and he had raced over the hill. "Wild Dog offered us one kindness: he knew this cavern and led us to it."

"You met them there?" asked Old Many Feathers, Two Bears aged white-haired uncle.

"No, but we suspect the Raven-Enemy killed or wounded one of their party. We found many hoof prints outside the cave's mouth and much blood inside. You have heard no more of them?"

The old man shook his head. "Not since we drove them from our village."

When Two Bears noticed the color draining from his sister-in-law's face, he quickly added: "The blood was not Light Bird's. The Raven-Enemy and she have vanished—like smoke from a spent fire."

"Whose was it?" asked Spotted Long-knife.

"One of Wild Dog's party," Little Turtle answered. "Who, we cannot say. We tracked hoof-prints from the Muddy River, hoping they would lead us to Light Bird, but they cut toward Red Fox's village. Tomorrow we will travel there to question their elders."

The old uncle, whom Joshua surmised held a place of importance, nodded. "Where does this Raven-Enemy live?"

"Near the place the sun settles down to rest."

"What makes you certain Light Bird was in this cave?"

Pretty Face handed him the cross. "We found this. I carved it for her last Christmas."

"And these," groaned Preying Eagle. He held his woman's gaze as he drew the long black spirals from his pouch. "They were caught in a pelt stained with the proof of her purity. The Raven-Enemy has already taken her his woman."

Accepting the strands from his hand, she pressed them against her cheek.

"I will track him down," cried Pretty Face, "and kill him as we would a crazed wild-cat!"

"How?" asked Running Deer. "You and I scoured the cliff together. Did you find a trail?"

The young warrior tightly clamped his jaw. His tracking skills were a secret source of pride, but he had not found as much as an oddly bent blade of grass. "No," he bit out, glancing from his grandfather to his mother. "It was as my uncle recounted. An eagle seemed to have carried them away."

"You said this enemy lives near the sun's bed," stated Spotted Long-knife. "Toward the cold wind or the grasses that blow with fire?"

"We do not know," answered Little Turtle. "Only Stands-Alone has seen one—during the Moon of Ripening Cherries. He told us the warrior appeared worn and ragged, like one who has traveled far from his village. He and his sons broke off from our party to find the place he spotted him, hoping the grass there remembers something."

Running Deer gravely shook his head. "They will find nothing. The wind blew strong during the Moon of Long Nights churning the grass in many directions, and the Moon of Hunger blanketed it with snow. But no one, not even this Raven Enemy, can escape the sight of the Almighty."

This I call to mind and therefore I have hope: Because of the Lord's great love we are not consumed, for his compassions never fail. They are new every morning; great is Your faithfulness.

Lamentations 3:21-23

Chapter 10

HOLDING HIS STAFF HIGH, Pacing Wolf rode down a lane between endless lodges while a herald proclaimed his victory throughout the village. Only the old and frail remained by their small cook-fires. Young warriors rushed forward in a frenzy of congratulations, and ululating women trailed behind them, appraising Light Bird as if she were a stolen mare. Several regarded her with pity, perhaps thinking of lost daughters. Others glared at her with hate—and disappointment that her captor kept her securely on the back of his mount.

The procession halted as an important-looking middle-aged warrior disentangled himself from the crowd. What he was to Pacing Wolf, Light Bird could not decide. They bore no resemblance of face or form. Still, she sensed deference in her captor's carriage and beheld warm approval in the lines of the older man's face. His gaze leaped quickly over Large Man's scalp, bow, and war club, and then came to rest lingeringly on her.

"You have gained your enemy's soul, his weapons, and his woman—and much honor from our young men; but when the grass turns green, you will see Foxes sneaking beneath your door-flap."

Her captor's eyes gleamed while receiving this older warrior's praise, but when he heard his final pronouncement, she felt his back stiffen. It made little sense to her, an enigmatic riddle that she had no time to solve. A throng of women was engulfing the horse and tugging her legs as if they meant to pull her down. Tightly clinging to her enemy-husband, she hoped he would shield her from their grasp, but he wrenched her arms free and forcibly slid her to the ground.

As Light Bird struggled with both her footing and composure, a firm hand slipped under her arm and a woman a bit older than her captor held her upright. "What do they call you?" she asked.

"She is Small Doe-Woman," declared Pacing Wolf, giving Light Bird a look that dared her to correct him.

"I am Never-Sits, your husband's sister. I will take you to his lodge."

Light Bird glanced back at Pacing Wolf, but he had dismounted and melted into the revelers. His sister pushed through the pawing hands until, at last, they arrived at a prominent dwelling close to the main path. Her slanting eyes and rounded features revealed nothing of her thoughts, but her level tone was a welcome contrast to the preceding frenzy.

"Go in," Never-Sits instructed, holding the door-flap aside.

Light Bird did as instructed, but before she could offer her thanks, the woman slipped off into the deepening shadows. The dwelling held nothing but a large buffalo-hide bag stowed beside a willow-frame bed and the few sparse possessions needed often by a warrior. A shield, different than the one hanging from his sorrel, was propped up against the lodge-cover; several drying saplings waited to be shaped into bows, and a few well-worn bridles awaited mending.

Looking up, she spotted a pipe overhead, stored in calfskin, and two crooked staffs fringed with long strips of willow bark. She wondered what they were. Her men-folk owned nothing like them, but even if her captor were home, she would feel too shy to ask. Putting another fear to rest, she sighed with relief.

He has already given his dead woman's belongings to her mourners, and either he has no other wives or they all live apart from him.

Four main lodge poles held up his dwelling with a number of narrower poles laid between them. It was much larger than any she had seen during her sixteen summers. If she stood on her father's shoulders, she doubted she could peek out the smoke hole. Wondering if she might live here, she began examining its cover's workmanship. The stitches were overly large, as if sewn by someone with poor eyes, and many seams were in need of repair.

She surmised his dead woman had owned a mirror, which was common now that white traders hauled their goods in wagons: someone had wedged a peg into a lodgepole at just the right height for a typically sized woman to study her reflection. Light Bird had never owned one, but she had bought one for Corn-Tassels to take to Boston. "So you do not forget who you are," she explained, as her pleased friend hugged her tightly.

As she fingered the spot where the object might have hung, the unexpected memory provoked intense cravings, not only for Corn-Tassels but for her friend's whole family. Though they did not actually share her blood, their mothers' white skin and close friendship had cast them as kin in the eyes of their people; and having only brothers, Light Bird looked on Corn-Tassels as an older sister. *She will soon come home. What will she think when I am not there to welcome her?*

← ← ← → → →

"ANNA MARY—Valuable Woman—and I have something we need to tell all of you," confided Spotted Long-knife as he and his extended family were enjoying an evening meal in Brought-Us-the-Book's dwelling. "We have been holding off because of our sorrow over Light Bird."

The gravity of his tone drew even Straight Arrows' ears, though the young warrior's eyes were thoroughly occupied. They searched Spotted Long-knife's daughter, discovering unfamiliar aspects of her well-known landscape; only he could not decide if the four summers she had lived in her father's village had changed her for better or worse. Her eyes returned the young white warrior's glances and her dress was immodest. It clung closely over a curving form that was foreign to his memory.

She had barely entered womanhood when she last traveled east, so he had always thought of her as she was in childhood: spindly as a newborn colt. Though he found the alterations appealing, he could not decide which seized his attention most: promises they held for his future or fear that she might burst through the flimsy fabric. He had been relieved when she removed her ugly white-woman's headdress to show she still owned lovely honey-colored hair. The sun had glistened all through it when she was little as if her braids had captured its rays and held them prisoner.

"An old family friend," relayed her father, "made me known to the Commissioner of Indian Affairs. He asked me to work as a liaison of sorts for the U.S. government and possibly, later, to run for office."

Wooden Legs cocked his head, thinking he could not have heard his son-in-law correctly. "The evil white-father who forces our brothers to leave their lands? We wondered why you again wear the night-sky coat of a long-knife."

"My people have recommissioned me. Jackson is no longer their chief elder. They have chosen another man, Van Buren, in his place."

"But these wrongs have not stopped," persisted his father-in-law. "Last summer we had heard they robbed a large people of their homes in the mountains and forced them to cross the wide river that flows from our headwaters. You would help this man?"

"I would help your people and others like the one you describe—but I cannot do this by hiding the things I have learned from you. I am no longer a young warrior like Straight Arrows here; I have become engaged in a different kind of fight. I hope to help lay good groundwork for the fair and decent treatment of all tribes. You have kindly adopted me into your family, but I am still a member of my own. How, in good conscience, can I remain here when I can better serve both your people and mine by returning to them?"

"What of our daughter and her two children?" asked Joking Woman, glancing from Valuable Woman to Corn-Tassels and Curly-Haired Boy. "Would you take them from us?"

"When I return to Boston, your daughter and grandson will go with me, but we will visit you as often as feasible. My son soon begins his formal education."

"And your daughter?" asked Preying Eagle, knowing what was uppermost in his eldest's mind.

"She has spent sufficient summers in both worlds to make her own decision. I ask only that you give her the same opportunity Running Deer granted Brought-Us-the-Book: several moons to listen to the Lord. He will tell her where her heart will find rest."

They turned toward the freshly arrived young woman and nodded assent as her blue eyes, peering up into Straight Arrows' penetrating black ones, dropped to the floor.

"And you, my daughter," Wooden Legs addressed Valuable Woman. "You want this also?"

Valuable Woman tucked a stray auburn curl behind her ear. "We have prayed hard over this, Father. This village is my home, but Spotted Long-knife and I are one flesh. I will go where he goes."

Their tidings did not surprise Brought-Us-the-Book, she had known such a decision was just a matter of time, but Valuable Woman's choice of words sent her thoughts to the place they usually wandered of late: her daughter.

One flesh. What is the man like who has stolen Light Bird and what does she feel within his dwelling? When Running Deer had betrothed her to Preying Eagle, she had felt as if she had stepped into a river too deep for her to maintain her footing, and yet God had provided her both strength and direction. *The Lord is worthy of my trust. "He is faithful in all He does."*[31]

When everyone grew quiet, she realized they had turned to her for an answer. "I am sorry; I was not listening. I was thinking of Light Bird."

Spotted Long-knife studied her face: it looked haggard from the past days' sorrows. *Am I willing to leave Abigail to the same chances?* He knew Straight Arrows would love and cherish her, but as Light Bird's fate so vividly attested, wars between tribes often brought rapid and unalterable changes. In addition, Indians of every tribe were being sandwiched in on each side: America to the east, the newly born Republic of Texas to the south, Oregon Territory to the west, and land too bitterly cold for habitation to the north. *What will become of them?*

"My brother asked if you regret your decision?" replied Running Deer, her father-in-law. He did not specify which decision, for he could have meant only one.

Brought-Us-the-Book shook her head, though somewhat sadly, as the question again brought her daughter to mind. "No. How can I regret the path the Creator set before me? He has given me all my heart could desire and more. Vengeance and injustice dwell everywhere; and before He formed me—or Light Bird—within the womb, He knew we would come to this sorrow.[32] I only hope I have prepared her well enough to follow Him alone."

"She is His," Two Doves assured her gently. "The Holy Spirit will bring all that you have taught her to memory and teach her things which you could not."

"But how," blurted Corn-Tassels, "can she endure a loveless marriage?"

Joking Woman felt embarrassed by her granddaughter's lack of tact and manners. "Do you remember her so poorly that you ask this question? When her captor's grief subsides, how can he help but love her? Old Many Feathers was mourning his first wife when he captured Quiet Woman, but you see what it is like between them."

"But what of her?" Corn-Tassels rushed on. "How can she love a man who has taken her against her will? I would hate him for the rest of my summers!"

Everyone grew quiet as they recognized the insult to Old Many Feathers, Two Doves' brother, and to their customs regarding the spoils of war.

"Would you, little one?" Two Doves asked. "And whom would you be hurting?"

Corn-Tassels looked down at her hands. "Myself."

"That is right," Two Doves nodded. "When the Creator made women, He knew their strength would not match a warrior's. He gave us different weapons to wield and hearts that are like water. We adapt and find a way. She will have much pain, as you will also—whatever path you walk. But if she clings to Jesus, she will also find peace that passes our ability to fathom, peace that no warrior can give her, no matter how loving and kind. I remember when you were only as tall as a foal. You loved cherries more than any child I have known. Do you remember when we used to pick them together?"

"Yes," nodded Corn-Tassels, perplexed by the change of topic.

"Where did we find them?"

"Cherry trees," the young woman shrugged.

"And if we had gone searching for them in the tall grasses, would we have found any?"

"No."

"But we may have found onion or garlic to season our stews. It is the same. Many people, not just women, crave what their heart is missing; but they search in places they can never find it. They delight for a time in the many good things the Almighty has created, but only by seeking Jesus can they satisfy the deep longings of their hearts. Ask your mother or your aunts. Pick women with husbands you admire—the kind you hope one day will offer your father many horses to gain you. They will all tell you the same. God has created all of us with an emptiness that only He can fill, and no enemy can snatch us away from Him."

"But what if he is evil, like the one who cut my aunt's…" Glancing at Brought-Us-the-Book's scars, faded but still evident on her cheeks, she feared she had probed too far. "I am sorry. I did not mean to remind you."

"You have said only what we have all been thinking," her *aunt* answered, "but if you will listen, my mother has already answered your question. Look at Daniel or Shadrach, Meshach, and Abednego. All four were bound and led from their people, yet God had a purpose for allowing that enemy to take them. He has not forgotten Light Bird. Pray that her husband will treat her kindly, but know that even if he does not, the Almighty will neither leave nor forsake her."[33]

As Valuable Woman listened to their patient answers, her stomach felt like a cavernous pit into which a huge rock had dropped. Her husband's family loved her, and she enjoyed Boston, but she was always eager to return home. She could not imagine living there always and only visiting this village occasionally.

Wooden Legs, as if reading her heart, asked her husband, "When do you go?"

"Lieutenant Wilson and I hope to visit the tribes that signed O'Fallon's treaty ten summers ago; but with your permission, I would like to leave your daughter and grandchildren in your care. Until the Moon of Changing Seasons, we will go back and forth between your band and these other tribes and then head east when the leaves begin to yellow. Which enemy did you tell me stole Light Bird?"

Running Deer, Light Bird's grandfather, handed him the arrow Pacing Wolf had tied to Wild Dog's blood-soaked shaft. "They bear Raven-Enemy markings."

Stroking his auburn beard, Spotted Long-knife shook his head. "I cannot recall a tribe listed by that name, but we will search for her wherever we go."

The eyes of the Lord range throughout the earth to strengthen those whose hearts are fully committed to Him.

2 Chronicles 16:9

Chapter 11

STARING DISPIRITEDLY into her memories, Light Bird did not notice the tiny fingers that lifted the door-flap or the pair of large eyes peeking through it. She was glad that Never-Sits had left her alone and relieved her captor had neither made her an object of the revelry coming from the center of the village nor forced her to listen to him recount the details of his vengeance quest. Hearing a sound, she turned to find her sister-in-law hauling in a bag of round, golden gourds.

"Come in," urged Never-Sits, gesturing to someone outside. "Come meet your new mother."

Mother? Looking past Never-Sits, Light Bird found a well-dressed little girl, about four summers old, framed in the open lodge-door. She felt stupid; she had not thought of children. Her captor, she guessed, possessed as many summers as Standing Elk, and Standing Elk had two. *Her mother must have been very beautiful—she looks nothing like him.*

"Come," Never-Sits repeated, but though the child stared openly, she would not budge. "Come! Your new mother is waiting."

"No!" the little girl cried, planting her feet firmly as her aunt began tugging her forward. "When sun sleeps, she will grow owl ears!"

"Who told you this?"

"Eats-With-Fists."

As the child strained to gain her freedom, Never-Sits glanced at her brother's captive bride, not much older than a child herself. "Is the sun sleeping now?"

The little girl nodded.

"Does she look like an owl?"

The befuddled child shook her head and stopped struggling, but she stepped behind her aunt's skirt as Light Bird knelt to greet her.

"I am called Light…"

"Your father has named her Small Doe," his sister interrupted. "Can you tell her what we call you?"

The little girl bolted.

Never-Sits sighed. "She is Among-the-Pines. I am sorry she was rude. She carries much grief in her heart. It will lessen as the days grow warmer."

Nodding sympathetically, Light Bird felt every bit the unwelcome intruder. *His kinsmen do not want me thrust into his dead woman's place any more than I wish to take it.*

"You are hungry," stated Never-Sits, handing her a bowl of cooked meat and then retrieving another sack. "This is for tomorrow. It contains dried apple rings and buffalo strips."

Thanking her sincerely, Light Bird placed the food stores by the dwelling's inner wall and picked at the bowl. She felt too ill at ease to eat, and even more so when she heard women's voices calling to be admitted.

"They are The-Women-Who-Talk-Against-Each-Other-Without-Fear," explained Never-Sits. "They have come to welcome you."

The name did little to make their identity clear. Light Bird had been raised to talk against no one. She tried, nonetheless, to prop up her flagging confidence while Never-Sits invited them in. She recognized many from the pawing crowd, but they surrounded her now with everything necessary to run her new home.

"She is too thin," pronounced a harsh-looking old woman, pulling back the excess doeskin of Light Bird's dress to reveal her youthful figure. "When we break camp, she will lag behind."

A second old woman, more heavily wrinkled, peered up warmly into Light Bird's face and smiled. "Pacing Wolf owns many horses. You will not need to walk."

"And she will not be thin for long, I wager," chuckled a much younger woman, patting her own rounding belly.

Laughter erupted from the group, but the harsh one continued to poke and prod Light Bird as though she were a pony offered for purchase.

"She will bear nothing!" clucked a tall, well-fed woman, carrying a belly only slightly smaller than the other. "When Jackrabbit hears of her clan brother's butchery, she will ask the spirits to dry up her captive's insides."

"We will see," countered the more heavily wrinkled grandmother. Her black eyes twinkled as she examined Light Bird's dress. "Jackrabbit would do well to hold her tongue. Pacing Wolf has handed this girl the fates of her younger daughters and also her own once Marks-His-Face meets death."

"And Pacing Wolf," added the harsh-looking one, "is no fool."

"Someone has done fine quill work on your dress," observed the twinkle-eyed grandmother. "If you also possess this skill, I will adopt you into my sewing guild."

Light Bird felt too timid to confess the work was her own, but the old woman's approval set her more at ease until Pacing Wolf unexpectedly drew back the flap. Once he ducked in, the women scattered, leaving behind only his sister and the kinder of the two wrinkled old women.

"Where is Among-the-Pines?" he demanded, looking around the lodge.

"With my daughter," answered Never-Sits. "She can stay in Mountainside's lodge until…until her new mother has grown accustomed to your home."

Nodding a brief thanks, he jerked his head toward the door, and his sister and the old woman also ducked out.

Light Bird felt shy after spending the past hours away from him. Although she could not say his relatives had made her feel welcome, she understood women's ways. Covertly watching from the other side of the fire, she saw that he had returned her kinsman's scalp to his staff and painted a new red stripe across his right legging to show he had drawn fresh blood.

Pacing Wolf was relieved that he had finished recounting the past days' exploits. Normally, he took pride in the approbation of his leaders and relished the awed expressions of the Good Young Men. Tonight had been different. He had walked a cliff-edge between details that might increase his clansmen's regard for the young doe and those that might deepen her shame.

She looks no worse for the womenfolk's appraisals, though she is watchful, and I cannot tell what she is thinking.

The guarded expression in her large liquid eyes renewed his gut's uncomfortable twisting. Hunts-For-Death, his adopted father, had been correct. When new life emerged from the snow-watered soil, his desire for her might yield shame and disgrace. The same men who had just been praising his valor would declare she had made him weak, and his Fox rivals' taunts would deafen his ears.

I have handed her good reason to hate me, and the moons that pass before the grass greens are too few to lessen her sorrow. Wild Dog should have chosen the haughty goose. She could warm my bed while the snows still linger, and then I would be grateful to the Fox who snatched her. But this doe...

"I will gather wood for your fire," offered Light Bird.

"It is there," he snapped, glancing at the door.

Light Bird ducked out to get the bundle and set it within reach of the fading embers. Though his sudden change of humor chafed, it did not surprise her; and when he told her to tend the fire and go to sleep, she felt relieved. Forming a tripod of sticks over the embers, she softly blew them to an amber glow.

Pacing Wolf slipped under his buffalo robes, but her pursed lips so roused his ardor, he turned his back lest she altogether rob him of will. *She tugs at my insides,* he muttered while pulling up the covers, *but if she hopes to own my heart, she will be disappointed.*

AS DAYLIGHT BROKE across the horizon, Light Bird emerged from Pacing Wolf's dwelling and looked down the path they had ridden up yesterday. The village reminded her of a woman's hair, parted straight down the middle to form two sides. Turning, she spotted Never-Sits chatting with the two eldest women who had come to the lodge last night.

"Come," called her sister-in-law. "I will show you the best place to gather wood."

Light Bird followed her in the direction opposite the river to which her captor had taken her to bathe before sunrise. Winding between the dwellings, she felt amazed by their vast number.

"We are called the Many Lodges,"[34] offered Never-Sits, "the greatest of the Sparrow Hawk bands. When the grass begins to green, Those-Who-Live-Among-the-River-Banks and the Kicked-in-the-Bellies will join us. Pacing Wolf told Mountainside, my husband, that your people possess far fewer lodges. I had thought Those-Who-Cut-Off-Our-Heads were many."

Light Bird was a bit bewildered. She had never known anyone who cut off a head. Guessing Never-Sits referred to the Allies, she explained, "We are many bands who live apart. Last summer, when our people gathered for The Dance, my feet grew sore while I walked from one end of the camp to the other."

As the two climbed up a slope, picking up fallen branches and twigs beneath the trees, Never-Sits examined the whole of Light Bird's attire. "You will need cooler clothing for summer."

"I brought nothing," she shrugged, wishing for the fine pair of moccasins that her mother and Quiet Woman had finished beading shortly before her capture. *I speak as though I came here by choice.*

As if reading her thoughts, Never-Sits responded, "Many mothers were disappointed to see you atop Pacing Wolf's sorrel. They hoped one of their daughters might gain his heart."

Unwilling to offend, Light Bird was unsure what to answer. She certainly did not deem her abduction a privilege. "All can see he is a fierce warrior."

Never-Sits could not help but smile. *By chance or intention, my brother has chosen well. His new bride possesses prudence, though she guards her tongue better than her eyes.* "We have gathered enough kindling. Come, we need to fetch water for our morning meal."

Within a few steps of Pacing Wolf's dwelling, his sister stopped. "When I was not much older than you, I also had to leave my family—for a warrior from Those-Who-Live-Among-the-River-Banks. The man I live with now, Mountainside, is of our band but he belongs to a different clan. His lodge is over there, by that tall tree." She pointed across the road to some trees in the distance. "You know the way to the river?"

Light Bird nodded, surprised by the disappointed she felt that his sister must leave her. Never-Sits did not possess inviting ways, but she had been helpful and had expressed an inkling of how it felt to be misplaced. After retrieving the water sacks her captor's clanswomen had given her last evening, Light Bird descended the steep bank.

"Lord, I feel so alone," she admitted. *"Even You seem far away, and yet I know You do not change with my surroundings. Help me to walk by faith, not by sight."*[85]

"The morning is warm," called an old bent form stooping by the river's edge. Her folds of wrinkled skin reminded Light Bird of her grandfather's mother, Red Woman, who had gone home to the Lord some years ago. She had adored the old woman.

"Yes," replied Light Bird. "Summer will come early." *She is the old one who approved my quillwork.* "The way is far and all uphill. Let me carry some of your sacks."

Readily consenting, the old woman snickered, "Pacing Wolf told us he stole you right out from under your suitor's nose!"

Light Bird simply nodded in reply. She did not care to be discussed by these strangers, but this woman was the friendliest of those she had met, and by now the whole camp would know any private detail her captor had wished to divulge.

"Does your heart long for him?"

"N-no," Light Bird stammered, taken off-guard by so personal a question. "Wild Dog was like a sickness. He brought discomfort when he came and relief when he left. I did not desire his notice."

As the old woman smiled with approval, her plentiful creases all but swallowed her eyes. "A wild dog may pant after a doe's tender flesh, but what is he against a fearsome wolf?"

This grandmother is like his sister, thought Light Bird. *She admires my captor and thinks I should feel grateful I am his woman. She would not feel happy if my brother carried off her granddaughter—though, in fairness, I would think such a girl fortunate.*

The old woman's aching bones had traversed too many summers to allow conversation while they walked, but when they gained the village, she clutched Light Bird's arm and whispered. "A gentle doe is more pleasing than a snarling cat."

What the grandmother meant, Light Bird was not certain, but she had neither time nor temerity to ask. The shriveled old woman quickly ducked under a nearby door-flap, but as Light Bird turned the enigmatic comment over in her mind, she smiled. *I think the Lord may have offered me a friend.*

Once inside her captor's dwelling, Light Bird heated some of the gourds that Never-Sits had brought last night, seasoning them with the dried meat, and then looked for something useful to do. She carefully opened the large buffalo-hide bag she had noticed last evening and found a neatly folded, light-colored scalp shirt decorated with porcupine quills across its shoulders.

Mother would love the workmanship, she thought, running her hands over the intricate design; but her fingers recoiled as they touched human hair running down the sleeves. Not once had she felt pity while adding scalps to Straight Arrows' shirts, nor had she given any thought to their former owners' families.

As Pacing Wolf entered his lodge, he spotted his scalp-shirt in Small Doe's lap and, tossing her his latest trophy, bade her look in the bag for needles. Large Man's shriveled skin made her stomach queasy, but she complied without hesitation. Had her captor been crueler, she might be holding much dearer scalps.

Pacing Wolf squatted down, lifting Large Man's hair from her lap and holding it out between them. "If I had not killed your kinsman, he would have handed you to the shamer."

Light Bird nodded, so nervously fingering his shirt's black fringe, he pointed to each line.

"Blackfoot. Yellow-Legs. Blackfoot. Flat-Head. None are from Those-Who-Cut-Off-Our-Heads."

Surprised that he bothered to reassure her, a smile faintly played about her lips. A less attentive warrior would have missed it altogether, but it pried Pacing Wolf's heart open just wide enough to allow his lips to soften. Hoping to divert her attention, he withdrew some folded red sheepskins he had tucked under his arm and handed her a knife that she recognized immediately. He had removed it from the back of her belt the evening he unwrapped her from her robe.

"You will need these."

As he unfurled the red sheepskins over his knee, spilling them over the scalp shirt on her lap, Light Bird quietly gasped. They had been sewn into a skirt and blouse, covered neck to hem with rows of costly white elk's teeth.

"Where…how?" she murmured, glancing up into keen black eyes that reflected her pleasure. Not only was she astonished he obtained such well-made garments in so short a time, but also that he troubled himself with the expense.

"Kills-Behind-Her-Dwelling, the old one, my grandmother."

Light Bird had trouble finding her voice. She felt unreasonably disappointed that they were not from him after all and intensely grateful toward the thoughtful woman who had sent them.

"The one who stayed behind with your sister after the others left?"

Pacing Wolf nodded.

"They are beautiful," she whispered, running her fingers over the elk teeth. "Why does she give…"

She can see your worth, he thought. He was well aware his grandmother had disliked his dead woman. "My clansmen come tonight to celebrate my success. You will wear this when you serve them."

Though his answer did not surprise her, the prospect so deadened her fleeting delight that she cast her eyes downward. She did not mind the labor, she had been helping her mother and grandmother prepare feasts for many summers, but to be gawked at like a trophy would heighten her shame. Knowing she could not avoid it, she turned her mind to practical considerations.

"I do not have food for many."

"I go now—to hunt. You will use the meat for the meal and the hides as you wish."

Kills-Behind-Her-Dwelling ducked in, greeting them both with a wide toothless grin. Spotting the skirt and blouse, she beamed. "I cured the hides myself and sewed on each tooth with my own hand."

"They are beautiful," Light Bird replied, though she felt awkward accepting a generous gift from a woman she barely knew.

"A bride needs proper clothing. My grandson has given me an appaloosa in trade—the one I ride when we break camp."

Light Bird looked up at Pacing Wolf with a mixture of gratitude and surprise, but he felt more agitated than pleased. He hated the way his heart responded—panting after each scrap of her approval—and he found her surprise insulting. *Does she think I am unable to provide?*

"Elk-teeth are costly," she blurted out, seeing his lips had turned down.

Rising to his feet, he ended the discussion, brusquely ordering her again to wear the skirt and blouse that night before abruptly ducking out.

"Do not let your heart grow bitter, little one," his wrinkled grandmother counseled. "He has eaten much sorrow."

And he has also ladled up much! Light Bird wished to retort, but she was too grateful for the old woman's friendship to say so aloud.

He has not despised or scorned the suffering of the afflicted one: he has not hidden his face from him but has listened to his cry for help.

Psalm 22:24

Chapter 12

WHILE LIGHT BIRD added Large Man's hair to the seams of Pacing Wolf's scalp shirt, she could not push Wild Dog's mother from her mind. She had not known Swallow Woman well, but Wild Dog's aunts belonged to her grandmother's weaving guild.

They will be grieved when they learn of Large Man's death, and what I now do would disgust them, but God alone knows the days of a man's life.[37] *Besides, the Sparrow Hawk is right: Large Man would have handed me over to his cousin, who would have...*

Light Bird shivered. *I do not understand the rapid change of Wild Dog's heart. He and my father are like darkness and light. My captor stole only Wild Dog's pride, and yet his anger burns so hotly that he would also destroy me. He stole me from my father, but my father asked the Lord to bless him.*

Repeating Preying Eagle's requests, along with new ones of her own, she realized something that turned her lips upward. *The vast prairie may separate me from my family's embrace, but it can never separate me from their hearts.*

Completing her task, Light Bird began reworking many of the garment's seams, wondering with each stitch about the woman she had replaced. Many were crooked or loose, like the ones in her enemy-husband's lodge cover, contrasting oddly with the shirt's skillfully executed embellishments.

Never-Sits called for admittance, interrupting her thoughts, and though Light Bird felt out of place inviting anyone into a dwelling that was not her own, she was eager to be occupied with something other than dismal recollections.

"You do not wear my grandmother's skirt and blouse?"

"I do not want to spoil them while butchering game for the feast your brother holds to..." Light Bird's eyes dropped to the neatly folded shirt, "to honor his...victory."

As deep crimson blotches spread over her new sister-in-law's throat, Never-Sits felt moved with pity. From the morning she had carried her first bundle of wood, she had lived in fear of meeting the same fate.

"Grandmother worked many nights making them for…" Never-Sits stopped herself, realizing she would need to speak ill of the dead was she to explain further.

The color of Light Bird's neck deepened. She had not considered why the old one had sewn the garments. Perhaps they were intended as a gift for Never-Sits or the woman Wild Dog had murdered. Unable to think what to say, she was relieved to hear her captor call her new name.

"Small Doe!"

Ducking out of his lodge, she looked up as Pacing Wolf, vibrant from exertion, shoved two wooly animals off the back of his sorrel. As they thudded to the ground, she wondered what sort of creatures they might be. They were almost the size of wolves, wore short curling brown fur that was white across their hindquarters, and owned stubby tails.

"What do you call them?" she asked Kills-Behind-Her-Dwelling, who had come out of her nearby lodge.

"Has-Face-for-Earrings."

The name did nothing to help Light Bird understand what they were, but as she examined their heads, she knew immediately how they had earned it. Buffaloes had pushed-in noses, but these strange creatures possessed pretty muzzles, soft and rounded. Cocking her head this way and that, she was unable to decide whose faces theirs resembled most closely—deer or rabbits, but when she knelt to split the first one's hide along its spine, she was pleased to find an ample quantity of meat.

Never-Sits pointed up to the heights. "They live farther up but come down to graze where the snow has already melted. Stay away from the males. They are large, tall as a young deer, and have huge curved horns that hang from the sides of their heads, like so." She drew circles in the air, springing up from her temples, around toward the back of her head, and then curving forward near her jaw.

Light Bird could not imagine such a thing.

"When they wish to mate, they will harm anyone who gets in their way."

Kills-Behind-Her-Dwelling chuckled under her breath, nudging Light Bird with her elbow. "They are no different from warriors—always trying to prove who is strongest or to gain the choicest of the females."

The description was so unlike Light Bird's men-folk that she peeked up at her captor's sister to see what she might say, but Never-Sits looked away as if embarrassed her grandmother spoke so freely. Glancing from one to the other and back again, she revised her assessment of the younger: *She is not disapproving but timid—a trait I understand well.* Caught often between uncertainty and good manners, Light Bird contented herself mostly with listening.

While they were dividing the mutton to roast from the mutton to boil in a tasty stew, Kills-Behind-Her-Dwelling looked up at the sun. "Go—it grows late. Change into the elk tooth garments. The fire will complete our task. Never-Sits must look after her husband's meal, and I will brush your hair."

Light Bird hesitated. She appreciated the old woman's offer but she no longer owned a brush. Kills-Behind-Her-Dwelling quickly grasped her predicament.

"You go inside," she insisted. "I will come to you shortly."

True to her word, the old grandmother ducked in while Light Bird was pulling the elk tooth blouse over her head, and her face folded into countless happy wrinkles. "You look like a proper Sparrow Hawk bride eagerly awaiting her proud husband."

Acutely conscious that she was neither, Light Bird silently unfastened her braids and accepted Kills-Behind-Her-Dwelling's ministrations. The old woman had fetched her own porcupine tail and drew it through the waving tresses, finding them nearly as fascinating as her grandson had.

"When Pacing Wolf dies in battle, many clansmen will contend for your hair."

"Why?"

Kills-Behind-Her-Dwelling shook her head, astounded that a properly raised girl would need to ask. "You do not have a mother or grandmother?"

"Yes," replied Light Bird, unable to fathom the connection. "I have both and many aunts."

"Have you noticed the long braids my grandson and his companions wear?"

Light Bird nodded. Every man she had seen in his prime or older wore braids that fell well below their waists. A few swept past their hips, and many men wore three or four.

"When your husband travels to the Mystery-Land, you will cut off your hair and give it to his clansmen and war society brothers."

"Why?"

This child needs much instruction; it is good Pacing Wolf has brought her to us. "They commemorate his valor by weaving it in with their own and will gain a share of his strength."

"I do not understand."

Kills-Behind-Her-Dwelling sighed. "Your kinswomen have taught you nothing? Hair is the home of the soul—you must care for my grandson's carefully."

Light Bird wondered if the old woman's mind had been wandering through strange visions. She had never heard anything like this.

"Why else would a warrior keep his enemies' scalps? By taking their hair, he binds their souls to the earth so he will have fewer opponents in The Land Beyond."

Light Bird silently considered how she might respond. The Creator's Book said He alone could destroy the soul in hell,[38] but she hesitated to openly challenge his grandmother's notions. She wanted neither to show disrespect nor to offend one of her only two friends among this strange people. Unsure whether prudence or cowardice kept her tongue still, she asked Jesus to tell her what to say.[39] Before He answered, however, Kills-Behind-Her-Dwelling began again.

"I see the way you look at my grandson. No—do not protest. For many years I have watched women when the warrior they desire is near. Some pretend not to notice while posturing to exhibit their finest features. Among-the-Pines will be one of those if Jackrabbit has anything to do with it."

"Jackrabbit?" Light Bird asked, hoping to divert the conversation to less unnerving ground.

"The little girl's grandmother. Marks-His-Face' woman. They live among Those-Who-Make-Their-Homes-On-The-Outer-Edge. When my grandson is near, you keep perfectly still—like a frightened creature—but your eyes follow him carefully."

What she says is true, Light Bird conceded, *but only because I am uncertain how to act.*

"Why should you not desire him?" the aged woman prodded. "Because he is your father's enemy?" Moving forward to peer into Light Bird's eyes, she saw clearly she had hit the intended mark. "You are not the first woman to be snatched, little one. Warriors have stolen their enemies' wives and daughters since He-That-Hears-Always created us."

"My father's aunt was born of another people."

"Then you know what will happen over time, but all will go better if you do not resist. Your kinsman grieved us all, and Pacing Wolf mourns hard for his son, but even a fierce wolf prefers a doe to a snarling cat. Treat my grandson as you would a warrior whose lodge you hope to share. Smile when you catch his eye, and when he is near you, do not shy away. Draw closer—so close you catch his scent."

As Light Bird recalled the smell of sweet tobacco, she began feeling like a bone caught between two dogs. Part of her welcomed his grandmother's counsel. She had been longing to speak with Quiet Woman about such things. The other part felt repelled. The old one had gone far beyond what was polite on so short an acquaintance and had—by speaking of her fate aloud—stolen the faint hope she was having a night terror from which she might soon awaken. Worse yet, she had uncovered something Light Bird wanted desperately to keep hidden even from herself. While she had gone about her chores, her captor continually crept into her thoughts. She stole glimpses at passing warriors, wondering if he were near; and when she heard a man's voice or the mention of his name, her ears pricked alert.

With each stroke of the brush, the quavering old voice continued droning. "You cannot fight a rushing river…let it carry you where it wills. You gain nothing by struggling…you will end in the same place, only bruised and battered from the journey."

The words seeped into Light Bird's heart like the green paste her mother used to draw poison from a wound. They unknotted her aching loneliness even as the brush smoothed out her tangles.

"He will soon fill your thoughts so often, you will have no room for sorrow; and when your belly grows large and round, your family will fade away like a pleasant dream. A woman's heart is like the rich, dark soil we turn over to receive our sacred tobacco seed. It cannot stay empty for long, so plant your crop wisely, tending each new shoot lest thorny weed overrun your heart."

As the old one began weaving Light Bird's waves, Pacing Wolf stepped through his lodge door. Light Bird turned her face away, afraid he might notice her warming cheeks. She had no way of telling how much he had overheard. Before they had sufficiently cooled, the gnarled old fingers placed the porcupine tail into her small hand.

"Take this, my little one; I have another. Tend to your husband's hair and remember all I have told you. The Men-Who-Speak-Against-Each-Other-Without-Fear will be here shortly, and I will return to help you serve."

After the old woman had bent and hobbled through the flap, Pacing Wolf fastened it shut. Neither he nor Light Bird spoke, both were busy trailing separate reflections; but when he turned to present his bare torso, years of watching her mother and tending brothers told her what to do.

She took the clothing he had been wearing, folded it away, and retrieved the scalp shirt she had earlier repaired. Holding up its sleeves to receive his hands, she drew them up his arms and then pulled the neck-opening over his head.

His warmth was disturbing, but she resisted the impulse to step backward. After tugging the hem down over his hips, she smoothed the shoulders into place; and when his steady gaze flushed her with uncertainty, she concentrated her on examining her stitches.

He followed her eyes to the improvements. He had often been ashamed of his dead woman's carelessness, and when his mouth curved up slightly, a frail twinge of satisfaction wriggled up through the soil of Light Bird's heart. All at once, she could stay put no longer and, searching for a good excuse to escape his gaze, offered to brush his hair.

Pacing Wolf was tempted to reiterate his grandmother's admonitions. He had enjoyed her slight touches while attending to his clothing and wanted to prolong them. Instead, he reminded himself of her age, how well she had taken the last four days' changes, and that necessity would teach her what words could not. Sitting cross-legged atop his buffalo pelts, he prepared for a harsh raking of his hair. His dead woman punished him this way for every trivial complaint.

As Light Bird unwound his long braids, he found her touch was as soothing as her voice; and when she rubbed his herbed grease between her palms, the pleasant aroma permeated the air. She eased his frustration as she smoothed out each tangle, allowing his mind to wend where it willed, but it soon stumbled over his adopted father's warning.

"When the grass turns green, you will find Foxes sneaking beneath your door-flap."

His back grew stiff as he imagined her cool fingers easing another warrior's tensions, and the look in her thickly fringed eyes as she circled around to face him increased his determination to keep her.

I will steal her heart as I have stolen her body and allow no rivals to snatch either.

Light Bird had felt him stiffen and detected a hardness flickering through his eyes, but she was at a loss to understand either. Knowing nothing else to do, she tentatively touched the thatch of hair that sprouted above his forehead.

"My men-folk do not wear this," she explained. "I do not know how to make it stand."

Turning her greased palms upward, Pacing Wolf added a pinch of clay, pressed her hands together, and rubbed them back and forth between his own. He weaved her fingers in and out of each other to distribute the tacky substance evenly and then drew them upwards through his close-cropped hair.

Her eyes, so close to his own that he could see the division between iris and pupil, held such a plain desire to please, he began to feel ashamed. He had shown horses more patience than he had this young doe. They also held a quality he could not name, reminding him of a deep, tranquil pool he had once found hidden beneath a clump of cottonwoods on the open prairie.

As he remembered the coolness of its water against his skin, he wondered where she had acquired such unassailable grace. It defied her circumstances, easing something in him also, something as hard to define as the quality itself. So profound was the feeling that he fleetingly wondered whether she was of the earth or like White Buffalo Woman in the stories of old.

No, he decided, faintly shaking his head as he recalled the softness of her skin. *She is made of flesh and blood.*

"I do not do this well?"

"No!" he answered, meaning to deny—not confirm—her worry, but it was too late. His terse retort had turned her eyes wary, and he could see her pulling inside herself. As he wondered how to draw her out again, he began to perceive a pattern. His tone, like a stone dropped into that tranquil pool, possessed the power to disquiet her stillness.

"You have done well," he murmured, curious to see if retracing his steps might restore her calm. "My own thoughts disturbed me."

Her eyes so brightened, he sorely wanted to caress her cheek, not only to feel her skin beneath his fingers but also to test how she might respond. He decided to wait. She was already moving behind him to weave his braids, and while she tied their ends, they heard several male voices approaching.

Light Bird melted into the shadows as he welcomed Hunts-For-Death, the older man who had met him when they first arrived in camp, splendidly arrayed behind an eagle feather fan. Several others ducked in after him until the dwelling became filled with amiable masculine greetings.

The fruit of that righteousness will be peace; its effect will be quietness and confidence forever.

Isaiah 32:17

Chapter 13

LIGHT BIRD SLIPPED outside to tend the meal Never-Sits and Kills-Behind-Her-Dwelling had helped her prepare. She had hoped to the older woman by the cook-fire; she was not sure whom she should serve first. Piling a trencher with roasted ribs, she took a deep breath, ducked back into the lodge, and began perusing the assorted warriors' finery for tokens that might indicate their rank.

The conflicting array was perplexing. In her mother's dwelling, the greatest reverence was due the aged, particularly those who had distinguished themselves in battle. Several such warriors sat opposite her captor, but he had invited the man with the fan to sit to his left—the place her father gave to the guest most honored. Lowering her eyes, she knelt before the one pair of leggings she readily recognized, but a sudden hush loudly announced she had violated their custom.

"Your captive woman offers you the highest honor," chortled the warrior with the fan. "Does she possess great fear of you or display her desire?"

Color crept up Light Bird's neck, but before her husband answered, a grim-faced man cut in. "Even young rattlers possess deadly bites. Before you take her into your bosom, instruct her with the back of your hand."

"Do you speak from habit?" replied Pacing Wolf, gently enclosing Light Bird's hand beneath the platter. "I thought you took Sparrow Hawk wives." After casually selecting a meaty rib, he guided her toward Hunts-For-Death.

"Short Neck takes women from the Kick-Bellies," another clansman snickered. "They are all like the thick, rabbit-eared horses that pull the white trader's wagon. They learn only from sharp blows."

Guffaws erupted across the lodge, but an aged voice cut them short. "Listen to me, you Good Young Men. Treat your women well. Do not beat them. When you are wounded, who stays by your side? When the wasting sickness comes, who sits by your bed while your clan-brothers sleep? If you are wise, your heart will chew my words thoroughly before swallowing. A fool will spit them out to make room for counsel more to his liking."

Pacing Wolf turned toward his honored guest. "My captive's suitor was evil but shrewd. He chose her from a line of women renowned for respecting their husbands."

"Then hurry," laughed a younger warrior. "Lead us to her village so we can snatch her sisters!"

As Light Bird's eyes darted up, Pacing Wolf shook his head. "I did not see any sisters, only a grandmother whose eyes are dim. I will gladly show you where to find her. My woman enjoys her company."

When their laughter died down, Hunts-For-Death leaned over toward his host. "What is she called?"

"Small Doe. Her people called her Light Bird, but the name does not fit."

"Yes," nodded the honored guest. "Her neck and eyes remind me of the animal, and she possesses its gentle and quiet spirit."

Light Bird felt relieved when the trencher was nearly empty. She had never sought the center place within her circle of cousins and desired it far less amidst this group of male strangers. As she was about to duck out, however, she noticed a latecomer's unfamiliar leggings and knelt down to offer the few ribs that were left.

"If I captured such a woman," the latecomer told his neighbor, "I would treat her as gently as a newborn foal."

Light Bird glanced up, startled by his boldness, and met finely shaped eyes, brimming with warmth. Through nearly sixteen summers, she had never felt such a marked attraction. Immediately dropping her gaze, she hurried out into the cool night air.

Pacing Wolf smiled. Only the hard of hearing could have missed Goes-to-Battle's challenge, but betraying anger over a woman would draw his clan brothers' contempt. Once the door flap had fallen shut, he leaned over toward his guest of honor. "When our war societies cut new staffs, he may take her. Three moons are enough to tire of any woman."

When Light Bird heard boisterous laughter, she began to breathe a little easier. The man with the fan had almost continuously engaged her husband's attention, and though Pacing Wolf's eyes were keen, he could not have seen her reaction. Her back had been turned.

"Lord, is my heart so faithless? I am married less than four days and am already attracted to another!"

"You look pale," noted Kills-Behind-Her-Dwelling, joining her by the stew pot. "Are you ill?"

"No. I am well."

"I could not make my old bones hurry. Serve Hunts-For-Death first. He leads our clan and will be the next One-Who-Leads-the-Moving-Band. Seven summers ago, he adopted Pacing Wolf into his war society, The Lumpwoods, and possesses great influence over him. Take care you do not offend him—and do not forget to smile at your husband."

It is too late, thought Light Bird as she held two bowls steady to receive ladles full of stew. Mindful of the old woman's warning, she stole a few glimpses at the clan leader's face as she knelt down to serve him. He received his bowl without looking up, but whatever he thought of her, his high regard for her captor was plain.

Their clansmen spoke of many things, some strange to her, some common; but when their talk turned to buffalo they sounded so like her uncles and brothers, she soon became lost in her duties. Accustomed to such gatherings, she blended so well into the background that all but two pairs of eyes forgot she was there. One, she pointedly avoided. The other left her thoughts no longer than the bowl left her hands.

As Pacing Wolf watched her slipping in and out of his lodge, he felt charmed by each encounter with her alert and observant eyes. They increased as the meal wore on, so dividing his attention from his guests that he began to listen only absently. Once, she offered him a shy but lovely smile, so ambushing his heart that it hurtled down blind tunnels whose end he could not fathom.

No enemy has stood against me for many summers, but this doe turns me into a wobbling pup.

When at last his guests had finished eating, he took off his moccasins, withdrew his pipe from its quilled bag, and loaded the bowl with tobacco and bear root. He acknowledged the four directions of the wind, circulating the pipe around the circle until each man's aromatic breath became inseparable from his neighbor's. Pointing the stem toward the heavens, after each man had taken an appropriate number of puffs, he signaled for her to carry the remains outside and sprinkle them on the earth.

Tucking the empty pipe into her belt, Light Bird gazed up at the stars while tiptoeing gingerly through her memories of the evening. Pacing Wolf had pressed several seeds into the susceptible soil of her heart, and she thought a few might already be sprouting. Considering how best to nourish them, she decided to retreat to his dwelling, but her plan came to a sudden halt.

They are in it! she realized. *I have nowhere to go.*

Before she could think of what she should do, a strong tug on her sleeve pulled her gaze downward. "You cannot wait here," smiled his toothless old grandmother. "Come to my lodge. I own many robes to receive your tired limbs."

Light Bird gratefully accepted her invitation. The cold was already turning her breath into misty vapor, and she had not thought to fetch her buffalo robe. Hoping to return the old woman's kindness, she followed her into a nearby dwelling and helped her lower her knotted frame onto a pile of pelts. She was about to begin rubbing the thinly skinned legs when her hostess raised her head to listen. Light Bird heard it also: feet padding hurriedly in their direction. The faintest trickle of excitement compelled her eyes to the opening door flap, but instead of Pacing Wolf, she saw his handsome clansman.

"I thought it might be you," chuckled the old woman as he came to sit beside her. "You have not yet outgrown your boyish impatience."

"It grows cold, Grandmother." He grinned. "I will make your fire brighter."

While he began to stir the embers, Light Bird withdrew into the shadows. *He looks much like Father and Straight Arrows,* she thought, relieved he did not glance her way. All three had strong cheekbones that descended sharply toward rock-carved chins, and noses as straight as well-made arrows. *But their brows differ. Father's overhang his eyes like the edge of a cliff. This warrior's are finely arched, like the wings of a soaring swallow.*

"My cousin's new bride is very young. Before the grass greens, she may find his disposition tiresome."

"And if she did?" his grandmother snapped. Her sharp tone surprised Light Bird, both forbidding and demanding this younger grandson's answer.

"When the sun increases its warmth," he smiled, "her happiness will increase also."

Kills-Behind-Her-Dwelling laughed. "You are too sure of your handsome looks. Do not force me to take up my knife against you."

"Alone? Pacing Wolf will do nothing. He risks too much by raising his ax."

As Light Bird listened, she felt confounded. Their banter made her think of a pile of broken pipe pieces: some lovely, some soiled, but all unconnected. Though she appreciated this cousin's kind wishes, she sensed something odd in his manner. Then, when their conversation turned to foxes, she grew doubly alert. The last time she had heard them mentioned, her captor's back had stiffened. Wanting to know why, she tasted every word, but though she chewed each carefully, they were impossible to digest.

Light Bird began wondering when Pacing Wolf's guests might leave. His handsome cousin had said they were gambling, raising prickles on her skin as she thought of Black Swan, a friend from her family's village. Two summers past, a warrior from another band offered her father eight horses to gain her, and the flattered young woman could speak of little else until her father accepted. Light Bird had assumed her happy, but when they met again at The Dance last summer, only her friend's weary outer shell looked the same.

"I ache with loneliness," Black Swan had confided. "His sister is kind enough, but his brother's wives do not like me."

"But what of your husband?" asked Light Bird, assuming all marriages were as happy as her parents', her aunts', and her uncles' were.

"He gambles most evenings. I see him only when he loses."

She pulled back her loosely woven braid to reveal a large purple bruise that extended far into her hairline.

"Little cousin, marry a warrior from your own band. Your mother and aunts will provide you company and your men-folk will require him to treat you well. Even his mother never interferes. She only shrugs and tells me, 'The Creator made women to please warriors, and warriors to please themselves.'"

Light Bird had heard the old saying before. It had been handed from mother to daughter for generations, but she knew the Creator well and was certain He did not regard women so lightly.[40]

Pacing Wolf could not concentrate on his game. Between turns, he eyed the door, wondering where Small Doe was keeping warm. She had not yet ventured to Never-Sits' side of their village, and his old grandmother was probably fast asleep.

Goes-to-Battle is no doubt sniffing for her scent.

His handsome cousin had been stirring up his jealousy all evening, slowly and carefully, like a ladle churning up morsels hidden at the bottom of a pot. Unlike the young Fox, Pacing Wolf was obligated to stay with his guests.

Hunts-For-Death, aware his Lumpwood son was growing restless, leaned against his shoulder. "Why do you waste time playing with these over-stuffed bucks when a well-formed young doe awaits you in the darkness? Go. Find her."

A wide grin was all the reply the older man needed. Hunts-For-Death rose, signaling to the others, who also stood to their feet—all except one Good Young Man who was intent on winning. His older cousins began to tease him.

"Will you play until the sun wakes up? Otter-Woman hopes you will watch for her. Perhaps Crazy Bear will give you a place to sit inside his dwelling."

Catching their hint, the young warrior bid their host farewell, and each man went in search of softer company.

Light Bird was too unsettled by her memories to notice a second, softer set of treads heading toward Kills-Behind-Her-Dwelling's lodge. She startled when the door flap opened, and as her captor darted flinty eyes from her to his young cousin, her stomach knotted.

"Come!" he commanded, stretching out his hand, but though she quickly scrambled to her feet, the tight grip of his fingers confirmed he was angry.

Once they slipped into his dwelling, she occupied herself by replacing the backrests his guests had pulled toward the fire and smoothing into place the pelts they had taken from his bed. Pacing Wolf said nothing. He simply stretched out his arms so she could remove his scalp shirt, and from years of practice, she promptly responded. While she carefully lifted it over his head, he dropped his hands possessively about her hips and drew her closer.

Where, he wondered, *is the shy attention she offered me while serving? She is as wary and watchful as she was in the cave.*

Retracing her steps through his memory of the evening, he found much to commend and little for which she might feel shame. Serving him before Hunts-For-Death was nothing. She had shown sense and raised him in the eyes of the other Good Men. Taking the shirt she held, he tossed it over the willow headboard, but when he lifted his hand toward her face, she flinched. He caressed her cheek anyway but asked himself once more what had aroused her fresh fear.

He did not fault her for Goes-to-Battle's obvious interest. She had conducted herself with polite and proper modesty, and though he had been irked to find his young cousin in their grandmother's lodge, he had noticed Small Doe had seated herself as far from the man as she could.

"I am not like my clansman, Short Neck," he murmured, softly brushing a straying strand back into her hair. "I will not strike you."

The effect of his tenderness was immediate. Her legs felt like green twigs holding up a heavy stone, whether from relief, exhaustion, or the unexpected weakening in the pit of her stomach, she was not sure; but as she crumbled against him, her hands reached out to gain support. Misreading the agreeable gesture, he responded immediately, pulling her closer and wrapping his arms around her back. He wondered afresh as he breathed her sweet fragrance, just what sort of creature he was holding and to what spirit he might attribute his good favor.

In the morning, he decided, *I will ask about her strange book-god and the kind of offering he desires.*

No temptation has overtaken you that does not pursue us all. God is faithful. He will not let you be tempted beyond what you can bear. When temptation closes in on you, He will show you a path that offers an escape.

I Corinthians 10:13

Chapter 14

"OH MAMA!" CRIED Corn-Tassels as she ran her fingers down the doeskin dress Joking Woman had made for her homecoming. "It is lovely, but how can I go about so...so...uncontained? I feel naked without my corset. Just imagine what old Mrs. Van Cleef would say!"

As she dimpled deeply, her mother tossed her a sympathetic look. "You need never see the Van Cleefs again. They will certainly never call on us here." Pushing an escaping auburn curl from her forehead, Valuable Woman stepped back to admire her daughter. "You look beautiful! After all these years, my mother can still make as small and neat a stitch as she did when I was a child."

Genevieve would say it looks like a sack, thought Corn-Tassels. *It shows nothing of my figure.*

Aware her daughter wanted to protest, Valuable Woman added, "Give it a week. Soon you will wonder how you ever forced yourself into those awful corsets. I cannot bear them."

Corn-Tassels did not argue. A prickly shrub had already snagged the trim on her traveling dress, and she did not want the few others she had brought from Boston to become soiled while doing chores. Staring down at her bulky, fur-lined moccasins, she concluded that they, too, were horribly inelegant, but she was grateful for their warmth. This morning, she had crunched through the meadow on a layer of frost.

"Mama, do you think he still wants me?"

"Of course he does."

Valuable Woman knew exactly who she meant and could not have been happier. Straight Arrows had grown into a fine and trustworthy warrior, and her daughter could wish for no better mother-in-law than her own dearest friend, Brought-Us-the-Book. Best of all, the marriage would permanently link Spotted Long-knife and her with this people she loved so dearly.

Once they had enrolled Corn-Tassels in finishing school, their yearly visits to Boston had so lengthened, Valuable Woman occasionally feared they would never come home. Over the past winter, as Spotted Long-knife explored the possibilities of serving in the government, she had felt desperately torn. She tried to be excited for him—he grew more so every day—but she felt threatened. If their daughter married Straight Arrows, they would continue to visit as frequently as feasible, even after Joking Woman and Wooden Legs went home to Jesus. If Corn-Tassels married one of the Van Cleef brothers or some other white man, Valuable Woman knew what it would mean for their family. Curly-Haired Boy showed a decided preference for building and engineering over the frenzied games that trained warriors for battle, and her husband was inclined to encourage him.

"I wish my hair were not so light," mumbled Corn-Tassels, calling her mother back to their conversation. "It makes me stand out so from the other…untouched women."

Her cheeks grew warm. The expression so typified her grandparents' language, candidly proclaiming the most intimate details in the course of everyday conversation. How differently she had felt during her first years away. Her classmates had gone to great lengths to avoid reference to any natural function whatsoever. She had thought them ridiculously prim.

And now I have become just like them. As mother said, I must give myself time.

Hearing giggles at the door, she called permission for her cousins to enter and was soon entangled by more arms than a fly in a spider web. They lifted and petted her loose yellow hair as they had while they were children, clucking like a flock of little hens. She missed Light Bird sorely. Although Light Bird was four years her junior, Corn-Tassels had always appreciated the girl's quiet temperament, so unlike her own.

Light Bird reminded me of a buried treasure whose value could only be recognized once it was unearthed. I wonder if anyone in the strange territory she now calls home will bother to uncover those riches.

Corn-Tassels remembered the dread she had felt each time her father announced they were going east. Her eldest cousins mocked her childhood, dubbing it "life among the savages," and she hated the myriad of restrictions imposed by what they considered "polite society."

Oh, but I will miss the balls and soirees, and all the gentlemen lining up to fill my dance card...

As she pictured these cousins who were surrounding her in ball gowns, she could not help but giggle. They would feel as scandalized by her "life among the white men" as her Boston cousins had been about her life here.

Here or there, I seem bound to shock someone!

"Straight Arrows is going to come for you when the sun sleeps," confided Smiling Girl, her youngest cousin. "He told my brother. Walks-with-a-Limp says all your children will have yellow hair, but I told him it is not true. Brought-Us-the-Book's children all have black."

"Would it be so awful if they did?" replied Corn-Tassels, a bit more sharply than she had intended. Her cousin only voiced what she had been thinking earlier.

The whole group burst into laughter as if the very question was absurd.

"Are all white men like the long-knife who came with your father?" asked Talks-to-Birds. "His eyes followed us last night as we gathered our wood. My brother says if he does not stop ogling my cousins and me, he will…"

"He is just trying to learn our ways," Corn-Tassels interrupted, a little surprised she fervently wished to defend him. "He is a good man, very thoughtful and considerate."

"And handsome!" teased Smiling Girl, doing as her name implied. "But we are not the only ones his eyes often follow. My father thinks…"

This time, Valuable Woman cut in. The last thing she wanted was a bunch of silly girls jeopardizing the fine foundation her husband had laid for peace between their people. "Our family came to know him well on the long journey home. Corn-Tassels has been helping him learn our language, so when he is near, you had better keep your thoughts to yourself."

JOSHUA SCALED THE nearby promontory, hoping for a better view of the village and some much needed time alone. He easily picked out his mother's childhood friend among the women—the setting sun illumined the brown tones in her braids—but as she stooped over, the black-haired infant on her back set him wondering how she lived as she did. He was familiar with the large stone home in which she grew up. It was the finest in Skippack, and though he had been told her grandmother disdained ostentation, he also knew the family had employed a full staff of servants.

Imagining his mother stooping beside her, he began to chuckle; but when he glimpsed a blond woman moving toward the water's edge, the laughter died in his mouth. A warrior loomed above her, feathers haphazardly poking out from shining black hair. It fell loosely over a highly decorated robe that he had wrapped around them both.

Who can tell where he is putting his buffalo greased hands? How can the Major permit it—or Miss Anderson? He must stink something awful.

Joshua remembered the moment he had first seen her. Major Anderson had met him in Washington, and the next week the two traveled north to retrieve the Major's wife and children from his parent's home outside of Boston. The family had retired by the time he and her father had arrived, so he had gone to sleep without meeting one of them. The next morning, he arose with the sun. Eager to begin his new adventure, he felt too restless to stay in bed and too well-bred to explore the house, so he slipped out quietly to walk the countryside.

While a thick mist kept him along the paddock fence, he heard hooves pounding at a full gallop, and peering in their direction caught sight of the rider's long, golden hair. It swirled out behind her gloriously, like the goddess Diana come down to visit man. Surely no earthly maiden would choose such a time, fogged in no less, to exercise her horse. He was captivated, and more so when he noticed her seat: rather than secure her leg around a pommel, she rode astride with no saddle at all. He could not believe his eyes, but she sped toward him and leaped to the ground without mishap.

"Who is she?" he whispered, whether aloud or not he was not sure, but she quickly turned her head and spotted him leaning against a fence-post. Her face looked aghast, as if she had caught him peeping into her bedroom window; and when he burst into laughter, he half expected her to throw her crop at him. She hastily disappeared into the mist instead.

For the rest of the day, he looked for her in all the places Anderson took him, but how did one inquire after an unknown goddess? Not until that evening, at a ball held in her honor, did he discover she was Major Anderson's daughter.

"Abigail," said her father. "I would like you to meet Lieutenant Wilson. He will be accompanying us on our journey west."

As Joshua watched recognition dawning across her face, he feared she might choke. She turned bright red and appeared to have swallowed her tongue.

"Do you like to dance, Lieutenant Wilson?" asked the elder Mrs. Anderson. "My granddaughter has earned a reputation as quite an accomplished partner."

"It will be my pleasure," he had replied, holding out his arm before Abigail could bolt. "I am certain Miss Anderson has many accomplishments."

After a brief glower, she recovered her composure and let him glide her into line with the other dancers, but all through the first set, she refused him any but the barest pleasantries.

"You needn't worry," he whispered as the dance steps brought them together. "I have not given away your secret."

"I am sorry, Lieutenant Wilson," she blushed. "You must think me terribly rude. Grandmother does not approve of young ladies riding on horseback, particularly astraddle 'like a savage.'"

He wanted to tighten the arm about her waist but did not dare. "How can I resist such a charming apology? Does your father approve?"

"He does," she dimpled. "In my grandparents' village, women who do not ride quickly develop very tough feet. But while we are staying with Grandmother Anderson, he wishes me to abide by her restrictions."

Joshua cocked his head as the next steps briefly swirled her away and then back again. "Do they not live here, in Boston?"

Abigail laughed, "I'm afraid I've made myself as clear as this morning's fog. I meant my other grandparents. The Indian ones."

"Indian?" He had spent much of the morning with her mother. Her skin was far paler than his own, and her hair was a lovely shade of auburn.

"I am surprised Father has not told you. My mother was raised by an Indian couple in the village to which we journey."

"I knew she had been orphaned, but she seems such a refined woman. I can't imagine…" It was now Joshua's turn to be embarrassed. If he were to succeed in his new position, he must learn to speak his mind less frankly.

"Don't worry, Lieutenant Wilson; I am quite used to surprise about my upbringing. You will find my grandmother's people as refined in their own way as anyone here. I am quite anxious to return to them."

Her back had stiffened and her smile seemed forced, betraying her determination to conceal the offense she had taken; but whether she did so for his sake or merely to please her father, he could not tell.

As Joshua now watched her—standing on tiptoe to whisper in the warrior's ear—he turned away in disgust. She had been raised to this life, but he just could not imagine her creamy soft arms elbow deep in a buffalo carcass.

←←← →→→

AS BUDS UNFOLDED on the white-barked trees, the passing nights eased Light Bird's fear of the warrior who kept her warm. The morning sun, however, proved itself an enemy, flooding her with dread as it infiltrated his lodge's smoke-hole.

Aside from cooking each day's early and late meal, her role as a wife made few more onerous demands on her than the role of a daughter. She fetched Kills-Behind-Her-Dwelling's water as she had Two Doves' for most of her life; and when the old one's hands ached, Light Bird gladly mended her sundry garments. In some ways, she worked less. She had only one warrior's clothes to wash or hides to scrape and cure

Lying awake, listening to her husband's even breathing, or while performing tasks within his dwelling, she could almost imagine herself at home. Once she stepped outside his lodge-flap, the foreign camp closed in like a summer storm.

His clanswomen reminded her of those tightly packed white-barked trees. Their kind and number promised shelter, but their branches lacked sufficient spread to provide any but the most illusory comfort or protection. Worse yet, working alongside them day after day made her acutely aware of all she used to take for granted and had lost forever.

At home, she had sewed each shirt with her mother or aunts. Gathering morning or evening firewood and water provided time for chatting with her cousins or listening to her grandmother's stories. Even skinning and cleaning her brothers' kills was made pleasant by the company of her womenfolk. Here, she worked alone. Pacing Wolf's sister usually stayed on the other side of the village, and though his grandmother was kind, an unexpected cold snap most often kept her by the fire.

Why do I torment myself with such memories? My old life is like the winter grass: new life cannot sprout until it dies.

Most troubling of all was her loss of the Scriptures. She had read them since childhood and listened to them each night, but now they seemed irretrievably confined to the deepest recesses of her memory. The only verses she could readily recall were carved into the songs her people had often sung. Her brothers could recite whole chapters. Her parents had encouraged her to do likewise, but she had continually put it off for another day. Helping her mother with her three youngest took much time, and her other chores had seemed never-ending. Besides, like every girl in her village, she planned to marry a warrior who knew the Scriptures well and had not anticipated the past half-moon's vast changes. She had known enemies sometimes captured women, but she had not expected to one of them.

Unable now to remedy her lack, she mouthed silent songs so constantly that the Women-Who-Talk-Against-Each-Other-Without-Fear had begun to call her Talks-to-the-Wind. She did not care, as long as she could concentrate on what comforted her most—Jesus' love and faithfulness; but whenever possible, she slipped into the woods beside the river to find refuge from their stares.

Climbing carefully up the steep rise with her evening water, she spotted Pacing Wolf atop the cliff, scowling harshly.

"Where did you go?" he demanded as she reached the top. He had been looking for her well over an hour, his throat constricting with panic as he recalled the gory details of his dream.

"I have been by the river."

His eyes narrowed. He had never known her to lie, but he had searched the banks from the cliff several times and had not seen one sign of her. "Stay with my clanswomen—you are safer."

She nodded but looked sadder than he had seen her since her first few days in his lodge. "I am loneliest while I am with them."

He had not considered this and hated his inability to provide her a solution. His dead woman far preferred their company to his. Recalling why he had been looking for her, he said, "I have brought you two elk."

Forcing the ends of her lips upward, she voiced the first thoughts that occurred to her heart: "My father would be pleased to know you provide for me well."

Pacing Wolf's lips turned downward. "I do not need an enemy's approval!" Even while the words were leaping from his mouth, he wished he could recall them, and the defeat he saw passing through her eyes made him feel as if she had taken an ax to his gut. "I have dropped them by my lodge," he told her and quickly strode away.

Light Bird sank down on a rock beside the path, unable to decide what upset her more—her inability to anticipate what might anger him or that he had forbidden her to steal away. It seemed a small thing, too insignificant to cry over, but she felt she had lost something precious, a last thing that belonged to her alone. Dropping her head in her hands, she began to pray.

"You are hurt?"

Looking up, she saw a warrior outlined by the sun. She could not distinguish his features, but the warmth in his tone announced his identity: he was the clansman who owned swallow wings for eyebrows.

When she did not answer, he bent to examine an ankle, probing it as she had done to Two Doves' the morning Pacing Wolf snatched her from the meadow. Shaking her head "no", she drew her legs up under her skirt and wished he would go away. She felt impolite ignoring his kindness, but in her village, a woman did not speak with a strange man. To do so might invite his attention. Worse still, she craved the tenderness in his touch. Casting her eyes back over her shoulder, she scanned the cliff for Pacing Wolf—whether for his guidance or because she feared how he might construe his cousin's concern, she was not sure—probably both.

Aware of her discomfort, Goes-to-Battle rose. "You must be careful. These rocks are smooth from many moccasins. You will slip if you do not tend to your way."

Nodding briefly to acknowledge his warning, she felt thankful he bounded up the trail too quickly to require her to say anything else. She picked up her water sacks and ascended the same path at a pace that guaranteed he would be long gone.

←←←   →→→

"I SIMPLY CANNOT!" muttered Corn-Tassels as her mother handed her a knife.

Valuable Woman looked at her daughter sympathetically. "Have you forgotten how?"

"No—I remember. I just cannot bring myself to do it!"

The petite redhead drew the blade across the soft underside of the doe's throat and let its blood drip into the grass.

"How will you dress Straight Arrows' kills when I return to Boston? He may bring you many, sometimes several in one day."

When Corn-Tassels refused to look up, her mother knew something troubled her beyond feeling squeamish.

"It is not just this, Mama," she confided, slipping into English. "It is everything."

"Come inside. Your father is with Preying Eagle and your brother with Straight Arrows. I do not expect them to come back for a while."

Corn-Tassels followed her mother into her dwelling and flopped down on her bed. "I do not know what is wrong in me. For four years, I have eagerly wanted to come home, but now that I am here everything is so strange. I used to hate going to Boston, and when father said I must stay there for so long I thought I would just die. Now I find myself wishing I were there!"

"You have grown unaccustomed to our ways," her mother murmured. "I remember several times when you begged your father to take you home with us. Just give yourself time."

"I do not want time—I hate it here! I spend my days doing servants' work and feel constantly in need of a bath. How can you stand this drudgery day after day?"

"How else can we eat or have clothes to wear?"

"We can buy cloth!"

"Yes," her mother nodded. "The trader will be here soon, but he will not bring us food...and why buy fabric when we already have skins from your father's kills?"

"It is not just the work, Mama—it is Straight Arrows. I sense that he is disappointed in me and frankly, I am not sure I am not disappointed with him."

"In what way? He is respected by the elders and the image of his father."

"It is not that...it is..." At a loss to express her feelings, Corn-Tassels twisted the chain around her neck. "If I accept him, I accept all this," she explained, encompassing the dwelling with a sweep of her arm. "It is not what I want. He is not what I want...at least I do not think so. Oh, I am so confused!"

"Have you grown so proud while you were away or afraid to face hard work?" She hoped it not true, but could not fathom another explanation.

"I do not think so...but I am not sure. It is not the labor that bothers me...I just feel so...so wasted here...just another woman gaining calluses on her knees so her family can eat."

Valuable Woman rubbed her pale freckled hands together, surprised and a bit offended that her daughter held their womenfolk in such low esteem. She had always been proud to do any task that contributed to the welfare of their tribe. "And how would you be of greater use in Boston?"

"That is just it—I do not know. There are times that I wonder if I have just grown lazy and then I try harder to adapt to things here. At others, I feel so restless that I cannot stand another day let alone a lifetime. Please do not mention this to anyone and certainly do not mention what I said about Straight Arrows. You are right, of course. He has grown into quite the handsome and successful warrior—any untouched woman would be proud that he wanted her. The trouble is not with him, but me...but he knows. I can tell by the way he looks at me sometimes."

"He still loves you, I am sure. He had quite a struggle forgiving your father for taking you away, and every year when we came home, he was among the first to greet us. Of course, he wanted to see us, but all his questions were about you."

Corn Tassels looked down at the hands on her lap, unable to reply. Naturally, her mother would try to convince her to ignore her misgivings. She could think of nothing more wonderful than living with this people for the rest of her days.

But what if Straight Arrows dies in battle? Joking Woman and Wooden Legs are old, and my cousins...they are not truly related to me and owe me nothing. Remaining here as a widow or marrying another warrior is untenable— and what if I bear Straight Arrows children? Not only would his father and brothers prevent me from taking them away, no one in Boston would take me in if half-breeds were part of the bargain.

"Perhaps you should talk to Brought-Us-the-Book. She had to make the same decision and I am certain she remembers how she felt."

Corn-Tassels nodded, aware of the similarities of their choices. *But she is Straight Arrows' mother...how can I expect her to say anything that might jeopardize his happiness?*

Many are the plans in a man's heart, but the Lord's purpose prevails.
Proverbs 19:21

Chapter 15

WHEN LIGHT BIRD awoke and turned toward the place her husband normally lay, she let out a deep moan of relief. She was alone. *Oh God, forgive me.* She thrust her dream's details from her thoughts, but the swallow-winged warrior kept tenderly whispering to her memory. Pulling the covers over her ears, she asked the Lord to keep her from temptation and then prayed in the pattern He taught His disciples.

"Father in heaven"[41]...

As the familiar words brought her earthly father to mind, she pondered their meaning more deeply. They not only proclaimed the Creator's position above all things but also affirmed her relationship to Him and all the love and protection His fatherhood implied. Pacing Wolf had stolen her from Preying Eagle, but no one could separate her from God.[42]

Thank You for making me Your own, Lord, and for my father's clear example of Your love. Your name is holy.[43] *Glorify Yourself through me as..."*

"Small Doe!" called a quavering old voice. "Are you in there?"

Light Bird sat up, pulling a robe over her chest. "Come in, Grandmother."

"Get up, child, and hurry! The white trader has driven his long-eared horses over the prairie and his wagon is heaped up high."

Among-the-Pines pushed past her great-grandmother's skirt, gaping as if grasping for the first time where her father's captive slept.

"Dress quickly!" urged Kills-Behind-Her-Dwelling. "The Women-Who-Talk-Against-Each-Other-Without-Fear are swarming him like bees!"

When she noticed a sudden sadness flicker through Small Doe's eyes, she inwardly shrugged. *She must get used to the child and the child to her.*

"Go ahead, Grandmother," Light Bird replied. "I do not need anything."

"Not need anything? You have less than any woman in this village!"

Forcing cheer into her voice, Light Bird smiled, "The next time he comes, I may be first in line."

At once, Kills-Behind-Her-Dwelling understood the trouble: Small Doe had nothing to trade. She had not lived in the village long enough to have sewn spare garments and the Women-Who-Speak-Against-Each-Other-Without-Fear had provided her with only the items necessary to avoid embarrassing Pacing Wolf before an enemy. As stubborn as her grandson, the crafty old woman knew exactly how to coax his new bride outside.

"I will need help carrying my trades."

Hastily weaving her braids and donning the elk tooth garments, Light Bird caught up with her husband's daughter and grandmother as the trader was uncovering more goods. Kills-Behind-Her-Dwelling had not exaggerated the women's rivalries beside his wagon. Each bargained fiercely, asserting the superiority of her wares when a coveted item was at stake. Grabbing both of her charges by the wrists, the old woman cut a path for them through the crowd.

Light Bird's gaze fell upon a lovely mirror. Its sea-green enamel was just the color of her mother's eyes. Running her finger along its back, she felt seized by a keen desire to own it. She had not given her features much thought at home, but she now wanted badly to learn if they were pleasing. Sighing wistfully, she put it down. Such a beautiful item would fetch a far better price than she was able to give. The dress she had been wearing when Pacing Wolf snatched her was all she could truly call her own.

The trader, a tough-looking man in his mid-forties, had been listening to three ancient hags bicker over a length of ribbon when he noticed Light Bird steal up quietly across from him. As she glanced up from the mirror, her eyes grew so wide that he looked down to see which item had caught her attention: a stack of Bibles printed for the Sioux.

Last autumn, a ginger-haired ex-cavalryman living in the Dakotas had asked him to give them out in every tribe who spoke their tongue. The trader had hesitantly agreed, caring little for missionaries or their message, but the thinly concealed joy in this young woman's eyes almost made the space they took worthwhile. He had not seen a face so radiant since he left Missouri. Why they interested her, he could not imagine. She would no doubt understand the words if someone read them aloud—their languages were very similar—but who would she find that could?

"What would you trade for this, sir?" she asked in perfect, even refined, English.

The trader's wide mouth dropped open. *This little gal is full o' surprises!* He did not go for Indian women, but it crossed his mind that this one might come in handy. He could use a translator to help with trade and he hankered mightily after female companionship during the long summers away from his wife.

Maybe I kin make a bargain with'er Pa that'd suit us both. If she turns to carpin', I can pass'er off as Spanish an' sell her to a brothel or a Don.

"Where'd you learn English, girl?"

"My mother."

"Yer Mother?" He supposed a Crow woman might find it useful—they could haggle the paint off a wagon—or maybe her ma was some trapper's half-breed. "You read?"

"Yes," she nodded happily.

"Go get yer Pa. We'll see if we can work sumthin' out."

Pacing Wolf climbed the heights to join Hair-Up-Top and Hunts-For-Death as they weighed whether their band should stay along this river or travel across the Echata.

"As the sun approaches our doors tomorrow," Hunts-For-Death told him, "we will break camp."

Pacing Wolf kept his face impassive, but he did not welcome this news. He was not looking forward to seeing his dead woman's family. Though his ears attended to both the two older men, his eyes wandered toward his lodge. Kills-Behind-Her-Dwelling was pushing Among-the-Pines inside. Any moment he might catch sight of Small Doe's graceful form. He did not wait long. Her neatly parted crown ducked into the sunlight moments after his grandmother and little daughter, and the three began weaving toward the trader's wagon.

A supple grin slipped over his lips as he watched her hand pass slowly over a small object, the color of the Great Water to the Wind. It lingered there for a time, but as she moved down the wagon toward the trader, she fixed her gaze on something he could not make out. She began bouncing on the balls of her feet, reminding him of a little girl trying to control her hunger while her elders took the first share of a roasted buffalo hump; but after she spoke with the trader, her head and shoulders began to droop. He wished he were down there. His dead woman had been her most charming toward him when she wanted something new.

As Light Bird picked up his grandmother's goods, he wondered what she had desired. She was obviously reluctant to part with it. She kept glancing back longingly as Kills-Behind-Her-Dwelling led them from the wagon, but by the time Pacing Wolf made his way down to the village, she had gone.

"The girl," he spoke to the trader, "she want what?"

After conducting rapid business with one woman after another for over an hour, the trader would have retorted irritably had he not happened to glance up at the speaker. He had worked the plains and surrounding mountains for many years and knew the significance of each mark on a garment. One word from this warrior could toss him into more trouble than a beehive in a heap of grizzly bears.

Pacing Wolf nodded toward his lodge, "The one who possesses the spirit of a young doe."

The trader hesitated. He suspected the young chief meant the gal who spoke English, but he needed time to assess how they might be related. If he were the gal's brother, he might sell her for the right price; but if he were her husband or a suitor, he might not take the offer kindly.

Assuming the trader had not understood, Pacing Wolf scoured his mind for the words in English. "Woman like small deer—small woman deer. Face good—like fresh snow—no cut, no holes." To clarify his meaning, he first stroked his cheek and then sliced his thumb across it to indicate scars. Lastly, he pecked indentations with his finger to depict marks left by spotted fever. As an afterthought, he added: "Big eyes—round."

Pacing Wolf's description confirmed the little gal's identity but did little to answer the trader's questions about their kinship. Back east, a man might describe a sweetheart this way but never a sister. Indians, however, ascribed all sorts of unexpected traits to people—even other men. In the missionary's village, he'd heard one warrior call another Pretty Face. The warrior's English did not offer much help either. It lacked her quality, but that was easily explained. A daughter would naturally spend more time with her mother than a son. On the other hand, this tribe had been at peace with the United States dating back to Jefferson's exploration of the Louisiana Purchase. Many of its people spoke an odd word here and there.

"Tall or short?" the trader asked, trying again to buy more time.

Pacing Wolf held his flattened hand level with his nose.

"Speak English?"

Pacing Wolf did not know. She had said she had a white mother, but he did not want this foreigner to think him ignorant about his own woman. "She want this," he replied, pointing to the only lake-colored object in the wagon.

Concluding the man was her sweetheart, the trader calculated how he should reply. An eager suitor might buy her anything he mentioned. Slowly stroking the reddish gold stubble at the bottom of his chin, he perused the heavier goods left in his wagon. He had quite a lot of trouble getting his mules to haul it up the mountain. The more he lightened his load, the easier time they would have going on to the next stop. Still, the warrior had walked up and pointed out the only other item that particular gal had touched. He decided he had better tell the truth.

"Well, she looked at that a while," he answered, picking up the mirror and flipping it over so Pacing Wolf could look at his reflection, "but she really wanted this." Handing Pacing Wolf a Bible, he watched him turn it over and over as if trying to discover its appeal. "It's the Good Book written in Sioux."

Pacing Wolf had not heard of the last word, but another stood out from the rest. "Book?" he questioned. "White man's Spirit-book?"

"Yep. That's it. She said she could read it."

Pacing Wolf casually laid it back on the pile. He would offer several horses to invite her smile, but he did not like this trader. His yellow-green eyes reminded him of the great hungry cats that stalked the mountains. He also knew if he betrayed his interest, he would pay too much.

Quicker witted than his fearsome opponent realized, the trader chewed over the sort of swap he might make. If he demanded a high price, the warrior might deem him dishonest and bar him from the village—or worse. If he gave him the Bible, as the missionary intended, he risked insulting the man's pride. "Two good buffalo hides for both," he offered.

Yellow-Eyes places little value on his god's book, thought Pacing Wolf. "One."

"One?" The trader acted insulted, though he would gladly have accepted a hide for the mirror and thrown in some beads as well.

"One!" replied Pacing Wolf, holding up a single finger for emphasis.

"One it is," the trader nodded. "You're as good at trading as you are at raiding."

Accepting the compliment as his natural due, Pacing Wolf ducked into his dwelling, relieved that Small Doe had not been present to see how cheaply he had obtained the gifts. He grabbed the pelt closest to the door flap, intending to take it directly to the trader, but he stopped when he felt a spot that was wet. Touching it with his tongue, he tasted salt and knew he had accurately read her disappointment. Why she wanted it, though, was beyond his ability to fathom. The object had reminded him of a pouch with its sides left unsewn, crammed full of dried tobacco leaves.

After completing the exchange, Pacing Wolf hurried back into his lodge and hung the mirror on the peg. Next, he retrieved his best leggings, cut a few stitches along a seam, folded them around the book, and stashed them back into his large leather bag. Slipping out onto the path, he looked all about before crossing to the other side. Several Good Men had gathered there, and though he felt too distracted for conversation, their location offered an excellent view of the way from the river.

In a short while, Small Doe trudged up the rise, hauling their morning water. Her eyes were on the newly sprouting red grass, but as she drew near enough to catch her husband's voice, they darted upward. That brief glance was all the encouragement he needed. He dashed across the path, leaving his surprised friends to think whatever they pleased.

The moment Light Bird stepped inside she noticed the mirror. Removing it from the hook, she touched it almost reverently. She felt amazed Pacing Wolf had bothered to buy her a gift and delighted he had chosen the very one she wanted. Turning her head from side to side, she assessed the shape of her eyes and brow, the length of her nose, and the hollows beneath her cheekbones. They looked angular, almost sharp, and nothing like Among-the-Pines': the only hint she had of features formed to his liking.

Stealing up silently, Pacing Wolf brushed aside the door-flap. Her pleasure in his gift was plain, but while he watched her eyes begin to cloud, the shining surface caught his reflection.

Her lips curved sweetly. "It is lovely," she murmured, clutching the mirror to her chest as she turned.

Although he had known her only a moon, he felt as though he had been waiting for this moment all of his summers; yet, once he received her smile, his tongue refused to loosen. Squatting to retrieve the folded leggings from his bag, he pointed to the ruined stitches.

"I have split them."

Light Bird wondered when he had done so. He had not worn the pair since the night she had made a feast for his kinsmen. When she took them from his hand, they felt so unexpectedly heavy that she nearly dropped them, and out of their folds slid a dark rectangular object. Her mouth fell open, then she hurled herself against him, throwing her arms around his neck.

When she drew away, a rapturous smile broke across her face. It lit her fine-boned features like the fresh morning sun captured on the surface of a placid lake. "How did you know?"

"I watched you from the ridge," he grinned.

"You are as generous as you are clever and skilled. My father would have welcomed you."

As the words were leaving her lips, she wished she could pull them back. They were not true. Though her captor possessed many admirable qualities, her father had rightly refused to let anyone court her who did not cherish a relationship with Jesus, and he would never have given her to an enemy.

Pacing Wolf bristled. He did not need her father's approval, but her undisguised delight assured him she had not meant to stick a barb in his side. Seizing the chance to besiege her heart, he swallowed a sharp retort and laid his hands about her hips. "He was wearing few tokens when he searched the cave, but the respect his brothers offered spoke well of him."

His tactic paid off. She relaxed against him, relieved that he was not angry and profoundly grateful for something too vague for her to put into words. By acknowledging her father, Pacing Wolf had somehow relieved her of the compulsion to choose between the two: husband and father, present and past.

Feeling a bit emboldened, she added, "His lance and war bonnet are heavy and he is much respected in our councils. I have watched you often amidst your clansmen; you are much like him."

At a loss for a reply, Pacing Wolf pulled her closer. Her admiration had exceeded his hopes and far outstripped any his dead woman had offered. His clansmen had long held him in high esteem, expecting he would one day lead them, but his dead woman most often treated him with contempt. Laying his cheek against Small Doe's hair, he began wondering again about her spirit-guide.

"What do you call him?" he asked her.

"Preying Eagle."

"Not your father—the spirit whose words live in this white man's book?"

"Many things," she smiled. "The Creator,[44] the Most High,[45] the Almighty,[46] the Eternal One,[47] and like you: He-Who-Sees-All-Things."[48] Opening the cover, she showed him the pages. "These are His words written in the tongue of my people—almost the same as the Sparrow Hawks'."

"You read these markings?"

"Yes. Each has a sound." Turning to Genesis, she pointed to the title and pronounced each of the symbols until they combined into a word he recognized.

"Go on."

She read about the first two days of creation, similar to the Sparrow Hawk tradition that says He-Who-First-Made-All-Things wandered over the water before creating life,[49] but when she glanced up and saw him frowning, she stopped.

He waved his fingers forward. "Go. Go on."

She happily continued, pointing to each word she read. The sound of her voice pleased his ears. He had drunk more of it by chapter's end than he had through all the weeks she had warmed his lodge, but when she came to Adam taking Eve, he heard her falter. Glancing at her reddening cheeks, he picked up the trail of her thoughts and trotted eagerly after them, closing the Book and setting it aside.

Kills-Behind-Her-Dwelling lifted an eyebrow. She had brought the new beads Small Doe had promised to sew around her collar, but though it was mid-morning, her grandson's lodge-flap was fastened shut.

As she was turning away, it fell open. "I wish to come in," she called, surprised further when she heard Pacing Wolf answer. She had seen him last with Hunts-For-Death up on the high ridge. When she took in Small Doe's appearance, her eyes began to twinkle. The girl's long spirals swirled loosely about her flushed, bare shoulders and her eyes shown particularly bright.

The old woman began to back out, assuring Small Doe she would come later, but Pacing Wolf waved her in.

"I go," he assured her, but he paused while his luminous bride was settling her dress into place. As she began weaving her braids, he asked, "What offering does he require?"

"Offering?"

"The book's spirit. What does he require?"

"Nothing…he wants only our hearts."

The old woman watched her new granddaughter pick up and thumb through a curious object. She could not say what it was, but the girl seemed delighted to hold it: tiny dimples twitched persistently about the corners of her mouth. Kills-Behind-Her-Dwelling had not known she possessed any. She had seen Small Doe's lips turn up politely, but even then, they had conveyed more sadness than joy.

Light Bird found a Psalm she knew well and pointed to the text. "See." She knew her husband could not read it, but she wanted him to know she spoke the Creator's words, not her own. "'The sacrifice the Creator desires is a broken spirit. He will not despise a broken and a contrite heart.'"[50]

Pacing Wolf strained to catch the meaning. "What is this word—contrite? We do not use it."

"It means sorry, ashamed of the wrong you have done."

Pacing Wolf sat stiffly, turning down the corners of his mouth. "I have taken just vengeance against your clansman, no more."

Glancing first at Kills-Behind-Her-Dwelling, Light Bird quietly assured him, "I meant no offense. We are all born with a desire to cut our own trails—I as much as you. The Creator wants us to walk His path with Him."

Twisting around to show her his back, Pacing Wolf touched two scars starting below his shoulder blades and snaking forward beneath his arms. "From youth, I've pierced my flesh and hung from the pole so my spirit-guide would give me visions. I honor the four winds each time I smoke—I do not need this contrite heart!"

Light Bird stifled a sigh, wondering how her mother made her father and grandfather understand; but before she could think of an answer, Hunts-For-Death began calling from outside. As Pacing Wolf got up and slipped out, Kills-Behind-Her-Dwelling shook her head. She had not understood the strange word either, but she wished her grandson had kept silent. All the brightness had drained from his young bride's eyes.

"Do not let the thorny weeds take root," she advised, holding out the beads she had bought.

Nodding solemnly, Light Bird put them in her pouch. She knew his grandmother intended to help but wished the old woman would go. She wanted to climb into the lap of the One who could truly soothe her, particularly now that she had His Word to read.

"A voice speaks to each of us," Kills-Behind-Her-Dwelling continued. "Pacing Wolf's often shames him."

Small Doe looked up, suddenly interested in his grandmother's counsel. "What do you mean?"

"As a boy, he carried much tenderness in his heart, but he has dug a deep hole to hide it in, piled it with dirt, and stomped it down tightly. He hates the sorrow he has handed you."

Small Doe's eyes softened while she listened to the old woman, though she tilted her head to one side. "But you heard him. He…"

"I heard the little boy that cried when he thought I was asleep."

"Why?"

"Sometimes the dead plague our hearts."

As before, Small Doe did not know what to make of his grandmother's assertions. Thinking of nothing better to say, she confessed, "I do not understand."

"He could not stop his mother's bleeding."

Small Doe wanted to know more, but since Kills-Behind-Her-Dwelling stood up to leave, she did not press her to speak further. "I will try to sew the beads on your dress before the sun takes his rest."

"If you can," the old woman replied. "If not, you can do it later."

Small Doe stared blankly after the bent form, even when the door flap fell back into place. She was not sure what the old woman had meant but suspected Pacing Wolf blamed himself for his mother's death. Picking up her new Bible, she found the one passage she had dependably remembered all through the past moon, eager to read the verses that surrounded it.

> It is commendable to bear up under the pain of unjust suffering because you are conscious of God. How is it to your credit if you receive a beating for doing wrong and endure it? But if you do what is right and suffer patiently this is commendable before God. God's Anointed One left you an example. You were called to walk in His steps. 'He committed no sin, and no deceit was found in His mouth.' When they hurled insults at Him, He did not strike back. When He suffered, He did not threaten. Instead, He kept entrusting Himself to Him who judges justly. He Himself bore our sins in His body on the tree so that we might die to sin and live for righteousness. His wounds have healed you; for you were wandering off on your own path but now have returned to the guide and protector of your souls.[51]

I just told my husband that Jesus desires us to walk with Him—how could I have wondered what this passage meant! Jesus came to earth knowing what he would suffer so that we might know Him. How can I expect any different? "A slave is not greater than his master." Her mouth dropped open as she read the next verses—the answer to an unspoken plea:

> In the same way, women, submit yourselves willingly to your husbands, so that if any of them do not obey the word you may win them—without talk—as they observe your pure and respectful behavior. Do not wear your adornments on the outside—weaving your hair, wearing necklaces and earrings and fine dresses, but hide in your heart the imperishable quality of a gentle and quiet spirit, which is precious in the sight of God. This is how holy women of old who hoped in the Creator adorned themselves: they submitted to their husbands. Sarah obeyed Abraham, calling him her master, and you are her children if you do what is right without giving way to fear.[52]

Oh Lord, how good You are—giving me the answer before I asked! Help my behavior to attract Pacing Wolf to You, and keep my words from getting in the way!

With a heart full of joy, she wove the final rows of a gift she had been making for him. She had had difficulty obtaining the materials but was doubly glad now that she had made the effort.

Lord, you are my Creator. I will exalt You and praise Your name. For You have accomplished wonderful things—things You planned long ago in perfect faithfulness.

Isaiah 25:1

Chapter 16

ONCE SHE HAD COMPLETED her early morning chores, Corn-Tassels slipped into Brought-Us-the-Book's dwelling. "My mother said you were looking for me."

"Yes, though I fear I am intruding. Valuable Woman says you are not sleeping well and are eating little."

Corn-Tassels warily shifted her blue eyes. "I have had much on my mind lately."

As a pink hue tinged her *niece's* cheeks, Brought-Us-the-Book suspected what it was. She handed Corn-Tassels a breastplate to occupy her hands as Two Doves always had when she wanted to talk. "You have young eyes—would you mind loosening these sinews? I wish to add to the bottom. Pretty Face has grown quite tall."

Corn-Tassels nodded, happy to help.

"When I was about your age I also struggled over a momentous decision."

"Oh, Auntie," the girl sighed, relieved by the invitation to unburden herself. "I am so confused. How can I know what the Lord wants? I was born and raised here—surely that was not by accident—but Boston has changed me, and I do not know how to change myself back."

"Why do you think you need to?"

"I am sure mother has told you," the girl frowned. "She very patiently listens, but she does not understand. A new world has opened for me—a world I am not ready to leave forever."

Brought-Us-the-Book smiled. "I felt like that when I came here."

"But you stayed...though it must have been hard."

"My 'new world' was here, and staying was honestly the easier choice. I could not bear to leave."

"Were you not scared? How could you trade your whole life for...for this other?"

"I heard from God."

"But how? I fear I may hear wrongly or that mother is right and I have grown proud."

"Hearing is less difficult than muffling other voices, though seeking counsel from those you respect deeply is always wise?"

"Mama cannot imagine preferring anywhere else and Papa...he refuses to tell me what he thinks. He says to seek the Lord's will, not his."

A private smile crept across Brought-Us-the-Book's lips. "Perhaps he has learned over the years that the course that seems logical is not necessarily the one God chooses. Only He knows the future."

"I suppose you are right, but it would be so much simpler if he were like the fathers here and insisted I do as he desires. Though Mama wants me to stay, I suspect Papa does not, so either way I choose, I will grieve one of them."

"The Lord did not create you to make either of them happy—or Straight Arrows. He had his own reasons, just as He did for creating them."

"But what about honoring my mother and father? Should I not try to do as they wish?"

"Yes—and your father wishes for you to do God's will, not his. Your mother does also, despite her distinct preferences."

"Then how do I choose?"

Searching the earnest young face, Brought-Us-the-Book recalled the moment Corn Tassels decided to place her feet in Jesus' footprints. "If you stay here to please others, you will find only bitterness and resentment. The Holy Spirit lives inside of you. He will guide you into all you need."

"But I pray and pray and hear nothing."

"Then perhaps you simply need to wait longer for His answer. Do you remember asking me to carry Light Bird around on your back when you were little?"

"Yes. I was four, maybe five."

"When I strapped her cradleboard onto you, you began wobbling from the weight and nearly fell over. I was foolish to have given in, but you were so eager to try, and I wanted to make you happy. If you asked to carry this one, though," she glanced over her shoulder toward the babe on her back, "I would agree without a thought. If God is still keeping His will to Himself, He has a good reason, and even if you are ready to learn it, someone else may not be."

"When He told you to stay here, did He speak aloud?"

"No, though I would not rule out the possibility since He did so to several people in the Bible. Usually, He speaks through His Word or even circumstances—especially those that are not of our own choosing—as He did with Esther and Daniel."

"Do you...do you think this is what He has done this with Light Bird?" As Brought-Us-the-Book's green eyes clouded, Corn-Tassels wished she had not asked.

"I can come to no other conclusion. Before He placed her in my womb, He numbered the days of her life.[54] Troubles come that no amount of wisdom and planning can prevent, but the older I grow, the more deeply I become convinced that these—and our responses to them—are the moments that matter most. Think of Joseph. He was obeying his father when his brothers sold him to slavers, and his faithfulness to Potiphar got him tossed into prison. Can you imagine how dismayed he must have felt? Yet, with every step, God was preparing him for his eventual role. Recently I again read those chapters and felt amazed by something I never noticed before. Not only did Joseph trust God; God trusted him. If Joseph had clung to bitterness, he might have executed his brothers.[55] Their families would have starved, nullifying God's promise to bless all people through Abraham's offspring."[56]

"Do you think we will ever see Light Bird again?"

"Perhaps. Joseph and his father were reunited. More than praying for God to bring her back, though, I am praying for her faith not to fail."[57]

WHILE PACING WOLF and Light Bird were finishing their morning baths, they heard a herald shouting along the river. "Men, bring your horses! Women, throw down the lodges!"

Hurrying back to the village, Pacing Wolf gathered his weapons and war-shield and left Light Bird to pack his belongings. *My belongings*, she corrected herself, for most were given to her by his clanswomen. As she was laying the sturdiest lodge poles parallel to each other on the ground, he rode up with several horses in tow.

"You will ride this one," he told her, adding as she craned her neck to search a group of little girls, "Among-the-Pines travels with Never-Sits."

Why then, she wondered, *did he bring me a second mount?* Before she could ask, he had already ridden off to join a large group of assembling warriors. She shrugged, noticing he had also supplied his grandmother with two horses. Fastening his lodge poles along each side of her mount, she spread their lodge covers between them and began piling them with household goods.

"Not that way!" scolded Does-Not-Cry, the shorter of the ripe-bellied woman who had welcomed her in Pacing Wolf's lodge. "Watch what I do."

Instead of forming a travois, as Light Bird's womenfolk always did, Does-Not-Cry tugged her second horse behind an ornately saddled roan. Hoisting up her two lengthiest lodge poles, she fastened their front ends on each side of the wooden saddle and their back ends to the second mount. She then spread her husband's lodge covers between the two.

Light Bird thanked her and did likewise. It seemed an awkward way to haul things but had answered her question.

"My people did as yours do," Does-Not-Cry told her, "but this way is better. We travel faster."

As Light Bird glanced up in surprise, the woman smiled.

"I also am a captive—from the Grass Lodges who live toward the…" The woman dropped her gaze to her belly, caught Light Bird's hand, and firmly pressed the palm over a hard bulge. "You see?" she laughed when Light Bird felt it. "Already my small-thing wrestles like a warrior! He has been pushing hard against me all morning, impatient to be out. I hope he will wait until we make camp."

"Perhaps you should wait," suggested Light Bird, "and join us later."

Does-Not-Cry's eyes grew wide. "No—I cannot! The Lumpwoods would beat me and cut up my husband's lodge. They might even maim his horses. Better to bear my small-thing while crossing the Echata."

Light Bird felt appalled, particularly because she had learned that Pacing Wolf was a member of the group. She hoped her new friend exaggerated but did not prod further. Does-Not-Cry had heaved her cumbersome belly over the elaborately decorated saddle and was moving her horses into line behind a scowling warrior.

Alone, Light Bird was uncertain how to proceed. Pacing Wolf had disappeared. Searching the assorted faces, she spotted Among-the-Pines and Never-Sits atop ponies within a crowd of strangers and Kills-Behind-Her-Dwelling struggling with her mount. While she tried to think of a way to help—her own horses might bolt if she left them—the swallow-browed warrior ambled into view.

He is as kind as he is handsome, she concluded while he tugged the old woman into position beside her; but she averted her eyes when he glanced in her direction. Though she credited the Creator—not him—for his well-formed features, she admired the care he gave his grandmother more than she wanted to show. As she listened half-heartedly to their conversation, she felt seized with a desire to cover her ears.

"Why is Pacing Wolf' captive riding with old women? She should ride behind him so all can see he is proud of her beauty."

His grandmother snickered in reply. "When you chose the Foxes over the Lumpwoods, I was surprised, but I am no longer. You possess a fox pup's cunning and were drawn to your own kind!"

Goes-to-Battle laughed. Wheeling his mount with a swish of her tail, he plunged toward a group of Good Young Men, but his comments rubbed a raw spot on Light Bird's heart. As she surveyed the Many Lodges, she saw many highly decorated Good Men moving into place just ahead of their wives. They formed a stunning procession. Young brides sat on wooden saddles with large fringed bags perched just behind them. Attired in the finest of garments, each adorned her horse with her husband's highly ornamented shield and proudly flaunted the tokens that hung from his lance.

Light Bird felt forgotten. Dressed simply in her doeskin, no one could tell to whom she belonged or even that she was newly married. Still, she was grateful Pacing Wolf had provided her a mount. As she looked around, however, even this small comfort lost its power. The Many Lodges owned such a wealth of horses that no one traveled afoot.

"You will not find him," his grandmother interrupted. "When the grass last greened, Hair-Up-Top chose the Lumpwoods as our soldiers. They ride ahead to protect us from attack or behind to discipline stragglers. Those," she pointed to her swallow-browed grandson and his companions, "are the Foxes and these others are Muddy Hands. Over there you see the Big Dogs."

"I do not understand," Light Bird replied, annoyed by the woman's uncanny ability to read her private thoughts. "Only the young or old of my menfolk travel with the women."

"We are too many. When the grass begins to green, Hair-Up-Top may honor a different war-society. The Lumpwoods are the strongest—but one battle could lessen their ranks."

Although Light Bird did not entirely understand, she did not wish to ask many questions. As with any large group of travelers, interruptions were plentiful and confidentiality did not exist. Instead, they rode silently for several hours.

Does-Not-Cry had been correct. By suspending their goods above the ground, they progressed rapidly. Light Bird was surprised, though, when the throng began pulling to a stop. The sun had not yet begun yawning and was far from drifting off to sleep.

"Are we making camp?"

"Not yet," replied Kills-Behind-Her-Dwelling, nodding to a point ahead of them. "We have come to the Echata. The snow melting in the mountains has made it swell. Our crossing will not be easy."

Slipping down, the two guided their horses closer to the water. Men, women, and children were scurrying up and down the bank, fishing out driftwood or breaking dead limbs off nearby trees. They fashioned them into rough rafts across which they lay their lodge-poles and spread their largest coverings. Then, upon these they placed their loads, gathering up and tying the covers' ends to keep their possessions dry.

The whole undertaking fascinated Light Bird. Only while en route with Pacing Wolf had she crossed a large river, but wrapped in her pelt she had glimpsed little. Taking out her knife, she imitated her husband's womenfolk but stopped—stunned—when an untouched woman a few lengths away shed her dress. Wrapped in a skin that barely covered her from waist to knee, the girl proceeded to paint red stripes around her waist, wrists, and ankles and then waded into the water to swim behind the first raft.

"That is Otter Woman," said Kills-Behind-Her-Dwelling. "Do as she does—this is not a time for modesty. When your dress becomes heavy with water, the current may carry you away."

Light Bird felt mortified. After she helped the old woman onto their hastily constructed raft, a clansman came up alongside and guided it out into the Echata. Clinging to the rear, she followed it into the swirling water, determined to take her chances rather than shame herself.

On a high ridge, Hunts-For-Death laid his spyglass across Pacing Wolf's outstretched palm. During the Earth Lodges' council by the Knife River, a blue-coated Long-knife had offered him the tool in exchange for marking a paper that guaranteed settlers safe passage through Sparrow Hawk territory. Hunts-For-Death had been glad to do so. The white men lacked the sense to stay where the air was cool and game plentiful. They settled the hot plains or drove their clumsy wagons into the land of a poor and dirty people who traveled in canoes and ate fish.[57]

The tool had proven useful. When he peered through its long-eye, he could search up and down the riverbank and spot game high on the mountain. Nothing he had seen alarmed him today, but judging from his Lumpwood son's expression, the younger man did not agree: he glowered intently through the long-eye at the river below.

Last spring, Pacing Wolf had felt proud when their Real Chief had chosen the Lumpwoods to protect their people for yet another summer. It proclaimed their strength and superiority over their rival war-societies, but he had not liked leaving Small Doe to cross the Echata alone. She might not know to paint red stripes on her torso and limbs to keep the water monsters from attacking.[58] As he searched the immense jam of rafts near the narrows, he located his grandmother atop her bundled goods, holding her moccasins and blanket.

Small Doe cannot be far, he thought; but as he pointed the long-eye toward the rear of the raft, his heart plummeted like a stone. She was wearing her one-piece doeskin. Her face looked pinched as she strained against the current in its water-soaked weight, and though she clung on tightly, he feared she could not do so for long.

While he was asking her book-god to notice her plight, his throat constricted in panic. An elderly clansman lost control of his raft, and the river was swirling it straight toward Small Doe's head. In fascinated horror, he watched it knock her beneath the rushing surface. The swiftest eagle lacked speed enough to dive down the cliff to save her. As his grandmother's raft surged forward, another immediately took its place until one after another filled every opening on the crowded river.

Pacing Wolf seethed with helpless frustration. Even if Small Doe mustered the strength to surface, she would be trapped beneath driftwood and pawing hooves. All at once, he saw her head bob up, pitching his stomach into his throat, but the turbulent Echata dragged her back under.

Save me O God, for the waters have come up to my neck! I sink into the muddy deep where there is no foothold. I am plunged into deep waters. The floods engulf me.

Psalm 69:1-2

Chapter 17

LIGHT BIRD GULPED a mouthful of air and sank again beneath the churning water. It pulled her down—further and further—until she was too tired to fight any longer. She almost felt relieved that the struggles of the past moon were over. As her limbs went limp, she was enveloped by an overwhelming sense of euphoria and thought she heard Red Woman, her father's grandmother, singing her to sleep. She could almost feel her mother's gentle fingers stroking the tension from her forehead and a verse, learned long ago and then forgotten, coaxed her lips into a peaceful smile.

I shall behold Your face in righteousness. When I awake, I will be satisfied with beholding Your form.'[60]

Her father disrupted her bliss. Shoving his arm around her waist, he heaved her onto the neck of a swimming horse and forced her limp fingers into its thick mane. Water ran freely from her mouth while he hoisted her hips across the animal's broad back, but she was too exhausted to do anything but sputter.

Tenderly, he brushed back the braid that clung to her lips, but as she offered him a wan smile she grew confused. The eyes peering back at her were warm with concern, but they were topped by finely arching brows.

Terror, relief, and elation shot through Pacing Wolf in rapid succession, leaving him reeling until the clansman who saved her turned his head. *The red grass is just sprouting,* he muttered, *and already my cousin is trying to steal her.*

He hated the jealousy that wrestled down his joy; but even more, he hated all Goes-to-Battle's quick rescue implied. The young warrior had been staying close to Small Doe, offering the kinds of assistance that made his desire for her clear. Equally irksome was the debt Pacing Wolf now owed. It bit him like an insect burrowing into his hide. The expense was nothing, he had plenty of fine horses in his herd, but to reward a rival for wooing his wife set his teeth on edge.

Still, he groaned, *if he had not been sniffing after her trail, she would be sleeping tonight beneath the covers of the Echata. I will give him my best mare's yearling.*

"Look!" Hunts-For-Death commanded. Without the aid of the spyglass, he had been unable to see what was agitating his war-society son, so he had trained his attention on a minuscule speck moving into the mouth of a distant valley. Other specks followed, drifting leisurely along one of the Echata's slender, slowly flowing daughter.

Following his adopted father's gaze, Pacing Wolf returned the spyglass and hurriedly set out to tell He-Who-Leads-the-Moving-Band that they had spotted buffalo. He found old Hair-Up-Top high on a brother-ridge, but by the time he reached him, someone else had already done so. Flanked by a pair of elderly warriors, the aged Real Chief was lighting his pipe.

Pacing Wolf took up a position behind them with the other assembling Lumpwoods and watched the wind carry the sweet-smelling smoke toward the herd. Recognizing the sign's significance, each began congratulating his brothers about the hunt they would enjoy, but all became quiet as a particularly keen-eyed warrior directed their attention back into the valley.

"The far ones are picking up speed," he told Hair-Up-Top, who in turn addressed several of the Lumpwoods' Good Young Men.

"Before the sun wakes, climb up here to see how they are moving. If they travel swiftly, watch for an enemy and then hurry to my lodge."

LIKE A HUNGRY HAWK, the red sun hovered between the mountains as the last driftwood crafts bumped against the swollen Echata's other bank. Up and down the river, the Women-Who-Talk-Against-Each-Other-Without-Fear heaved their lodge poles up and hastily covered them with hides. Kills-Behind-Her-Dwelling and Light Bird were already gathering sticks for their evening fires as excitement started spreading like a fever. Men, women, and children abandoned their chores when they spotted Hair-Up-Top riding his painted stallion down from the ridge, his headdress and white hair flowing out behind him in the wind. Light Bird thought he looked magnificent.

"Young Men," he called to those who ran to greet him. "Cut limbs and dry them. The buffalo we spotted run like an enemy is chasing. Fill your quivers and make your bowstring good. Bring extra sinews—if yours breaks and you have no other, the enemy will kill you. We own no teeth or claws to protect ourselves—arrows, knives, and axes are our weapons. Make yourself ready.

"When the enemy charges, stand firm and keep your hearts brave. Look around you—we have few old men. If your spirit-guide wants you to grow old, you will. If he wants you to die, you will die. We have heard the spirits are looking for their children; perhaps you are the ones they are seeking. Look at our Good Men. They have many horses and their lodges are tall. Consider the way they live and live like them. Go up the mountain, fast and make an offering. Ask your spirit-guide for strength so that one of you may one day lead our people. I will not always be with you."[61]

As Pacing Wolf rode in procession behind him, he noticed Small Doe standing beneath a cottonwood a short distance from his gathering clanswomen. She was holding herself with surprising elegance for one who had just tasted death. Her face betrayed nothing. Like all who had lived beyond childhood, she had learned to subdue her emotions; and yet as he drew nearer, he found more than an impassive expression. He found the subtle quality that had brought the hidden pool to mind. He found peace.

His own insides churned like the flooding Echata. Her near-drowning had left him vulnerable and hungry—hungry for something the mere possession of her could not satisfy. He wanted her to welcome him gladly after a hunt, to hold joy in her eyes when he returned safely from battle, and to mourn when he died for more than a loss of status and provisions. He wanted what his mother had given to his father—her heart.

ALONE THAT NIGHT inside his dwelling, Pacing Wolf tried to pick up a trail to the secret place she hid her thoughts. Neither mentioned the crossing. Light Bird was afraid her lack of sense had shamed him, and he feared he might expose too much. Instead, they worked by firelight with tongues that refused to loosen: he, whittling arrow shafts, and she, mending her dress. Completing the task, she hung the still-damp garment from a peg, but before beginning to sew another, she withdrew something she had hidden at the bottom.

"I have made this to protect your throat from enemy arrows and knives." Across her palm, she held an intricately woven choker for him to examine. "I traded a skin for the buffalo bones."

Pacing Wolf stared hard at her gift. He could tell it had taken her many hours to complete, and her artistry made it worthy for Hair-Up-Top, but suspicion sprang up within him like a sentinel determined to guard his vital parts. Sparrow Hawk men adorned themselves elaborately, but none wore the protective coverings of her clansmen. If her band trailed the buffalo, her gift might mark him for death. *When,* he wondered, *did she make it? She wears the look of the skittish young doe that she wore in the cave.*

"You do not want it," she murmured, casting her gaze to the ground. *It would have been better had the water carried me downward.* Crumpling it into a tight ball, she would have flung it into the flames had he not gripped her fist.

"Would you draw your uncles' war clubs to me?"

Light Bird's eyes flew up in obvious surprise. "My uncles?"

"Buffaloes do not run unless someone chases."

"You heard my father in the cave," she reminded him, trying to pull away from her hand. "They do not seek vengeance. I meant you good, not harm."

He distinctly remembered where he had heard those words before: in the alcove while she was praying to her book-god. He also knew the Blackfoot were more likely than her band to follow this herd. They lived toward the wind and, like Sparrow Hawks, needed to replenish their supply of meat now that the snow had melted. Having trotted down this path, however, his pride would not allow him to forsake it.

"Your young brother was not of the same heart."

Recalling Pretty Face's prayer, she could not contradict him, but she did not think her men folk hunted this far from home. Still, her natural instinct was to protect them.

'I gave you my promise—if you spared them, I would not leave you."

"You are not a prisoner!" he flung back at her, sharply disappointed she felt only debt. "If you wish to go—GO!"

As he nodded toward the door, tears stung Light Bird's eyes, but she felt too hurt to reply. She stared silently, instead, at her clenched fingers.

After prying the open, Pacing Wolf grasped the choker and thrust it aside, but the feel of the small, tightly woven bones reminded him of the hide she had traded—a flawless hide he had carefully chosen to replace the one-piece garment that nearly ended her life. Ripping the dress from the place it hung, he tossed it into her lap. "This one is no good. Make more like these." He tugged at the elk-tooth covered blouse and skirt she wore.

Nodding acquiescently, she picked up his scalp shirt and inspected each seam while silently eating her heart. *You shame me and then cast me off? You are little different than Wild Dog. Where am I to go? I cannot cross the Echata alone!*

Finishing her task, she slipped between his buffalo robes, scooted as far from his side of the bed as she could, and turned her face toward the lodge coverings. Pacing Wolf was too tense to sleep. Staring at the buffalo robe wrapped tightly around her back, he inwardly grumbled. *My cousin need not turn her heart from me; I do this well enough myself!*

HIDDEN WITH HIS clansmen along a ridgeline, Goes-to-Battle carefully watched the progress of the Blackfoot below. "Enjoy your captive doe while red grass sprouts," he prodded his war-party leader. "She lies awake while you are snoring, dreaming that I will come for her when the grass greens."

Pacing Wolf was in no mood for his cousin's needling. By wearing Small Doe's gift, he had hoped to soften the pain he had handed her last evening, but she did not seem to have noticed. She had said nothing this morning beyond what was needed and her parting look bespoke no hope he would return.

"What is a woman between brothers," he shrugged. "When she whistles for you—go to her!"

As low snickers erupted around them, Goes-to-Battle clenched his well-shaped jaw. Nothing invited more ridicule than bending to a woman's bidding, but he was sure his cousin was not as indifferent as he pretended. Twice during the past moon, he had seen him pass over easy but scarred prey in pursuit of a flawless coat, and early last evening a boy had brought him a fine colt from Pacing Wolf's herd. Goes-to-Battle recognized the animal instantly and thought the payment too high for an unwanted woman's life, but while he contrived a subtle way to bring up the gift in front of their clansmen, his cousin caught him off guard.

"Did you like the colt?" asked Pacing Wolf casually.

"I have often admired him; he will make a fine buffalo horse. Why did you send him to me?"

Pacing Wolf slid his handsome cousin a sidelong glance. "If you had not helped my woman, I would have been cold last night...and what is one horse when I have so many?"

Goes-to-Battle seethed but dropped the matter. His cousin had handily stolen his only weapon and then used it to attack him. He would bide his time. After the girl had thoroughly ensnared his cousin's affections, he would expose the weakness in Pacing Wolf's heart for all the clan to scorn.

As the Blackfoot slipped into the narrower end of the valley, Pacing Wolf rose up on his haunches. "I will relay your intentions to my woman," he grinned. "I enjoy the sound of her laughter."

With a blood-curdling cry, he rushed down the hill, his war party swiftly behind him. The bright early sun gave them aid, blinding their enemies' eyes as it crested the ridge and turning their silhouetted forms into frightening faceless specters. They forced the Blackfoot into the creek and up the butte, overwhelming them on every side.

Pacing Wolf repeatedly tore into the fray, determined to keep Small Doe from warming an enemy's bed or his daughter from becoming an old woman's slave. As he jerked a Blackfoot warrior off a white mare, two well-attested warriors plunged forward and pinned him in a dry run-off.

BY LATE MORNING, scavengers began to swarm the sky. Lumpwoods looped ropes around their dead enemies' necks and dragged them into a deep gully. Their clansmen caught the scattering horses or chased down fleeing women and children. The choicest women were yanked up onto the backs of warriors' mounts. The less desirable were slain where they hid or wounded and left to die. Children ran crying after mothers, and elderly women ran crying after their grandchildren. The healthy were allowed to join their kin, but the weak or too old were beaten away.

From a watching place on a towering ridge, Hair-Up-Top and the other highest-ranking Good Men perused the narrow valley. Their hearts were full and satisfied. They had led their warriors to great victory, warned the Blackfoot to stay out of their hunting grounds, and gained much that was good for their people: packhorses laden with the fresh buffalo meat and household possessions still bundled between lodge poles.

AS THE FIRST REPORT of victory rippled through the camp, Light Bird sought the privacy of Pacing Wolf's dwelling. "Lord, how am I to welcome him? You heard him last night—he told me to go. I had hoped You brought me here to read the Word, but to whom? Most of the women treat me as an enemy and my…my husband…does not want me."

"He wrestles with his own heart." She recalled something her mother had once said when her father had spoken harshly. *"When you marry, remember this and you will avoid much pain. Even the most loving warrior acts like a hungry wolf until he consumes what troubles him. He will bite if you offer help. Cut a wide path and trust him to return to you."*

Seized by a sudden need to see if he was safe, Light Bird laid aside her misgivings and ran to the place his kinswomen were gathering. All day, she had been dancing between pleas that the Lord would protect him and shoving away the grim possibility that he might not return alive. He had said little that morning as he left, and his face had told her even less. He had painted the whole of it deep crimson except for the areas around his eyes. These, he had painted bright ochre—like yellow leaves floating on a pool of blood. Even now, she shivered at the memory, and hoped the Blackfoot, not her brothers, faced him.

He must care something for me. Why else would he have bought me gifts? Their parting, however, argued otherwise. She had not expected him to caress her cheek and pray as her father did with her mother, but she had hoped he might at least bid her farewell. Instead, he simply rode away. Only then did she spy her choker around his neck.

"Lord, he has handed me much pain, but I…I…please bring him back."

Brandishing three new trophies atop his lance, Pacing Wolf headed for Hair-Up-Top's lodge. He towed several horses laden with fresh buffalo meat from the Blackfoot's hunt last evening and could already hear the crier calling the poor to come feast. In front of these, he led two captives. The first, he had pulled from a hiding place within some tall shrubs. Her long loose hair fluttered about her face and clung to her ripening belly. The second was the lovely white mare he had followed down the runoff. Quick of mind and foot, she had taken much skill to capture; but the harder she tried to outwit him, the more determined he became to gain her. He hoped she might provoke Small Doe's smile and ease the tension between them. *What will her eyes say when she sees I am alive?*

Had a Hunts-For-Death not carried him to safety after their last battle, he would still lie in a gorge toward the wind. Flung across his sorrel's back, he had listened to the Good Young Men hailing his courage. He had stood, unyielding, as the Flat Heads attacked. His clanswomen had ululated loudly, all but his dead woman. She narrowed her eyes as if cursing the blow that only grazed his head.

Retracing the path of their courtship, he was appalled by his own gullibility. He had never possessed the teasing banter that poured easily from his cousins, making the women of their neighboring clans question his tender qualities. One day, however, their doubts ceased to matter. A woman, quite like the proud goose he meant to steal instead of Small Doe, swayed past him, her almond eyes extending invitations that even he could not miss.

Believing his daring had distinguished him above his rivals, he followed his people's custom, concealing all but his eyes in a buffalo robe to see if other suitors approached her father's lodge. He was surprised when Speckled Horse failed to come. Nearly as handsome as their cousin Goes-to-Battle, the young warrior had been courting her for several moons, sending her ponies to ride whenever they broke camp and helping her family guide their goods across the Echata. After several nights of watching yielded no rival, Pacing Wolf fetched the required quantity of game that proved him able to provide. Her father accepted him with alacrity, handing Pacing Wolf his daughter after so few days that Never-Sits needed to section off a place for them in her lodge.

Grateful for his good fortune, he credited the generosity of his spirit-guide; but before the new moon regained its brightness, he suspected the scheming of a little trickster-spirit. His bride had grown cold and unwelcoming, turning away whenever he tried to touch her. When she continued to do so for another moon, he contemplated casting her out, but a small mound had already begun to form under her belly. A handful of moons later, her mother offered him the red and squirming small-thing Hunts-For-Death named Among-the-Pines.

Small Doe is as different from my dead woman as her namesake is from the lazy naked buffaloes the white men prod across our grasslands.

As Pacing Wolf approached the cottonwood, he spotted her; but instead of wearing yesterday's tranquil expression, she glanced anxiously from one Good Man to the next. Then, the moment her head turned in his direction, relief broke like a sunrise over her face. Immediately, her mouth began to move with joyful ululations, but as her eyes flitted past him, they clouded with pain.

He has snatched another captive! Lord, how much shame must I bear? Turning quickly, she fled past a group of wailing women and refused to stop until she reached his dwelling, but instead of ducking inside as she intended, she stopped. She could not take refuge there—at any moment, he might arrive with his new prize, ripe with a child who could replace his son. *How can I face him...and not only him—her? She does not want him, I know that well, but she already carries what I can only hope to give.*

Drawing her hands across her stomach, she wondered what it held inside. Her belly looked as flat as the day he had taken her, but her mother had always conceived easily. *I am being foolish...he took me less than two moons ago...surely it is too soon to tell.* Knowing the band would gather shortly in the camp's center, she ran to the water's lonely edge and ducked within a thick stand of pines.

Small Doe's departure puzzled Pacing Wolf as much as her ululations had made him proud. Dropping his load at Hair-Up-Top's door, he entrusted his horse and Blackfoot captive to a young cousin's care and casually ambled toward his lodge. To chase after her would expose him to shame.

He planned to draw her alone into the thick grass and give her the white mare; but when he shoved aside his door-flap, he saw that the lodge was empty. Turning back toward the camp's center, he wondered where she might have gone; but when he overheard an untouched woman admiring Goes-to-Battle, jealousy spewed from his heart like hot mist from the earth's belly. He cared nothing for her praise; it had reminded him of his young cousin's position in the parade: just beyond his own left shoulder.

Which of our faces washed Small Doe with relief? My cousin offers pretty words and plucks her from death; I have offered her grief upon grief.

Spotting his grandmother, he crossed the path and asked her in a low, calm voice if Small Doe had the Blackfoot scalps he took, but the old woman only shrugged. "I do not know. I did not see her. When I went to your lodge, she was already gone." As he started to walk away, though, her knotted fingers grasped his arm. "Treat her kindly when you find her. She has borne her sorrows well, but today her head hangs low."

Briefly acknowledging her concern, he trotted toward Never-Sits' side of the village, cursing himself once more for the harshness of his tongue. His sister's lodge was also empty and the moccasin prints spreading from it went in too many directions to yield a distinct pattern. When he saw a slender form within a small group of women who were displaying their husbands' loot, he picked up his pace; but when he reached them, he found a sweetly smiling young untouched woman from a neighboring clan. Her mother looked quite pleased that her daughter had drawn his notice, but he went on his way, ignoring them both.

She cannot have vanished, he assured himself, but once he was out of earshot, he began muttering to her book-god: "I am Pacing Wolf. Do you hear me? Small Doe is my woman. If you see her, show me where she is."

As he approached the Echata, he stopped and stood as still as stone. The corner of his eye had caught a movement low to the ground, but it had been so swift and subtle he was unsure of its direction. Keenly alert, he melted slowly into the shadows of another cottonwood and waited. His clansmen were making a festive ruckus; a healthy mountain cat would cut a wide path around them, but one that was wounded or sick...

Catching a second, farther set of movements, he realized the animal was not alone. A crouching form slithered stealthily some distance from the place he had picked up the first, obscured by shadows on the steep embankment. Pacing Wolf calmed the blood racing swiftly through his veins, fitted an arrow against his bow, and inched so close that his ears picked up the faint sound that must have drawn them. A kit inside a cluster of dark pines was plaintively mewling. It was clearly distressed, probably stuck on a high branch, but the quality of its crying somehow did not fit. When the creeping shadow peeked cautiously above the bank, everything suddenly shifted sharply into place. Up from its crown stood two eagle feathers.

Turn toward me and be gracious, for I am lonely and tormented. Relieve the troubles of my heart. Free me from my anguish.
Psalm 25:16-17

Chapter 18

PACING WOLF STIFLED his war cry and relaxed his weapon. He could not explain why: perhaps pity for the captive woman weeping for her husband; perhaps sympathy for the warrior who was risking his hide to retrieve her. Had the Blackfoot carried off Small Doe, he would be crawling around the outskirts of his enemy's camp this evening.

Let him have her, he decided. *He shows courage, and her captor is stupid or careless.*

The second Blackfoot slid against the bank while his brother crept up to the stand of trees and made a soft, identifying call. At once, the weeping ceased and he hastily slipped between the thick branches; but instead of quietly guiding the woman to safety, he roughly dragged her into the open. Her slim fingers clawed desperately at the calloused hand clamped over her mouth, as round, frightened eyes pitched Pacing Wolf's heart into his throat.

With an ear-splitting shriek, he leaped forward. The startled Blackfoot flung Small Doe to the ground. Pacing Wolf slammed against him, thrusting a blade deeply into his belly as they rolled down the bank to the water's edge. The second Blackfoot, hearing others rushing towards Pacing Wolf's cry, plunged quickly into the Echata. Its swirling waters grabbed him like a fallen branch, rapidly hurling him downstream while arrows showered the foam around his dark, bobbing head.

In horrified relief, Light Bird watched her husband deftly slice away his opponent's hair before turning his red and yellow-painted face toward her.

"Do I need to tie you to my lodge pole?" he bit out. "I told you before— stay with the women. Do not go off alone!"

Thrusting the bloody scalp into her hand, he dragged her through the gathering crowd toward a line of exultant women dancing in the center of the camp. She joined them gladly, brimming with gratitude, though she understood neither how he happened to appear when he did nor why he would risk his life to save her.

All the terror and relief of the past moments gushed forth in her song, surprising and pleasing both her hero and hearers. She praised his courage, described his swiftness of thought and arm, thanked him for the generosity he had shown to one born of an enemy, and announced how thankful she felt for his protection and care. Had she dared to look into the eyes of his clansmen, she would have found new respect and approval in all but two: they glowered with envy and frustration.

Light Bird trained her eyes on the silky black trophy that both inspired her steps and refuted her fears. A warrior would risk little for something he did not value. When she took her place with his grandmother, however, something quite different arrested her attention. Kneeling between Hunts-For-Death and the white-haired elder they called Hair-Up-Top was her husband's new captive.

Tears streamed freely from the woman's eyes, dribbling down her chin onto arms tied securely across a swollen belly. Light Bird wished she could wipe them away, but another, less generous impulse began clamoring for her notice. The captive's face was flawless, her nose straight and round-tipped, and though her lips quivered and twisted uncontrollably, they were wide and full.

As Good Men awarded honors to their fathers, sons or brothers, The-Women-Who-Talk-Against-Each-Other-Without-Fear prepared a great feast. The Lumpwoods mocked the Foxes, claiming the greater coup they had counted proved their superior skill and courage. The Foxes volleyed taunts of their own, poking fun at any hint of Lumpwood weakness. While she served them, she listened half-heartedly, pricking up her ears only when she heard her husband's name.

Crossing to the rowdy Foxes, she quickly learned to keep her eyes low. The Lumpwoods had taken what she offered with the polite reserve due to another warrior's woman, but the members of this rival war-society treated her like prey. They furtively stalked her with their eyes, and if she happened to look up, they endeavored to capture her interest with their sly looks and smiles. She wanted none of them. Her conflicting emotions shouted louder than they did, each claiming preeminence until two youths led the captive away.

Weaving back toward the Lumpwoods, she searched for the pair of leggings that had enfolded her Bible; and when a calloused hand caressed her own beneath the trencher, she glanced up in quick relief.

He did not go after her!

Rather than Pacing Wolf, however, she found his handsome cousin. She jerked her hand away so swiftly, she nearly upset the platter, but not before she noticed the warmth corralled in his eyes. It promised much for which she deeply longed and provided a sharp contrast with her husband's last glare.

God forgive me, she prayed, hoping the dusky sky had hidden her heightened color. *I owe Pacing Wolf loyalty, not only because he is my husband but for saving me from that Blackfoot!*

Slipping through the Lumpwoods, she no longer looked for her husband. She was afraid of what he might uncover if he read her face. Instead, she concentrated on one aim: avoiding the swallow-winged brows and the welcoming warmth she would find beneath them. They turned up everywhere she served, and although she assiduously kept her eyes to the trodden grass, she was soon able to pick out their owner's good-humored laugh among the other boisterous warriors.

"I am tired," murmured an old woman close to her elbow, and looking down she found Kills-Behind-Her-Dwelling. "These Lumpwoods will taunt those Foxes long into the night. I am going to my lodge."

Light Bird accompanied her home, though every successive footfall increased her trepidation. She dreaded meeting the Blackfoot captive and much more seeing her with Pacing Wolf, but neither did she want to stay alone among the revelers. Never-Sits was busy serving Mountainside's clan, and she had not seen Does-Not-Cry all evening. Supposing the latter's small-thing might have chosen this night to enter the world, Light Bird decided to seek her out in the morning.

Once she had arrived at Pacing Wolf's lodge, Light Bird stopped to listen for any murmurs or movements. He had made her his woman on the night he had snatched her; he might do the same with this other, though the Blackfoot's obvious encumbrance might gain her a reprieve. When she heard nothing from within, Light Bird assumed they were already sleeping, so she silently slipped inside and glanced around. It was empty.

Sighing with relief, she pulled her attacker's scalp from the small purse about her waist, hung it on a peg to dry, and readied herself for bed. She began to wonder as she slid into her customary place, however, if he would want her there. The new captive was close to giving birth; he might offer her the most comfortable spot. Taking out a worn lodge covering, she fastened it between several poles and the lodge lining to section off an area for herself and then lay down in the buffalo robe she had worn the day he snatched her.

She felt exhausted in every way but could not sleep. Staring at the lodge lining, she listened for their footsteps, trying to thwart the images that kept bounding through her mind. Where would she find Pacing Wolf sleeping in the morning—in a separate robe or warmly curled against the Blackfoot's back? Multiple wives were so common, even among her own men before they knew Jesus, she had once asked whether another woman might be of help with their family's chores. Now, she understood the revulsion that had leaped into her mother's green eyes.

Lord, I know You would want me to be kind to her, even welcoming—but how can I? She is a rival—an enemy!

Her childhood village had endured several enemies' onslaughts, but she had never comprehended the cost of loving one. Though the past couple of moons had been very difficult, her role as Pacing Wolf's woman had also brought unanticipated rewards. This Blackfoot captive threatened the little she had gained. Even her ability to help with chores would be limited. Indeed, so close to giving birth, she was more likely to increase Light Bird's load.

A woman began loudly wailing in the distance. The Many Lodges had suffered few losses and the Lumpwoods none; but as she prayed for the unknown mourner, she was struck by the enormity of the challenge she faced.

How do I tell them of You, Jesus? How can I get them to listen and believe me? Your path is as strange to them as their ways are to me.

Mindful of the odd things his grandmother had said about the soul, she left her pallet, took down the scalp, and turned it over.

At least I had no husband to grieve. This hateful thing was dear to some woman—perhaps the very Blackfoot Pacing Wolf captured. Its owner snuck up the bank for a purpose, probably to retrieve his woman.

Shivering, she recalled the warrior's arm crushing her ribcage, the odor of his body slick with sweat, and the calloused fingers she had clawed for breath. *He was sharply displeased to discover I was not Blackfoot but Sparrow...*

Light Bird stopped in mid-thought, torn between her first inkling of belonging to this people and disgust that her heart had strayed so quickly from her own. *How many seasons did it take Quiet Woman to think of herself as an Ally?* Concluding she owed this new feeling to her attacker, she hung his drying scalp on her side of the tattered curtain.

If he was not this captive's husband, he may have been her father or brother. She did not choose to come here any more than I did and cannot escape her fate. We are the same.

As Light Bird began sifting through last evening's conversation, she realized this was not quite true. *The soreness of my heart has clouded my memory. Pacing Wolf never said he did not want me: he said I was no longer a prisoner. He set me free...and I will not let the destroyer steal my peace.*

Flinging back the door-flap, Pacing Wolf startled Light Bird from her reverie. His loose hair hung damp about his chest, as though he had been bathing, and only the deepest creases around his eyes showed traces of yellow paint. As he took in the alteration of his home, he tipped his chin toward the partition she had constructed.

"What is this?"

"I thought you might want privacy with your...captive."

His face betrayed nothing of his mood or whether her efforts pleased or annoyed him.

"If you prefer, I will sleep in Kills-Behind-Her-Dwelling's lodge."

As he searched her face, several disconnected bits of information fell into place: the pain that had replaced her relief, her unexpected flight, and the way she had avoided his gaze while singing of his valor.

She ran when she saw the Blackfoot captive—this was why she wept!

Suppressing a grin, he yanked down the old lodge-cover and tossed it aside. "She is for Hair-Up-Top. His only woman died during the Moon When Wolves Run Together and his daughters serve Good Men in other bands. She will keep his old bones warm at night and the small-thing she carries may bring him laughter."

Light Bird was speechless. Her assumptions—alone—had caused her heartache, and each had proved false. When he scooped up her buffalo robe and signaled for her to accompany him, she followed without hesitation. He led her through the cool night air up a dark slope covered with moving shadows she knew to be horses. All the while, she kept thinking of the last verse she had read yesterday.

"You are her daughters if you do not give way to fear."[62] *My foolishness might have cost him his...*

Before she had finished the thought, her husband located his herd. They had approached it so silently, they took the youth who guarded it unawares. Jumping to his feet, he brandished his knife and prepared to face an enemy; but Pacing Wolf's sorrel, picking up his friend's scent on the late evening breeze, began nickering a welcome. The youth relaxed, a sheepish but bright smile breaking across his face, while several horses joined the soft chorus.

Pacing Wolf and she weaved among them; but one, lighter in color, shied away. "Here," he said, drawing Light Bird to stand in front of him. "Let her smell your scent." He extended her hand beneath the mare's nose, near enough to accomplish his purpose but far enough away to let the animal choose its own course.

"She is lovely," Light Bird whispered.

"She is yours."

"Mine?"

As she glanced up at him over her shoulder, the quarter moon did not allow her to read his expression, but something in his closeness hinted what was in his heart.

"She is like you," he breathed into her hair. "Shy and watchful but also spry and intelligent. She will make you a fine mount."

As he slipped his arms about her waist, Light Bird leaned back against his chest. She felt too overwhelmed to speak. He had said nothing of love or desire, but the warmth in his tone and embrace made her feel safe enough to rest her head in the curve of his neck. His response was immediate, but as he pulled her closer, she slid a hand over his arm and felt a crusted gash the length of her finger.

"You are hurt!"

"A fly bite," he smiled, leaning his head down over her shoulder. "Your gift kept me from graver harm." Taking her hand, he ran her fingertips across the small bones of the collar he still wore.

"I have been praying for you all day," she admitted. "He-Who-Sees-All-Things kept you safe."

Nuzzling his cheek into her hair, Pacing Wolf possessively tightened his embrace, wondering again about her strange spirit. He seemed more a friend than a god.

"Why did you not keep her for yourself?" she asked.

"My sorrel shows more courage and I have trained him well for battle."

"No, the Blackfoot woman. She could soon give you a small-thing."

"I do not want her small-thing," he chuckled softly. "And I do not want another woman. I am having enough trouble keeping you safe."

I will rejoice and be glad in Your steadfast love because You have seen my affliction. You have known the distress of my soul, and You have not delivered me into the hand of the enemy. You have set my feet in a broad place.

Psalm 31:7-8

Chapter 19

LIGHT BIRD NESTLED into a thick, curling buffalo fur on her husband's bed. She had awakened from a pleasant dream about him, and though the details were rapidly escaping she relished the bits she had captured. She wished his arms still enfolded her, wished she could return to the wonders of the last evening, wished always to feel such unexpected joy and security.

As she envisaged how he might greet her this morning, she grew reticent. She was now certain he was glad to have her. His protection and gifts made plain what his words did not, and she could not miss the warmth in his embraces. Still, the two moons she had lived as his woman had not taught her to predict his turns of temper.

Ducking out into the dawning light, she found Among-the-Pines sitting near the door and bent down to the little girl's height. "Have you been waiting long?"

The child simply motioned with her chin. "There."

Following its line, Light Bird spotted a bent form hefting a basket up the ridge. "Come," she suggested, tossing a gentle smile to her little stepdaughter. "We will help her."

Among-the-Pines responded immediately, trotting after Light Bird like a small dog; but when they reached the old woman, they found her heavily creased eyes clouded with sorrow.

"Where are you going?" asked Light Bird, lifting the basket from the thin, gnarled hands.

"To Does-Not-Cry."

Light Bird looked blankly at Kills-Behind-Her-Dwelling, uncertain what she meant. If Does-Not-Cry had delivered her baby, she would have been too weak to climb the mountain.

"Pacing Wolf has not told you? Our losses against the Blackfoot were small but grievous—our Good Men revered her husband greatly for his loyalty and valor."

Light Bird's mouth fell open. Not only did she feel stricken with sympathy for her new Grass Lodge friend but also by the suddenness of death. She might easily have lost Pacing Wolf.

"Has she born his little potbelly?"

The old woman nodded her head sadly. "When they brought her husband's body into his lodge, Does-Not-Cry cut her arms so deeply that her small-thing lost all strength and hurried off to catch up with his father. She is on the cliffs above and will come home to what—an empty dwelling stripped of her husband's possessions and no father or brother to provide for her? Better that she, not her small-thing, had died."

Light Bird felt so deeply grieved, she did not know how to offer the old woman comfort, but she determined to do as much for Does-Not-Cry as Pacing Wolf would allow. She followed Kills-Behind-Her-Dwelling through the pines and up the mountain, but before they caught sight of the young woman, they crossed an irregular line of red splotches, most of them half-dried to a dark shade of brown.

"We will need to tie her on her horse when we break camp," the old one clucked. "She will be too weak to ride."

They followed the trail as it wound around the eastern side of the cliff until the trail of dark drops abruptly stopped, but Does-Not-Cry was not there. While the two women wondered aloud which way she might have gone, Among-the-Pines clutched onto Light Bird's leg and started tugging her elk-toothed skirt.

"What?" asked Light Bird.

"There!"

When she followed Among-the-Pines' small finger to the rocks below, she found a sight so horrid she immediately spun away. Pressing the little girl's face against her skirt, she motioned for Kills-Behind-Her-Dwelling to look down also. Does-Not-Cry lay dead on the rocks and the smell of death had already drawn several hulking vultures.

Quickly, Light Bird hefted the child onto her hip and guided Kills-Behind-Her-Dwelling back the way they had come. She had not known Does-Not-Cry well. She had been too caught up in her own sorrows to make the effort. Now, she could never make amends.

As they passed along the Echata, Light Bird searched the faces of latecomers fetching water. Many were still strangers, but the one she looked for stood out sharply from the rest. Her hair hung loose and her long dress was made of deerskin, much like the ones Light Bird's tribeswomen wore. When Light Bird noted the Blackfoot's round profile, she could not help thinking of her newly deceased friend, and her heart, so torn by jealousy last night, grew warm with compassion. The captive's belly stuck so far out that she had difficulty reaching down to fill her water-skins, and no sooner did she lift one than she lost hold of the other.

Setting Among-the-Pines on her feet, Light Bird told her to help Kills-Behind-Her-Dwelling tote the basket home and then hurried to the Blackfoot's aid.

"I will fill them," she offered, plucking the skins from the bank, but the confused stranger only stared. Supposing the captive might doubt her intentions, Light Bird smiled up over her shoulder as she bent to fill the bags. When she straightened, she nodded toward the woman's burgeoning impediment and then pointed toward the white-haired leader's lodge. Whether the Blackfoot understood was not clear, but her face relaxed as she responded in a musical, though indecipherable, tongue.

"I am Pacing Wolf's woman," Light Bird enunciated carefully. "They call me…Small Doe."

The words formed uncomfortably on her tongue. This Blackfoot could not know that she was also a captive; yet, as Light Bird considered how to tell her, she realized this was no longer true. Her own will betrayed her; and though she felt awkward calling herself the new words, it stirred pleasant memories of the man who had named her.

The Blackfoot merely shrugged, but her face showed a keen interest in something taking place over Small Doe's shoulder. A girl, a summer or so older than Among-the-Pines, walked behind a tall woman Small Doe immediately recognized as one of The-Women-Who-Talk-Against-Each-Other-Without-Fear. The child hauled a water sack so heavy that it slowed her pace, irritating her keeper; but when she caught sight of the Blackfoot captive, she abruptly dropped it and broke into a delighted sprint.

The annoyed clanswoman grabbed sharply hold of the small shoulder, flinging the girl backward onto the hard-packed ground; but the child scrambled up, straining to break free. She was no match for the scolding woman, who snatched up the empty skin, thrust it into the tiny hands, and dragged her charge back toward the Echata.

The little girl's head twisted backward, her eyes pleading with Small Doe's companion for protection and relief, and her bewildered face crumpled as the Blackfoot silently but decisively shook her head. Seeing no other choice, the girl tromped compliantly beside her ill-tempered keeper, but her slumped shoulders and hanging head loudly proclaimed her misery.

When Small Doe returned her attention to the Blackfoot woman, she beheld such agony that her own bereavement seemed trivial. She had no way to offer consolation and was struck hard by last night's horrible ironies. While she lay newly contented, even happy, within Pacing Wolf's arms, Does-Not-Cry and this captive were enduring unspeakable losses—losses not merely of childhood dreams and expectations but of beloved husbands and children. Sighing deeply, she asked the Creator to comfort her own mother and incline Hair-Up-Top's heart toward mercy.

Maybe, she is the reason that Jesus brought me here.

Once Small Doe returned to Pacing Wolf's lodge, she sliced thin strips from the buffalo flank he had held back from the feast and fashioned a rack of twigs she had cut from green saplings. Her thoughts danced elsewhere, every step pressing a tender seed into the unspoiled soil of her heart. She admired her husband's generosity to the poor and, though she sympathized with the Blackfoot woman, his concern for his white-haired leader.

As she thought of his other prize, captured specifically for her, the seeds she had planted split their protective coverings, allowing plentiful roots to wriggle out in search of further nourishment. They did not need to wriggle far. With each fresh memory of him hurtling toward the Blackfoot warrior, new shoots sprouted toward the warming sun. Only from her father or brothers would she have expected such an impassioned defense.

His grandmother's advice was very like a verse she had read in Philippians: "Whatever is true, whatever is worthy of esteem, whatever is just, whatever is pure, whatever is lovely, whatever is worth recounting, if there is any virtue or anything to be admired, train your heart to consider these things."[63]

While she marveled over the happy gains these instructions had yielded, a slight commotion drew her attention up the central path. Children and dogs were scurrying to make way for a group of Good Men who had exited Hair-Up-Top's lodge. As these warriors headed her direction, Light Bird busied her hands, hanging strips on the rack to dry; but when she spotted her husband's Lumpwood father, anticipation began nipping at her like a pup after his boy's ankles. Pacing Wolf was sure to be among them.

While she covertly perused their ranks, her heart made a sudden leap. A keen pair of eyes collided with her own, rushing blood into her cheeks and turning her normally adroit fingers clumsy. How she had once judged her husband less than handsome, she could not fathom.

Dropping her gaze, she forced herself to resume her task; but glancing up as he passed by, she found his eyes still lingering on her warmly and a grin so full of teasing, it weakened her knees.

As Pacing Wolf returned his attention to the path ahead, he spotted a cluster of strutting young Foxes approaching from the opposite direction. He drew himself up to his full height, assessing their tokens as he would an enemy's. Several returned his challenge, but the most handsome among them was too busy to notice. His eyes were fixed on something just beyond

Pacing Wolf's shoulder, and his lips were twisting into his most charming smile.

Pacing Wolf tightly clenched his jaw, but as he glanced back at his cousin's quarry, he relaxed. Small Doe's cheeks were still aglow, like twin ridges painted by the morning sun, but her long, black lashes never fluttered upward. Wondering to what length his rival might go to have her, he calculated the days remaining until the Lumpwoods made new staffs.

Goes-to-Battle's concentration broke as a quick, sharp finger jabbed his ribs. "Her husband has hawk's eyes," warned his companion.

"He will do nothing," the handsome warrior scoffed. "He is not a fool— he knows he cannot keep her."

"Do not be too sure," cautioned his friend. "She paid you less notice than a passing dog."

"Huh," grunted Goes-to-Battle. "Did you see her cheeks? They were bright with color. Do you think they warm for my ugly cousin? He owns nearly twice her summers. She kept her eyes low because she fears him."

"You risk too much," a more seasoned Fox agreed. "He is a Lumpwood but also a useful ally. The Good Men say he will one day lead your clan."

"If you fear him, old man, stay home when I fetch her." One misgiving, however, nagged Goes-to-Battle. If Pacing Wolf did indeed frighten her, she might refuse to leave him. He and his Fox brothers would need to snatch her forcibly; and if they failed, he would earn much ridicule and severe reprisals. While taking stock of his chances, he stumbled over a pleasing prospect he had not yet considered: he would laugh at his cousin's helpless desperation as he carried her off. *And who will stop me? Only our old grandmother will rally to her aid.*

WHEN PACING WOLF ducked into his lodge, two smiles greeted him. One offered a sincere but quiet welcome. The other eagerly demanded his attention.

"We saw Does-Not-Cry, we saw Does-Not-Cry!" chirped his daughter. "Big birds with naked heads stood on top of her, pecking like this!"

With morbid glee characteristic only of the very young, she hopped atop Pacing Wolf's buffalo pelts, hunching her shoulders forward as she rhythmically attacked her imaginary prey. Her father watched politely, but his thoughts trailed Small Doe's fading smile.

"I have seen her," he replied, "but look—your mother is offering you a bowl. Take it to Kills-Behind-Her-Dwelling. She will be hungry."

The little girl frowned. She was not finished with her story and still wanted his attention. Nonetheless, she grabbed the dish and scampered out to do his bidding.

"You are hungry?" asked Small Doe, dipping out another.

"Yes," he nodded, "but I eat in Hunts-For-Death's lodge."

He read clear disappointment in her dark eyes, but she did not protest. Instead, she fetched his leggings with the red painted stripes. Pointing out three fresh lengths of black hair, she told him, "I sewed them here. Your scalp-shirt possesses too many."

Pacing Wolf looked pleased that she had noticed and began fingering her work. "All Blackfoot; none are Those-Who-Cut-Off-Our-Heads."

Small Doe smiled at the game he revived, but her heart felt too unshielded to maintain his gaze. She was almost happy that he had stolen her, certain no other warrior could rouse such strange but wonderful stirrings. She felt hesitant and eager at once, vulnerable and yet astonishingly secure.

As he lifted her chin, he found eyes soft and yielding, like well-ripened fruit begging to be picked. He wished Hunts-For-Death did not require him tonight. He preferred her charms to the pipe he would smoke with his society brothers and looked forward to hearing more of her book.

He had not understood why her spirit-guide unleashed the earth's headwaters and drowned all the people outside the giant canoe,[64] and yet, if the story was true, her god possessed much power. Something more than this, though, compelled him to listen—something in the book that called to his heart.

Perhaps it was the words themselves. They had power to discern his hidden motives and express his secret thoughts. "It is not good for man to be alone,"[65] had drummed within him long after she read it, and he was more than willing to "be fruitful and multiply."[66] If the other women who walked this book-god's path were like Small Doe, Braids-His-Tail's suggestion had great merit. Each of his clansmen should steal a woman from her village.

Sliding around to his back, Small Doe unwound his long braids and began gently separating each tangle, but her fingers began to quiver as they came across coarse new strands.

Are they Does-Not-Cry's, she wondered, *or her husband's?*

Pacing Wolf reached behind and pulled her around in front of him. Smoothing the crease between her brows, he ran his fingertips across her forehead, down along her temple to her cheekbone, and caressed the side of her face. Does-Not-Cry's husband had assailed the two Blackfoot warriors that pinned him in the gully. If he had not, his own long strands or Small Doe's lovely spirals would lengthen his clansmen's braids tonight.

"I am glad to honor him this way and gain a share of his strength. He was a Muddy Hand, a rival, but he fought with great courage."

As he ran his thumb across her smooth lips, he wondered how quickly he might slip away from the Lumpwood feast. Not since his mother's death had he felt this compelling need to protect and care for a woman. His heart had been a hollow cave, devoid of inhabitant and relieved but briefly by his dead woman. Only the thrill of hand-to-hand combat made his blood run swiftly, and cheating death often had earned him much acclaim.

Snatching Small Doe had changed everything. If Hunts-For-Death offered him a Lumpwood death-staff this year, he would refuse it. In the past, accepting the staffs had risked him little. If he had perished, his apple-faced woman would have returned to her father's lodge without a tear, and their daughter…he had never known a girl to walk more closely in her mother's shadow. Small Doe was like neither. He would not leave her to cower beneath a bush while he sought glory on some far-off ridge.

No, I will stay where I can keep her safe. Where could she go if I journeyed to my fathers? He did not search his mind long for an answer or need to fear that she might starve. *Goes-to-Battle would be swift to claim her.* Even so, the thought made his blood roil.

"Was the Blackfoot woman alone when you found her?"

"Umh?" His thoughts had traveled so far that he was not sure what she had asked him.

"The Blackfoot captive—the one you gave to the white-haired elder you call Hair-Up-Top. The one who rides a spotted horse. Was she alone when you found her?"

Pacing Wolf nodded, curious to know why she had asked the question.

"She bears much pain."

"Her time is soon."

"Not only in her body—in her heart."

Pacing Wolf was as surprised by Small Doe's statement as he had been by her question. *She, of all women, should understand a captive's grief—does she mean to toss her pain into my face?* Tamping down his rising defenses, he grew curious to know how the two had met.

"She speaks our tongue?"

"No, but I was helping her carry water when a child came upon us. I suspect she is the Blackfoot's daughter. Great pain ran through both of their faces."

He nodded gravely, making fresh sense of her concern.

"She is little older than Among-the-Pines, but her misery showed plainly. The Blackfoot bit her lip and turned her face away to spare the child from her keeper's wrath. It was hard to watch."

Hearing his daughter and grandmother coming, Small Doe tucked her concern away and began attending again to the thatch of hair that stuck up above his forehead. She would not acquaint one so young with a fate she might meet if her father were killed in battle.

As Kills-Behind-Her-Dwelling bent beneath the door-flap, Among-the-Pines barged past her. The dimness within the lodge shaded Small Doe's face but did little to conceal Pacing Wolf's intense interest. Catching her great-granddaughter by the dress-sleeve, the old woman began a hasty retreat, but her grandson waved her forward.

"Stay. Small Doe is alone tonight. I eat with the Lumpwoods."

PACING WOLF SAT in Hunts-For-Death's lodge, feasting for a second night. When the weather warmed, the Lumpwoods' number would become so large they could not dine indoors. Those-Who-Live-Among-the-River-Banks would drift north from the Muddy River, and the Many Lodges would descend the mountains. Most of these bands would stay together all summer; others might break away now and then to chase the herds.

He wished the Kicked-in-the-Bellies would continue to sojourn along the Outer Edge. He had honored Marks-His-Face with his vengeance quest, but he feared the man might not be satisfied to leave things as they were. Toward the end of last summer, he had begun pressing Pacing Wolf to claim his two younger daughters.

Pacing Wolf dreaded the day. He would never know another moment's peace. Pretty Crow Woman was the image of his dead wife and equally vain and selfish. The youngest, Yellow-Fish, took after their father; but since she idolized her older sister, she acted often as her fool.

Furthermore, he could not refuse Jackrabbit, their mother, the right to raise Among-the-Pines. Antipathy for his dead woman had stunted his affection for the child, as well as a sharp suspicion she was Speckled Horse's daughter; but under Small Doe's guidance, the girl might grow into a woman worth supporting. Jackrabbit's influence would ensure that she did not, and any ground Small Doe had gained would be lost.

The gathering bands offered one bright possibility. Goes-to-Battle might fall in with the Whistle Waters, their mothers' clan. They were the most independent of Those-Who-Live-Among-the-River Banks and frequently left the main body of the tribe to pursue game.

Perhaps, he mused, recalling Small Doe's attentions earlier, *it will not matter where my handsome cousin summers.* Years of war-parties, however, would not let him rest on his recent victories. He had learned to hope for the best but plan for the worst. Unseen events had a way of arising when least expected.

The right offering may persuade her book-god to help me, he thought, but he was not sure what he should offer. The words she had read in His book were plain: He did not desire sacrifice. *What was the word she used?* It had been strange to him and repugnant. *Contrite... "a broken spirit and a contrite heart." How is any man to offer this? Her guide is better suited to women.*

Still, as he considered the path down which this spirit had guided Small Doe, he could deny neither His wisdom nor His strength. Her acquiescence in the cave had sprung from an astute assessment of her situation, and she had kept each vow she had made.

"You are far from us," observed the white-haired leader, seated between him and Hunts-For-Death in the place of first honor.

Embarrassed the old chief had caught him wandering, Pacing Wolf coaxed Hair-Up-Top to follow a different trail. "Does the Blackfoot woman please you?"

The white braids jiggled. "I was just telling you so, though I wish I was younger. A pity to waste such supple flesh on these stiff hands. Why did you not keep her? When her small-thing is born, he would do much to heal your grief."

Pacing Wolf also nodded. "My healing comes. But though the suns grow warmer, cold nights spent alone are long and miserable. I do not want this for you."

The old man gave him a look of appreciation. "From childhood, you have been aware of the needs of others. You will lead our clan well and one day, I hope, our whole people. My heart ached when I heard that the spirits had handed you sadness."

"I find solace already."

The old eyes twinkled. "I have seen. Hunts-For-Death pointed her out while she served us last night, but I fear for you when the grass turns green."

Pacing Wolf darted him a wary look, and Short Neck picked up the path of their conversation. "Goes-to-Battle makes his intentions plain. What woman can resist him?"

Hunts-For-Death leaned forward. "My Lumpwood son owns a strong heart. He will not dishonor himself for a woman."

Turning towards Braids-His-Tail, Short Neck lowered his voice just enough to draw every man's attention. "We will see. A man who turns weak for a soft pair of eyes cannot be trusted with hard decisions. He forfeits the right to lead the band."

Several younger Lumpwoods nodded in agreement and slid questioning looks in Pacing Wolf's direction. The most daring among them added, "I would not follow such a man. Who knows what he might do if his woman began calling?"

When their laughter subsided, Bites-With-Dog, Hunts-For-Death's nephew, rose to Pacing Wolf's defense: "If his Cuts-Off-Our-Heads woman prefers Goes-to-Battle, he will let her go."

"She will not want to," Hunts-For-Death interjected. "Have you seen the way she gazes after him—like a warrior longing to greet the morning sun."

"I have noticed this also," observed Crazy Bear. "I will wager my new mare that she refuses Goes-to-Battle."

Braids-His-Tail elbowed Short Neck in the ribs and sniggered. "Your wives gaze after you as they gaze at thunderclouds—hoping you will pass by without unleashing your fury."

Short Neck shot him a warning look, briefly silencing the group, and then turned his hard glare toward Pacing Wolf. "I will bet a war-horse that your captive goes with him and a foal that you will follow after her."

Aware the ruff on Pacing Wolf's neck was rising, Hunts-For-Death steeply upped the stakes. "I will wager my herd that he will let her go."

Hair-Up-Top raised a leathery hand, signaling for them to desist, and their talk soon followed trails less thorny. Turning back toward Pacing Wolf, the old man counseled, "Quiet your heart about the doe. I have seen that Fox pup licking her hand, but she quickly brushes him away. These men understand little. I am old and have spent my heart foolishly—caring more for our Good Men's praise than the warmth of a woman's love. If not for your gift, I would shiver in my bed this night. No woman comes willingly to a man too old to give her children."

Hair-Up-Top's candor caused Pacing Wolf greater discomfort than Short Neck's heckling, but when he tried to divert the conversation, the white-haired leader would not let him.

"Seize your woman's heart as you would a hard-won trophy and do not allow another to claim it. As a man grows old, pride becomes a poor companion. I have had eighteen women; your gift makes nineteen. One by one, I cast them aside—all but the woman who recently died. These men laud my strong heart, as their fathers did before them, but I wonder who will mourn me when I die.

"Oh, yes," he continued, "I know what you are thinking. I have sons and grandsons, Good Men young and old who will vie for a portion of my hair to gain my strength. Daughters and granddaughters will cut themselves in grief, but whose gentle hands will cradle my head as I drift into the mystery land or stroke my brow to ease my pain—the Blackfoot captive you have given me? No. When the grass turns green, a younger man will come to my lodge, and she will go with him willingly. At least by then, the nights will have grown warmer."

Shifting uneasily, Pacing Wolf saw a chance to deepen Small Doe's admiration. "The Blackfoot has a daughter."

Immediate interest raised the old brows, encouraging Pacing Wolf to confide further.

"While Small Doe and she filled their water-skins, they came across a Blackfoot girl. Both her face and your captive's displayed great pain."

"Hmmp," the Real Chief snorted. "Did your woman tell you who kept this child?"

"'A tall woman of our clan.' Crazy Bear's wife, I am guessing."

Earnestly contemplating the information, the old one resolved to speak with his clansman, but feeling Hunts-For-Death's hand at his elbow, he turned to take the pipe. Sucking in the sweet tobacco, his eyes became glazed and his mind traveled to far off memories when his arm was still strong. Pacing Wolf accepted the pipe in turn, intermingling Hair-Up-Top's counsel so thoroughly with his thoughts they became less distinguishable than their swirls of their smoke.

Delight in the Lord, and He will give you what your heart desires.
Psalm 37:4

Chapter 20

LIEUTENANT WILSON CLIMBED the precipice, hoping to steal a few private moments, but when he reached the top, he spotted a lone woman intently watching the sunset. She looked as if her mind was miles away. Not wishing to intrude, he began backing silently toward the path he had just ascended, but she had already sensed him and turned around.

"Joshua—do not go."

"I did not want to disturb you, ma'am." He thought her a fine looking woman, though the years had been less kind to her than they had been to his mother. Contrasting the lives the two had led, he did not wonder at the difference. His mother diligently protected her complexion from the sun; his godmother's skin had become so tanned that only her green eyes and the glint of brown in her hair betrayed her parentage.

"You aren't—honestly. I know I'm being foolish, but I come here each evening and gaze as far as my eye can see, hoping Light Bird will ride over the horizon. When do you and Spotted Long—I mean, Major Anderson—visit the Pawnee?"

"We leave tomorrow before sunrise."

"Already? I feel that you just arrived. The Major is impressed with your heart as well as your mind. He says you care much about our people."

"I have you to thank for that," he smiled. "I used to swipe your letters and read them so often that I could probably recite each one."

"You must have been very bored," smiled Brought-Us-the-Book, "and I can just imagine what you thought of all our back and forth about husbands."

"Well," Joshua laughed, "I did not memorize *all* the portions of your letters."

"Are you finding it difficult to pick up the language?"

"Yes ma'am, but the Major's…uh, children, have both been quite helpful."

"I believe the Pawnee language grew from a different root, but at least you should be able to communicate. Our people have been warring with them before Old Many Feathers was born, and more than a few women and children have been captured on both sides. They cannot help but pick up a few of the others' words. I regret that I have not taken good advantage of this time to get to know you. You must think me a negligent hostess."

"You have had a lot to occupy you. I cannot begin to think how Mother would have coped if my sister, Lisa, was kidnapped."

As she peered into his dark, sympathetic eyes, she thought again of his Uncle Tommy. "She would take her brokenness to Jesus, though it is far from easy to leave it there. She must be quite proud of you."

Turning back to the sun, the two watched together until it lay down in its distant bed.

"I pray that her husband is kind," she sighed.

Joshua did not answer. Until this year, his mother had considered his little sister too young to be brought out into society, let alone be sentenced to live as the wife of some savage miscreant. He grew angry just considering the possibility and could not help contrasting his godmother's husband with his own dad. John Wilson was a man to be reckoned with—a good man, a fair man, but not one who would stand idly by if his daughter had been kidnapped and forced into an unwelcome marriage. In his fairer moments, though, he admitted Preying Eagle had followed every lead. How could any man chase an enemy who made no tracks to a destination he did not know?

Frustrated with his inability to offer his godmother solace, Joshua blurted out the question that was often in his thoughts. "Do you regret your decision to stay here?"

"No. I count myself privileged beyond anything I'd dreamed—not only to have brought the gospel to this people but also to be loved by a man whom I grow to respect more with each passing season. I cannot imagine why the Lord has been so kind to me, except, of course, that He is generous by nature."

The smile that lit her face was quite genuine and made her look years younger. He had not seen it often; she reserved it mostly for private gatherings. Aside from this, she often reminded him of Corn-Tassels, though less given to impulse. Thinking of the latter, only brought him back to his godmother's men-folk, particularly the tall son—so much like his father—who would soon consign Abigail to live as a drudge.

"But surely," he prodded, "you regret how life here has exposed your daughter?"

"Life here?" She cocked her head as though his question made little sense, but the lift of her chin informed him she had caught his meaning. "Evil is everywhere, Joshua, and revenge is an inherent part of human nature. Why else would God have made such a point of telling us to leave it to Him? To protect her from harm, I would need to keep her out of this world, not this village. God has thoroughly convinced me His heart is good, and though I would not say He caused the man to take her—He never tempts anyone to sin—His hands were not tied while He watched him. She is no more hidden from Him than Esther was while in the harem of King Xerxes."[67]

"So you think we are to simply accept what happens as fate—much like Hindus?"

"By no means. God allows us to make choices, and insofar as we can see through the Scriptures the way we should go, we should make them."

"But your daughter did not choose to be carried off."

"No, but she has choices now. She can live for God's glory with the Raven-Enemy and trust that He has not forsaken her, or she can hate those around her and become bitter toward Him. I would ask a question similar to the one Mordecai asked Esther: How can we know that He does not have a special purpose for her there?"[68]

"And the Major's daughter? Do you think he should risk allowing her to remain here as well?"

Brought-Us-the-Book began to see what lay beneath her godson's questions. She had noticed his marked interest in Corn-Tassels and his aversion toward her eldest son.

"Surely, the Major will consult our Lord's heart on the matter. What that may be, I cannot pretend to know, but I assure you that my son would not wish her to stay if God does not. I assume I can say the same for you?"

Joshua could only nod and mutter, "Yes, by all means." Inside, however, he grew determined to present the Lord, and Miss Anderson's father, with quite a different proposal.

←←← →→→

AS THE MANY LODGES neared a vast lake, Kills-Behind-Her-Dwelling searched a large band of Sparrow Hawks merging into their ranks. She scrutinized the warriors first and then the women, as if uncertain they were friend or foe, though her other clanswomen appeared as relaxed as they had been all day.

Wondering what—in the old one's mind—set this band apart from the others who had lately joined them, Small Doe glanced up at the ridge where the Lumpwoods were keeping watch. A stream of warriors, obviously friendly, melted into their lines, but her constant companion pulled her many-wrinkled lips into a sour-looking scowl.

"What troubles you?" asked Small Doe.

"They are Kicked-in-the-Bellies. Jackrabbit and Marks-His-Face will be among them."

Although Small Doe had heard the names, she could not remember why they were significant; but she was relieved when she saw Hair-Up-Top signal for the tribe to stop. Her white mare had proven even-paced and eager, and the warming soil had painted the valleys with lovely purple and yellow flowers; but whether from the increasing heat or lack of water, she had begun to feel weak.

As she gazed up at the ridge, she saw the many-feathered stranger who was talking with her husband abruptly wheel his horse and hasten to a group of women wending toward Mountainside's clan. Pacing Wolf followed closely on his heels, but the throng quickly swallowed them both.

Suddenly, a shrill shriek split the air. Small Doe could not at first discern its direction, but as the cry grew louder she spotted a strange woman, older than her mother but younger than Two Doves, rushing her mount toward their clan. The stranger's eyes bulged and her lips drew back like those of a frantic horse.

Watching absently, Small Doe began to wonder if Kills-Behind-Her-Dwelling was her target and grew alarmed when the old woman prodded forward her spotted mount, harnessed in tandem with another, to meet the woman's charge. The stalwart pony balked and backed until it looked like it might rear.

Small Doe instantly dove for its bridle, but before she grasped hold of it, the mad stranger grabbed her belt, yanked her off her white mare, and tumbled down with her to the rocky soil. Gripping Small Doe's braids with surprising force, she aimed to beat her face against a stone.

"No!" cried Pacing Wolf, leaping from his horse. Grabbing the woman's wrists, he swung her off her feet and suspended her mid-air.

The stranger began spewing curses, kicking her feet toward Small Doe's head. "She is not fit to take the dead's place!"

"Stop—you will not do this!" ordered Pacing Wolf, his face and voice full of menace.

"Let her down," the many-feathered warrior demanded. His face, tattooed with a circle on his creased forehead and a line beneath his lip, looked much older than the woman's.

"My debt is settled!" spat Pacing Wolf, dropping the madwoman on his farthest side, away from Small Doe.

"I curse her belly!" the woman snarled. "Your small-things will all die before they see the sun!"

"Come," the tattooed man commanded, hefting his wife up behind him with difficulty before turning toward Pacing Wolf. "You have honored your vengeance quest, but do not forget the rest of our agreement."

Wheeling his horse with surprising grace, he began to trot away, but his woman grabbed the reins of Among-the-Pines' mount, pulling the pony behind them. Small Doe scrambled up quickly to rescue the child, but Pacing Wolf put out his hand.

"She is Jackrabbit, my dead woman's mother. She has just learned what Wild Dog did to her daughter." Watching Marks-His-Face retreat, Pacing Wolf absently mumbled for Small Doe to raise her skirt, but she did so with such modesty, he wondered if she was aware of the rivulet of blood dripping down her leg. "Up!" Squatting down, he brushed a thumb over her scraped knees, declaring, "Your wounds are not deep," but the eyes he raised to hers clearly wished to know if she felt much pain.

"No," she shook her head. "Your quickness kept me from harm."

Her reply faintly raised the corners of his lips, but before she could return his smile he had leaped onto his mount and was galloping toward the ridge.

The Blackfoot captive, whom Hair-Up-Top had named Last Woman, guided her horses up beside them. She asked no questions, knowing her efforts would be wasted, but nodded inquiringly toward the scraped knees.

Small Doe smiled and shook her head in reply, but Last Woman was no more satisfied than Pacing Wolf had been. With considerable effort, she dismounted, withdrew a pinch of black salve from her pouch, smeared it across the abrasions, and then nodded to assure her friend that she would heal nicely. Small Doe smiled in thanks, but as she looked up, she noticed Last Woman's daughter riding after Among-the-Pines.

"Come back," she called, but until the child heard the command in her mother's musical language, she did not give up. The little girl halted, staring longingly after her small playmate until she could no longer distinguish Among-the-Pines from the other Kicked-in-the-Bellies.

Kills-Behind-Her-Dwelling muttered, "They will ruin her."

"When will she come home?" asked Small Doe.

"Never," replied the old woman. "Jackrabbit is her dead mother's mother. She has the right to raise the child."

The news was as unexpected to Small Doe as it was disappointing. At home, the father's clan would have kept the girl. Among-the-Pines had been unpredictable, warm one moment and balky the next, but Small Doe had grown to care for her. Sighing sadly, she realized she still had much to learn. The Sparrow Hawks looked much like Allies, but their customs were a continual surprise.

Too weary to delve further, Small Doe grasped her white mare's reins, but in deference to Last Woman's condition, she did not mount. Instead, the four companions led their animals side by side toward the amassing camp. Each walked in silence for most of the distance. Kills-Behind-Her-Dwelling was too disgusted to talk, and the two Blackfoot captives were unable to offer much more than smiles and nods. Losing Among-the-Pines would greatly hinder their communication. The little Blackfoot girl and she, adjusting more rapidly to each other's languages, had acted as the grown-up's interpreters.

Small Doe could only guess how Hair-Up-Top discovered Last Woman had a daughter. She was far too in awe of Pacing Wolf to ask if he had conveyed the information, but the morning after she had befriended the Blackfoot, the old leader had led a lovely mare and her foal to Crazy Bear's lodge. Honored to receive such a visit, Crazy Bear was quite willing to grant his Real Chief's request, but he refused to take the man's gift, telling him it was not necessary. Hair-Up-Top insisted. After a time, Crazy Bear gave in, accepted the horses and sent the child, along with gifts of clothing, to her mother.

Small Doe wished she could have been there when the old leader returned home with his surprise. Both mother and daughter had looked radiant that evening when Small Doe went with them to fetch water; and when the old man happened by, they gazed after him with gratitude that transcended speech.

Once Hair-Up-Top indicated they would make camp, Small Doe's friendship with the Blackfoot captives presented her an unforeseen difficulty. His lodge—used frequently for councils—required longer, sturdier poles. Since Last Woman was close to delivering her small-thing, Small Doe took on the task of tossing the first pole into place; but after two attempts, she began considering whom she might ask for help. Pacing Wolf was still performing the duties of a soldier, and his grandmother's knotted arms possessed little strength.

As she was trying a third time, two well-muscled arms reached around from behind her and hoisted the cumbersome pole from her hands. She guessed who owned them without turning. Indeed, he so regularly appeared when she needed help, she had fleetingly wondered if he was an angel. The firm torso he brushed against her back argued otherwise.

Slipping out from between his arms, she stood aside while he positioned the heavy pole into place and then stepped forward to hold it steady while he braced the next against it. He did the same for each, neither speaking nor waiting to be thanked; but the smile he tossed her while striding away was like the sun breaking through a dreary rain.

As she glanced at the tall Blackfoot, she saw her press her lips into a hard, straight line before telling her daughter something in their sing-song tongue.

"He no good," the child announced, tilting her chin toward Goes-to-Battle's smoothly muscled back. Gesturing for Small Doe to bend down, Little Blackfoot's short, padded fingers took hold of her chin and guided her to look up toward a line of watching warriors on the ridge. "He much good." At once, Small Doe picked out Pacing Wolf among them, but in case she had not, the little girl drew a circle around her face. "Red." Next, she pointed to her eyes. "Yellow."

"He is called Pacing Wolf," smiled Small Doe. "My husband."

The little girl grinned broadly. "He say Old-Hair trade horse. Get me."

Her words were imperfect but their meaning unmistakable, confirming Small Doe's suspicions. Looking at her captive friend, she asked, "Pacing Wolf told Hair-Up-Top about your daughter?"

After Little Blackfoot ran over and conveyed the question to her mother, a lovely smile brightened the solemn face. "Good," Last Woman nodded, looking toward the ridge. "Man good."

Small Doe smiled happily. They were the first Sparrow Hawk words she had heard her friend use, and she was proud that the kindness of her husband had inspired them.

SMALL DOE HUNG her husband's pipe and medicine shield inside his freshly tossed up dwelling and turned her thoughts toward their late meal. It would be a simple fare of dried meat and vegetables boiled in a buffalo hide kettle she suspended over a tripod. Adding a little spring onion she had found near the lake, she eagerly snatched a few moments to read her Bible. Returning to John's Gospel, she picked up where she had left off the day before.

> Jesus lifted up His eyes to heaven and said. 'Father, the hour has come to glorify Your son so that He may glorify You. You have placed all tribes under His authority so He might give everlasting life to all You have given Him. This is what everlasting life is: knowing You, the only true God, and Jesus, the Anointed One, whom You

have sent. I have glorified You on the earth by completing the work You gave to Me to do.[69]

"Lord, this is what I want also—to complete the work You have given me to do. My efforts seem feeble and useless, but You are able to do anything. Please let me speak what You want to be spoken and do what You want to be done. Use me in any way that You will and make me like Jesus, who did not turn back though He knew suffering awaited Him."

While she considered what it might cost her when He answered her prayer, her mind wandered toward her new Blackfoot companions.

"Lord, would You also please comfort Last Woman and help me, somehow, make You known to her? She has endured far worse than I have and does not have Your Holy Spirit to console her. Her husband is probably dead, and the man she belongs to now is likely older than her grandfather, though he does seem kind." Recalling the happy smile on Little Blackfoot's face while she looked up at Pacing Wolf on the ridge and the difference in Last Woman since mother and daughter were reunited, Small Doe felt both grateful and proud.

"Lord, You are unspeakably wonderful, and though…"

Hearing Small Doe speaking within his lodge, Pacing Wolf halted. He had hurried home once he had finished his duties, but he was not in a temper to greet a group of women. When no other voices answered, he realized she was talking with her spirit-guide and paused, torn between two desires: his eagerness to see how she had fared after Jackrabbit's assault and his regard for her spirit-vision. His people both respected and considered them private, but as he decided to turn away, she said something that arrested his breathing.

"…I am glad you gave me to him. His heart is like his arm: strong and ready to act. I am proud to call him my husband."

Pacing Wolf stilled every muscle, longing to hear more, yet he also felt compelled to flee. His feet decided for him, carrying him swiftly back to the ridge and up a cliff he knew well. Dangling his legs high above the encampment, he filled his lungs with the cool evening breeze as it swept the perspiration from his face.

Perhaps she is not woman-flesh after all, he supposed, but as he pondered the possibility, a passage she had read last night began ringing like an echo through his thoughts:

> How much more harshly will a man deserve to be punished if he tramples the Son of God under his feet, considering the blood of the covenant that has set him apart as unclean, and insults the Spirit of Grace? For we know the One who said, 'Vengeance is Mine, I will

repay,' and, 'The Lord will judge His people.'" It is terrifying to fall into the hands of the living God.[70]

Did my vengeance-quest insult this spirit? He grabs hold of me like an enemy. Feeling all the terror the verses described, guilt pressed him down like a crushing rock, and Jackrabbit's assault added to its weight, squeezing him until he could hardly breathe.

Jackrabbit is vicious and has much influence among her clanswomen. They will treat Small Doe harshly, but I cannot take her back. He remembered Wild Dog's stinging pronouncements as if he had heard them yesterday. *Still,* he thought, *she might fare better with her own than here.*

"Spirit of the Book," he cried aloud. "I am Pacing Wolf of the Sparrow Hawks. I have snatched a woman who belongs to You. You know her as Light Bird, but I have called her Small Doe. We are one flesh like the man and woman You first made; and like him, I want to keep her. If You wish to strike me, here I am, but who will bring her meat when she hungers or skins to keep her warm?"

Crouching like a man prepared for an enemy, he half-expected lightning to pierce the sky, and yet he did not feel aggression toward his woman's god. He liked to listen to the book, though it sometimes made his insides quake. Surmising the absence of her god's immediate wrath implied acceptance of his terms, Pacing Wolf rose to his feet.

"I will care for her well!"

Trotting home with a lightened burden, he cautiously entered his lodge. Small Doe's brow was pinched together, but when she saw him, her face softened with clear relief.

"I will get your supper."

As she headed toward the door, Pacing Wolf pulled her to him and ran his hand around the back of her neck. "You are well?"

Small Doe smiled, touched by his concern. "Yes—only worried that you had fallen down a ravine."

As he searched her large round eyes, he mulled over the vow he had made to her book-god. He would happily risk his life to keep it. He despised the evils to which his revenge had exposed her, but he could not wish he had left her as she was. *A hungry man cannot wish his full bowl was empty.*

Small Doe grew self-conscious under his intense scrutiny. Laying her cheek in the crook of his neck, she smoothed her hand across his shirt and contentedly breathed in the smell of sweet tobacco.

"Little Blackfoot told me what you did for her mother and her. Worthy warriors care for their own, but you have shown mercy to an enemy's family. I am privileged to belong to such a man."

Pacing Wolf's throat constricted. Pressing her closely against him, he nuzzled her hair, relishing the feel of her hands as they wound around his waist and wended up his back. When he had last thanked his spirit-guide for a woman, she had severely disappointed him. This time, he would offer thanks to Small Doe's book-god.

Whoever this spirit-guide is—He-Who-First-Made-All-Things or some lesser spirit—He takes much pity on the wounded of heart.

You, O Lord, are compassionate and gracious, slow to anger and flowing over with love and faithfulness.

Psalm 86:15

Chapter 21

During the Moon of Green Grass

STRAIGHT ARROWS STRODE toward Valuable Woman's dwelling, still unsure of what he would say. He could not remember a time when he did not wish to marry Corn-Tassels; the whole village knew and expected this. Still, something between them had changed—she had changed, saying anything that came into her head whether or not she was asked.

What did they do to her at that school? He had come to hate the word. It had meant separation and sadness, and now ruination. Even Curly-Haired Boy, Corn-Tassels' brother, often squirmed in her presence—not that he could throw stones. School had changed him also. He preferred reading to hunting and seemed reluctant to join their battle games. During the most recent one, he had helped his team hold their line, but he fought without heart. *I would not want to meet an enemy with him alone.*

He hated to disappoint their father, whom he had held in high esteem since childhood. Spotted Long-knife hunted buffalo with the daring of an Allied warrior and never shied from a just skirmish. Straight Arrows' own father would understand his decision and might even agree with it. Although Preying Eagle was too polite to say anything, he held censure in his eyes whenever Corn-Tassels barreled like a wild colt into matters that were not hers to enter. His mother suggested that he give her more time.

"Their people," Brought-Us-the-Book explained, "define submission more broadly than ours. A husband expects his woman to give him the final say, but many men are like Spotted Long-knife. He wants to hear Valuable Woman's opinion and wishes her to offer them even if he does not ask."

Straight Arrows bristled. "Father values yours. He tells me often that he asks you when he is uncertain of the Creator's way."

"I know and I was not complaining, but not every warrior is like your father. Also, I have always held a unique position here. When I first brought The Book, no one else could answer our elders' questions. Each culture interprets respect in light of its own customs. You must both let the Lord guide you."

The Lord...

Since Straight Arrows was ten, he had walked I-Am-Savior's path, but lately the Creator seemed strangely quiet, and though his father answered his questions, he would not tell him how to choose. When Straight Arrows asked how he had known whom he should marry, Preying Eagle said only, "I recognized your mother: she was bone of my bone and flesh of my flesh."

I do not recognize Corn-Tassels.

Praying yet again for direction, he came to a complete stop within sight of her mother's dwelling. The young long-knife her father had brought from Washing Town was waiting next to Valuable Woman's door, wearing a borrowed courting blanket. Straight Arrows had noticed his marked attentions many times, but he had not paid them much mind. No respectable untouched Allied woman would consider such a man. Like Corn-Tassels, he spoke whenever a thought came into his head and to whoever was nearby, young or old, male or female.

As he watched Corn-Tassels greet the young long-knife, her expression told him all he needed. He turned to retrace the path to his mother's dwelling, surprised by the reaction of his own heart. Rather than jealousy or anger, he felt lightness and relief.

Corn-Tassels' stomach thudded to her feet as she recognized the retreating warrior's back. On the way home from their trip to the Pawnee's village, Lieutenant Wilson had asked her father for permission to court her, but she had felt so horribly disloyal to Straight Arrows that she at first refused. Her father, however, was insistent.

Why did Papa consent? she fretted, though she already knew the answer. Try as she had to push away her feelings, they crept out unexpectedly and often. She fidgeted whenever Joshua was near, and if he spoke to her directly, she flushed or made such nonsensical responses that she sounded ridiculous. Scolding herself for acting like a schoolgirl, she reasoned his attentions away. *He seeks me out so he may converse without first translating his thoughts, and as father's aide, he cannot be rude.*

During the journey from Boston, he had been charming and had kept her secret about the morning rides; but her eagerness to see Straight Arrows had so captured her thoughts, she lacked time to consider anyone else. As she grew less sure of her commitment to live in this village, though, Joshua had begun to seem like an island to a sea-tossed sailor.

"He will have to wait his turn as I have waited for mine," murmured Joshua, following the direction of her glance. "How can I present my suit while you're looking at my rival?"

Surprised by his candor, Corn-Tassels colored but smiled brightly. In many ways, the Lieutenant was like her father: confident, intelligent, and forthright.

"This is not a bad custom," he teased, wrapping her in the blanket, "though we would raise quite a few eyebrows on a street in Boston."

"Has it been difficult for you—adjusting to such different ways?"

"Tremendously," he laughed. "I am afraid several of your cousins are expecting me to ask their fathers for their hands. I've made the grave mistakes of observing them while they engaged in chores and smiling when our eyes met."

Corn-Tassels dimpled deeply, remembering Talks-to-Bird's comments. "You are right, I am afraid—one cousin especially."

"That hasn't been the hardest, though. On our trip out, I'd grown used to speaking with you at will. Here, if I want your opinion or even look your way, one of your uncles starts breathing down my neck. Your rival looks at me as if I'd bared fangs."

Imagining their thoughts of him, Corn-Tassels again dimpled. She had noticed, from the first, his unfaltering ease with ladies. He was not a cad, but his attentive and direct way of looking into a woman's eyes would lead many to suspect he thought them singularly special.

"Should I ask you what my chances are," he goaded playfully, "or lay out reasons why you should choose me over him?"

Corn-Tassels' dimples faded. She had no idea how to answer—she had only just now admitted to herself how strongly he attracted her.

"I did not mean to make you ill at ease," he smiled. "While we are wrapped in this blanket, must I call you Corn-Tassels or may I call you Miss Anderson? I don't mean to insult your upbringing, but to call you a tassel of any sort, let alone one found sprouting from a common vegetable, seems absurd."

She could not help but laugh. "Miss Anderson would be fine—or Abigail if you like."

His left eyebrow shot up, but he noticed she still had not replied to his original question. Thinking it better not to force an answer, he pursued his own course.

"Abigail, then," he murmured, lowering his voice to an enveloping rumble. "The good Lord has not placed a woman on earth that would suit me half as well as you. Anyone with sight can attest to your beauty, and your abilities to understand the customs and language of these people perfectly complement my goals, but my mind was made up about you that morning in your grandfather's meadow. A mealy-mouthed and insipid woman could never suit me. I want a wife who can face challenges without disintegrating in a heap of weeping, a partner—not a servant or a slave. When I saw you atop that mare, her back as bare as a newborn's, I knew you were extraordinary; and once we danced that evening, I never wanted you to leave my side."

"I...I am not sure what to say."

"Then say yes," he cajoled boldly. "Say you will marry me."

"I cannot," she told him frankly, but she rushed ahead when she noticed the sparkle in his brown eyes dim. "I didn't say I will not. I cannot without Father's permission." She did not know what had come over her. He seemed to have drained her desire to resist.

Joshua's perfectly matched white teeth lit his entire countenance. "I already asked him, and he has given it—providing you were willing."

"You...you asked him?" she repeated. "Then yes, I will certainly marry you."

As she reeled from the suddenness of her decision, she marveled that she had wondered what to do at all. Like a well-designed garment, marrying him fit perfectly into place. The many evenings she had spent within Straight Arrows' blanket had felt discordant, like two instruments out of tune, though she had adamantly argued the contrary with herself. One evening, she had even hidden her face when Joshua came upon Straight Arrows and her without warning. Now she understood why: her heart had known all along to whom it belonged.

A warrior makes plans in his heart, but the Lord gives a fitting answer to his tongue.

Proverbs 16:1

Chapter 22

AS SMALL DOE bent to fill her water skins, the rising sun shimmered across the lake. It was a cool but glorious spring morning, and since some of the clouds of her grief had lifted, she could appreciate the beauty of this new territory she called home. She had never seen a lake so clear, and the encircling peaks brought to mind the protective edges of a bird's nest. As she recalled her first sight of them, her stomach unexpectedly knotted. They had seemed much like Pacing Wolf that day—fearsome and forbidding—but the responses both inspired in her now were far more agreeable.

Hearing youthful whispers behind her, she was about to turn around when two hands shoved hard against her back. Her face painfully smacked the frigid water, grazing against a sharp stone. Stunned beneath its surface, she grew vaguely aware of an odd mix of sounds: bursts of muffled laughter, harsh scolding voices, and the answering tattoo of scurrying feet. The latter died away as she pushed up on all fours and, glancing behind her, caught sight of two girls running up the path toward the village. The taller one, perhaps fifteen summers, gained the lead over her companion but slipped as her soaked moccasins hit a patch of grass. Distantly behind them, a very small girl was desperately clutching an object while she scrambled to keep up. It slid from her grasp, arresting the little girl between the desire to retrieve it and the need to escape.

Not until a bright red splotch pierced the water's surface did Small Doe realize that she was bleeding. Putting her hand to her temple, she felt someone helping her to her feet. Her mind felt a muddle as blood splattered a warrior's sleeve and set her to worrying it might spoil the finely worked fringes. Instinctively backing away, she tried again to stem the flow, but the warrior impeded her efforts by pulling her hands away.

"Stop squirming!" he commanded, pressing a cold, wet sleeve against her wound.

She complied at once, certain she would find swallow-winged brows if she dared to lift her eyes. Where he had come from, she could not fathom; she had seen only women near the lake.

"What did I tell you?" a familiar, aged voice began upbraiding. "They will ruin her!"

Making no sense of the comment, Small Doe wondered if Kills-Behind-Her-Dwelling's mind had begun to wander until she remembered Jackrabbit taking her stepdaughter's away. *Among-the-Pines!* She had thought the youngest child familiar, but everything had happened so quickly. *I would not have expected this of her.*

Goes-to-Battle lifted the moistened buckskin from her wound, pulling back Small Doe's attention. She smiled up at him cautiously. She felt impolite ignoring his kindness, and his grandmother was close by; but instead of setting her loose, he slid his hand firmly down to the small of her back. Small Doe stiffened, though she told herself he meant only to hold her steady, and sidled away from him as soon as possible.

Kills-Behind-Her-Dwelling stood atop the bank, her arms outstretched and her forehead furrowed. The creases softened slightly as she saw that Small Doe's wound was not deep.

"I will take you home, my little one," she cooed. "You will need something dry to wear."

Small Doe nodded absently. She was busy searching the path for Among-the-Pines and her heart for an excuse for the child's behavior. "Perhaps they are afraid I will turn her father from her."

"Afraid of you?" the old woman sneered. "You should be afraid of them!"

Thanking Goes-to-Battle, his grandmother asked him to pass her Small Doe's water sacks. He did so readily, plucking them from a limb that jutted out into the water, filling them up, and dividing them between the two women.

Small Doe felt a bit unsteady as they climbed toward the village, but she reached the top without further mishap and then retreated to her husband's lodge. Lighting a fire, she slipped out of her wet garments and hung them beside it to dry, but before she could don others, Kills-Behind-Her-Dwelling called impatiently for admittance.

Small Doe grabbed the nearest buffalo robe, hastily wrapping herself before sitting down with her mending; but when she looked up to greet her elderly friend, she met her husband's eyes instead. He was amused by her unusual state of undress, but before he thought of a polite way to tell his grandmother they wanted privacy, he spotted the drying blood just inside Small Doe's hairline.

"What is this?" he asked, squatting to examine the jagged gash. His fingertips were as gentle as his tone, but Small Doe wished that he had not noticed. Her heart ached for Among-the-Pines and she did not want the incident to come between them.

"I fell into the lake," she mumbled, dropping her gaze so suddenly that his eyes naturally followed.

He found her making large careless stitches that conflicted—as did her answer—with all his previous observations. During the three moons that had passed since he had taken her, her tongue had never proven false—but neither had her balance. He knew it to be excellent and her hands unfalteringly steady.

"The rocks that made you slip—where are they?"

An edge had crept into his voice, alerting Small Doe that he suspected something. *He often watches from the heights with other Lumpwoods. He may have seen everything that...* All at once, she pictured herself with his handsome cousin, and as she imagined how they might have looked from a distance, her fingers began such quivering, she tucked them beneath the garment on her lap.

"I did not slip on a rock," she murmured. "I was bending down to fill my water sacks."

Pacing Wolf nodded. He despised a false tongue and would have been keenly disappointed had Small Doe fallen into his trap. There were no rocks large enough to stand on this side of the lake. Still, her wary glances told him she was hiding something.

"Slip?" the old one scoffed. "She was pushed!"

Pacing Wolf wrinkled his brow. "Pushed—by whom?"

Kills-Behind-Her-Dwelling opened her lips, but Small Doe hastily responded. "I did not see. When I lifted my head, no one was near, though two older girls were running up the path. The tallest one's moccasins were wet."

Pacing Wolf's eyes narrowed. He suspected who they were and would not allow the incident to go unchecked. What he could not comprehend was her reluctance to accuse them.

"Did you see Among-the-Pines?"

How he guessed this, Small Doe could not imagine—unless he had indeed been watching from the heights. "I saw a girl around her age but the distance was great."

"I *know* it was her!" spat Kills-Behind-Her-Dwelling. "She dropped this on the path—the small-thing I sewed for her last summer. She carries it often."

Pacing Wolf took the well-worn rawhide doll, turned it over in his hand, and peered searchingly at Small Doe. "Why did you hold back?"

"She is young and has already lost her mother. To separate a daughter from her father would be cruel."

Pacing Wolf clenched his jaw. Her choice of words was like a knife thrust into the ribs though he read no accusation in her eyes. Rising abruptly, he ducked through the door, flinging back the flap as if it intentionally impeded his progress.

Small Doe stared unhappily at the doeskin on her lap, exasperated by his rapid turn of temper. All the ground she had lately gained seemed lost, and she wondered again if she would ever understand him.

"He looks for Marks-His-Face—the old man you met with the tattooed circle on his forehead. He will speak with him about his daughters. When Pacing Wolf bargained for their older sister, he agreed to take them also as they came into womanhood. Pretty Crow Woman did so last summer."

Small Doe's stomach sank, and thorny weeds began pricking her well-tended heart. They crowded the tender shoots she had so carefully nourished and burst into seed before she had thought to pluck them out.

"He wants another wife?" she murmured. "Do I displease him?"

She was already sure of the answer. His eyes had turned from keen to flinty before he strode away. They contrasted sharply with the other pair springing vividly into her memory. She could almost feel the warmth of his cousin's caress, so startling her, she grew newly aware his grandmother was telling her something.

"You mistake what I am saying, little fawn. Pacing Wolf does not go to claim her. He tells Mark-His-Face what she has done and threatens what will happen if she harms you again."

"The girl who dunked me? She is his dead woman's sister?"

"Both of those girls are, but that was no playful dunking. Among-the-Pines may have thought so, but Jackrabbit's two daughters—you must be wary of them."

Small Doe touched the tender swelling. "They meant me harm?"

"Perhaps, perhaps not," shrugged Kills-Behind-Her-Dwelling. "But if we found your body floating toward the Echata, they would shed no tears. The older one covets your place. With you to warm his bed, Pacing Wolf will make her wait—perhaps for so many summers, she will grow eager for another warrior. Let us hope so. If she begins to cast her eyes about, what can Marks-His-Face say? Pacing Wolf is no longer young and foolish, and if she is determined to have him, she will not find his lodge to her liking. As head-wife, you hold her fate and those of her younger sister and mother in your hands."

Thinking of a life spent near Jackrabbit and her daughters made Small Doe feel ill. In addition, she felt ashamed. She had vastly misjudged her husband and been swift to disregard the very qualities in him for which she had recently given God thanks. Eagerly tearing out the prickly weed's roots, she asked the Creator to restore her clean and faithful heart.

"You have nothing to fear," offered the old grandmother. "Mark-His-Face will keep them away from you. He began walking before I became a woman, so he knows he will soon travel to the Mystery Land. If he angers Pacing Wolf, who will care for them? He has no sons. But Pacing Wolf must prod him softly. When old Hair-Up-Top rests his white head, Short Neck, Marks-His-Face's cousin, bends down to see if he is still breathing."

Small Doe cocked her head.

"When one leader dies, the Good Men choose another to follow—usually for the kinds and numbers of coups he has counted. When old Hair-Up-Top passes, the Many Lodges will elect Hunts-For-Death to lead our band. Our Good Men will also want him to replace Hair-Up-Top as the Sparrow Hawk's Real Chief, but the Kicked-in-the-Bellies will naturally prefer Marks-His-Face. Once that is decided, they will select a new leader for our clan. Some wish to follow Short Neck, but most prefer your husband. Both have counted many coups, but though Pacing Wolf is young, he has always cared well for the needs of our people. This is why the spirits keep him alive. Every summer he accepts one of the Lumpwoods' death-staffs, and every autumn he returns to us whole. Short Neck is older, but he owns a cruel temper."

"What is a death-staff?"

The old woman sighed, wondering once more how Small Doe had grown up so ignorant. "That is one, up there," she answered, pointing to the crooked staff hanging beside Pacing Wolf's pipe.

Early on, its dangling curls of willow bark had drawn Small Doe's curiosity; but whenever Pacing Wolf entered their dwelling, all else faded quickly from her mind. As the moons came and went, she had ceased to give it thought.

"Very soon—as the sap begins to run and the grass turns green—our war societies will cut limbs or saplings to make into standards they will bear into battle. The Lumpwoods will then cut four long rods, which two warriors who have proven their courage will make into these death staffs. They will bend the tops of the first and second until they curve down to point toward the ground. Hunts-For-Death made that one. They leave the other two stakes straight, like the ones there, above your door flap."

Small Doe had seen numerous straight rods, whittled to a point on one end, pinned over the doors of Lumpwood lodges, but she had not understood their significance. "Do they serve a purpose?"

Kills-Behind-Her-Dwelling nodded. "A remarkable one. When an enemy charges, the warriors who have accepted them leap from their horses, thrust them into the ground, and stand to fight between them and the enemy. They will welcome death rather than retreat. Only when another Lumpwood yanks it loose may these staff-bearer flee to safety. The Foxes make staffs also, but the Muddy Hands and Big Dogs use ropes."[71]

As Small Doe glanced up at her husband's staffs, her stomach grew upset. The grass had already begun to green. "How do they decide who must take them?"

"All the Lumpwoods will gather in Hunts-For-Death's lodge. He is a great war-leader. After he has filled and lit his pipe, he will offer it to a warrior he particularly admires."

"Must that warrior smoke it?"

"No, and no one takes this honor lightly. If a warrior is not ready to die—perhaps because he feels his medicine is weak or he wishes to enjoy his new wife—he will hang his head low, asking Hunts-For-Death not to see him. He bears no disgrace. But a warrior who is ready to give his life for his people will leap up, give his war cry, and accept the pipe. Pacing Wolf has accepted four staffs. Count them: two crooked and two straight."

Small Doe had already done so and was inwardly praying that he would hang his head. "Marks-His-Face is neither Lumpwood nor of your clan. How does he threaten my husband?"

"Not just Pacing Wolf—the whole clan. And what threatens the Many Lodges threatens our whole people. As leader of the Kicked-in-the-Bellies, his voice holds much sway. While my grandson was married to his daughter, Marks-His-Face favored him, but if Pacing Wolf breaks faith now, he may use his influence in favor of Short Neck."

War cries interrupted further explanation, followed by pounding hooves. Fearing the worst, Kills-Behind-Her-Dwelling grabbed several weapons while Small Doe slipped into the dress she had been mending; but when they peered outside, they saw only a party of Lumpwood soldiers rushing toward a blue-coated long-knife that had ridden over the ridge. Pacing Wolf was among them. A second long-knife trailed the first, but the bright sun showed clearly that neither brandished weapons.

I know this man, thought Small Doe. His uniform was unfamiliar and his cap obscured his features, but she recognized the way he sat his horse. All at once, she started running toward the middle of the camp, knowing they would escort him there, and praying while the Lumpwoods engulfed him, they would not deem him a threat.

She could barely contain her excitement. When he trotted past her, though, she thought she had been mistaken: his eyes flitted through her without a hint of recognition. As she trailed his progress to the large central dwelling, Hair-Up-Top emerged and pulled himself up to his full height; but once the long-knife dismounted, the gathering warriors so swallowed both that she could see nothing.

Not until she dodged clear of a mounted Lumpwood was she able to catch another glimpse. The throng about her parted, clearing her doubt along with her view. Merely a good leap across the path, the long-knife was removing his cap and running a gloved hand through his flattened hair. It was damp with sweat from the arduous journey and slightly lightened by scattered white, but the brilliant sun, high in the sky, showed it unmistakably tinged with auburn.

I wait for You, O Lord. For it is You, my God, who will answer when I pray: "Do not let those who boast against me rejoice when my foot slips."

Psalm 38:15-16

Chapter 23

SMALL DOE FELT baffled by Spotted Long-knife's snub, but she was determined to find any excuse she could that might bring her close to him. Running home, she grabbed all her food-stores and returned quickly to Hair-Up-Top's lodge.

"A large party of warriors is gathering outside," she told Last Woman. "I have brought what I have to help you make a feast."

Her Blackfoot friend smiled and whispered something to her daughter in their musical tongue, and the girl slipped out. To where, Small Doe could only guess, but she came back quickly carrying additional supplies. Pointing to items they might pleasantly combine, the two women made a stew in Last Woman's cook-pot, roasted meat over a cook-fire, and were softening greens on a nearby rock by the time the men began to wander inside.

Small Doe tried covertly to engage her white *uncle's* eyes, but each time she succeeded he turned away. Her imagination whirled with plausible explanations, but one by one they failed the test of reason. At last, she decided she could do only one thing: trust him.

Keeping her eyes low, as she had learned to do in this company of warriors, she listened intently to all that he said. Little of it was interesting—he spoke mostly about keeping peace with the men of his white tribe—but when he tried to convey greetings from an elder he called The President, he could not find the correct word. Her father's tribe, from whom he had learned to speak their language, did not follow an elected leader but a Council of Elders distinguished for their wisdom. As he discussed this difficulty with his aide, Small Doe knelt beside Pacing Wolf with a bowl of greens.

"Batsetsi-kyashe," she whispered. "This is the expression the long-knives seek."

Pacing Wolf widened his eyes, but he quickly recalled what the trader had asked him. Beyond his fleeting embarrassment, he had not given her ability to speak English another thought. He leaned over to Hunts-For-Death and repeated what she told him.

"Batsetsi-kyashe—the Real Chief the white leaders follow."

Major Anderson nodded. "Yes, our...would you give me the word again?"

"Batsetsi-kyashe," replied Hair-Up-Top, tilting up his lips as he nodded at Small Doe.

"Our...Batsetsi-kyashe," continued the Major, "has asked Lieutenant Wilson and me to visit the tribes who live between the white men toward the rising sun and the place it settles to sleep. He offers you the friendship that his father enjoyed with your fathers."

A number of Good Men nodded and began murmuring to their neighbors. Many, including Hair-Up-Top and Hunts-For-Death, had attended O'Fallon's council and drawn their mark on his paper.

While patiently waiting for them to resume their discussion, Major Anderson surreptitiously glanced at the silent warrior to whom Light Bird had spoken. "You understand English well," he told Pacing Wolf, leaning behind Hunts-For-Death, who sat between them. "Would you consider accompanying me as a translator and guide?"

Rather than answer, Pacing Wolf looked at his war-society father, but as Hunts-For-Death offered no reaction, he replied candidly, "My woman handed me the word. She has a white mother."

Major Anderson was certain he meant Light Bird—the two had exchanged several glances in addition to her helpful whisper—but he needed to confirm the exact nature of their relationship. If he spoke to her or even smiled in her direction, he might endanger his own standing and mission with the tribe's leaders. They could not trust a man so closely aligned with an enemy, and paying undue attention to another man's wife might place him on the wrong end of a knife.

"Which is yours?" he prodded, knowing he would not easily find another opportunity.

"There—coming in," replied Pacing Wolf, nodding toward the door. "With eyes like a doe's."

The Major took full advantage of the chance to study her face. He wanted to assess the condition of both her health and spirits. When she knelt well within his hearing, he confided, "I recently saw a white woman who looks much like her. Could she be your woman's mother?"

Joshua's eyes shot up. He had thought she looked familiar, but his godmother's blue-green eyes and brown hair had blurred the connection. Hunts-For-Death, who observed his reaction, eyed him suspiciously. "She is of Those-Who-Cut-Off-Our-Heads," he informed the Major. "You are brother to her people?"

"I do not know this name," replied Major Anderson, fearing he might have overreached. "How did they earn it?"

"Long ago, when Hair-Up-Top's mother still carried him," explained the watchful clan leader, "they defeated many of our Good Men in battle. When our fathers went out to bring back their bodies, they found them without heads."

The Major wrinkled up his nose and sharply drew down the corners of his mouth.

"Why did you not take this white woman from them," asked Hair-Up-Top, "and return her to your tribe?"

"I have come to ensure peaceful relations between our peoples, not to interfere with another man's family—and even if I possessed a brother's rights, I doubt she would come away. She looked well and content aside from mourning the recent loss of a daughter."

Approving the answer, Hair-Up-Top addressed a complaint he had earlier ignored. "You say the white settlers are angry that my Good Men have taken a few of their naked buffalo. They drag their carts through our lands and shoot our antelope and elk. Do they think it is right to take from us but offer nothing in return?"

Pacing Wolf listened while the two discussed this and other grievances, but his eyes followed Small Doe. She had been ducking in and out all afternoon so often and inconspicuously that no one else paid her any mind. After the Good Men had at last depleted the numerous bowls and trenchers she offered, she had taken up any minor task that would keep her in the lodge.

He suspected he knew why: the grieving white woman was likely her mother, and she hoped the older long-knife might say something more. He was equally certain that the man would not. The white woman had been of merely passing interest, and Hair-Up-Top had asked his question only to uncover the stranger's thoughts.

When Hunts-For-Death leaned away to say something privately to Hair-Up-Top, Pacing Wolf turned toward the spotted white man. "Where do you sleep?"

"In the open."

Pacing Wolf shook his head. "You will sleep in my lodge."

The Major accepted readily but returned his attention to the whitehaired elder. He had summered with the Allies for two decades, and, among many things, they had taught him to respect a warrior's uncanny aptitude for reading another man's thoughts. The scarlet stripes across this one's leggings proclaimed he did so better than most. Few tokens were won by strength but by a keen ability to anticipate an opponent's next move.

During the course of the discussion, the young warrior's interest in Light Bird had grown increasingly obvious. He had proved a careful listener, making comments only when they contributed well; but each time the Major glanced his way, his eyes were avidly trailing her movements. The rest of the man's face told him nothing. Like all warriors worthy of the name, he carefully kept emotion from his features. He might merely find her form appealing or be watching for signs that betrayed her close tie to their guests.

When all parties had exhausted their various topics, the Major bid the Lieutenant good night at Hunts-For-Death's dwelling and followed Pacing Wolf to a nearby lodge. Coming across Light Bird had been a clear answer to prayer. He hoped her husband might answer another. Warriors loathed performing chores women typically did. If Pacing Wolf agreed to act as a scout, he might take her along to attend to his needs.

When Small Doe saw Spotted Long-knife ducking into her husband's dwelling, she bubbled with inward happiness. Outwardly, she donned her usual reserve, unsure how he wished her to act. On one hand, their private setting permitted her more freedom. On the other, he had purposely concealed their relationship from Hair-Up-Top and might wish to do so from her husband. To hide her indecision, she busied herself by spreading out buffalo pelts for his bed and retreated to the background to await her husband's lead.

Picking up a sapling he had cut to form a bow, Pacing Wolf jerked his head toward his guest and grinned at Small Doe. "You have much to ask the long-knife and the night grows old."

Her eyes danced with happiness, rewarding his heart, but Major Anderson remained guarded. Aware he was there by his host's grace, he addressed her in their common language.

"Your husband tells me your mother is a white woman. Are her braids the color of rich soil and her eyes the color of your lake?"

"Yes," she nodded, "but they change often. Sometimes they are more like the sky before a rain."

"I have seen such a woman with a tribe across the grasslands. She belongs to a warrior they call Preying Eagle."

Small Doe smiled. "He is my father. Are they well?"

"They seemed so."

Hoping he might venture into matters more private, Major Anderson glanced at Pacing Wolf to see how carefully he was listening. The warrior sat apart and appeared absorbed in his task, but the Major decided to remain cautious. He could better serve his *niece* by winning her husband's trust than by offering him cause for alarm.

"I heard several say they miss you deeply. You appear to be well loved."

"I am," replied Small Doe, though she was not sure he meant there or here. She had noticed his frequent glances at Pacing Wolf. "I miss them also."

"How did you come to live here? It is far from your home."

"A warrior belonging to my people shamed my husband's wife and slew both her and his son."

"I am sorry to hear such a thing," replied the Major, looking to see how Pacing Wolf reacted.

"When my husband followed his tracks, he overheard him plotting to shame me also."

The Major's eyebrows both shot. No one had told him this detail. "What happened?"

"His keen mind and strong arm kept me safe. If you travel the path back over the prairie, please tell them so and that his vengeance quest was just."

"I will. I am sure learning this will give them comfort."

"Please also tell them," Small Doe added, slipping into English, "he is not only courageous but caring toward the weak and poor. I lack nothing and have even found happiness in his lodge."

While Small Doe was describing him, Pacing Wolf stood to switch the sapling he was shaping for another that leaned against the lodge cover, but when he resumed his place he turned to sit with his back to them.

Major Anderson was unsure how to interpret the change, though he was certain it was deliberate. It likely signaled permission for them to ignore him and speak freely or might merely indicate he found their conversation dull, particularly if he assumed they would continue in English. Contemplating his back, the Major wondered just how much English her he understood. Light Bird had supplied their word for President. Still, both itinerant peddlers and the U.S. government had long-standing contact with this tribe and a trapper named Beckworth had lived among them for several years. Her husband might have acquired the rudiments of the language from any of them.

"He appears to be a fine warrior," replied the Major, adopting English also.

"He is highly respected among this people and gentle and generous with me." Blushing deeply, she rose, took the mirror from the peg, and showed him its enameled back. "He noticed I wanted this and purchased it from a trader last month, but this gift," she smiled, bending down to withdraw her Bible from Pacing Wolf's large leather bag, "is my dearest treasure."

Major Anderson's eyebrows again darted up. "Well now…I have seen one of these before!"

"He often asks me to read it to him."

"Any warrior worth his breath provides for his woman, but your husband shows both attentiveness and perception."

"While you visited my village, did you see my brothers—are they all well?"

"There were many warriors there and my stay was brief, as it must be here, but I saw no signs of any sickness."

"My grandmother hurt her ankle on the morning my husband...rescued me. Did you see a woman limping?"

Major Anderson glanced nervously at Pacing Wolf, fearing what her eager tone and hurried volley of questions might betray, but the muscles in his back worked in steady rhythm with his chores. Signaling that she should slow down, he took a long, reflective pause before answering.

"I do recall a silver-haired woman who favored one foot. Other than that injury, she looked well."

"And her husband," ask Small Doe, controlling her enthusiasm with difficulty, "the gray-haired elder they call Running Deer?"

"If I were able, I would give you an account of every person there," he replied, pointedly nodding towards Pacing Wolf's back, "but I cannot."

Comprehending the delicacy of her *uncle's* position, Small Doe stepped onto a less hazardous trail. "This place where your President lives, is it far from us?"

The Major nodded. "Yes, we traveled hard for weeks."

"Where are the other members of your band?"

"Only my aide and I are here. My wife and two children stayed behind with her father and mother. I have a son a bit younger than you and a daughter a few years older."

Small Doe knew this, of course, but continued the game. "If she is older than I am, she must be married."

"Not yet, but a young man asked for her. Both her mother and I esteem him highly and believe the Almighty planned the match."

Small Doe smiled happily. Spotted Long-knife could only have meant Straight Arrows. He and Aunt Valuable Woman loved her siblings almost as much as they loved their own children, but he seemed to be having difficulty maintaining her gaze. Unable to think of a safe way to ask why, she contented herself with her joyful thoughts. If her life was not quite as she had imagined, at least her brother and her friend's dreams remained intact.

As Pacing Wolf laid leather to the second bow, the embers began fading until he no longer had light enough to work. Propping the partially crafted weapon against the lodge lining, he sat down on their bed and tossed back the covers.

"Come," he commanded Small Doe and then tilted his chin toward the pallet she had laid for the long-knife earlier. "We sleep."

Both complied willingly, grateful he had arranged a private visit. But as Small Doe balanced the tops of three thick sticks over the warm embers, she began to feel awkward. She imagined the day, nearly sixteen summers ago, that her father had placed her tiny, pot-bellied form in Spotted Long-knife's freckled arms. Of course, she had been too young to see at the time, let alone remember the event, but it had signified a guardianship of sorts—a pledge of care should her father die in battle—and was among the important events that her intimate family regularly recounted. How would he feel as he watched her climb beneath the covers of a strange and enemy warrior?

If the Major was embarrassed, he hid it well, slipping into his pallet across the lodge and turning over. Small Doe did likewise, wriggling back until she felt her husband's chest, but she was too elated by what she had heard about her brother and Corn-Tassels to fall asleep.

Pacing Wolf encircled her with his arm and gathered her more tightly against him. He had been lying awake while she coaxed the embers, treading back carefully through each step of her conversation with the long-knife. Many of their English words had been unfamiliar; but between those that he knew and the tones of their voices, he pieced much of their meaning together.

Something false kept nipping at the back of his mind, though he was not sure if it lay in what they had said or in the participants themselves. He had felt it from the moment she spotted the stranger ducking in behind him. He had hoped she would be pleased, but he had not expected such a greeting to dance in her eyes. The long-knife, in contrast, held himself like a tightly reigned horse cautiously picking his way along a dangerous ledge. Determined to know why, Pacing Wolf considered accepting his guest's proposal until Small Doe distracted his attention. She was smoothing her hand up over his arm, warmly caressing every hill and valley.

Nestling his face against her hair, he meandered unhurriedly among the words she had used to describe him—admiring words that so swelled his heart, he had turned his back so they could not see. He would take her with them if he accompanied the long-knives. She would be of great use, but as he imagined the desire she might stir within an enemy, he discarded the idea.

What guarantee did he have that they would welcome the long-knives or consider their treaty? They were more likely to kill them, and him, and what would become of Small Doe then? No, he could neither take nor leave her. The assurances Marks-His-Face had offered concerning his daughters had been too weak.

When he nuzzled her soft ear lobe, she twisted in his arms and began tenderly exploring the firm muscles that spanned his chest. "Thank you for asking the long-knife to sleep here," she whispered. "He has promised to tell my parents I am glad I belong to you. I hope he will return their way soon."

Pacing Wolf lay his forehead against the crest of her hairline. He had worked out a hint of this from their conversation but to hear her clearly say so in his own tongue overwhelmed him. During the past three moons, he had noticed her eyes increasingly trailed him and her smiles held both sweetness and welcome. He also often inwardly recounted the grateful pride she had expressed to her book-god, but such freely offered affection exceeded anything he expected.

Women, young and old, admired his skill and all knew he could provide well. He had hoped these capabilities might secure her allegiance, but he had not thought himself capable of arousing anything deeper. Not once during nearly four summers had Among-the-Pines' mother offered him such tenderness. Unable to account for it, particularly considering the great suffering he had caused, he concluded it grew from the exceptional quality of her heart.

Most women store bitterness in a loosely covered earthen pot and ladle it out freely. She flings hers away like a bird she wishes to set free.

Toss all bitterness, rage, anger, brawling, and slander, out of your heart, along with all forms of spite.
Ephesians 4:31

Chapter 24

LIKE THE AIR BEFORE a cloudburst, the Sparrow Hawk village felt charged with excitement. Women scurried for shelter while packs of warriors prowled like wolves sniffing the wind for the scent of a herd. Small Doe did not see Pacing Wolf among them. He and the other revered leaders had sequestered themselves in Hair-Up-Top's lodge debating which war society should act as soldiers during the coming year.

As she wound between the dwellings, several clanswomen slipped from their husband's lodges and headed toward the very tumult others were trying to avoid. They were dressed in fine garments, highly adorned with costly shells or beads, as if they were untouched women anticipating the arrival of eligible warriors from another band—only these women were married and a few were as old as Small Doe's aunts or mother.

The nearest to her was nearly knocked down by a warrior riding up the central path crying out Hair-Up-Top's decision: the Foxes were to act as soldiers in place of the Lumpwoods. Small Doe sighed with relief. Pacing Wolf need no longer patrol while they traveled or be among the first to take a position against their enemies. Only one concerning question remained.

"When will we know whether Pacing Wolf has accepted one of the Lumpwoods' death-staffs?" she asked his grandmother.

"When the Lumpwoods stream from Hunts-For-Death's lodge, watch to see which two warriors take the head and which two take the rear of their procession. These four will have accepted the stakes. Hair-Up-Top will not accept one," she assured Last Woman, who had come out when she heard the crier. "He is too old to fight on foot."

Toward evening, the Lumpwoods did as Kills-Behind-Her-Dwelling predicted, singing loudly to inspire the assembling crowd. Small Doe craned her neck. Pacing Wolf was not at their procession's head, but before she could see who was bringing up the rear, they divided into four strands.

"What are they doing?" she asked his grandmother.

The old woman smiled. "There—the first in each line—they bear the new staffs."

Whether Hunts-For-Death had not offered one to Pacing Wolf, she had no way of knowing, but Small Doe felt weak with relief.

"Look!" Kills-Behind-Her-Dwelling nudged her. "They have chosen your husband to craft the new staff. This is an honor! Only one who has struck the first blow against an enemy is qualified to make it."[72]

"How can you tell?"

"See the birch rod he carries? Look at the top. He has bent it down to form a crook like the staff that hangs in your lodge beside his pipe. Remember? I described this to you the day Pretty Crow Woman pushed you into the lake. Crow-Face, the man who follows him, is the new staff-bearer."

"I do not know him," replied Small Doe.

"He lodges across the path with Those-Who-Live-Among-the-River-Banks. He is from the Whistle Water Clan, like Pacing Wolf's mother, and is a cousin. See, they are going into Short Neck's lodge."

As Pacing Wolf and Crow-Face ducked out of sight, the Lumpwoods sang taunts to the other war societies, and Kills-Behind-Her-Dwelling explained to Small Doe what her husband was doing.

"He will shave one of Short Neck's thinner lodge-poles to the proper size and splice the crooked birch rod one end, winding deerskin around the splice to secure two pieces tightly together. Lastly, he will wrap the whole staff with strips of otter-skin. Oh—he is already coming out! See? There is the new death staff. See the otter tails dangling down?"

Small Doe did, but she grew too interested in what her husband was doing to offer more than a cursory nod. He had grasped the curved end of the new staff, thrust it through the skins above the door flap where Short Neck's wives had pinned the lodge cover together, and was executing the steps of a carefully planned dance.

"One summer," he proclaimed when he had finished, "a Lumpwood handed me a staff like this one. I struck the first blow against the Flat Heads. He-That-Sees-All-Things looked down and saw the strike was good. It was clean. May Crow-Face follow my example! May arrows fly past without lodging in his flesh!"

When Pacing Wolf offered the death-staff to Crow Face, a riot of war cries arose; and once Crow Face launched into his own dance, the Lumpwoods broke into a fresh singing.[73] Small Doe beamed with pride. When she had first seen her husband's lance, she had been awed by his number of trophies, but many reckless warriors were brave. While she looked around at his clansmen, she caught a glimpse of the esteem in which they held him. If he opened his mouth to speak, his clansmen clamped theirs shut to listen.

Were this not proof enough, Small Doe noticed the woman she stood behind nudge her daughter. "Take note of this one," the woman whispered. "When Hunts-For-Death travels to his fathers, Pacing Wolf will lead our band. And when the sons you will one day bear have grown tall, he will lead our whole people. The spirits have told this to Old White-Belly."

As Small Doe glanced at his grandmother, she saw Kills-Behind-Her-Dwelling was not listening. The old woman had bent down to whisper in Little Blackfoot's ear. The child's eyes grew round as acorns, and as soon as the old woman straightened up, she hurriedly scampered off. Small Doe was curious to know what startled the child, but before she could ask, Kills-Behind-Her-Dwelling resumed her instruction.

"The Foxes make staffs also, as I told you already, but though the Muddy Hands and Big Dogs also choose champions, they offer them ropes instead of stakes."[3]

Once the crowd dispersed, Kills-Behind-Her-Dwelling accompanied Small Doe to her lodge, but rather than duck inside, she looked pointedly in all directions and turned back toward the central path. Small Doe was too relieved to wonder what her old friend sought. She had been trying to think of an excuse to turn her away without offending. She wanted to be alone with Pacing Wolf. Not only was she delighted he would not carry a Lumpwood death-staff, but also she wished to confess a happy secret she had been saving.

Although she had been afraid to grasp her hope too tightly, she was now certain the Lord had answered the request she made in the cave. Only once during her three moons on The-Cliffs-With-No-Name had she needed to dwell for a time in the Women's Lodge, and every morning lately, she had awakened feeling nauseous. Last Woman had guessed her secret. Earlier in the day, while plucking lance-tipped leaves from beneath tiny yellow flowers, Small Doe had needed to stop on the hillside to rest. Last Woman slid her a look of concern but then broke into a wide, knowing grin. Stretching her hands across Small Doe's abdomen, she felt its size and firmness.

"He come." Last Woman held up seven fingers, one crooked in half, followed by a gesture to signify the moon.

Small Doe nodded happily. "During the Moon of Frost on Dwellings."

"Man know?"

Small Doe shook her head. "I have probably confused him. The last time Hunts-For-Death sent him scouting over several nights, I slept in the Women's Lodge. I felt too embarrassed to admit I lacked the courage to sleep without him. This place is still strange to me and…I…I have learned painfully what can happen to a woman who is alone."

Small Doe touched the scar near the hairline, left by the gash she received when Pretty Crow Woman had pushed her in the lake; and when she noticed Last Woman's quizzical expression, she laughed at her own silliness. Without Little Blackfoot to translate, Last Woman may not have understood anything she had said.

Glancing at the drowsy sun, she turned her thoughts from that conversation to Pacing Wolf. *What is keeping him so late?* Nothing was working as she hoped. Once Little Blackfoot had finished Kills-Behind-Her-Dwelling's errand, she had slipped—unasked—into Pacing Wolf's lodge and been following Small Doe so closely she nearly tripped her several times. Kills-Behind-Her-Dwelling had come over also, and though Small Doe had hinted she hoped for privacy, both seemed determined to scoop their late meals from her cook pot. She did not have the heart to turn either away.

While Small Doe knelt to check her wilting leaves, a smile lit her face: Pacing Wolf was ambling toward her with a boisterous group of Lumpwoods. He grinned as their eyes met, quickening her pulse; but when he spotted several Foxes loitering across the path, his face turned to stone.

Small Doe wondered at the sudden change. The warriors had been standing between the lodges when she had last turned her roasting venison, but she had been far too preoccupied to pay them any mind. As her husband crossed the lengthening shadows, she read menace in his eyes, and his posture held the tension of a wildcat preparing to attack.

Small Doe could not make sense of it until, after she had brought the meat inside and was serving her husband, the door-flap flew open. Startled by such rudeness, she glanced up to find Goes-to-Battle dressed in his finest.

Little Blackfoot bolted past him, knocking into the two Fox warriors who were ducking through the opening. Evading the hands that shot out to grab her, she fell into the soft dirt, scrambled up, and dashed down the central path.

Small Doe looked at her husband, but his eyes, as hard as obsidian, were fixed on his handsome cousin. Goes-to-Battle did not seem to notice. He strode straight to the place she stood ladling greens and held out his hand. His expression held such tenderness, she peeked over her shoulder, and during that instant he closed the slight distance between them. Uncertain what he wanted, she handed him the bowl.

Goes-to-Battle smiled warmly and took it, but he set it out of the way. "I have come for *you*. There are three of us—your husband can do nothing. You will no longer live as his unwanted vengeance trophy. You will be my woman, chosen and prized."

As he reached toward her cheek, she stepped backward. She had never heard of such a thing, but three of his words stood out sorely: unwanted vengeance trophy. Shrugging them off, she turned to Pacing Wolf. She was stunned he would allow the man to speak and act so freely and hoped he would command him to leave. Instead, he levelly returned her gaze.

"My cousin is handsome. If you want him, go with him."

Small Doe could not credit her ears. "I…I do not want him," she sputtered. "I want you."

A hint of satisfaction flickered so swiftly through his eyes, she thought she had imagined it; but instead of tossing his cousin out, he resumed his meal, slowly chewing each morsel. When at last he had emptied his bowl, he glanced first at his cousin and then at the two Fox witnesses.

"You heard her—she does not want him. But if she has made his heart so weak he cannot live without her, he may have her."

Small Doe's legs began wobble so that she reached for a lodge pole to steady herself. "You…you cannot mean…not after…"

"Come," said Goes-to-Battle, raising his chin. "He will not stop you. You are my woman now."

"No!" cried Small Doe, shaking violently as she turned to her husband, "What have I…I done that you…you no longer want me?"

Pacing Wolf's gut so twisted, it took all his strength to stay seated. He would gladly risk his skin to keep her, but if he yielded, his clansmen would thrust him aside, and Short Neck's temper would toss them into peril.

Kills-Behind-Her-Dwelling wedged herself between them. "Leave her, you cocky fox-pup. She does not want you."

"You are old and cannot remember how desire feels." Pushing her away, he seized Small Doe's wrist and began dragging her toward the doorway.

"*Please!*" begged Small Doe, buckling her knees so her weight dropped to the floor. "Do not let him take me!"

Pacing Wolf sprung to his feet, but the flap again opened and Goes-to-Battle felt a sharp lance tip against his throat. "You go!" bit out the tall Blackfoot captive. Her eyes snapped as she pressed the flinty tip into his flesh, pricking his skin until drops of blood trickled into the beads hanging from his neck. His two Fox brothers were unwilling to touch her. All knew she was their Real Chief's last woman, and he would not be pleased if she or the babe within her were harmed.

Goes-to-Battle released Small Doe. "He may have her," he sneered, brushing his hands together as if ridding them of grime. "I do not need a cast-off captive."

Curling her knees to her chin, she wished once again that the earth would swallow her whole. *This was why Little Blackfoot would not leave me, and why Kills-Behind-Her-Dwelling refused my hints.* As a small, soft arm curved gently around her back, Small Doe turned to face her tiny look-out.

"You safe," whispered Little Blackfoot. "Bad warrior go. Mother go—dish food for Old White-Hair. I sit by door. Call help if more come."

"Thank you. Tell your mother I am grateful. She spared me much. Where is Kills-Behind-Her-Dwelling?"

"She go. Say Good Man make talk with friend-woman. Not stand between." As the child noticed Pacing Wolf scowling, she nervously slid outside to keep her promise.

What will become of me? Small Doe wondered, burying her face so he could not see her tears. *Lord, how could I have been so mistaken, and what of his small-thing growing within me? You heard him—he does not want me.*

Pacing Wolf stood frozen, at a loss for words to explain what he had said. No Sparrow Hawk woman would have expected any different. She would have admired the strength of his heart, felt proud that she was the object of another warrior's desire, and appreciated the freedom to make her own choice.

Squatting down, he wound his hand behind Small Doe's neck and gave it an affectionate squeeze, and when she did not look up, he ran his fingers down her jaw and lifted her chin. He wished he had not. Her eyes held the pain they had in the cave, and she dropped her head as quickly as he let it go. Not knowing what else to do, he demanded the one thing he hoped might please her.

"Read to me from your spirit-guide's book."

Furrowing her brow, she did as he bid, turning to a passage she knew well in Paul's letter to the Ephesians.[74] "Women, yield to your own warriors as you do the Lord, for a warrior is the head of his own woman just as God's Anointed is head of His own people. He is their Savior. As they yield to the Anointed One, so wives are to yield to their own husbands in everything."

As Pacing Wolf listened, he began to understand much that he had found pleasing. His dead woman had acquiesced to him only grudgingly, afraid he might disgrace her by casting her away.

"Warriors," she continued, "love your own women just as the Anointed One loves those who yield to Him. He gave His life to keep them for Himself and washed them clean with the water of His Word. He did this to present them to Himself as a glorious bride: pure and for Him alone, without spot or wrinkle."

As he pictured her graceful form as they washed each morning, he could not recall a wrinkle or mark of any kind, but when she read, "for Him alone," he shifted uncomfortably. Although, like this Anointed One, he had offered his life to keep her from the Blackfoot, he saw he had violated the book-spirit's instructions by offering her to his cousin.

"A warrior ought to love his own woman as he loves his own body. In caring for his own woman, he is caring for himself. No one hates his own flesh but nourishes and cherishes it. This is how the Lord cares for His followers. We are parts of His body, of His flesh, and of His bones. For this reason, a warrior must leave his father and mother and be joined with his woman: the two become one flesh. This is a mystery, to show how those who follow God's Anointed are joined to Him. So, every warrior must love his own woman as he loves himself."

Waugh! thought Pacing Wolf, clenching his jaw. *How can her book-god demand this? What if she turns bitter and begins to complain?*

He had eaten a belly full of carping from Jackrabbit, and his dead woman had been growing more like her with every rising sun. Had she not been murdered, he doubted he could have borne her sharp tongue much longer. Looking at Small Doe's slender form, curled up tightly like a turtle, all his protests died away.

She is less like my dead woman than the white men's blotchy naked buffaloes are like her namesake. But how does a warrior possess this…this love for his woman without becoming like a dog loping at her heels?

He had once known such a man and found him repugnant, as did all the Good Men of his clan. They had shut him out as if he had no kin, and no one could say what had become of him. As he thought of Small Doe's father and uncles, they did not strike him as weak, and each held the other in obvious esteem.

What would her spirit-guide have me do? He-Who-Made-All-Things created women to please warriors, not warriors to please women. I will keep her as long as she pleases me, and if she does not I will cast her out—it is my right!

Small Doe noticed his face had hardened, but she was not surprised. She had purposely selected the passage to point out his shortcomings. Instead of feeling satisfied, however, her conscience felt stricken. God had not given her The Book so she could use it as a weapon, and she regretted the defenses against it her selection had likely aroused. Even if she could retrieve the words, though, she could alter nothing. Her husband had made his feelings for her achingly clear.

A loud voice outside interrupted their thoughts, calling, "A Lumpwood's woman has come to our Fox brother of her own free will and is here for everyone to see!"

As the Foxes broke into a song, acclaiming their triumphant member, Never-Sits stuck her head inside Pacing Wolf's entry. "Mountainside's brother, Bull-Will-Not-Fall, has stolen Short Neck's youngest woman. Do you have any elk teeth you would like to sell? We need to prepare her wedding clothes."

Clearly baffled, Small Doe stared at her sister-in-law. "No, not one."

Pacing Wolf seized her wrist and pulled her out among his cheering rivals. Short Neck's youngest wife was riding down the path behind a proud Fox warrior. On her cheeks, she had painted the red stripes of a captured bride, and her gaze—once she located her husband—brimmed with insolence. Short-Neck held his head high, and the firelight reflecting off his eyes showed she had hurt nothing but his pride.

As Kills-Behind-Her-Dwelling sidled up to her, Small Doe asked, "Why does he do nothing? If my tribesman's wife was unfaithful, he would pull her from the horse and slit her nostrils."

"Why?" the old woman replied.

"Because she betrays him."

"Short-Neck is a cruel man. What woman—given a choice—would stay with him?"

"But he is her husband."

The thin old shoulders shrugged. "If he wished to keep her, he should first have learned to keep his temper."

Small Doe was as confounded by her friend's reply as she had been by her young neighbor's wanton behavior. Soon another cry went up, and the Foxes led a second, third, and fourth woman down the central path. Each looked about them triumphantly, as though they had counted an awe-inspiring coup.

Small Doe found the entire scene dismaying, but when she caught a glimpse of a young Muddy Hand whose wife rode away with a Big Dog, tears stung her eyes. Not only did his rivals mock his undisguised torment, but his society brothers also heaped up spiteful insults, declaring only the hungriest woman would want to warm his robes.

Small Doe wished she could assure him this was not so. Of all the men in the village, she admired him most. His features were ill-formed and he wore few trophies, but he possessed one quality that set him apart. He knew how to love.

"Come on!" called her old friend, tugging at her arm while their clanswomen moved across the path. Dragging Small Doe into a strange dwelling, she urged her to carry off a lovely antelope skin. "You can make Pacing Wolf a new breach-cloth, and look—here is an awl—you need one."

Small Doe refused both, handing them back to the man's little sister, who sat watching helplessly while her home was stripped bare. As soon as she could, she returned to Pacing Wolf's lodge and gathered up her few things. She felt relieved to escape the frenzy, but now that she was alone, she needed to consider where she might safely sleep. If this village belonged to the Allies, the dwelling would belong to her, but Sparrow Hawks considered lodges a husband's property.

Perhaps, she thought, *Kills-Behind-Her-Dwelling or Last Woman will shelter me,* but she quickly discarded the idea. Hair-Up-Top might not welcome another mouth to feed, and Kills-Behind-Her-Dwelling was likely to defer to her grandson. *Pacing Wolf once told me I am free. When Spotted Long-knife returns, I am sure he will be willing to take me home.*

Feeling a flicker of hope, she tucked her Bible safely into the folds of her doeskin dress and let her eyes roam over the remaining belongings. Each had been mended, made or tended by her hands, and each held its own memories. Searching the past days for anything she might have done to displease him, she wondered whether she would ever trust her instincts again. She had thought he had begun to love or at least want her.

As she was about to duck outside, Pacing Wolf ducked in. He looked surprised when his eyes fell to her bundle. He had hoped all she had witnessed outside might make her understand. Pressing his lips into a grim line, he glanced past her shoulder to her mirror still hanging on its peg.

"You do not want this?"

Small Doe shook her head. "When I use it, I will remember that you once…that I thought you…" She let the sentence drop, afraid he might rebuff or mock the fragile memory she voiced.

Snatching her bundle, he tossed it on the bed. "You are my woman."

Holding up his arms, he waited for her to remove his scalp shirt. Small Doe complied as she had each day, though she felt greatly confused both in mind and emotions. When he pulled her against him, she retreated to the secret place within herself. Hoping he might draw her out, he brushed his fingertips into the loosened hair above her ear; but in place of his shyly affectionate woman, he found a spiritless thing, devoid of protest but also of welcome.

You men, how long shall my honor suffer shame? How long will you love words that are useless and seek after lies? Know this: the Lord has set apart the godly for Himself. He hears when I call to him.

Psalm.4:2-3

Chapter 25

SMALL DOE WONDERED if the village would ever awake from its engulfing night-terror. Warriors from each society pulled wives from their rivals' lodges. Their brothers urged them on or reciprocated so heartily Small Doe was no longer certain which women lived nearby.

Neighbors she had greeted daily during the past three moons now lived with clans across the central path, and women she had rarely seen had taken their places. Most had purposely provoked their new partners' interests though several had needed to be persuaded. A few clanswomen had refused to leave their husbands and their wishes were respected, and one other, like Small Doe, required her womenfolk's aid.

On the sixth night, the revelries finally quieted, but only the most mundane aspects of Small Doe's life returned to normal. Evenings became torturous. Pacing Wolf continued to provide for Small Doe but was increasingly taciturn. She spoke even less. While offering her to Goes-to-Battle, he had uprooted all the tender shoots she had carefully nourished, and she did not know how to replant them. Even worse, she was uncertain if the rivalries might start up again and became nervous when she heard warriors approaching the lodge.

The days grew longer but little better. Pacing Wolf relieved her of his presence, frequently scouting, hunting or keeping council with Hair-Up-Top; but his dead woman's mother was like a cut on her hand that broke open during each new chore.

One cloudless afternoon, Kills-Behind-Her-Dwelling found Small Doe washing clothes with Last Woman. "The sun is growing warm," the old woman told her. "Leave your wash on a rock to dry and gather up your sewing. My guild meets today. Only the most skilled of hand are invited—and I wish to adopt you."

Small Doe smiled with pleasure. Though her husband's clanswomen had not been hurtful, they were distrustful of strangers, and she privately hoped that her skill with a needle might bring her a measure of acceptance. She might have gained it already had she possessed half of Does-Not-Cry's lively temperament, but even her own cousins back home considered her reserved.

Glancing apologetically at Last Woman, she hurried back to the village, retrieved a blouse she had been adorning, and met her husband's grandmother on the path. The corners of her lips curved into a smile as they stopped before a lodge belonging to Mountainside, Never-Sits' hulking husband. As she ducked inside, however, the first eyes she met glared cruelly in return.

"Why do you bring this Cuts-Off-Our-Heads daughter?" Jackrabbit demanded. "She is too young."

"She may be very young," nodded White Moccasins, the old woman who had pulled back Small Doe's dress to assess her thinness that first evening in Pacing Wolf's lodge, "but look at her work." Taking the blouse from Small Doe's hand, she displayed the quills worked artfully into the bodice. "Can Pretty Crow Woman do this?"

Jackrabbit grunted, cowed into silence by her husband's old aunt; but her frequent, disdainful looks at Small Doe provoked Kills-Behind-Her-Dwelling. "You have missed many stitches. Perhaps you should pay closer attention to what you are sewing or have your eyes grown dim?"

"When I was young like this unwanted woman," she retorted, "I could see the smallest spider crawling on my shoulder. Now, I see only far away—but who needs sight when I have stitched for so many summers?"

Never-Sits glanced sympathetically at her sister-in-law, but Small Doe seemed not to have minded the comment. Had the two been more intimately acquainted, she would have recognized that Small Doe deliberately maintained a pleasant expression. Inwardly, she gripped hold of a verse from a Psalm. *"I will guard my ways so that I do not sin with my tongue. I will bridle my mouth, so long as the wicked are in my presence."*[76] *Lord, help me show kindness to Jackrabbit. Her dim eyes may account for the poor seams in Pacing Wolf's lodge—perhaps I will offer her help with her mending.*

"The color of this blouse is lovely," commented another guild-member. "What have you used to dye it?"

Before Small Doe answered, Jackrabbit cut in: "Pacing Wolf despises the color."

"Does he?" asked White Moccasins. "I have lately seen him wearing a shirt of that shade. He seemed very pleased with it—or perhaps the admiration of his new, young bride adds pride to his carriage."

Small Doe's grateful eyes darted up to meet White Moccasin's, but a piteous wail coming from the central path grabbed each of the guild-members' attention. They rushed outside where a neighbor whispered, "Loping Coyote—his woman was found dead."

The woman next to Small Doe sharply drew in her breath. Forgetting her sewing, she ran toward the wailing.

"She is Loping Coyote's sister," explained the guild-member who had complimented the color Small Doe had dyed the blouse. "She knew his woman well."

A pall fell over the group as they wondered what had happened. "She has fewer summers than Otter Woman," remarked Never-Sits. "Is there sickness in their clan?"

No one could answer her question, but after a time, when they had returned to the lodge, Jackrabbit and White Moccasins resumed their conversation. "Pacing Wolf has reason to walk proudly. He has been talking with Marks-His-Face lately about Pretty Crow Woman. All know that he has wanted her since she was a girl, and she grows eager to live with him. Ask Never-Sits. She saw him in the shadows near our lodge one evening, warding off any Good Young Men who might desire to court her."

Small Doe felt sick while she waited for his sister's answer, but Never-Sits kept her eyes low and said nothing. *I have wondered where he spends his evenings,* thought Small Doe sadly. *I am not surprised. We eat our meals in silence and sleep without touching.*

Wanting desperately to talk with Jesus, she found a ready excuse to withdraw: she needed more quills to complete her design. When she entered Pacing Wolf's lodge, however, she found him talking with Hunts-For-Death. Their grave expressions announced they needed privacy, so she hastily snatched up her Bible and trotted to Kills-Behind-Her-Dwelling's empty dwelling. Opening to I Peter, she reread the verses she had so often of late.

> It is commendable to bear up under the pain of unjust suffering because you are conscious of God. How is it to your credit if you receive a beating for doing wrong and endure it? God's Anointed One left you an example. You were called to follow in His steps. 'He committed no sin, and no deceit was found in His mouth.' When they hurled insults at Him, He did not strike back. When He suffered, He did not threaten. Instead, He kept entrusting Himself to Him who judges justly.[77]

"Lord, I feel such a fool for thinking he might love me, but even before I loved You, You suffered for me so horribly I hate to read of it. Please give me this kind of heart toward Pacing Wolf—a heart that cares more for him than my own happiness—and give me the same for Kills-Behind-Her-Dwelling, Old Dog Woman, and my captive friends—even Jackrabbit. I am glad…"

"Small Doe?" called a child's hesitant voice. "You inside?"

She recognized it instantly and popped her head outside. "Yes. Is something wrong?"

Little Blackfoot bobbed her head up and down while tugging on Small Doe's arm. "Come. Friend small-thing—come fast."

Uncertain if Last Woman's small-thing was coming quickly or the child wanted her to run, Small Doe snapped her Bible shut. The child's short legs were surprisingly swift. When they entered the Real Chief's lodge, the tall Blackfoot was on her knees trying to raise herself off a soaked pelt. Beads of sweat dotted her brow, and the bottom portion of her skirt was wet.

"The Women's Lodge is not far," Small Doe assured her. "I will walk you there."

Last Woman nodded her head, more docile than Small Doe had ever seen her; but once they entered the place and she knelt on the straw, she clutched hold of Small Doe's arm.

"I have never helped bring out a potbelly," admitted Small Doe. "Let me get Kills-Behind-Her-Dwelling,"

"No!" Last Woman moaned. "He come!" Small Doe looked anxiously at Little Blackfoot.

"When did her pains begin?"

"By lake. You and old friend go."

Small Doe stood uncertainly, watching Last Woman's labored breathing. "Go, quickly. Get your Blackfoot kinswoman."

"No," the little girl replied. "Woman say no."

Knowing nothing else to suggest, Small Doe knelt on the straw and prayed aloud. "Lord, You are the Creator-of-All-Things, including this small-thing that needs to come out. Your word says You care for the widow and orphan. Please help…"

When she heard Last Woman groan deeply, Small Doe opened her eyes just in time to see her bear down, and then a tiny wet form wriggled out. Last Woman scooped it up, smiling broadly, and lifted her blouse to nurse. Pointing to the cord that connected her to the baby, she mumbled something to her young daughter.

"Cut," translated Little Blackfoot.

Too amazed for words, Small Doe did so; and after the babe finished his first meal, she took him in her arms. He was beautiful like his mother, and as Small Doe cleaned him she half spoke and half sang:

"O Father and Creator-of-All-Things, we give you praise for the tiny life I hold. Be his Protector and Guide throughout all his days and teach him of Your ways. May his arm possess strength and his heart possess courage, but most of all, make it like the heart of the mighty warrior, David—a heart fashioned after your Own."

Enrapt in the wonder of his birth, she paid little attention as her friend said something to her daughter; but when they had finished, the child touched her sleeve. "Warrior—he Pacing Wolf or dead lodge-man?"

"Pacing Wolf is my first husband, my only husband," she laughed. "The warrior David I spoke of was the Real Chief of a tribe that dwells across a wide water where the sun wakes up. He was handsome and brave, but most importantly, he walked in the steps of the Creator with a whole heart."

As Little Blackfoot translated the words, Last Woman looked greatly puzzled.

"Where find steps?" Little Blackfoot asked on behalf of her mother.

Small Doe smiled and opened the Bible she had dropped on the straw. "They are here. 'See. This is what their leader David said of Him:

> I love the Almighty because
> He hears my voice and my pleas.
> Because He listens to me,
> I will call on Him as long as I draw breath.
>
> I was caught in a death-snare,
> the pangs of the grave gripped me,
> I felt deep distress and anguish.
> Then I called on the name of the Almighty,
> "O Lord," I pleaded, "Save my life!
>
> The Almighty is generous and righteous,
> our Creator is merciful.
> He preserves the simple-hearted:
> when I was brought low, he saved me.
>
> Return to rest, my soul,
> for the Almighty has been kind to you.
> For You, Lord,
> have kept my soul from death,
> my eyes from tears,
> my feet from stumbling.
>
> I walk in the path of the Almighty
> in the land of those who live."[78]

"Who this all-mighty?" asked Little Blackfoot.

"My people call Him Old Man or the Eternal," replied Small Doe. "In this village, they call Him He-Who-First-Made-All-Things."

"Mother say she want meet. She want make talk like this Real Chief."

Small Doe was astounded. "She needs only to ask. He is here now and waits to welcome her."

"Then she want Him. She want walk His steps. You teach."

Smiling from ear to ear, Small Doe nodded. "That will make me very happy, but I go now to show her small-thing to Hair-Up-Top."

God, You are so good! Who could have known You would use this man-child's birth to open a way for me to speak of You! She felt such joy, she could barely keep a smile from her face as she wound through the many lodges. When she circled around to the tallest one, though, she froze. Mature males were arguing within. The white-haired leader would want to see the boy, but she could not interrupt him.

The voices stopped and the flap flew open so abruptly that Small Doe shrunk back against the lodge-cover. Four older men abruptly exited. One, who was strange to her, passed by without giving her a glance. Marks-His-Face assessed her curiously. Hunts-For-Death nodded a brief greeting, and old Hair-Up-Top warmly searched her face. Caught between gratitude and awe, she waited for him to speak.

"You are Pacing Wolf's woman," he stated while poking a finger into the small-thing's palm. "Who is this?"

Surprised that he remembered who she was, Small Doe looked up into eyes that welcomed her to speak. "Last Woman's small-thing—a son."

"She is well?"

"Yes." She smiled, pleased he had asked. "She rests in the Women's Lodge."

"Good," he answered, turning to address Hunts-For-Death. "You will name this small-thing and care for his mother when I die." Hunts-For-Death consented without remark and the old man turned back to Small Doe. "You find our ways strange."

Unsure whether he was making a statement or required an answer, she simply nodded.

"A young warrior's heart is a wild pony. If he does not train it well, it will carry him over gullies he does not wish to leap or toss him into brambles—and if he hits the ground hard enough, his head becomes confused. He will stagger about, unable to understand which way he is walking. Our people will not follow such a man. A worthy leader's heart is a seasoned war-horse, steady and unafraid. It refuses to bolt when it sniffs the scent of a mare carried by the wind and will not cower when it faces an enemy. Our people need such a leader—and only such a man will they follow."

Small Doe nodded politely, enjoying his fatherly tone and the notice he was paying her. Supposing he spoke about of Pacing Wolf, she hoped he would say more; but once Hunts-For-Death began speaking of a war party,

Small Doe slipped silently away. Returning to the Women's Lodge, she laid the infant in its weary mother's arms.

"Hair-Up-Top was very pleased with your small-thing and asked how you were. He is a kind man."

As Last Woman enthusiastically nodded, Small Doe began wondering what kind of man her Blackfoot husband had been. Not once, since Hair-Up-Top had restored the child to her, had she seen Last Woman display a single sign of mourning.

Pointing toward the bit of sky peeking through the smoke hole, Small Doe observed, "It has grown late. I need to finish my chores, then I will return with something to eat."

Weeping may last while the sun sleeps, but when the sun awakes, he fetches new joy.

Psalm 30:5

Chapter 26

PACING WOLF'S STOMACH tightly knotted. He had found his freshly washed hunting shirts laid out to dry beside the lake, but he had not seen Small Doe since she had ducked out of his lodge. For the brief instant that she had thought herself alone, he had read misery in her unguarded eyes and remembered well her habit of finding comfort in lonely places.

Searching the surrounding bank, he discovered several petite moccasin prints. They were old, most likely made before the waking sun had lapped up the dew, and blended inextricably with others as they neared the heavily trodden path. The sun had been high overhead when he had parted with Hunts-For-Death. It now cast a deep pink glow below the trees as it settled down to rest; and though his grandmother and sister had remained with their guild, both told him Small Doe had not returned.

Hunts-For-Death's grim tale nipped sharply at his feet. Bites-with-Dog had been scouting for buffalo when he spotted a small war party passing near the Lion's Head, all wearing Cuts-Off-Our-Heads' breastplates. While hurrying home to raise the alarm, he stumbled across Loping Coyote's woman lying in the woods, recently shamed, with her small-thing cut out of her mounding belly. Pacing Wolf was sure she was not the intended prey; she had simply been in the wrong place.

Bounding up the hill, he spotted his grieving tribesman atop a warhorse, a blue and yellow shaft held high above his head. He was calling loudly to his clansmen, impelling them to follow him toward the Lion's Head; and for an instant, Pacing Wolf found the impulse to join him overwhelming.

It is my duty, and I can protect Small Doe best by destroying Wild Dog. Yet, I will offer his party little while my heart is here, searching for her everywhere. I will follow afterward when I am sure she is safe.

As the sun began sinking down between the peaks, panic began biting him deeply. She had not gathered any twigs for their cook-fire or retrieved fresh water. Neither was like her nor could he plausibly explain her neglect. Recalling she had been clutching an item to her breast while she hurried out his door-flap, he raced back to his lodge and began rifling through her belongings. A pouch full of quills lay atop her unfolded sewing, but he could not find her book. Cold with dread, he cursed the day he had bought it, certain she had wandered off alone again to read.

She craves her god's thoughts as a doe craves water. Did the Blackfoot warrior teach her nothing!? I will break her of this habit if I have to beat her!

Striding down the central path, he eyed the periphery of the village for clumps of trees large and dense enough for Small Doe to hide in until he, at last, spotted her graceful form weaving briskly through the lodges. Relief replaced his panic, but such anger spewed up within him, it swallowed both whole. Seeing her veer toward the lake, he whipped his legs to a gallop.

Small Doe felt happier of heart than she had since Goes-to-Battle tried to steal her. Fearing she might become frightened, her grandmother had never allowed her to assist in her younger siblings' births, but she had found the process wondrous. Touching her flat belly, she thought of the small-thing nestled inside it and of Hair-Up-Top's enigmatic description of its father.

As rapidly approaching footfalls pulled her from her reverie, she turned to see Pacing Wolf sprinting so swiftly in her direction, he scattered dogs lured to cook-fires by the smell of roasting meat. She stepped off the path, not wishing to impede his errand; but as he drew nearer, she saw his face was dark with rage. Wondering what had happened, she stepped back between two dwellings, but rather than pass by, he roughly grasped her arm.

His chest was heaving as he pulled her to him, and beads of sweat were glistening across his brow. "I have told you before, but you refuse to listen! Stay with the other women and do not go off by yourself!" Yanking the Bible from her hand, he ripped apart the binding.

Gasping, she grabbed for the fluttering paper, but he gripped her shoulder, pulling her upright, and with a few swift movements snatched the fallen pieces and tossed them onto a neighbor's burning coals. Wrenching free, Small Doe lunged to pull them out, but the thin pages had shriveled and turned black before she could grasp them. Clutching her hands to her mouth, she watched the last remnant disappear into ash.

Small Doe staggered away and entering her husband's lodge fell to her knees in despair. "O God, how could he have done such a thing?" she murmured. "He robbed me of innocence, of dreams, of my heart, and now he robs me of my only consolation. I can bear no more!"

PACING WOLF MOUNTED his sorrel and took to the heights. He wanted to escape the sound of her crying. It accused him of cruelty, and now that his fears were relieved and his anger was subsiding, he could not shove its echo from his mind.

"What has happened to your woman?" asked Hair-Up-Top as Pacing Wolf joined him on the ridge. The old leader had spotted Small Doe setting out toward the lake to retrieve her clean laundry. Her head hung low between slumped shoulders, and she picked her way down the dusky path with unusual care. "Has she fallen in a wasp's nest? Her eyes are swollen. Here." He offered Pacing Wolf his spyglass. "They brimmed with joy when I spoke with her earlier."

Pacing Wolf quickly jerked his head around to peer into the leathery face. "You spoke with her? Where?"

"She brought me my last son—the small-thing the Blackfoot captive carried when you gave her to me. He is healthy and fine to look at like his mother."

Pacing Wolf dug his fingers into his horse's mane, feeling that the earth had given way beneath him. Straightening his posture, he turned away from the old man's gaze, but Hair-Up-Top's eyes missed little. They were as good as any youth's, and years of war had trained his skills of observation.

"You regret giving her to me?"

Pacing Wolf stared uncomprehendingly for a moment and then narrowly shook his head. "No—you make me see that I have been unjust to my woman."

The aged eyes studied him thoughtfully, but Hair-Up-Top was not willing to pry into his young friend's private matters. Trusting Pacing Wolf to set them aright, he wheeled his horse to a sentry's call.

"Look." The old man pointed. "The long-knife and his hairy-lipped brother return. They bring a yellow-haired woman with them."

Turning his mount also, Pacing Wolf studied the small party with renewing suspicion. The long-knife had seemed forthright enough when he last visited and would not bring a woman if he intended the village harm, but like a raven atop an eagle's nest, something about him did not sit right. The visit, however, was timely. If he carried word of Small Doe's parents, this would cheer her more than anything Pacing Wolf could think to do. Replacing her Book was impossible: the white trader was not likely to come again until the leaves began to turn yellow.

SMALL DOE PAID little attention to the warriors and children running toward the center of the village. She felt too desolate to care and was busy catching up on the chores she had neglected while assisting Last Woman with the birth of her son. As she dished up a bowl of meat to carry to the

Women's Lodge, she saw the youth who tended her husband's horses approaching her cook-fire.

"Pacing Wolf wants you to bring food to Hair-Up-Top's lodge," he told her.

Assuming the old leader was hungry and had no one to cook for him, she gladly heaped the bowl high, choosing the bits she suspected were the softest. She would return and bring Last Woman her portion afterward, but the youth shook his head.

"Not that." He looked from the dish to the kettle. "This—food to fill many bellies." As he had apparently been instructed to commandeer her whole supply, Small Doe could do nothing but watch him carefully lift the heavy, hot bag on its tripod and lug it away. "You serve," he called over his shoulder.

Small Doe felt irritated: Last Woman needed food to keep up her strength. Besides, Pacing Wolf was sure to be sitting among the number that gathered in Hair-Up-Top's dwelling. She could not decide which she felt stronger—sickness of heart or dismay from his recent outburst.

What, she wondered, *did I do to cause it, and how am I to face him amidst a crowd of warriors?*

As she considered Hair-Up-Top's earlier kindness, she grew ashamed and reminded herself that it was him, not her querulous husband, that she had been summoned to serve. Spotting Little Blackfoot running up the path, she called for the youth to wait, bent down and handed the full bowl to the child.

"Can you carry this?"

"No need. Old White-hair's girl take food. Mother eat."

Relieved and impressed with the old chief's thoughtfulness, Small Doe smiled. "Tell your mother I will not be able to return to her tonight. My husband wishes me to serve Hair-Up-Top."

The child nodded, smiling as if she already knew, and ran off swiftly toward the Women's Lodge.

When Small Doe ducked into the Real Chief's lodge, her breath caught in her throat: next to her husband sat Spotted Long-knife! She did her best to subdue her emotions, but as she noticed the blond woman behind him, she could barely keep from bursting. Corn-Tassels looked away, as her father had on his previous visit, but not before her cheeks started dimpling. Calmly rising, she followed her friend out of the dwelling and would have grabbed and hugged her if not for the watchful eye of Hair-Up-Top's daughter.

When they eventually found themselves alone, Corn-Tassels gushed, "We were overjoyed when Father and Joshua arrived home and told us they had found you, though Father had quite a time restraining your men-folk.

You must tell me everything! What is it like for you here? And tell me all about your husband."

Glancing cautiously toward the flap, Small Doe replied, "We will talk later—after they go to sleep."

Pacing Wolf noticed Small Doe's heightened color and the looks she kept darting toward the long-knife's daughter, and all at once his earlier suspicions met their answer. *She knows this yellow-haired woman.* Watching Corn-Tassels made him certain. Less used to hiding her feelings, her cheeks kept twitching. *They have come to take her.*

He tensed as he thought of the war party the scout had spotted that morning and wondered if they were connected with these long-knives. The older one had already repeated a desire to take him with them as a guide. Once they were safely away from this village, they could easily toss him from a cliff.

Leaning toward Hunts-For-Death, he whispered: "I wish the yellow-haired woman and her father to sleep in my lodge tonight. My woman speaks English and may learn what lives in their hearts."

"Good," Hunts-For-Death replied. "The other will stay again in my lodge."

AS THE MOON floated high in the sky, Small Doe lay watching her husband's ribcage slowly rise and fall with the breathing of deep slumber. Corn-Tassels had grown so still that Small Doe wondered if she slept also. Peering at the girl's dark form, she whispered very softly: "Are you awake?"

"Yes," Corn-Tassels answered immediately. "Is he asleep?"

"Yes," replied Small Doe, "but speak English in case he awakens."

"I cannot tell you how devastated we felt when we heard what had happened. It must have been horrible for you!"

"It was at first. I was terrified. He is a fierce and accomplished warrior, but he treated me well and proved thoughtful."

"Father said he is a good man."

"He cares much for his people and all say he will lead them one day."

"And you? Does he care for you?"

Small Doe hesitated. She wanted badly to confide in her friend, and yet she did not want her mother to know how miserable her life had recently become. Infusing her voice with as much cheer as she could muster, she replied, "He never beats me and is an excellent provider. Not once have I gone without anything I might need."

Corn-Tassels sighed. "I am glad. I hate the thought of you being unloved."

Small Doe quickly changed the subject, afraid she could not keep up her brave front. "How is Straight Arrows?"

"He is well. Everyone is well—your mother and father and the rest of your whole family."

"Have you married yet?"

"Last week, but I did not want to say so until I saw how you fared. I did not want to add to your troubles."

"What do you mean? We have wanted to be sisters for all of our lives."

Corn-Tassels hesitated. "I did not marry Straight Arrows. I married Joshua, the white man who is with us."

Small Doe lay silent for a time. "The young white man with hair hanging over his lips? You have never wanted anyone but Straight Arrows."

"Oh, Light Bird. Nothing turned out the way I planned, but I wanted to tell you myself. That is why we took care not to mention it earlier among your husband's cousins."

Small Doe, remembering the pain she had felt when Standing Elk married, could readily imagine how hurt her brother must feel. "And Straight Arrows—is he…is he…alright?"

"Yes. Truthfully, he is relieved! I think he was in as much a quandary as I was—expecting to marry me but then finding we no longer fit together. Do you remember that verse my mama used to say all the time?"

"Which?" asked Small Doe. "She said many…and what is this word—quandary?"

"A puzzling situation. Whenever she heard us talking of husbands and babies, she would quote Proverbs 16:1. Don't you remember?"

Small Doe smiled. "'The plans of the heart belong to a man, but the answer of the tongue is from the Lord.' I wonder if she knew inside herself all along."

"I do not think so. She was the most disappointed of all that we did not marry, but she had never imagined herself marrying someone like my father. I came home intending to marry your brother, but I just couldn't. I can't explain why. He is more handsome than ever and has earned tokens that show his courage, but I simply do not belong there anymore—not permanently. I feel like I went away an Ally and came back a white woman."

"What did your grandparents say?" asked Small Doe. "Joking Woman was very eager to have you home."

"They are not happy. I suppose it is natural for grandparents to want their grandchildren around them, and you know how they feel about Straight Arrows."

"Do you love him—the long-knife?"

"Yes—so much! I am continually amazed by how much I can love a man I have known this short while. I only met him in Boston the weekend before we traveled out here."

"I understand," sighed Small Doe, tears spilling over the rims of her eyes. She was glad that the darkness hid them.

"I would hate to be cut off from my family. You must be so lonely. Can you love him? I mean your husband… after…what he did?"

Small Doe lay silent, quite puzzled that her friend could have heard. Then, she realized Corn-Tassels meant his vengeance quest. "Wild Dog murdered his woman and son."

"But how do you stand it? How must you feel when…when he touches you?"

"He is fearsome, but he is also gentle, and his heart seemed tender toward me…"

"Seemed? Did something happen?"

"Will you promise not to tell Mother? I do not want her to worry or think me unhappy."

"Yes, of course."

"He no longer wants me."

"That is not possible—who would 'not want you'? Are you certain?"

"Y-es…he…"

Hearing her friend falter, Corn-Tassels touched her cheek. "You are crying."

"I…I always thought if I were the kind of wife Scripture tells us to be, any warrior would grow to love me, but it is not so. I do not understand it. Perhaps he does not like my smell or he finds me ugly. I am nothing like his dead woman."

"No one could find you ugly. Maybe he is still grieving. It has only been four moons. Give him time."

"I would, but I do not have it to give."

"What do you mean?"

"He just sat by as his cousin demanded that I go with him, eating his dinner as he waited for me to leave!"

"He did nothing?"

"No. At first, I thought he was testing me. This cousin is very handsome and has been kind and attentive. Once, he kept me from drowning."

"Do you…prefer him?"

"No!" cried Small Doe, her voice cracking, "but though I made that plain, Pacing Wolf still urged him to take me."

Corn-Tassels gasped. "What kind of warrior does such a thing?"

"I do…do not know. My father would have killed him rather than let him take my mother—or died trying."

"So would mine. So would any warrior I know."

"I feel so ashamed," sobbed Small Doe, unable to stop weeping.

"You are not to blame."

"Maybe there is some lack in me."

"Something is lacking in him!"

Small Doe nodded, though it was too dark for Corn-Tassels to see. "How do I respect him now? The Scripture is clear: a wife is to revere her husband, but how can I after what he has done?"

"He is not worthy of respect. A husband is to love his wife like Christ loves the church!"

"Yes, but that does not offer me an excuse to shirk my part. I just read those scriptures. They are two independent sets of instructions: one for wives and the other for husbands. If a wife may withhold respect unless her husband has earned it, what of the love she wants from him? May he stop loving her if she does something that does not please him? That is nothing like Jesus' example and would keep the whole passage from making sense."

"I never considered that," answered Corn-Tassels, pausing to mull over what her friend had said. "Yet, it reminds me of those passages about loving our enemies. Jesus could not have meant we should love them only after they loved us. If they did that, they would no longer *be* enemies! How did you fend off this cousin?"

"A Blackfoot captive I befriended rescued me."

"Oh," Corn-Tassels let out a deep sigh. "I will not tell your mother. She would just die."

"I wish *I* could die!" Small Doe choked out. "What will happen when the next man comes? His cousin paid me much attention, but I did nothing to encourage him—nothing!"

"Do you love him?"

"No. He was just there all the time, whenever I needed him."

"I mean your husband."

"Oh. Yes," she admitted. "I wish I could stop. Somehow, when he stole my body, he also stole my heart. I am a rabbit caught in a snare, unable to rest and unable to pull away."

Corn-Tassels smoothed a wet tendril back from Small Doe's cheek. "I've never known anyone so cruel."

"These warriors are not like ours. His grandmother, and even the white-haired leader we served tonight, tried to make me understand, but their ideas are so strange. They might as well have told me horses fly! I just cannot make myself comprehend them. They think a warrior proves his heart is strong by throwing his wife away."

"But it is just the opposite! Strength of heart and strength of commitment go hand in hand."

Small Doe shrugged, unable to defend the point. "I know, and there is more. This afternoon I learned he plans to take another wife—a girl he has long wanted—the sister of his dead woman."

Corn-Tassels felt as if her heart might break. She lay glaring at Pacing Wolf's back, so still now he might have stopped breathing. She wished he had. All words of comfort failed her, dropping from her mouth before they could form on her tongue. "I wish we could take you home."

Moonlight glinted off Pacing Wolf's eyes. Small Doe's words had cut through his heart. He longed to pull her into his arms, to tell her how desperately he desired her. He wished he could make her grasp the strength it had taken to sit calmly while his handsome cousin wooed her, the trust his restraint had earned him from the Good Men, and what the choice of him over Short-Neck might mean for his people's future. Even if his tongue was skilled, he could not tell her now. She would not believe him.

The darkness shall not hide from You, but the night shines as the day. Darkness and light are alike to You.

Psalm 139:12

Chapter 27

"WHAT HAVE YOU decided about this long-knife's request?" Hunts-For-Death asked as Pacing Wolf and he drew near the departing white men.

"Bites-With-Dog speaks the white man's language well. Let them take him or some other."

Hunts-For-Death nodded, turning his attention toward the yellow-haired woman who was chatting with Small Doe. "What has your woman learned?"

"Nothing," answered Pacing Wolf. His heart still stung from the feelings she had confided, but they were of no value to his Lumpwood father. "They made only woman talk."

Hunts-For-Death drew down the edges of his mouth, and Major Anderson, seeing them approaching, urged his horse forward. He had been grieved by all he had overheard and praying for a chance to reconnect Light Bird with her parents. "You are certain you will not come with us?"

Pacing Wolf shook his head. "My path is here."

"Then your woman," ventured the Major, a bit startled by his own audacity. "I would like to hire her. She would be of much use."

Corn-Tassels and Small Doe immediately stopped talking and grew perfectly still. Pacing Wolf did also as last night's whispers stampeded through his memory. He was not sure he could give her up. Pointedly glancing beyond the two long-knives, he observed, "You have few horses. How will you pay me?"

He cared nothing about the price; he wished to stall for time enough to sort out what lay in his heart. Her fear of other warriors was unfounded; the festivities were over. No one could lay claim to her again until the grass greened next spring, and few would have the nerve to try unless she offered them an invitation. His inability to reach across the chasm of her pain, though, might make her heart vulnerable to the appreciative looks of his rivals. Many were sure to want her—already she had gained a reputation for hard work and faithfulness.

This may be the answer to my prayers, thought Small Doe. *I could go home,* but instead of feeling happy, she felt as if a wildcat was ripping her apart. Her stomach dropped as she envisioned Pretty Crow Woman slipping in to take her place. Despite all that had happened between Pacing Wolf and her, they had become one flesh, and she no more wanted to be torn from him now than she did on the evening that Goes-to-Battle tried to take her.

"Name your price," Spotted Long-knife repeated. "I will bring you as many horses as you ask."

As Pacing Wolf turned toward Small Doe, he clearly read her turmoil but mistook its source. "Her services are not for sale—I give her to you. Go quickly—gather your belongings!"

While she watched him stride away, her feet felt as heavy as boulders. She wanted to run after him, to beg for him to reconsider, but they would not move. Besides, she had begged him to keep her before and gained nothing.

"May I first say good-bye to two friends?"

Major Anderson assented readily, but the look in her eyes made him doubt what he was doing. *She is the man's wife, but I cannot look the other way while he passes her from warrior to...*

The Major left off his thought as their white-haired leader approached him with another warrior. "This man is called Bites-With-Dog. He is a Good Man and knows your tongue well. When my hair was black, the lost son of Big Bowl, who led the moving band, came back to us from the white man's land.[79] Bites-With-Dog used to dog his heels."

The man's ability to speak English is hardly the point, thought Major Anderson, but after pressing Pacing Wolf to join them for this purpose, he could hardly decline this other's offer of service. "All right. As soon as Pacing Wolf's woman has gathered her belongings, we will head out."

Small Doe took Corn-Tassels by the wrist. "Come quickly. I want you to meet Kills-Behind-Her-Dwelling and Last Woman."

As they weaved hastily through the lodges, Major Anderson could not help remembering them as little girls.

"Kills-Behind-Her-Dwelling," he heard his *niece* call. "May we come in?" At once, the girls ducked into the lodge and out of his view. Glancing at his guide, he realized how inconvenient the man's presence would prove. In addition to being an unnecessary expense, they would need to keep up their charade—at least until she was safely home. He did not want the man slipping away and raising a war party against them.

As Small Doe looked into Kills-Behind-Her-Dwelling's dear, wrinkled face, tears prickled her eyes.

"What is this?" the old woman asked when one of them escaped its bounds. "Never once, in all these moons of sorrow, have I seen you cry."

"I have come to say good-bye, Grandmother."

"What do you mean, good-bye? What of Pacing Wolf? Does he go also?"

"No. He has given me to this woman's father." She indicated Corn-Tassels. "You know how it has been between us since Goes-to-Battle tried to take me."

The old woman staggered backward. She knew perfectly well this was no wish of his. Surely, Small Doe had mistaken something he had said. "Who will fetch my firewood and haul my water? How will I eat?"

"Perhaps his dead woman's sister will help you. Jackrabbit said he courts her."

"Pah! Do not believe all you hear. Pacing Wolf loathes Pretty Crow Woman!"

"He does not tell me what he feels, but if he ever speaks of me, please let him know that I loved him. I love you, too, and deeply appreciate all that you have done for me."

Turning quickly, Small Doe ducked out, leaving Corn-Tassels to scurry out behind her. Longer of limb, her friend caught up quickly and they entered the Women's Lodge together. Small Doe knelt down next to Last Woman, who smiled at her welcomingly and caressed the tiny Blackfoot infant's head.

"Lord of all creation," she prayed aloud, "You are not confined as we are to one village or another. Watch over this little one and his dear mother and sister. Please show Yourself to them in a way they cannot mistake."

Once she had kissed the small-thing's forehead and hugged his sister tightly, Small Doe stroked their mother's frowning brow. "I am going back to my people," she told her plainly, "but you must tell no one this is where I go."

"Good Man's small-thing grow in you. You tell him?" asked Little Blackfoot for her mother.

"He has given me to this woman's father," she explained, bringing Corn-Tassels forward. "She has been like a sister to me since childhood and her father like an uncle. They will see me home safely."

"Good Man not want?" Last Woman asked again, her brow perplexed as she pointed to Small Doe's belly.

"He does not know and you must not tell him, or he may come to claim it. I am returning to my mother, as Little Blackfoot returned to you. Would you have me stay where I am not loved? Could Little Blackfoot keep watch by his door always?"

Last Woman shook her head. "Good Man," she pronounced carefully, "want Small Doe. Good Man want small-thing."

"I have no choice, and now I must go. Remember what I told you—ask the Eternal One to make Himself known to you. Thank you for all you have done."

"Mother not do," Little Blackfoot translated. "You she thank."

"She has done far more than she knows," Small Doe told her. "Before she came, my days were spent mostly alone; and if she had not kept me from Goes-to-Battle, I would be with him now. Tell her I will never forget her and will pray for her each night—and for you."

As she ran her hand down the back of the child's head, the little girl threw her arms around her and clung tightly.

"Let me go now," implored Small Doe, "before I lose my courage."

When Small Doe's voice began cracking, Last Woman was overcome with sorrow, but she pressed her lips together lest she make it harder for her friend.

Drinking in one last look at the tiny family, Small Doe ducked out before her face began to crumple. "They are waiting," she murmured to Corn-Tassels and ran up the hill quickly to hide her struggle.

Gathering her few belongings, she laid out Kills-Behind-Her-Dwelling's wedding dress on Pacing Wolf's bed and left a breastplate she had recently woven to protect his chest on his willow headboard. When she came to the mirror, however, she paused. *Using it will bring me pain, but at least I will remember that he...that I once...briefly pleased him.*

When she stepped out into the bright sunshine, she stopped. Her white pony was waiting for her, wearing a finely carved wooden saddle of a Sparrow Hawk bride and an intricately fashioned bridle. She did not know where Pacing Wolf had kept them—they had not been in his lodge. Feeling as if her heart might burst, she cast her eyes about to gain one last look at his face, one last chance to find something other than indifference.

He was nowhere to be seen. Having no other choice, she mounted the mare and guided her into line behind the others; but all the way out of the village she kept listening, hoping against hope that he would race up, grab hold of the bridle and turn her around. She heard only the sound of her horse's hooves.

HIGH ATOP THE ridge, Pacing Wolf followed the little party with Hunts-For-Death's spyglass. He was tired of causing her misery. He hoped the saddle and bridle would whisper that his heart had not been cut from stone and that he had wanted her to ride proudly behind him like the other brides. Urging his sorrel down the slope, he decided to trail behind them instead of the vengeance party hunting Wild Dog.

I will not force you to stay, but I will see that the long-knives deliver you safely into your old storyteller's arms.

With His feathers, He will cover you, and under His wings give you refuge. His faithfulness will be your war-shield and hiding place.
Psalm 91:4

Chapter 28

During the Moon of Making Fat

BITES-WITH-DOG, aware of the renegade shamers, led the long-knives and two women along the Stinking River past the holes in the earth that spewed water toward the sky. From there, they followed the Wind River and turned east toward a territory unlike anything Small Doe had ever seen. Mountains gave way to flat-topped ridges that wore striped war paint. They sprung toward the sky in peculiar shapes, and slender spires jutted up here and there like scouts scanning the horizon. As these melted into lowlands, they saw sporadic mounds painted to match their taller brothers.

Crossing the prairie was tiresome, but they made excellent time and arrived at the great falls near the Place of Pipes in a few days. No one had expected them, and though the sentries easily identified the Major and his entourage, they did not give much thought to the additional doeskin-clad woman. They were far more interested in identifying the foreign scout until a group of young cousins fetching their mother's water happened across the tired little party's path.

Talks-to-Birds dropped her water-sacks. "Light Bird! That is Light Bird!" she squealed excitedly, rousing the entire village as she ran to Brought-Us-the-Book's dwelling.

In hopeful wonder, women and even warriors poured out of their lodges or ran from the woods or the river; and as they neared their lost daughter, many broke into dances of glee. Their feet slowed, though, as they crowded close enough to peer into her much-missed face. She looked wan, and her smile, though brightly genuine, displayed defeat as well as happy relief.

"What did he do to her?" her mother whispered to Valuable Woman as they pushed through the crowd. "She looks nothing like your husband described."

Before her friend could answer, Small Doe leaped to the ground, plunged into her mother's arms, and clung to her tightly. Preying Eagle and her brothers circled closely around her, their joy warring with a powerful urge to mount a vengeance party. She no longer possessed the look of a girl full of hope and promise, nor did she wear the contented expression of a well-loved bride. She appeared old beyond her summers, a shattered ghost of her former self. At once, the crowd turned on Bites-With-Dog, yelping war cries as they yanked him from his mount.

"Stop!" cried Small Doe as their moccasins thudded against the Raven-Enemy's sinewy muscle. "He has done nothing!"

Her voice was no match for their pent-up fury, so she tried to wrench aside a younger cousin. Major Anderson leaped quickly from his saddle, also shouting. "This man is in my employ; I promised…"

Drowned by the din, his pleas also fell unheeded until Running Deer, Old Many Feathers, and Wooden Legs shoved through the throng. Interposing themselves between the newcomer and their many grandsons, they waited for the frenzied cries to quiet.

"Children, friends," Old Many-Feathers addressed them gravely. "Hear Spotted Long-knife. He has promised this man protection. Would you force him to break his word? I, too, burn with rage and share the vengeful impulse you wrestle to control, but Jesus paid for this man's sins just as He paid for ours—would you count His death as worthless? Let us go about our duties, and when this daughter of ours is ready to part from her mother, we will discover how everything is with her."

The old elder helped Bites-With-Dog to his feet as the crowd dispersed to their chores or homes. "I am sorry. My young niece is loved deeply by the whole band."

Nodding mutely, Bites-With-Dog watched the odd assortment of women leading Pacing Wolf's woman away. The one she had called mother wore hair the shade of a buffalo but owned eyes the color of a lake. On Small Doe's other side walked a woman whose braids were silver. Huddling around them all were the young yellow-haired woman of the hairy-lipped long-knife, another with braids the color of a red fox, and several plump, gray-streaked grandmothers. A party of men, some his protectors and some his assailants, accompanied the women into a large colorfully painted lodge.

Once they disappeared into Brought-Us-the-Book's dwelling, they fussed over Small Doe with all the affection her heart had craved for nearly four moons. After ascertaining that her health was sound, most of the men-folk went in search of Spotted Long-knife and spattered him with so many questions that he held up his hand for them to stop.

"She has not spoken much," the Major explained. "Something clearly took place between my visits. I gather a matter of repellent customs. On impulse, I asked if I could hire her, but her husband insisted I take her without payment. I know nothing more."

Despite their desire to give her time, they could no more restrain their joy than will themselves to quit breathing. Aunts and cousins brought special treats they had been saving for just such a celebration and laid them near Brought-Us-the-Book's door, and so many people inquired after her, the amassing assembly grew huge.

"I will go outside," Small Doe offered. "They are kind to care and I have missed them deeply."

Brought-Us-the-Book did not resist her daughter's wishes, hoping it might do her good, and Small Doe's grandmother and aunts nodded with approval. Once outside, Small Doe smiled shyly. She had not expected so many people. Eating a bit of each dish they offered, she then passed it to whoever stood next to her until one after another began calling out their thanks for her to God. Wrestling down the urge to retreat inside, she gazed into faces so full of love and compassion that she wanted to do nothing to dampen their joy.

BENEATH THEIR COVERS late that evening, Preying Eagle curved around Brought-Us-the-Book's back. "Has she told you what happened?"

"Very little and nothing of substance."

Small Doe was obviously asleep, but Brought-Us-the-Book suspected her sons listened eagerly from their pallets. She wished she had something more to tell.

"I just do not understand it. Spotted Long-knife had told us that her husband was a decent man and that she admired him greatly. What could have brought about such change? She seems utterly broken."

"Is she still married?" asked Follows-His-Shadow, Small Doe's seven-year-old brother.

Their mother shrugged. "I am not sure."

"Then what will become of her when Father dies?"

"She will live with me, like mother," Straight Arrows answered.

"Give me permission," offered Pretty Face, "and I will rouse a party to hunt him down. Spotted Long-knife now knows where he lives. Once we have put him in a shallow grave, no one can question her right to marry."

"You boys are like Spotted Long-knife's wagon on an icy hill," scolded their father, "slipping ahead of the horses. Old Many Feathers is right. We must seek the Lord and give her time. She owns no more summers than she did when she left us."

"She looks as old as Rising Wolf Woman, who already has two children," persisted little Follows-His-Shadow.

"She is very tired," his mother replied patiently. "When rest and love heal her spirit, you will think her young again."

"Enough talk," Preying Eagle decreed. He was having too much difficulty with his own emotions to rein theirs in also. "Go to sleep."

SMALL DOE ROSE before dawn the next morning and set about her usual chores. She gathered wood and water for her mother and grandparents and prepared their breakfasts without being asked. Their washing, however, she avoided. It would keep her too long in one place, encouraging conversations she did not desire. She was still confused by all that transpired and needed time before talking.

Even with the Almighty, she felt hesitant, though she had difficulty determining where her malady with Him lay. The Scriptures clearly promised He would draw near to her as she drew near to Him,[80] but she could not bring herself to do so. Her old Bible, which her mother returned to her that morning, brought her little joy. Verses such as "You of little faith," leaped out to accuse her every time she bent it open, leaving her with the feeling she had failed at everything.

As rest and love began bolstering her confidence, her thoughts started to swing in the opposite direction, filling her with questions about His tender care and faithfulness.

Why did the Creator let this happen? What purpose have I served? Perhaps He was asleep or considers me useless...

Round and round her thoughts went until she finally could not stand them any longer. Laying her cheek against her mother's heart, she spilled out her self-doubt and sorrow.

Brought-Us-the-Book felt so grieved, she had trouble responding. "Are you my child?" she asked when she finally found her voice.

Small Doe nodded against her shoulder.

"If you neglected to gather our sticks or fetch our water, or even if you ruined a garment I asked you to mend, would you still be my daughter or would I love you any less?"

She felt Small Doe shake her head, no.

"If I, who am so flawed, still love you dearly though you fail, can The Creator love you less? He loves you infinitely more than I do."

"You might feel disappointed in me."

"Only if you stubbornly chose to rebel—and that, more than anything, for your sake, not mine. I know that disobedience would only bring you pain. Of what does your heart accuse you?"

"Perhaps if I had more faith."

"If you have too little, where can you find more? Paul says our measures of faith comes from God. Did He fail you?"[81]

"No, but perhaps if I had been a better wife…if I had not grown angry with Pacing Wolf or felt hurt…or if I had loved him better…maybe then he would have loved me."

Brought-Us-the-Book closed her eyes, trying to tamp down both grief and frustration. "Satan accuses you, not the Holy Spirit. You would be less than alive if you had not felt those things. Hatred and holding bitterness are sins, but I already am confident you have not walked those paths. If you had, you could not have gained the happiness Spotted Long-knife noticed when he first found you. What happened between his visits?"

As she listened to her daughter's answer, she purposefully slowed and deepened her breathing. She was glad Pretty Face was not present; even Preying Eagle would not have been able to restrain him. *How could this man treat her this way? Lord, you said to forgive our enemies, but I will be able to forgive her captor only with Your help. It is one thing for someone to treat me badly…but to see what he has done to my precious child!*

All at once, she caught a glimpse of what her heavenly Father might have felt as He watched the way men treated His Son. Putting this aside to think on later, she asked, "Why did they kill Jesus? Because He failed to love them well? Even now, people cast Him away and then blame Him for the troubles that result. The fault lies in your husband's heart."

"But if Jesus knows the end from the beginning, why did He allow Pacing Wolf to snatch me? Besides reading the Bible to my husband, I spoke of Jesus with only one woman—and that was the day before Pacing Wolf gave me to Spotted Long-knife."

"He snatched you to sate his appetite for vengeance. Still, I am convinced that the Almighty works through us in ways of which we are not aware, ways that result from our obedience but far outstrip our imaginations. Naomi felt as you do when she returned from Moab. She even told the women to call her Bitter. Yet, God used her to bring about the birth of King David and even the Messiah.[82] She could not have foreseen this; she simply did as God directed by making her kinship to Boaz known. Joseph also[83]. As he obeyed God moment by moment, he surely did not imagine himself second only to Pharaoh, but we can see God planned that all along."

"You think God may have used me there even if I cannot see how?"

"I am certain He did—not because I am confident in you, though I am, but because I am confident in Him."

As Small Doe nestled gently against her, Brought-Us-the-Book felt her whole body relax. Both mother and daughter breathed in deeply and calmly, thankful they were together and each beginning to feel separate but related hope: the mother that her daughter would heal, and the daughter that God could use her, even in her weakness.[84]

AS THE HERDS became fat off the plentiful grass, Small Doe began smiling more often, but she still asked her mother to keep what she had shared to herself. She waited next to Valuable Woman's lodge, determined to do the same again with Corn-Tassels.

"Of course," replied Corn-Tassels to her request. "I respect your privacy, but my father already knows. He woke up while we were talking and asked me about it the next day. That was why he pressed your husband to sell you."

As Small Doe reverted to the pained look she so often wore, Corn-Tassels wished she had said nothing.

"My mother knows also. She will tell my father, but I do not like to think of others talking about me."

"Telling them would stop the gossip."

Small Doe's head shot up. "What gossip?"

"You know how people are. If you do not give them the entire story, they fill in the empty parts for themselves."

"What have they been saying?"

Corn-Tassels shrugged uncomfortably. "The kindest say your husband cast you out because you are the daughter of his enemy."

"And the others?"

Corn-Tassels looked down, wishing she had been more guarded.

"Tell me!"

"The cruelest say he found you displeasing—but no one believes that."

Small Doe opened her mouth but quickly shut it again, appalled that any who follow Jesus would be so unkind.

"Have you thought about suitors?" Corn-Tassels asked. "Before he courts you, a warrior will want to know what happened."

"Suitors?" The possibility had not yet occurred to Small Doe. "I am married and carry…" Small Doe stopped, not wishing to remind Corn-Tassels of the little Sparrow Hawk growing within her. Wild Dog had said her offspring would be vermin.

"Your husband gave you away. No one would blame you if you married someone else. Before my father and Joshua left this morning, Running Deer sought his counsel about it."

"They have gone—and Bites-With-Dog also?"

Corn-Tassels nodded. "They are visiting the Grass-Thatch-Dwellers."

"I am glad," confided Small Doe. "Not glad that your father and husband are away but to be free of Bites-With-Dog. He watches me often, and I am not sure what he wants."

"I noticed this also and do not trust him. He disappeared too frequently and for too long a time while we were on our journey."

"Yes. At first, I thought he needed privacy or that something had unsettled his stomach. What did Grandfather ask?"

"What The Book says about your situation. The verses Father showed him say you are not bound."[85]

Small Doe frowned. She knew her friend meant well, but she could not brush aside her moons with Pacing Wolf as if they had never happened.

"I should not have said anything—about either. Anyone who knows you also knows the sort of wife you would have been."

"Let them say what they will. He-Who-Sees-All-Things knows my heart—but I will not marry another. I belong to Pacing Wolf."

Not knowing what to say, Corn-Tassels repeated something she had heard often: "Give yourself time. You may feel differently one day."

Time, however, was something Small Doe was not to have.

Answer me when I call, O God of my righteousness! You have offered me room when I was in distress. Be gracious to me and hear my prayer.

Psalm 4:1

Chapter 29

WHEN SMALL DOE ARRIVED at her mother's dwelling, she found Standing Elk, the desire of her girlhood, waiting with a courting blanket. He smiled sheepishly in response to her widening eyes and spread the blanket open in welcome.

"Come. Your father has given me his consent."

"I cannot," replied Small Doe, wondering if Corn-Tassels had been trying to prepare her. "And how can you? We are both married."

Standing Elk's smile faded. "While you were with the Raven-Enemy, I-Am-Savior called my woman home to Him. Our potbelly was long in coming and she grew too weak."

"I am sorry," murmured Small Doe, her face crumpling with genuine sorrow. She had felt pricks of jealousy toward his wife, but she had never wished her ill. "I did not know."

"My sons need a good mother. Perhaps the Lord returned you to answer my prayers."

"There are other women in our village."

"Other women," he repeated, "but not a little bird whose chirping has always made me laugh. Please, come inside."

Recalling happier times, Small Doe almost wished she could. She would like to have offered him comfort. Unsure it would be right, however, she stalled. "Let me first speak with my father."

"Then I will come tomorrow evening."

She curved her lips subtly in reply and then ducked directly into her mother's dwelling. Finding her alone, she asked, "Why has Father given Standing Elk permission to court me?"

"Your father wants more than sadness to occupy your heart. Standing Elk's little potbelly will remember no mother but you, and the other boy is still quite young—his mother will also soon flee his memory. He is much like his father," she added with a twinkle, "whom I recall you pined after for nearly a moon."

"I was a child then and owned a child's heart. I do not possess it any longer."

"It was not so long ago. Four summers. He is older than we would have liked for you, but sometimes older warriors make better husbands—their heads are full of more than proving their courage."

As Brought-Us-the-Book watched her daughter's face grow somber, she remembered an occasion on which her own father had offered her the same advice. She had thought it exceedingly unwelcome. This courtship was not her idea, but she learned long ago to trust her husband—and also God's ability to guide his heart.

Mulling over her mother's words, Small Doe admitted, "My husband possesses one more summer than Standing Elk does and is, as you say, already confident of his courage. He is much concerned with the welfare of his people."

Brought-Us-the-Book was glad Light Bird could speak of him more freely; unopened wounds retain their poison. As she was about to encourage her to say more, though, Preying Eagle ducked into her dwelling.

"Where is Standing Elk?" he asked his daughter. "He was here waiting when I left."

"He promised to return tomorrow," she answered. "I told him I wished to speak to you first, and he granted this."

"Good. I wish you to accept his blanket."

"How can I? Would you have me commit adultery?"

Preying Eagle compressed his lips into a hard line. "Your Raven-Enemy husband ended your marriage."

Pulling out his Bible, he turned to the seventh chapter of First Corinthians and placed his finger below the fifteenth verse "'If a person who does not walk in Jesus' shadow wishes to part with his spouse, let him do so. The believing brother or sister is not bound. God has called us in peace.' See—you bear no guilt."

Small Doe's heart recoiled and fastened on a verse she noticed that came before it. "But look at what it says here: 'The unbelieving husband is sanctified through his wife and the unbelieving wife is sanctified through her believing husband.' This one below it also: 'for how do you know, wife, that your husband will not follow you onto I-Am-Savior's trail?' I did not want the Raven-Enemy, but he and I have become one. Can I pretend now that we are not?"

Brought-Us-the-Book saw her daughter's point and suspected where her malady lay: Light Bird loved him. *Still, he cannot love her, whatever she feels, or he would not have sent her away.* "Have you read the verses that come before them all?" she asked. "Look at thirteen: '...if a woman belongs to an unbelieving warrior who wishes to live with her, she should not leave him.'"

Small Doe brightened. "Yes. You see! His wife is to remain married to him."

"'*If he* wishes!'" answered Preying Eagle. "He gave you away."

Small Doe had no answer. *Father is right. Pacing Wolf clearly does not want me... and yet, I cannot do the thing he asks. It is unfair to Standing Elk.*

"I do not know why the Raven-Enemy sent Light Bird away," shrugged Brought-Us-the-Book, "but she is clearly in love with him."

"How does that matter," Preying Eagle retorted, "since he ended their marriage? She also once loved Standing Elk—I will allow him to court her."

Seeing Preying Eagle had come to a firm decision, both mother and daughter exchanged glances, each agreeing with the other to drop the matter. They would take it, instead, to the One who holds even the mightiest warrior's heart in His hand.

RAIN FELL IN torrents, but Small Doe did not mind. It might keep Standing Elk away. Since Spotted Long-knife had brought her back, she had been in constant company with her mother, grandmother, or Corn-Tassels. She loved them all dearly but could not bring herself to confide how often her heart ached for Pacing Wolf. Although her mother was sympathetic, she would not oppose her father. Two Doves so frequently gave thanks for her return that Small Doe was afraid she might hurt her grandmother's feelings by admitting she was unhappy, and Corn-Tassels thought Pacing Wolf was the devil wrapped in man-skin.

Smiling sadly, she thought, *In Pacing Wolf's village, I longed for my family. Here, I long for him. I am as I feared in the cave: a bird without feet, unable to find rest. I wish I could talk with Quiet Woman.*

Taking a handful of quills, Small Doe slipped out of her mother's dwelling and into her old aunt's. Several other women had the same idea, so Small Doe contented herself with studying Quiet Woman's face. It shared few features with the other faces in her dwelling. Although this aunt was older than Two Doves and Joking Woman, her skin was smoother and her face was much more round.

Has her plump flesh smoothed out the wrinkles, Small Doe wondered, *or do Puckered-Toes own fewer lines?*

Glancing from Quiet Woman to Corn-Tassels to her mother and younger aunts, she mused, *We are an odd assortment. Corn-Tassels and I were born in this village, but our hearts are divided between two peoples. Quiet Woman, Mother, and Valuable Woman were all born elsewhere, but their hearts dwell wholly here. Only Grandmother and Joking Woman possess one people, one place, and one heart.*

When Brought-Us-the-Book noticed her daughter's eyes lingering on their elderly aunt, she caught Two Doves' attention. Exchanging knowing glances with both Valuable Woman and Joking Woman, each made excuses to venture into the downpour—all but Corn-Tassels, whom her mother had to call.

Alone with Quiet Woman, Small Doe continued weaving in silence until she mustered the courage to murmur softly, "Did you yearn long for your first husband when my old uncle carried you off?"

The old woman took time to reflect before answering. "I hated Many Feathers at first—my brother's scalp-lock hung from his lance, but he was so handsome and very patient. My first husband was a great leader among my people, but he was hasty and rough—and older than your grandfather is now. Do you long for the Raven-Enemy?"

Small Doe nodded. "I have wanted to talk with you—even before—when he first snatched me. I do not know what I would have done then, had I not remembered your advice."

"The heart must survive, little one, even in circumstances we would not choose."

"My cousins do not understand. They see him only as an enemy, and I am afraid if I confide my feelings they will think I am not loyal to our people."

"They are young and think as you once did, but your heart has grown older than the body that holds it."

"Will I ever stop hurting?"

Quiet Woman shrugged. "I cannot know. Many women own aching hearts even while they share their dwellings with their chosen warriors. I will tell you what I have learned: toss your hope up onto Jesus alone. No matter where you make camp or what changes the passing seasons bring, He will hold you as fast as a sturdy lodge pole thrust firmly into the ground."

"I have done this...or at least I think I have," Small Doe answered, not sure she fully grasped her old aunt's comment, "but my heart aches still."

"It often will. David cried: 'My life is eaten up by anguish and my summers by groaning.'[86] Walking Jesus' path does not free us from hardship, but age offers more advantages than youth. When my granddaughters were little, their hearts were full of games and the dolls their uncles had carved them, but as they grew older these no longer satisfied.

They now delight in the dresses their mothers and I make, how they look in them, and which warrior's eyes they might catch. Soon, they will grow round with little potbellies and chase after laughing children who flee from them with glee."

Looking up from her weaving, she saw she was only confusing her grandniece. "This enemy warrior, did you love him from the first?"

"No," Small Doe replied. "He frightened me."

"But by the time Spotted Long-knife found you, your heart had changed."

Small Doe nodded.

"If he had kept you, how long would he have so constantly occupied your heart? You would grow round with his little potbellies, and he might look for another woman to meet his needs. How happy would you be then?"

Thinking of Jackrabbit's untouched daughter, Small Doe confided, "I would not be happy at all, but Many Feathers and Running Deer did not take second wives, even before they walked Jesus' path."

"No. The Creator blessed me even before I knew Him, but few men court women they have already won. They set their hearts on conquering fresh things—new women, riches, high standing among their people. Hearts do not stay still. They change as the seasons change, and so will yours."

"Are you saying my husband would someday stop loving me, even if he once did?"

"No, my little one. Many Feathers loves me still, just as Running Deer loves Two Doves and your father loves your mother. They love us more deeply than they did at first—not because our skin invites their touch or our forms yield them pleasure, but because they cherish the women who live inside these aging dwellings. But a warrior's eyes are not fixed on his wife's lodge, no matter how highly he values her. They follow the horse he sees running like the wind across the grasses or watch for an approaching enemy. What would become of our people if our menfolk thought only of their wives and how to please them, as your father did so often when he was courting your mother? I am saying this: Only I-Am-Savior never changes. He alone can satisfy that deep longing in your heart."

"But I have loved Him for as long as I have had thought."

"Yes, but while you are alone on your bed at night, you remember this Raven-Enemy who stole you and think you would be happy if you had won his love."

Small Doe nodded, albeit hesitantly, amazed by how well her aunt could read her thoughts. "Is this not natural? Is it not what Jesus wants a wife to feel for her husband?"

"Yes—it is natural and right, just as it is fitting for a son to enjoy the fine, useful gifts his father has given to him."

Small Doe cocked her head, wondering what path her old aunt was taking.

"I remember the many days your old uncle spent carving Runs-Like-Antelope's first bow and arrows. He keenly anticipated the glee that would leap into his son's eyes—and his hopes were well met. But soon Runs-Like-Antelope, who used to follow Many Feathers' shadow as closely as your young brother does Preying Eagle's, began spending most of his time with this gift. From the moment the sun awoke until it settled off to sleep, he ran through the meadows and into the woods hunting everything that moved. Many Feathers was pleased that he had handed Runs-Like-Antelope such joy, but while he waited each morning to greet the sun or tended his horses in the evenings, he longed to have his son nearby."

"But he could not have stayed beside Many Feathers always. Surely my old uncle knew he would grow up."

"You miss my point, little one...or perhaps you have offered me a chance to explain it better. This bow that Runs-Like-Antelope loved, does he still sling it over his back when he hunts?"

Small Doe chuckled. "No, it would be too small—a little boy's bow. He has probably forgotten it."

"Yes, long ago. If I asked each of my sons, none would know what came of it. But his father—what do you think Runs-Like-Antelope now thinks of him?"

"He is his closest friend."

As Quiet Woman watched Small Doe brighten, she knew her young niece was catching on. "Over his many summers, Runs-Like-Antelope has learned what will help you most if you too will learn it. Even the best gifts Our Father gives us do not last. Fathers and husbands are killed in battle, friends and then daughters wed warriors from another band, mothers and aunts go to their rest. Deeply love your husband, if you marry again, but set your heart on The Creator. He will never disappoint you. Drink deeply of His love. It will not fade—whatever else your life holds."

Slowly crossing the short distance to her mother's dwelling, Small Doe contemplated Quiet Woman's counsel. Something about it reminded her of the passage she had read so often in I Peter, but the connection between the two was too vague to apprehend. Lost in thought, she nearly did not notice the tall warrior wrapped in a blanket waiting next to her mother's door.

Who do I have in heaven but You? I desire nothing on earth besides You. My flesh and my heart may fail, but the Creator is the strength of my heart and my portion forever.

Psalm 73:25-26

Chapter 30

SMALL DOE SMILED a little shyly. "Let me put my weaving inside." When Standing Elk nodded, she ducked in to find her family eating its late meal.

"We would have called you," her mother apologized, "but we did not wish to disturb you and Quiet Woman."

"I am not hungry. Standing Elk is outside. I told him I would join him."

She could not miss the smile that crossed her father's lips or the pleasure in her first love's eyes when he greeted her outside. He was as handsome as she had always thought him—no, he was more so. Age had lent him measures of confidence and strength beyond those gained through quick reactions and able muscle. Unfolding his blanket, he welcomed her inside, and both found comfort from their sorrows.

"We passed them near the stream," Pretty Face told his family. "They are laughing as we all did together when we were children. I am guessing he will bring Father a string of horses before the new moon rises."

"He understands her loyalty to her Raven-Enemy captor," added Straight Arrows, "and thinks it commendable."

"Good," Preying Eagle answered, but with a flick of his eyes he warned his sons the door-flap was opening. "How is Standing Elk," he asked his daughter.

Follows-His-Shadow chirped, "I like him."

"I do, too," replied his sister. "He has made me remember many happy moments when we were younger."

"He is a good man and will be a good provider. I want you to accept his horses."

Small Doe smiled and took the bowl her mother offered, but she only picked at her food. She knew better than to argue with her father and admitted, at least to herself, that the qualities that once quickened her pulse whenever he was near had now ripened into all that they had formerly only promised. Were it not for Pacing Wolf, she would be thrilled he wanted her.

But when he holds me in the darkness, whose face will my heart see? And what of the little Raven-Enemy growing within me? I begged the Lord to create him for Pacing Wolf. How can I take a gift He made for one man and offer it to another?

Struggling to discover what the Lord would wish, she looked up at her father. "I desire to obey you in everything, but though the verse you read to me says I am not bound to my husband, does it grant me permission to marry another warrior? Perhaps it means I may merely live apart from mine."

Preying Eagle tightened his jaw, wanting to respond with patience he did not at that moment possess. He could tell by her tone that she honestly sought his counsel, but he wished he were more certain of his answer.

Seizing the opportunity offered by his pause, Small Doe set aside her dish, went to her portion of the dwelling, and withdrew her old Bible. "I have read chapter seven and found some verses that disturb my conscience. Here. Ten and eleven: 'A wife who leaves her husband should either remain without a warrior or go back to the one she left.' Did not Jesus Himself say that whoever marries a cast-off wife commits adultery?"[87]

Preying Eagle forced all expression from his face. He was weary of watching her pine after an unworthy enemy and found the verses she read confounding. He, too, wanted to adhere to the path of His Master and Friend, but he could not guarantee his life would last beyond this war-season. How could he provide for her until this enemy warrior died? The lots of unmarried, fatherless women were miserable. They lived by the grace of their brothers' wives, who greatly varied in generosity.

Brought-Us-the-Book spoke up. "I also read the chapter over again. Since the verses you have read come before the ones we looked at yesterday, Paul had taken them into account."

"Where is the quote of Jesus?" asked Straight Arrows, who was already searching for the verse. "I would like to read it."

Small Doe shrugged. "One of the Gospels that are much alike, but I cannot remember which one."

"Matthew's," replied their mother. "The fifth chapter, verses thirty-one and thirty-two. '...the law says a man can give his wife a notice that he wants to cast her off, but I say: a man who casts off his wife, unless she has been unfaithful, forces her to commit adultery; and whoever marries a cast-off wife also commits adultery.'"

Preying Eagle sat silently for some moments, pondering what she had read until Follows-His-Shadow piped up. "Why does he say 'unless she has been unfaithful'?"

"If she is unfaithful," his father answered, "she has made herself an adulteress." Looking at his wife, he added, "These words of Jesus are clear and our daughter accepts them, but how will we know when she becomes free? This Raven-Enemy might be gored by a buffalo tonight or live as long as Old Many Feathers. Standing Elk follows the Lord faithfully and will offer our daughter much happiness. And what of the little potbelly she carries?

Small Doe's mouth fell open. "Corn-Tassels promised me that she would not tell!"

"She has not," answered her father, "but did you expect to hide it long? Your mother could not help noticing the expected changes when you dress each morning."

Small Doe did not know what to reply. Her father was right, as he usually was. They would have no way of learning if Pacing Wolf died—and what about his son? She wanted him to have a father to guide him, a wise and caring father like her own.

"What of Old Many Feathers and Quiet Woman?" asked Straight Arrows. "If her husband is still living, are they adulterers?"

"He was old when my uncle took her," Preying Eagle told him. "If he was not killed during that battle, he is surely dead now. If not, Jesus has forgiven them. Would my uncle act justly to cast her off?"

Before Straight Arrows replied, Follows-His-Shadow again chimed in. "If He has forgiven Many Feathers and Quiet Woman, He will forgive Light Bird if she marries Standing Elk."

"His death was enough to cover all our sins,"[88] Preying Eagle answered, "but we are seeking the Creators path not looking for our own.[89] Would you disobey me, knowing that I will still love and forgive you?"

The boy took a moment to consider his reply. "No."

"Good. Your brothers and sister have possessed my trust from childhood. I hope you will always keep it also."

"And do not forget what Jesus told His disciples," his mother added. "'If you love Me, you will do as I have commanded.'"[90]

"Light Bird has done nothing wrong," interrupted Pretty Face. "Why should she pay for the Raven-Enemy's sins? My cousins and I can travel to this place of cliffs and ensure she is no longer married."

As all eyes turned toward her, they found her forehead had become pinched. "No—I do not crave his death. It would only bring me sorrow and the threat of vengeance from his clansmen."

"What do you want?" asked Straight Arrows.

As she considered his question, a slight smile had begun to play about her lips, partly from relief that her father's stance had softened, partly because she appreciated her brothers' love, but mostly because Quiet Woman's counsel was settling into her heart. "I have a husband who is kind, generous, and dependable. I will run to Him for protection, provision, and love."

"You go back?" asked Follows-His-Shadow, his small affectionate face suddenly awash with distress.

"No," she smiled at him. "The Creator is my husband. The Lord of Hosts. I will submit to all He has said clearly and wait for Him to make clear all that remains murky."[91]

Touched deeply by their daughter's faith, her parents exchanged resigned yet satisfied glances, but Brought-Us-the-Book turned to a practical matter. "You have not yet eaten. You are carrying a child and must keep up your strength."

Small Doe complied, while her father informed them all that the band would not meet for their Bible reading that night. The rains had turned the ground too muddy.

"I will care for my sister as long as I am living," Straight Arrows assured Preying Eagle. "And I will treat her son as if he were my own."

His brothers joined him, including little Follows-His-Shadow, unaware the eight summers that separated him from her potbelly, when it came, would amount to little.

As they called on their heavenly Father, Small Doe thanked God, aloud, for every one of them and silently for a new desire He had begun planting in her heart.

←←← →→→

PACING WOLF PAUSED on a high pinnacle, scouring the horizon for a way to reclaim his life. He could not remember when he had last eaten. Grief had so choked his parched throat, the smallest morsel hit his stomach like a heavy rock. His spirit-guide offered him nothing.

After stealthily escorting Small Doe to her family, keeping watch for roaming warriors and searching out ample water supplies, he had little desire to return to his home. Everywhere he looked, he would find her: in the choker she had woven, in the fringes of hair on his leggings and scalp shirt, even in the mended seams of his lodge cover.

Neither could he wait for Bites-With-Dog, as he had each night of their journey, to hear news of how she fared. It had been the same each day: she rarely spoke and never smiled. He wondered what her expression might hold if he snatched her back again.

When my people meet an enemy, I will dismount by Crow-Face's death-staff and fight beside him. I will welcome death. My clan would be better off following Short-Neck than a carcass of a heart picked clean by hungry vultures.

"Book-god, can you hear me?" he shouted hoarsely. "I am Pacing Wolf, your enemy, though I desire to be your friend. I did not mean to hurt Small Doe. I have given her back to her people and hope I have not done wrong. Watch over her, protect her, keep her warm and well fed. I can no longer do these things."

← ← ← → → →

"UNCLE." SMALL DOE addressed Spotted Long-knife the evening after he, Lieutenant Wilson, and Bites-With-Dog had returned from visiting the Hidatsa. "Will you ask your guide if he knows how Pacing Wolf fares?"

Spotted Long-knife studied her face while she was serving Two Bears and Elk Dog Man and wondered again if he should have brought her home. His conversations with Bites-With-Dog had given him grave doubts: had he not asked, Pacing Wolf would not have parted with her.

When she came around a second time, he told her: "Bites-With-Dog has not seen him. He returned to the Raven Enemy briefly after he guided us here, but Pacing Wolf was not there. His grandmother, who asked about you, said he left when we did and she has not seen him since. Their old white-haired leader supposes he is up in the mountains."

As her brow creased, her hand slid down to her stomach and his eyes grew wide. "I wish to talk with you," she whispered and then left the lodge.

He did not see her again until the next morning when Corn-Tassels and she were on their way down to the stream. "Come to Valuable Woman's dwelling after your chores," he suggested, "so we can speak privately. I do not want Bites-With-Dog to see us alone and make wrong assumptions."

When the two young women returned, he wondered whether Light Bird might feel more comfortable with or without his daughter, but before he posed the question, she told him he could speak openly. Corn-Tassels already knew all that was in her heart.

Turning to the second chapter of Peter's first letter, she read of the example Jesus set when He was treated unjustly. "I thought often of these verses while living with the Sparrow Hawks—the Raven-Enemy—and have been praying about a connection I see between them and something Quiet Woman told me."

Looking up, she saw that he patiently waited for her to explain.

"Jesus knew all that He would suffer, but He came to earth anyway—not to be pleased or find enjoyment but to bring those He loved to His father. How can I do otherwise?"

"What do you propose?"

"I want you to return me to the Sparrow Hawks. I want to go to those I love—they do not know our Father—and bring them to Him."

Spotted Long-knife dropped his eyes to the floor. He saw a host of difficulties with her plan and would not place himself between her and her father. "Are you certain you will find welcome?"

Small Doe shook her head. "No, but it does not matter. My husband will want the small-thing that I carry for him. It can be no other warrior's, and he knows this."

"What of this young woman he will soon marry?" asked Corn-Tassels. "Will she allow you to live with them?"

"I will earn a place in his grandmother's lodge by doing her chores."

Spotted Long-knife frowned. "What of food or clothing?"

"Pacing Wolf provides for her and is also sure to provide for me, not for my own sake, but for the sake of his small-thing. I know that you are concerned, Uncle," she added, clearly reading the doubt in his expression, "but though I am not explaining myself well, I am certain that God has planned this and will provide a way."

"Have you spoken with your father?"

"Not yet, but I have been praying for the Lord to direct his heart. Look at this verse in John's Gospel. I read it as my mother pointed out some others nearby." Turning to chapter fifteen, she read verse fourteen: 'Greater love has no one than this: that he lays down his life for his friends.' *They* are my friends and people for whom Jesus died, though they do not know Him. How can they unless someone tells them? I must go. How can I not?"

Corn-Tassels shook her head. "It is full of risk…"

"I risk no more than Jesus did when He left His home for us. All of you tell me continually that it hurts to see me sad. What greater joy can I have than laboring with my Savior at the task dearest to His heart? I know what I propose looks dangerous, but I am convinced it is the surest course. Look here, a few chapters back:

'Truly, I tell you: unless a seed falls into the earth and dies, it remains alone. But if it dies, it bears much fruit. The one who loves his life loses it, and the one who despises his life in this world will keep it to everlasting life. If anyone serves Me, let him follow Me; and where I am, there My servant will be also. If anyone serves Me, the Father will honor him.

"You see! I would risk more by clutching hold of safety. By placing my feet in I-Am-Savior steps, I gain everything."

Although it was not Small Doe's intention, her zeal offered her white uncle a rebuke. He began thinking of the days when salvation was new to the band. They regularly sent out warriors: first to bands within their own tribe and afterward to their enemies. New believers became part of their village and the sent-out-ones brought back wondrous reports of salvation.

Can I, in good conscience, argue against her desire when I heartily supported something similar so short a time ago? Still, many were treated brutally and others murdered. She is so young…and a woman.

His thoughts unavoidably brought to mind a conversation he once had with Brought-Us-the-Book on the catwalk of his former outpost. He had voiced the same concerns regarding her or something very like them. Whether Preying Eagle would accept her plan was another issue. He was fiercely protective of his children, and his people's custom granted him unquestioned authority over her.

"Very well. I can see you have thought it out and are determined to go. If your father consents, I will do as you ask—but I will not go against him."

"I knew you would help me," she smiled, "and with your frequent visits, how can Father protest?"

How could he not? thought the Major, as she gleefully slipped out of his wife's dwelling. *If Corn-Tassels asked the same of me, I could consent only if Jesus peeled back the sky and told me this was His will in terms too clear to deny.*

The heart of the most revered elder or war chief is a stream in the Lord's hand. He makes it flow wherever He wishes.

Proverbs 21:1

Chapter 31

AS CHERRIES GREW fat and ripened on their branches, Small Doe's most attentive aunts and cousins began to suspect that a tiny enemy was growing inside her. Her heart also grew full: full of love for a father who listened to the Creator's voice, even when his natural instincts screamed the opposite; full of appreciation for a mother who had taught her the Savior's steps were the surest place to set her feet; and full of gratitude for her white uncle who changed her desire into a plan. Not only did the Major guarantee he would visit her among the Raven-Enemy as often as possible, but he also divulged the horror he had initially felt when Brought-Us-the-Book had made a similar decision. As Preying Eagle considered the latter, he could hardly refuse.

"I know what Spotted Long-knife says is true," he confided to Brought-Us-the-Book on their bed that night, "but when you gave yourself to our people, I knew what you would find. What do I know of the Raven-Enemy, except that this young war-leader has made my daughter eat her heart in misery? How can I be sure he will adequately provide for her? He may snatch her little potbelly to give it to another and cast her away. And what of their strange wife-snatching custom? How many other warriors will force her into their lodges before she lays her head down for its final rest? It is vile."

"Spotted Long-knife said he once wondered if God took my father home to Heaven for this very reason."

Preying Eagle recoiled so sharply, his head rose off their pillow. "You believe God will kill me if I do not let her go?"

"No, I meant that God sees what we can only guess about, and she belongs to Him, not us. He is her father also and loves her even more than we do, though I found it much easier to trust Him through my own unknown dangers than I do for Light Bird's. Had my father been alive, he would never have given me permission to live here and certainly not to marry you." Stretching up in the dark, she ran kisses up his weatherworn cheek to his brow. "I cannot imagine living without you."

THE WIND HAD blown cold when Small Doe had first crossed the prairie. Her journey home had been pleasantly warm. This time, the heat was relentless. The two long-knives, their Sparrow Hawk guide, and she rose before the sun could bake the breeze and rode long after it had drowsily drifted to rest. The afternoons in between, however, afforded Small Doe a singular pleasure. As the sun ascended to its zenith, Spotted Long-knife resumed a habit he had begun while traveling to the Earth Lodges: looking for a shady place to eat, rest, and study the Bible.

Bites-With-Dog had at first thought this senseless, but as he listened to and observed the long-knives, a hunger began stirring in his secret depths that increased during their brief stays in Small Doe's village. Along with the long-knives, her clansmen possessed some inner satisfaction that he lacked, though he frequently climbed the mountains to fast, and some inward assurance that beat away the ravaging wolf of worry.

He could tell with one glance why her father and his brothers had reasons to feel confident. Their feathers proclaimed their courage and skill, though only two boasted tokens superior to his own. He found his employers utterly deficient. What had they done? He, himself, had counted grand coup, earning him a voice in the councils of his band. His spotted employer ran errands for a Real Chief who never bothered to speak with him, and the other—the one who allowed hair to encroach on his lips—seemed only to take up space by the fire.

The lieutenant made no sense to him. If a day atop a horse left the older long-knife too weary to caress Small Doe, what kept the younger long-knife from her? Bites-With-Dog did not think his yellow-haired woman posed a problem. Several trappers he knew took women among the Sparrow Hawks when they traveled far from the immovable wooden lodges they called "houses." The hairy-lipped man treated Small Doe as if she was his sister, which again circled Bites-With-Dog around to questions about her.

At first, he had asked them on behalf of his Lumpwood brother, but now he asked for himself. Why did not she rouse her kinsmen to avenge her shame, as a Sparrow Hawk woman would have done, and why would she remain faithful to an enemy of her father? He understood why she preferred Pacing Wolf to Goes-to-Battle, but her refusal of Standing Elk was incomprehensible. In order to explain, the Major introduced him to Jesus.

AS SMALL DOE spotted The-Cliffs-With-No-Name, her heart began pounding. *Pacing Wolf does not want you!* she told herself, but the smooth wooden saddle she sat upon stirred embers of hope. The thought of Jackrabbit's daughters quenched them quickly.

They may be living in his lodge already—or if not them, some other. Many untouched women in the village looked after him with desire. If he wanted me, he would not have given me away.

As they climbed steadily upward, the air in the hills brought welcome relief from the sweltering heat, but as they made their way through the pass, a stench of death assaulted their nostrils. Scaffolds, more numerous than they cared to count, rose up from the slope. These soon gave way to corpses wrapped in dug out cottonwood logs and finally to those who had been pulled outside the village on pelts and stashed between rocks.

Only dogs noticed their arrival, but even these did not bother to sound a warning. They were too busy with fresh carcasses to do more than raise their heads. They went from one to the other, gnawing anything that could not mount a defense. As Bites-With-Dog led their party down the central path, several weary warriors and women acknowledged them, but none seemed to care whether they stayed or went.

"Do not look," Spotted Long-knife advised Small Doe as they rode past a particularly disgusting sight. Handing her his handkerchief, he commanded her to tie it around her nose and mouth. "Small Pox. It is spread face to face, in the air that is breathed. Wilson, lead Light Bird back down the mountain. Bites-With-Dog and I will see what can be done."

"No—please," Small Doe swiftly responded. "Let me help."

Her uncle shook his head. "The danger is too great, especially for the baby growing inside you."

Small Doe hesitated until she heard someone crying within Hair-Up-Top's lodge. "I must—they are my friends."

"Very well, but put on my gloves and touch no one without them—and do not go near anyone with flat red spots or pustules. If you must, hold your breath in their presence—and keep that kerchief on! When the sores have scabbed over they present less risk, but they are still contagious until the scabs have fallen off."

Quickly dismounting, Small Doe ducked into Hair-Up-Top's large lodge and found her Blackfoot friend vainly trying to comfort her hungry small-thing. Last Woman's flesh hung loosely from her bones and the skin covering her once lovely cheeks was marred with half-hanging crusty blotches.

"You come back," Last Woman weakly whispered.

"Yes." Small Doe smiled, brushing the hair from her pitted brow. "I am home." As she picked up the baby, his lean scarred belly turned her sick with pity, and she fretfully searched for the other member of the family. "Where is…?"

"Ol' White Hair?" replied Last Woman, when she did not finish. "Him gone." As Last Woman tossed her eyes toward the smoke hole, Small Doe understood and, though saddened, she was not surprised. They had passed a scaffold adorned with Hair-Up-Top's war shield.

"Your daughter—where is she?"

Before Last Woman could answer, Little Blackfoot flung the flap aside and began backing in, dragging four heavy water sacks. Small Doe cried out with joy, so startling the child that she spun around swiftly, flung herself into Small Doe's arms, and hugged her tightly.

After a time, Small Doe gently pushed the little girl to an arms' length to examine her small face and limbs and smiled brightly when she saw only slight scarring. The child seemed to have suffered less than her mother and had apparently been the first of the three to both catch the pox and recover.

Once Little Blackfoot offered Last Woman something to drink, she patiently dribbled water over her tiny brother's pursed, smacking lips.

"We need to find him something to eat," Small Doe told her. "Lack of water has made your mother's milk dry up."

The little face crumpled. "I could not carry more," she cried, breaking into a heap of sobs now that someone else was there to shoulder her troublesome load. "Mother wash me when I hot with red spots. Then she hot and I wash…but lake far and old grandmother friend not come out…not go for water."

Small Doe pulled her close as foul smelling smoke wafted into the dwelling. "I will fetch plenty and the white men who brought me back will also do all they can. Kills-Behind-Her-Dwelling…is she…is she in her lodge?"

The young head nodded mutely, and Small Doe set her to her feet.

"I must go check on her. You stay here and care for your mother. I will come back as soon as I can with food for you and milk for your brother."

She would have to be careful, horses did not like to be milked. Gathering the empty water-sacks, Small Doe ducked out and almost collided with Corn-Tassels' husband.

"The Major, our scout, and I have been setting flames to the lodges that contain the dead, and we are marking large circles on the dwellings of the sick. You may bring them water and food, but do not go inside. Most spots on the living have begun to crust over and many of their scabs are already falling off, but with your baby, you should not take chances. I promised

Abigail to do everything I can to keep you safe—not to mention the many assurances I gave to your mother and father."

Small Doe smiled in return. At first, she had seen him as an intruder on her brother's happiness, but over their two journeys, many meals, and daily Bible readings, she had begun to see why Corn-Tassels loved him. "Have you found Hunts-For-Death?"

"Yes, in the home of his daughter—languishing but alive. How were your friends?"

"On the mend," she replied, glancing at the grazing horses, "but I need to find milk."

"The herds cannot catch it. Look for a mare that has recently foaled. Have you ever done it?"

Small Doe nodded and hurried to complete her task. Little Blackfoot was old enough to touch the pricked sack of milk against her brother's tiny cheek and lips until he started to root for it. Once Small Doe was sure he eating well, she forced herself to face the single task she dreaded most.

Lord, the lieutenant said nothing of Pacing Wolf, and I have not seen him anywhere. Have I come back too late?

She felt her feet might give way as she paused outside his lodge. Spreading a hand over the small firm mound beneath her ribcage, she took a deep breath and swiftly ducked inside. It was entirely empty and every possession exactly as she had left it. The breastplate she had woven lay untouched across the willow headrest and his grandmother's elk-toothed wedding dress lay spread out atop the bed. Awhirl with possibilities, she quickly ran to Kills-Behind-Her-Dwelling's lodge.

As she spotted the old form lying with her back to the door, her stomach, which had felt as if it had settled around her ankles, suddenly lurched into her throat. Dropping to her knees, she examined an exposed arm and found nothing but wrinkled skin.

The old woman moaned. "Put my arm down! I want to rest. I cannot get up."

Giving the thin shoulder an affectionate squeeze, Small Doe murmured, "Rest then, Grandmother. I will get you water and food."

Kills-Behind-Her-Dwelling twisted about quicker than Small Doe would have thought possible and peered at her with keen black eyes. "Small Doe…" She pronounced the name with wonder, stretching out a crooked finger and running it along the fine-boned young cheek. "You have come back. You must not stay…the new moon brought us spotted fever."

"I will be fine," Small Doe assured her. "Many are beginning to recover and are not contagious. The long-knives have marked all the lodges I cannot go in. Where are your sores or scabs?"

"I have none," she replied, chuckling softly. "Being a lonely old woman has its good side. Since you left, no one comes to me but the little Blackfoot girl."

"But you are sick."

"Not sick—old and tired and hungry. I have climbed back and forth from the village to the lake too many times, trying to quench my neighbors' thirst, and I have no more food. They have consumed all that I had to offer. Do not look so sad. Your mother surely told you that old women do not walk this earth forever, but this I-Am-Savior of your book…the one who cared for the widow and raised her son from his death-log…I have been speaking with Him—mainly about you and the child of my proud and obstinate grandson."

Dropping her hand to Small Doe's protruding belly, Kills-Behind-Her-Dwelling wanly smiled. "You see. My grandson is as virile as his father and grandfather before him. I knew he would not wait long to get you with child. Love him. He does not deserve it, but love him as I-Am-Savior loved the people He wept over on His way to their great feast.[92] You did not think I was listening all those times in your lodge, but an old woman hears…and sees. I have noticed much my grandson thinks he has hidden and also the feelings in the heart of the sweet granddaughter he has brought me."

Small Doe brushed her fingers across the old woman's wrinkled forehead, unable yet to ask what she most wanted to know. "Do not talk. You need your strength. I will fetch you food and fresh water. Little Blackfoot is feeding mare's milk to her little brother."

"Pacing Wolf is in the mountains…trying to starve his sorrow. A man does not grieve for a woman he does not love."

A sprout of hope began casting off its shell in Small Doe's heart as she pressed the gnarled hand to her soft cheek. "I will come back shortly." *At least if he is in the mountains, the pox will not reach him.*

While wondering how to get food for so many—apparently, there had been no one to hunt for some time—she thought again of the herd wandering the slopes. Donning the Major's gloves again, she gathered all the water sacks she could find and rushed up to locate the newest mothers among the mares.

THE HOLLOWS BENEATH Pacing Wolf's eyes had grown dark and deep. When he drifted to sleep, he met Small Doe begging him to keep her from Goes-to-Battle and would startle awake. The few nights he did not dream of her, he dreamed of his cousin, sneering as he stole the heart that most mattered.

He did not need to snatch her...I threw her heart away.

Again and again, he retraced the same twisting thoughts until he finally broke onto an open prairie that promised room to free himself from the brambles entangling his heart. *I will summer with the Whistle Water clan, where Goes-to-Battle has fled to hide his shame, and expose him for the poor-hearted weakling he is! Then, I will hunt down Wild Dog and rid the earth of him forever.*

While he was gathering up his weapons, someone called his name. The man sounded close, in his very ear, but as Pacing Wolf whipped around to see who it was, he found only the sun's first rays peeking over a distant ridge. Squinting into the dawn, he searched for anything that moved.

Pacing Wolf turned back toward the tree-line, supposing Hair-Up-Top had sent a messenger, but the shadows held only a lone elk whose attention he had drawn with his sudden movements. Briefly, he wondered if the animal had spoken—as in the ancient grandfathers' tales—but he concluded he was mind was mad from thirst. While taking a long draw of water, the fine hair on the nape of his neck stood straight up.

"Vengeance is mine. I will repay."

Wheeling swiftly, he grew uncertain if he heard the words aloud or whispered in his heart, but he recognized their source. *"It is a fearful thing, to fall into the hands of the living God."*

All at once, he understood the verse's import, as though a lodge flap were suddenly pulled back to reveal the contents of the home inside. *I should not have destroyed His book...but He does not threaten me. He asks me to leave Goes-to-Battle to Him.*

Spewing up from his memory was something Small Doe had once said: *"Ask, and He will show Himself to you. He came into the world to bring all people back to The-One-Who-First-Made-All-Things. His people called him Jesus; it means, 'I-Am-Savior.'"*[93]

"I-Am-Savior!" he shouted. "I am Pacing Wolf. I have spoken to You before. The 'contrite' heart you desire now lays in my chest. I give it to you. Do with Goes-to-Battle whatever You like—only let me know You as Small Doe knows you, not as a far off spirit but a brother or father and friend."

At once, Pacing Wolf felt bathed by a strange peace—an immeasurable peace that exceeded all the confines of his understanding,[94] a peace that made what he had felt in Small Doe's presence seem only a taste on the tip of his tongue.

"Show me Your path, and I will follow and lead my people there also."

WHEN THE SUN arose, Small Doe gathered everything edible she could find and climbed up and down the path to the lake so often, her limbs felt like water. Her mind was awhirl with clansmen, both living and dead, as she weaved back through the fires to Kills-Behind-Her-Dwelling's lodge. Mostly the young and strong had survived, though several small-things had perished.

She had never thought to offer thanks for loneliness, but it had clearly kept her closest friends alive. Their lack of companionship meant infrequent exposure to the fever. Were it not for Little Blackfoot's efforts to assist others, they might have missed it altogether. Small Doe resolved not to tell this to the child who had worked so tirelessly to keep both mother and brother alive.

The loss of Hair-Up-Top would deeply affect the workings of the tribe. She supposed Hunts-For-Death would take his place as He-Who-Leads-the-Moving-Band and possibly as Real Chief. Spotted Long-knife had informed her that the other contender, Marks-His-Face, Jackrabbit's husband, had succumbed to the pox. Inevitably, his name brought Pacing Wolf to mind, and she wondered when he would return and what new role they would choose for him to perform. She had not heard how Short-Neck had fared.

If he is dead, Pacing Wolf will be uncontested as the Many Lodges' clan leader.

As she considered all the changes, a new idea sprang up in her heart that made her marvel, and tears of gratitude began flowing in uncontrolled rivulets down her cheeks.

If Pacing Wolf had been here, he might have died...and so might his small-thing and I. Sending me home kept me from danger...and if his grief kept him away as his grandmother said... "Oh Lord, how many times I questioned Your care when all the while, You were keeping us safe!"

Entering Kills-Behind-Her-Dwelling's lodge, she knelt down with some cherries she had found that were nearly ripe for picking. "Eat as many as you can. I will look for more tomorrow."

When the old woman did not respond, Small Doe gently shook her, but her bony shoulder slumped forward.

"*No,*" Small Doe gasped, "*not now Lord. Not now that I am back...*"

Small Doe turned over the aged body, pulled it into her arms, and slowly began rocking back and forth. Rivers of grief flooded over her former streams of joy, but one hope pressed resolutely through the damp mud of her sorrow. *She said she spoke to Him often...perhaps I was not too late after all.*

You will call upon Me and come and pray to Me, and I will pay attention to you. You will pursue Me and find Me when you pursue Me with all of your heart.

Jeremiah 29:12-13

Chapter 32

WHEN PACING WOLF smelled the rising smoke, he hurriedly clambered down the steep decline. His thoughts leaped from one enemy who might be attacking the village to another, harshly chiding himself for staying away so long. When he reached a bend that allowed him a clearer view, he felt kicked in the gut. In place of imposing lodges lay charred heaps; and instead of the normal scurrying of clanswomen, he found an eerie stillness.

As he scrambled closer, his half-starved brain became befuddled. Crisscrossed lodge poles, beautifully clothed, jutted up between circles of smoldering ash, and grazing herds still covered the untouched slopes. *No enemy would have left them.* Descending to the path as quickly as his weakened legs would carry him, he made his way to his grandmother's lodge.

Small Doe gazed down at Kills-Behind-Her-Dwelling's peaceful expression. Her tears were spent, and the frail form in her arms no longer contained her beloved friend. As she laid it down, a noise at the entrance drew her attention, and Pacing Wolf unexpectedly ducked in. He stood transfixed as if confused between what he saw and the pleasures or torments of a dream.

From the moment her father said she could return, Small Doe had been swinging between eager anticipation and dread of this moment. Now that she faced him, she could not speak. It did not matter: her hand unconsciously moved to the slight bulge still hidden by the folds of her doeskin, telling him all she had kept secret.

Pacing Wolf, also, was speechless. Too many things assaulted him at once: the burnt lodges, some still aflame; the inexplicable absence of his clansmen; the slender and yet budding form kneeling by his sleeping grandmother's side...

Small Doe rose as his eyes traveled upward to her face but felt unraveled by his intense scrutiny. "On...on the night that you...took me and on...on many since, I asked the Creator to give you a son to…to…allay your grief. He has answered my prayer, and I…I could not keep His kindness from you."

Pacing Wolf only stared in answer, unable to awaken his brain or make his tongue form an intelligible response.

Mistaking silence for scorn, Small Doe again began to stammer. "I…I can live here, in Kills-Behind-Her-Dwelling's lodge…or with Last Woman. I ask nothing of you but food for our child and me…and…and that no one take me by force."

As he recalled her conversation with her yellow-haired friend, he wondered if she meant him or a rival. Clenching his jaw, he dropped his eyes to his grandmother, who still lay strangely stone-like on her pallet.

Small Doe realized at once that he could not know what had just transpired. "She is gone," she murmured, "but not because of the spotted fever. She wore herself out while feeding and fetching water for those too sick to leave their lodges."

The spotted fever... He gazed at his grandmother with the same awkward confusion he had been directing toward Small Doe and then knelt to place his fingers in front of her nostrils. Feeling no breath, he scooped up the lifeless form and spilled out the same sort of rhythmic wail that echoed from every sector of the village.

Small Doe felt helpless. She longed to offer him comfort and to help him make sense of it all but, instead, stayed still until she thought of the elk-toothed wedding garments. After all the old woman's kindness, the least she could do was dress her well for burial. Crossing the short distance to Pacing Wolf's lodge, she bundled up the blouse and skirt, savoring the memories they carried, and then paused before the breastplate she had woven for him.

He will not want it, she thought, snatching it up and stashing it in the bottom of his large buffalo-hide bag. While hurrying back to dress his grandmother, she spotted her white *uncle* and Corn-Tassels' husband walking up the central path. They pulled the kerchiefs from their noses when they saw her, but stopped when they heard cadent grieving from within the old woman's dwelling.

"Pacing Wolf," Small Doe responded to their raised eyebrows. "His grandmother just died."

They were about to ask her more when the warrior himself, hearing their voices, stepped outside. He, too, wanted answers. While he curtly greeted them, Small Doe attempted to slip around him to enter the lodge, but he gripped hold of her wrist.

"Where is Hair-Up-Top?" he asked.

"Dead," replied Major Anderson. "We saw his scaffold on our way yesterday, near the place the sun rises. It is spotted fever."

Glancing from the scowling warrior to Small Doe, the Major felt the same misgivings he had when he took her away. Neither of their expressions offered reassurance, but the circumstance of their reunion had not been happy.

"And Hunts-For-Death?" demanded Pacing Wolf, forestalling the questions he read clearly in the long-knife's eyes.

"He is sick in his daughter's lodge, but he will recover."

"Marks-His-Face?"

Lieutenant Wilson pointed toward the Kicked-in-the-Bellies' portion of the village. "Dead. That side got the worst of it. Here," he gestured toward the Many Lodges, "we found a few dwellings the pox has not touched. Light Bird..."

"Small Doe," Pacing Wolf cut in. "Her name is Small Doe."

The Lieutenant cleared his throat, tempted to say he had given up the right to dictate anything about her. "While...Small Doe...has been distributing the food she could find, we have been helping Bites-With-Dog mark lodges housing the contagious. We are burning those of the dead. We would prefer to give them a proper burial," he continued as distaste darkened the young war-leader's eyes, "but we do not dare to touch them."

Pacing Wolf's stomach churned, though he reluctantly acknowledged their good sense. Turning away, he pulled Small Doe into his grandmother's dwelling and left the two soldiers to stay or go as they pleased.

Once they had stepped out of earshot, Lieutenant Wilson muttered, "He appears to have appointed himself chief."

"For good reasons," affirmed Major Anderson. "As you learn their ways, you will also learn to read their emblems better. He is highly accomplished. A false move with him would ruin any trust we've built."

The Lieutenant conceded, twisting one end of his mustache. "Do you think she matters to him?"

"He has quickly reclaimed his authority over her. It's a start, and I suspect I've discovered why he gave her up."

Josh turned his head, intrigued by his superior's choice of words. "Up? I would have said he gave her *away*."

"What language were you speaking?"

"English."

"Did he have difficulty understanding what you said?"

After a moments' reflection, a smile slipped slowly beneath the dark mustache. "No," the Lieutenant answered, "not once."

"Where is Among-the-Pines?" asked Pacing Wolf as he led Small Doe into his grandmother's lodge.

"I do not know. I have never learned which lodge she lives in and the long-knives forbade me to go searching. Not only for my own sake," she added hurriedly, lest he deem her negligent, "but also because of..." She glanced down at her midsection, too unsure of his thoughts to continue. "I have brought your grandmother's elk-toothed garments. I will prepare her for burial."

While she drew the porcupine tail through the matted gray hair, Pacing Wolf studied her face. Tears had streaked her cheeks, and the gentle way she smoothed out each tangle stirred longings for her touch...her scent...her softness...

"She did not suffer. She was just tired, but she mentioned a curious thing. All the times she was present while I read you the Scriptures, I thought she was disinterested, but she told me she had been speaking with Him...with I-Am-Savior."

Pacing Wolf nearly mentioned he had begun doing the same, but as she eased his grandmother out of her sweat soaked garments and replaced them with her own blouse and skirt—the prized ones for which he had traded his grandmother a pony—his heart grew wary. Remaining silent until she stepped aside, he wrapped the old body, hoisted it onto his shoulder, and carried it to the place his clansmen had set their dead.

With little difficulty, he located a hollow cottonwood trunk and chopped it down to the size of his grandmother's shriveled form. He commenced yanking out the last of its rotten center until he heard Small Doe was whispering.

"'I am certain our Redeemer lives, and He shall stand at the last day upon the earth. And though our bodies decay, yet in our flesh shall we see God.'"[95]

Pacing Wolf listened intently, wishing she might say something further or explain the words; but as she looked up, he dropped his eyes and gently rolled his grandmother onto her side. Laying her inside the hollow, he curved her legs up toward her body[96] and lifted it next to Hair-Up-Top's burial log, out of reach of any wolves or dogs that might catch the smell of death.

Walking beside Small Doe back to the village, he wondered how he might leap the gulf he had created between them and whether she would welcome him if he found a way. He wanted her to share his lodge, but she had made it clear she intended to stay elsewhere.

"The Blackfoot captive and her children—are they well?"

"The scabs have fallen from Last Son and Little Blackfoot. Last Woman's have crusted over and are beginning to fall."

"You will sleep in my lodge," he told her, gripping her wrist and pulling her in lest she argue. She did not, but as he prepared for sleep, he realized the awkwardness of their arrangement. He did not wish to threaten her by insisting she share his robes, but neither did he want her to sleep apart from him.

Small Doe was as much at a loss as he. She yearned to sleep enfolded in his arms, as she was accustomed, but dared not assume she was wanted. Both wished Pacing Wolf was wearing a shirt. He could draw her close, as he used to, by holding up his arms for her to remove it. As this thought crossed her mind, she considered offering to brush his hair. Even if he did not want her, he would want his tangles removed; but after a day of fetching water and picking cherries, she was not sure her arms would comply.

While she was mulling the matter over, she suddenly sucked in her breath, dropped her eyes to her belly, and laid her palm over the slight swelling between her ribs. He dropped swiftly by her side, brushing her hand away to press his own in its place, and felt their small-thing squirming. Small Doe gazed into his black eyes, lit with keen pleasure, and longed to slip her hand over his, but fear he did not want her kept it pinned firmly to dress.

"He is vigorous like his father."

A glint of amusement curled Pacing Wolf's mouth, but concern for his eldest pressed his lips back into a grim line. "I go to look for my daughter and sister."

"I will come with you," Small Doe suggested, hating to quench the spark of intimacy just as it had awakened.

"No. Stay—sleep." He nodded toward the bed, but when he saw disappointment flitting through her eyes, he added: "I do not know what I will find. She may have the fever."

SMALL DOE AWOKE alone. She had slept so hard she could not remember when Pacing Wolf had returned. Looking around his lodge, she began to suspect he had not. Everything looked just as it had when he left last night.

As her heart assumed the worst, her memory became its ally, taunting her with Jackrabbit's claims about her eager daughter. She had been convinced at the time that Never-Sits would like to have denied them, but—if so—why had she not? By all accounts, Pretty Crow Woman looked much like Pacing Wolf's first wife who Small Doe felt sure was as beautiful as Among-the-Pines.

Rubbing a hand over her stomach in the half-conscious way of all ripening women, she thought of his small-thing growing within. *Pretty Crow Woman may attract his interest, but I carry something of him that she does not.* As Small Doe tasted her own thoughts, flavored pungently with pride and exultation, she let out an exasperated sigh. "Oh Lord, I learn so slowly. I sound like the verses Quiet Woman showed me."

When her ancient aunt had heard Small Doe was returning to the Raven-Enemy, she had invited her into her dwelling. "Remember what I have told you, and do not become like Leah. The names she gave her sons reveal where she built her hope. See." She flipped to Genesis. "The first, she called Now-My-Husband-Will-Love-Me.[97] She named the second, The-Lord-Heard-I-Was-Unloved-and-Has-Given-Me-Another-Son,[98] and her third, My-Husband-Will-Surely-Love-Me-Since-I-Have-Given-Him-Three-Sons.[99]

"Do you understand? She thought if she gained her husband's heart, she would finally be happy; but her longings were not satisfied until she sought the Lord to fill them. Look here—she named her fourth son I-Will-Praise-the-Lord.'[100] Do not take as long as she did to learn where to gain your joy."[101]

Small Doe read the chapter over again, praying that the Lord would forgive her continually straying heart. As she did, the jealousy she had once felt toward Last Woman sprang to mind, along with memories of the disappointed Blackfoot warrior who violently pulled her from the trees. *Lord, help me never to...*

"Small Doe!" Pacing Wolf interrupted her prayer, calling her outside.

When she hurried out to meet him, he tossed one of the soft-muzzled animals, Has-Face-for-Earrings, down from his sorrel and promised to come back with more. She withdrew her knife immediately, but as she watched him urge his mount back toward the mountains, she noticed his ribs sticking out on either side of his knotty-looking spine. *"He is starving away his sorrow"* she remembered his grandmother saying. *"A man does not grieve for a woman he does not love."*

Afraid of false hope, Small Doe busied herself with the animal's wooly hide, and once she had scraped and pegged it in the sun to dry, she scampered down the path to the lake. Up and down repeatedly, she hauled as much water as her arms could carry, distributing it to her neighbors along with the mutton when it finished roasting. By the time Pacing Wolf returned with an elk, she already felt exhausted. She was happy to sit with him a few moments, while he tore the meat off a hind leg she had saved.

"Bites-With-Dog hunts game for the Black Lodges and the long-knives are hunting for the Kicked-in-the-Bellies."

She studied his face as she listened, surprised he was including her in their plans. He looked several summers older than he had when she first met him, and hunger had carved deep hollows in his cheeks.

"The Many Lodges are no longer many," he scoffed, tossing the well-cleaned bone into the sun to dry.

"Did you find Among-the-Pines and Never-Sits?"

"They are sick," he nodded, "but like the others who are strong, they will recover."

"If you tell me where they are, I will bring them food."

"No. They are with Jackrabbit and her daughters in Mountainside's lodge. They live, but only Pretty Crow Woman's scabs have fallen off. She will see to their needs. Stay on this side and touch only the dwellings the long-knives have not marked."

Small Doe nodded, glad that he wished to keep her well, but his mention of his dead woman's sister wiped away the smile that had been tilting up her lips. *Jesus is ever faithful,* she told her heart. *He will never cast me aside.*

LAST WOMAN AND Little Blackfoot fell asleep with the sun while Small Doe struggled to stay awake. The days had begun to run together until she no longer knew how many had passed. Her knees were raw from kneeling over hides, and her back was so sore that she thought it might snap.

As she watched Last Woman's little potbelly empty his evening milk, she wondered if the air would ever smell fresh again. The stench of burned flesh hung on a breeze too slight to carry it past the village, and the fouled smoke clung to their dirtied lodge covers. She longed to hear a herald announcing they were breaking camp, though even if one did, the people were too depleted in both strength and spirit to move from the place.

Help soon came from an astounding source. While Small Doe was hauling yet another bunch of water sacks, the pound of hooves began shaking the ground. Soon, a long line of warriors rode into the village along with women on horses harnessed in tandem, one behind the other. Small Doe stopped, searching for some indication of who they might be: all Sparrow Hawk bands had gathered before the spotted fever struck. Not until she saw Goes-to-Battle could she guess their identity.

The Whistle-Water Clan! Kills-Behind-Her-Dwelling had said they were the most independent of the Sparrow Hawks, leaving the assembled tribe often in chase of game—and they had killed plenty. Horse after horse was laden with meat; she supposed it was buffalo from the amount. When they saw the extent of the devastation, they immediately joined in with the healthy and recovering, distributing needed encouragement along with their bounty.

They proclaim about the Creator: "He is my refuge and my hiding place, my God in whom I trust." Surely He will save you from the trapper's snare and from deadly disease.

Psalm 91:1-3

Chapter 33

LIKE AN UNWELCOME visitor, the spotted fever tyrannized the village and then vanished. Skin that was formerly smooth took on the appearance of soil turned over for tobacco planting, and the untended herds that had covered the slopes began wandering toward the grasslands. One wound, however, the spotted fever nearly healed.

As Small Doe observed Pacing Wolf from afar, she at last apprehended what the white-haired leader had tried to tell her: the sacrifice of one person's happiness might purchase survival for an entire clan. No matter how often or loudly her white uncle repeated his directions, his words fell to the ground like a flock of birds with broken wings.

Recovering warriors insisted they must honor their dead by giving them proper burials, and their women were determined to search infected lodges for scraps of food. The briefest instructions from Pacing Wolf sent criers throughout the village proclaiming prohibitions that stemmed the fever's spread. Had the Good Men deemed his heart weak, he could not have commanded their respect, and he amply proved their confidence in him was well-founded. He worked tirelessly, utilizing every resource available until the band's remaining vigor sprouted up through the charred and ravaged soil.

As soon as the Many Lodges were able to ride, Hunts-For-Death informed Pacing Wolf and the other clan leaders that they would move their people from "the village of death." All the Women-Who-Talk-Against-Each-Other-Without-Fear received the news gladly—all except Small Doe.

She, too, was happy to leave a place that had held such suffering, but their journey portended a final parting from the people of her birth. Spotted Long-knife and Hair-On-Lip, as the Sparrow Hawks had dubbed the Lieutenant, had helped as long as they could, earning goodwill and respect that no amount of talk could have tendered, but they had a mission to complete. Furthermore, having accomplished their goal so well among her husband's people, they would not be able to justify a swift return. As she glumly watched them ride away, she doubted anyone but Last Woman would speak to her during any given day. She could not have been more wrong.

As the tribe began to toss up their lodge poles beside a stream that trickled through the mountains, the women who had mockingly called her Talks-to-the-Wind invited her to join their conversations; and when Jackrabbit ventured into the Many Lodges' portion of the camp, they closed ranks around Small Doe like pines protecting a clear lake.

This was not all: Hunts-For-Death had kept his promise to Hair-Up-Top, moving Last Woman and her children into his lodge. While Little Blackfoot translated the Scriptures that Small Doe read, his other wives and their daughters could not help but overhear. Soon they gathered to listen, and she even noticed the fatherly leader lingering with his ear inclined toward his lodge-door.

AS THE YAWNING sun covered the horizon with a blanket of pink and coral, Bites-With-Dog tossed a good-sized deer over his horse's rump. "While I was with your woman's people," he told his new clan leader, "I learned why they call her Light Bird. She has the look of a doe but possesses the heart of a cliff swallow."

"Hmph," grunted Pacing Wolf, unsure he welcomed the intrusion on his privacy. Small Doe tormented him no less now than she had while she was away—always within his grasp but ever beyond his reach. She seemed happier since the fever had abated, but what had that to do with him? When he held up his arms, she slipped his shirt over his head and had begun again to brush the tangles from his hair; but beyond spreading his hand across her upper abdomen, he did not try to touch her. He was loath to provoke the wary look that still haunted his dreams.

"I have guided her on two journeys between our people and her father's, but if I glance at her, she flies away. Have you made her fear men or does she pine for you?"

Pacing Wolf did not reply. Though he had many questions about her stay in her parents' village, he was unwilling to disclose how little he had learned.

"I stayed with the older long-knife while there. He keeps a woman with hair as bright as fire."

When Pacing Wolf's eyes darted up, the corners of Bites-With-Dog's lips began to twitch.

"While they thought I was sleeping, she spoke of a warrior who had sung to your woman's heart when she was a girl."

"Why do you tell me?"

"He asked for permission to court her. Her father consented and instructed her to accept this man's horses."

Pacing Wolf said nothing, but Bites-With-Dog noticed that his hands, which had been busy securing the limbs of a buck beneath his sorrel's belly, had grown still.

"She refused."

Pacing Wolf narrowed his eyes but resumed his task. He trusted Bites-With-Dog, but he doubted the story. It was not like Small Doe to disobey her father. She loved and respects him too deeply.

"She is afraid," chuckled Bites-With-Dog, swinging himself onto his horse's back, "that her heart will see only you while she is with him in the darkness."

"She told this to the long-knife's fire-haired woman?" asked Pacing Wolf, forgetting to pretend he did not care.

"No—to the woman's yellow-haired daughter."

While Small Doe lay fresh hides atop the grass under Pacing Wolf's lodge, a female voice she did not recognize called from outside. "Come quickly! Pacing Wolf needs you!"

Throwing back the flap, Small Doe faced a young woman of about fifteen summers whose almond-shaped eyes snapped with urgency.

"Hurry!"

The woman took off toward the ridge, weaving through lodges into a stand of evergreens growing up the tallest of several peaks. Small Doe followed instantly, praying that her husband was not hurt, while the moccasins she chased summoned up a memory. She was sure she had never met her guide, but the round face, glimpsed intermittently as the girl glanced backward, nagged for recognition.

When the young woman entered a thicket of dark pines, she disappeared from view. Small Doe hurried through them, ascending the curving incline as quickly as the small burden in her belly would allow; but by the time she reached the other side, the high rocky crag began casting an oppressive shadow. Only stones, plummeting down a sheer drop ahead, offered hints of her guide's direction; and as the narrowing path further slowed her feet, Small Doe's concern increased to alarm. Within moments, she heard nothing.

Encouraged by all Bites-With-Dog had recounted, Pacing Wolf rode straight through the middle of the lodges. When he arrived at his own, however, Small Doe was not cooking their late meal, as he expected, nor did she duck out to greet him. Assuming his small-thing was slowing her pace, he called her name and dropped the buck near the door. Still, she did not come. Urging his sorrel toward the nearby Blackfoot captive, he watched her ladled food into a dish. "Where is Small Doe?"

Last Woman glanced up and then whispered to her daughter.

"She is in," replied Little Blackfoot, nodding toward his lodge. "We go from her not long."

"Girl!" cried Small Doe, but only the wind replied, raising prickling bumps on her legs as it lifted her skirt's hem. Continuing steadily upward, she grew thankful the sun had not yet closed its eyes; but once they began drooping heavily toward slumber, she could barely see the pathway ahead. She clung to the cliff's marred face, placing one foot in front of the other and refusing to stop until she thudded into a fallen boulder that nearly sent her tumbling backward.

Gripping it tightly, she paused to catch her breath and calm her rapidly beating heart. Inch by inch, she moved along the greatly narrowed ledge, gingerly pressing every spot with her toe before trusting it with her weight. When at last she wound around the boulder's other side, she felt sick with relief.

Her persistence yielded a welcome reward. Just up ahead, she heard leaves rustling. Small Doe hastened toward the sound, grasping tough roots that jutted from the jagged wall to secure her balance, but the rustling suddenly stopped.

Although Pacing Wolf tempered his gait, inside he tore about like a ravenous dog sniffing for any promising trails. Black clouds were gathering overhead, obliterating the moonlight, but he had not found a trace of Small Doe. He could not imagine where she might be. A fresh bundle of sticks leaned against his lodge and their water sacks were full.

He had noticed for the first time since she had returned from her people, she had hung the mirror he had once given her from its peg; and a brief search of the bag she had brought produced the tattered Book he had recently discovered her reading. He had not yet told her about the voice he had heard while fasting in the mountains, but now that the spotted fever and their ensuing journey had ceased to occupy all their waking moments, he longed to hear the Book's words again.

If she wished to leave him, even for another Sparrow Hawk lodge, she would have taken it with her. She was not likely to have ventured over to Never-Sits' side of the village, but knowing nowhere else to look, Pacing Wolf started out in search of his sister.

"Are you there?" called Small Doe, but in reply, she heard only labored breathing. For a moment, she wondered if it were her own breath echoing off the cliff. The blackness had grown dense, almost palpable, and so chilled with moisture that it clung to her braids and dribbled down her cheeks. Calling a third time, she began to shiver and wished she had grabbed her robe. Still, no one answered.

She inhaled deeply to quiet her chattering teeth while she stood straining to discern the direction of the breathing. It seemed to quicken and deepen with every cautious step she took until, at last, she could hear it quite distinctly. Fearing Pacing Wolf was wounded or so near death he was unable to speak, she rushed forward until a flash of lightning lit the sky. The hair on her neck stood on end. Just beyond reach of her outstretched hand hung a disembodied face, light-colored and queerly swaying.

Mountainside boomed a jovial welcome when Pacing Wolf called at his lodge. "It has been long since you last came to visit. Come! Sit in the place of honor by my fire. Many Good Young Men tell me fine things about you. They say you will lead our whole band when Hunts-For-Death visits the Mystery Land."

When his brother-in-law ignored the compliment, the older, larger warrior concluded the visit was not social. "Among-the-Pines," he called, assuming the man had come to see how his daughter had fared with the spotted fever, "Your father is here."

Pacing Wolf grew impatient when the child stepped forward and felt doubly irked when he noticed Jackrabbit, his dead wife's mother, sitting in the shadows beside Never-Sits. Were his sister alone, he would have enlisted her aid.

Looking down into Among-the-Pines' almond-shaped eyes, his heart felt heavy with guilt. He had not done right by the child. She could not help looking like her mother, though the close resemblance was not all that turned his heart away. His grandmother had been right: the child had begun displaying her mother's self-important ways. Jackrabbit would only encourage them.

Small Doe stood stock-still, her pounding heart drowning all other sounds. While washing clothes in the creek shortly after Pacing Wolf had snatched her, the Women-Who-Talked-Against-Each-Other-Without-Fear had spoken of a pale-faced evil spirit that inhabited their territory. She had dismissed their chatter and thought nothing more of it, suspecting they alluded to the light color of her skin; but on this lonely mountain, even the swirling pines seemed full of menace.

As lightning struck again, she noticed the head had drifted toward the ground; but as it struck a third time, she realized her mistake. The head was not floating. It thrust forward from a hulking form, snorting gusts she had mistaken for labored breathing. Round horns, roughly the size of her husband's small war-shield, protruded backward from either side of its bead-like eyes, jerking in rhythm as a front-hoof struck the dirt.

At once, she remembered Never-Sits' enigmatic warning to stay clear of the soft-muzzled herd animal's ominous mate. She pressed her body against the cliff's side, praying he would lack temerity to charge in such darkness, and carefully edged back the way she had come.

Collapsing on the boulder's other side, she sank down, scooting tightly into the crevice formed between it and the rocky wall. The beast was reputed to be sure-footed, but its sight, she supposed, might be poor at night. If it was not and he decided to plunge forward, the narrowed ledge might at least limit his ability to turn. He might pass her hiding place altogether or even plummet over the edge.

"I am taking my daughter," Pacing Wolf announced, surprising his own ears as much as those hanging from three gaping apple-shaped faces. As the child ran to Jackrabbit, he explained, "The fever has hit this side of the village hard. Your grandmother needs rest to regain her strength. Small Doe will care for you."

"Let her stay with me," cajoled Jackrabbit. "That foreign woman does not want her. She will take out her hatred for you on the child."

Hearing this, the little girl began to whimper, but Pacing Wolf grasped her firmly by the shoulder and steered her toward the door. "Your grandmother knows nothing of Small Doe. Has she ever been unkind to you?"

The child slowly shook her head.

"You will dwell in my lodge and treat her with respect, and she will love you as a mother."

As he stood erect, daring Jackrabbit to challenge him, he could not help noticing that Yellow-Fish, the younger of her two daughters, was behaving oddly. When he had mentioned Small Doe, her eyes grew wide like cherries then slid furtively toward her older sister.

Now that he gave thought to Pretty Crow Woman, he realized she had been acting quite unlike herself ever since he had entered her uncle's lodge. She usually proved eager to gain his attention, but tonight she was subdued, almost sullen. Recalling this same threesome had shoved Small Doe into the lake, he wondered what they had been doing earlier and how he might find out without offending Mountainside.

"Why did she crawl back here?" Jackrabbit questioned. "I will bet my best elk-toothed dress that her people cast her out when they discovered she carries your small-thing—if it is yours."

Pacing Wolf kept his face impassive. He refused to let her know how sharply her words provoked him or that he had often wondered why Small Doe had returned. He owned no doubts about the child. Although its mother's abdomen bulged only slightly, the babe had begun forming too long ago for a recent union. Rather than answer Jackrabbit, he addressed Mountainside.

"Small Doe is sensible and *obedient*. All warriors desire a woman with these qualities. Do you agree?"

Mountainside did so heartily but wondered what mischief his brother-in-law plotted. He had little love for either Pacing Wolf and had married Never-Sits only because his first wife needed help with chores. Supposing she complained about the way he treated her, he assumed her cunning brother was laying some sort of trap.

"Beauty fades with age," he shrugged, "but an obedient woman will always be appealing."

"Then our thoughts walk side by side," replied Pacing Wolf, but only a thickheaded warrior could have missed the changes he provoked as he stared at Jackrabbit's daughters. The elder one assiduously kept her eyes to the floor and the younger could not stop fidgeting. "If I could not trust a woman to do what pleases me, I would not offer her a place in my lodge. I would harden my heart if her uncle died in battle and let her wander like those who have no kin."

While Pretty Crow Woman shrunk farther into the shadows, Yellow Fish jumped to her feet; but before a sound left her open mouth, their mother yanked her back down.

"Even a cur will lick a hand that feeds it," sneered Jackrabbit, "until another offers tastier scraps! I have seen how your captive looks at you—like a dog cowering before her master!"

Eager to find Small Doe, Pacing Wolf clenched his jaw shut. Dragging his daughter into the chilly night air, he hoisted her up onto his shoulder and began trotting back toward his lodge.

"She came down?"

"Who?"

"New mother."

"Small Doe? You saw her?"

The little girl nodded her head and turned toward the higher mountains. "Up there."

Awhirl with questions he knew she could not answer, Pacing Wolf affectionately caressed her round cheek. The heights were dangerous on any night, much more so when a storm was brewing. Hurrying to Hunts-For-Death's lodge, he pushed Among-the-Pines inside, telling Last Woman to watch her, and dashed off before the Blackfoot could reply.

As Small Doe sat listening for a clatter of hooves, her thoughts turned to finding her husband. He had been markedly less harsh with her since she had come back, but he was sure to be angry when she did not come. *But I cannot go forward! Where could that girl have gone?*

Fearing her young guide might have fallen, Small Doe was inwardly retracing her steps for a turn she might have missed when she suddenly recalled where she had seen those distinctive moccasins. They had scampered up the path after dunking her in the river. *Pretty Crow Woman!* Laying her head against the huge rock, Small Doe recalled her aged friend's warnings. *She led me here on purpose...and Pacing Wolf...did he...*

Although he still rarely spoke, Small Doe could not believe he would conspire with the girl. His grandmother had confided he detested her, and she knew he would not endanger his small-thing. If he wished to be rid of her, he would simply have cast her out. Realizing her fear for his safety was unfounded, she let out a deep sigh of relief.

He did not need me—Pretty Crow Woman lied so I would follow her—but what will he imagine when he finds me gone?

Almost as an afterthought, Pacing Wolf grabbed his lance and flung a buffalo robe across his shoulder before running toward the pines. He hoped he was choosing the correct course. Thunder clapped loudly; the black clouds would soon let loose their torrents, turning the rocky mountain paths slippery slide.

As he mulled over Pretty Crow Woman's sullen silence, he suspected what Yellow-Fish would have said had her mother not interfered. Among-the-Pines went with them everywhere.

If Small Doe had fled, she would have headed toward the flatlands.

Jackrabbit's remarks chafed at his heart, though Bites-With-Dog's report sharply contradicted them. Pacing Wolf's own observations supported neither. When he had caught her eyes lately, they failed to brighten as they had before Goes-to-Battle tried to take her. They contained questions or looked away, but they never held hatred or bitterness.

The wind picked up strength, making the way treacherous. It tore at his robe and whipped pine needles across his cheeks. He welcomed their sting; it kept his mind alert and pulled it back to his task. Hurtling pebbles down the steep cliff as he raced along its craggy face, he barely had breath to pray.

"I-Am-Savior, please hear me. Small Doe is clever, but the night is cold and the rains will make her way slick. She might fall and break her limbs. She has only her knife to fight bears or wild cats that roam these mountains. I need to find her before she comes to harm. You brought her back to me; show me her trail."

Lord, teach me your way so I may rely on Your faithfulness. Give me a heart that is not divided, so I may fear your name.

Psalm 86:15

Chapter 34

AS A HIGH WIND threaded wisps of hair through Small Doe's lashes, it parted the clouds engulfing the bright full moon. Curling into a ball between the crag and boulder, she laid down her head and whispered between chattering teeth: "I feel like David did, Lord—utterly spent. 'Do not forsake me or stay far from me! Make haste and help me, O Lord of my salvation!'[102]" As she repeated the verses, her breathing grew calmer until, almost inaudibly, she began singing.

> 'How long must my soul bear pain
> and my heart hold sorrow?
> How long will my enemy triumph over me?
> Consider me and answer, O Lord, my God.
> Bring light to my eyes
> or I will sleep the sleep of death.
> Still, I have trusted in Your steadfast love.
> My heart will find joy in Your salvation."[103]

As the last lines lifted her hopes, she raised her voice slightly also.

> "The Lord hears when the righteous cry for help
> and delivers them out of all their distress.
> He is near to the brokenhearted
> and saves those who are crushed in spirit.
> Many are the afflictions of the righteous,
> but the Lord delivers him out of them all."[104]

By the time she began singing the second verse, joy began welling up in her heart. It started like a gentle brook bubbling onto dry ground; but as she finished, it was gushing like the mighty Echata. "He has not left me alone!" she laughed, suddenly understanding this was precisely what her father's old aunt meant. "'Better is one day'—even one moment—'in Your lodge,

Lord'—even in this cold and dark—'than a thousand elsewhere!'"[105] Lifting up her voice, she began singing the Psalm's refrain with jubilant abandon:

> "I will bless the Lord always.
> His praise will be always on my tongue.
> My soul boasts in the Lord.
> May the afflicted hear and be glad.
> "O magnify His name with me
> and let us exalt His name together.
> I ran to the Lord and He answered me
> and delivered me from all my fears!"[106]

As the bright moon stepped out from behind the breaking clouds, Pacing Wolf began to hear the faint sound of a woman grieving. He could not distinguish her words but was surprised the wind could carry her song so far from her lodge. Supposing the spotted fever must have taken her warrior, he wondered which of his tribesmen she mourned.

The higher he climbed, the clearer her song became until he concluded anguish had driven her up the mountain. She sang of her trust in the warrior's fierce heart, her admiration of his valor, and unashamedly boasted about his matchless generosity.

Such a woman should not be left destitute, he decided. *I will discover who she is and supply her a portion of my kills.*

As the woman's singing grew louder, Pacing Wolf grew puzzled. She no longer sounded as if she were grieving but expressing joy, even awe. He found himself growing jealous, wondering how any warrior could inspire such love. He had stirred nothing in his dead woman. She had been a wasteland, soaking up every drop of water and yielding nothing in return. *And in Small Doe, I...*

At once, he recalled where he had heard such praises: in the alcove near the slope of the cave and from within his own lodge. Scattering stones wildly, he plunged up the path, sure now he knew who was singing.

Small Doe heard a skittering of gravel close by, reminding her of the queer horned creature. Scrunching more deeply into the crevice, she kept very still, listening intently as a large dark form thrust itself through the shadows into the moonlight. When it abruptly stopped, a gust of wind picked up and unfurled a loose covering behind it, exposing the fringed leggings of a man.

She assumed he could also see her. If she were more daring, she could have touched his foot; but as the man ran his hand along the wall, she realized the boulder's shadow blocked her from view. Another strong burst of wind almost tore his robe away, but as he quickly reached out to grab it, the moon silhouetted his profile.

"Pacing Wolf!" she whispered. Afraid to believe her eyes, she reached out from the crevice to confirm he was not a dream; and the sound of her voice brought him such forceful relief, he forgot all his defenses. He followed her touch and squatted to enfold her against him so tightly her ribs hurt. She did not care. She clung to him like a frightened child while thunder, clapping loudly against the cliff's side, almost drowned his rhythmic murmurings.

He praised Him-Who-Hears-All-Things for attending to his cries, thanked Him-Who-Sees-All-Things for showing him where to find her, and worshiped I-Am-Savior for keeping her from harm. Small Doe drank in every cadent expression, her happiness etching them deeply into her heart.

As rain splattered on his stiffened hair, he backed into the crevice, pulled her onto his lap, and drew the thick pelt over both of their heads. She relished the warmth of his arms, and he delighted in the gentle way she nestled against him. When at last the storm abated and the moon shone bright and clear, Small Doe tumbled out the events that had stranded her there.

"The young woman disappeared…I was afraid you were hurt… a queer pale face hung swaying in the dark air…"

Pacing Wolf found much that she said an incoherent jumble, but her concern for his welfare was clear, adding to the hope Bites-With-Dog had offered. With uncharacteristic patience, he drew from her the necessary details for him to understand her story until she began to describe her young guide.

He fell silent, rigid with anger at his dead woman's sister and consumed with vengeful contemplations. He would marry Pretty Crow Woman as he had agreed with her father. No one, then, could question his right to beat her; but he not only found the notion revolting, it also pricked his newly sharpened conscience.

When her husband fell silent, Small Doe did likewise. She sensed his anger and wished she had not told him. It ruined the feeling of security his arms were offering and drove away his tenderness. As she lay stiffly in his embrace, growing increasingly wary as the moments stretched longer, he began to speak. His voice sounded so gravelly that she felt it reverberate in his chest.

"Vengeance is mine. I will repay."

The words so surprised her, she forgot her normal caution and sat up so she could see his face. When she asked him why he had said them, he broke into the brightest smile she had ever seen him wear.

"I-Am-Savior," he answered. "He spoke these words to me when I was wandering on these heights."

While her mouth dropped open, Pacing Wolf recounted their meeting and his commitment to walk in Jesus' shadow. Everything in her rippled with happiness. Savoring her reaction, he relaxed against the rock to consider how he might accomplish his pledge. He would encourage those who were willing to listen to her read the Book, and perhaps she could teach them to decipher the strange symbols that held its meaning captive. As she felt his chest expand in a deep, relieving breath, she nestled into the hollow of his shoulder.

"I want no other woman," he murmured, brushing his lips against her hair. "From my first glimpse of you with the silver-haired storyteller, I have wanted you; and you have become part of me, like my arms and my legs. Only in death will I give you up."

Small Doe raised her head again to look into his face, but she felt too overcome by all that overflowed her heart to maintain his gaze. Lying back against his chest, she listened to his strong and steady heart and sighed contentedly: "I am yours altogether."

God is living in your midst. He is a warrior who can deliver. He takes delight in you, and with His love, He will calm all your fears. He shouts over you with joyful songs.

Zephaniah 3:17

Epilogue

WHILE THE SUN rose over the flatlands, Pacing Wolf carried Small Doe down the mountain. Many of the Women-Who-Talk-Against-Each-Other-Without-Fear came running when they saw her, concerned her fire had stayed unlit throughout the night. The Good Men had chosen Pacing Wolf as their clan's new head, but Small Doe's diligence had gained her a place in their hearts.

As their health began returning, each asked their neighbors, "Who left food and water by my door?" The answer was always the same: "Pacing Wolf's Cuts-Off-Our-Heads captive." What one clan knew, others quickly learned until clanswomen whispered whenever she was present, "There is the woman who Kept-Us-Alive."

Bites-With-Dog added to her reputation, recounting his journey to Small Doe's people and her decision to return. Those inclined toward romance hailed her as courageous. Those who preferred the solidity of the mundane lauded her good sense. They were certain Sparrow Hawk warriors possessed superior strength, courage, and cunning to any others. Who would not return to them?

As for Jackrabbit's daughters, Pacing Wolf wanted Mountainside to punish them severely, but when Small Doe secured his heart she also gained his ear. "Blessed are the merciful, for they will gain mercy,"[107] she read, hoping if they repaid evil with good, they might open the girls' hearts to both her and I-Am-Savior.

Unfortunately, they did not. Over the remainder of the summer, however, one problem did resolve itself. Goes-to-Battle, who had wisely moved his lodge to the Whistle Water Clan, heard rumors about Pacing Wolf's intentions toward Pretty Crow Woman and wooed and won her for himself. Alas, when the Foxes fashioned their death-stakes the following spring, he also stole another Lumpwood rival's young wife, but Pretty Crow Woman did not mind. She left his lodge on the back of a hapless Muddy Hand's pony. Small Doe was learning quickly why so many grandmothers raised most of the tribe's children.

THE CREATOR'S GIFT for Pacing Wolf arrived during the Moon of Frost on Lodges. Four days after his birth, Pacing Wolf invited Hunt-For-Death to name him, and his Lumpwood father accepted gladly.

"On the mountain top I fasted," he told Pacing Wolf, "and my heart heard this name. He will be called Wolf-Who-Lays-Down for the rest he has brought you."

Responding after the custom of his people, Pacing Wolf promised Hunts-For-Death a horse when the boy could walk[108] and promised another to Bites-With-Dog for delivering the blessing.

"When we went out against the Yellow Legs," announced his Lumpwood brother, "I was the first to strike a warrior. The blow was hard, and the blow was good. I took the war-club from his hand; this deed was also good. May this child of my friend grow up like these deeds: full of strength, full of cunning."[109] To this he added a wholly new hope: "May he have the courage to place his feet firmly in the steps of I-Am-Savior, the One who has led us to life."

THE SUMMER WOLF-Who-Lays-Down began walking in Pacing Wolf's shadow, Among-the-Pines asked her stepmother, "Is it difficult for you to live among us?"

Small Doe stopped brushing the girl's hair for a moment. "I owned much sorrow when your father first snatched me, but I do not regret it. I feel much like a verse from a psalm we read last evening. "One who goes out weeping, carrying seeds for sowing, will return with shouts of joy, hauling his plenty with him."[110] You are part of that plenty, little one. The Creator has offered me love and purpose beyond all I hoped or imagined. He is truly worth trusting!"

The Spirit and the bride say, 'Come!'

Let him who hears say, 'Come!'

And let all who are thirsty come.

Let all who desire drink freely from the water of life

The One who testifies to these things says,
'Surely, I am coming quickly.

Revelations 22:17 and 20

Even so—come quickly, Lord Jesus!

Straight Flies the Arrow
A novel of love, loyalty, and wonder

Chapter 1

PACING WOLF SILENTLY edged out from under the buffalo robes he shared with his sleeping woman and pulled a hunting shirt over his head. In the dim morning light, her face appeared as smooth and her expression as childlike as it had the morning he had stolen her from an enemy village, but the slight mound raising the buffalo robe atop her mid-section belied the impression. She had already borne him one son, who was nestling peacefully against her far shoulder. He hoped the small-thing growing within her now would be another—this was no time for daughters. Caressing them both with his eyes, he tucked his sharpened knife into his belt.

I do not like leaving them.

In the days before he walked within I-Am-Savior's shadow, he would have entrusted her to Hunts-For-Death, his adoptive Lumpwood father, whom the Good Men had chosen as Real Chief once old Hair-Up-Top had traveled to the Mystery Land. As he now considered doing so, though, he could not rid himself of a vague but niggling anxiety.

Hunts-for-Death would provide for her well, he reasoned, running his thumb along his ax-head to make sure it too was sharp, *but she would not be happy. Her graceful form and features might awaken his attention.*

Although his adoptive father was far past his first vigor, many women still admired him. He kept three wives already, along with the Blackfoot captive old Hair-Up-Top left with him before he died. To this later woman, Small Doe was more sister than friend, but if Hunts-for-Death decided to take her into his bed, jealousy might compel the other three to treat her cruelly. At best, they would allot her the most grueling chores.

As his little son shifted, pushing aside the gleaming black hair that had hidden his diminutive features, additional misgivings about his Lumpwood Father crept over Pacing Wolf's heart. A cleft had begun forming in the common ground they had always shared. It had barely been perceptible at first—a slight crack in a grassless patch of prairie that had drunk little rain—offering Pacing Wolf hope that Hunts-for-Death might yet walk beside him along his new path. Lately, it had widened to a gaping ravine. Several Men-Who-Lead-the-Moving-Bands held The Creator's Book in contempt, not only because a daughter of a hated enemy introduced it to their tribe, but also because it condemned some of their traditions, causing divisions among the people.

Glancing fondly at his daughter, Among-the-Pines, curled in a ball beneath her own covers, Pacing Wolf wished she had already lived through enough summers to draw a warrior's interest. If she had, he could easily secure her a place to dwell if he did not return, and she was sure to offer a home to her young stepmother and toddling brother. They had formed an unmistakable bond. Pretty as his daughter was, however, a girl of seven summers was of little use to a man. She needed twice that many—and more summers were exactly what Pacing Wolf lacked.

As he wound down the river path to bathe, a gust of bitter wind set the fringes of his hunting shirt a flutter. The leafless trees provided little protection, reminding him again of the Old Ones' warnings. The approaching winter would be severe. He must hurry. A mere sliver of the current moon still hung in the sky; soon the Moon When-Deer-Shed-Their-Horns would be nipping at his heels. If the snows came early, they might strand him; and if they were heavy, as they had been the past winter, his Fox cousin or some other rival was sure to start sniffing around his unguarded den.

As Pacing Wolf slung the frigid water from his hair, he shook off the distasteful possibility. One by one, he considered other clansmen; and one by one, his heart turned each away. All the Good Men he most admired had wives, returning Pacing Wolf to his second objection to Hunts-for-Death. Indeed, few men tried in battle remained unmarried.

I will speak with Bites-With-Dog about his eldest, Held-Back-the-Enemy. He walks closely behind I-Am-Savior and though he possesses only one more summer than Small Doe, he displays much courage and good sense.

Last spring, the young man had used his bow to pin down a stray party of Grass Lodges while his older companions circled around to attack them from the rear, earning him a new name and token of valor. Pacing Wolf had not been among them, but as they had hunted the previous summer, he had seen Held-Back-the-Enemy encounter a great cat. The young man had stood perfectly still, bow drawn, as the animal approached and had not let his arrow fly until the cat's crouching haunches confirmed its intentions. From that day forward, Pacing Wolf had grown so impressed with his skill and courage, he had acted as his sponsor when the Lumpwoods last initiated new warriors into their society.

"I-Am-Savior," prayed Pacing Wolf, wringing rivulets of water from his long, sleek braids. "You know how it is between Small Doe and me. I have kept the promises I made the night she consented to become my woman, providing food for her belly and hides to keep her warm. Often, I have asked

You to protect my family, how can I do less for the Many Lodges? They have chosen me to lead our clan. Can I stay in my lodge and listen while they wail?

"You are The-One-Who-Sees-All-Things. Keep my woman and son from hunger while I pursue her evil kinsman; and if I have finished what You set before me to do on earth, receive me to Yourself.[1] I am not afraid of Wild Dog or to make the journey home to You; but Small Doe is your daughter—to whom should I entrust her and our children?

He-Who-Sees-All-Things will watch between you and me while we are hidden from each other's sight.

Genesis 31:49

End Notes

[1] Matthew 5:40
[2] Psalm 37:8
[3] Matthew 12:25
[4] Exodus 14:21-22
[5] 2 Kings 19
[6] Acts 12:1-18
[7] Book of Esther
[8] Psalm 33:4
[9] Mark 10:27
[10] Psalm 139:12, 16
[11] Revelations 20:1-3
[12] 2 Kings 23:10
[13] Proverbs 15:1
[14] I Peter 2:19-21
[15] Genesis 2:24
[16] Psalm 30:5
[17] Romans 8:28
[18] I Peter 3:2
[19] Proverbs 31:12
[20] Matthew 5:44
[21] Luke 6:28, Romans 12:19
[22] I Samuel 23:27
[23] Lamentations 3:24
[24] 2 Samuel 13:1-15
[25] 2 Peter 2:20b-23
[26] Corinthians 12:9
[27] Psalm 27:1
[28] II Samuel 13:1-14
[29] Genesis 34:2-5
[30] Deuteronomy 32:35, Hebrews 10:30
[31] Psalm 33:4
[32] Psalm 139:16
[33] Hebrews 11: 25
[34] Dale D. Old Horn, Dale D., and Tim McCleary, "About the Crow Genealogy: Political Organization," Library@LittleBighornCollege, retrieved 2007.
[35] 2 Corinthians 5:7
[37] Psalm 139:16
[38] Matthew 10:28
[39] Matthew 10:19
[40] Proverbs 31:10
[41] Matthew 6:9
[42] Romans 8:38-39
[43] Leviticus 20:3
[44] Genesis 1:2
[45] Genesis 14:18-20
[46] Genesis 17:1
[47] Genesis 21:33
[48] Genesis 16:13
[49] Curtis, Edward S. *The North American Indian.*, *Vol. 4*, p. 116 New York: Johnson Reprint Originally published in 1909, Northwestern University Library
[50] Psalm 51:17
[51] I Peter 2:22-25
[52] I Peter 3:1-6
[53] Deuteronomy 32:29
[54] Psalm 139
[55] Genesis 39:20
[56] Galatians 3:16
[57] Luke 22:32
[59] Edward S. Curtis, *The North American Indians*, *Vol. 4*, pp.8, 9-10
[60] Psalm 17:15
[61] Adapted from a speech by Chief Eelapuash (1830), Graetz, Crow Country: Montana's Crow Tribe of Indians. Billings: Northern Rockies Publishing Company, 2000, Library @ Little Bighorn College, retrieved 2007.
[62] I Peter 3:6
[63] Philippians 4:8
[64] Genesis 7:6
[65] Genesis 2:18
[66] Genesis 1:22
[67] Esther 2
[68] Esther 4:13
[69] John 17:1-4
[70] Hebrews 10:29-30
[71] Edward S. Curtis, *North American Indians*, *Vol. 4*, p. 15
[72] Ibid., pp. 12,15
[73] Ibid., p.16-17
[74] Ibid., p.17
[75] Ephesians 5:22-3

[76] Psalm 39:1
[77] I Peter 2:19-20
[78] Psalm 116:1-9
[79] Jim Beckworth
[80] James 4:8
[81] Romans 12:3
[82] Ruth 1-4
[83] Genesis 30-50
[84] 2 Corinthians 12:9
[85] I Corinthians 7:15
[86] Psalm 31:10
[87] Matthew 5:32
[88] Romans 8:6-10
[89] Romans 6:1
[90] John 14:15
[91] Isaiah 54:5
[92] Matthew 19
[93] Exodus 3:14: YHWH: "I am" or "I be" plus Hosea: "savior/ salvation"
[94] Philippians 4:17
[95] Job 19:25-26
[96] Edward S. Curtis, *The North American Indians, Vol. 4*, p. 35
[97] Genesis 29:31
[98] Genesis 29:33
[99] Genesis 29:34
[100] Genesis 29:35
[101] Jan McCray, *The Love Every Woman Needs,* Grand Rapids: Chosen Books, 1997, p.87-95.
[102] Psalm 38:21-22
[103] Psalm 13
[104] Psalm 34:17-19
[105] Psalm 84:10
[106] Psalm 34:1-4
[107] Matthew 5:7
[108] Edward S. Curtis, *North American Indians, Vol. 4,* p. 25
[109] Ibid. p.25
[110] Psalm 126:6

Author's Note

Light Bird's Song is a work of fiction, though several historical figures and events have been incorporated into the plot. I have intended to accurately reflect the culture of the Sparrow Hawk Nation whose territory encompassed thirty million acres along the entire length of the Yellowstone, Clark's Fork, Bighorn, Little Bighorn, Tongue, and the Powder Rivers. My primary source has been the late Edward S. Curtis' voluminous work entitled *North American Indians*. Published in 1909, it records first-hand accounts of everyday life among this fascinating people. For further study of the Sparrow Hawks, refer to the 4th volume.

As in *A River too Deep*, I have tried to avoid erroneous stereotypes, glorifications or denigrations, and have used this nation's own names and phrases, translated into English, to depict tribal structure, the physical characteristics of the locale, and items encountered in everyday life.

Concerning Scriptures written within the text: they are the fictitious translation of Major Anderson from *A River too Deep*. I have taken the liberty after consulting numerous Bible translation and an interlinear of altering the phraseology when necessary in order to render the verses understandable to a Plain's Indian population in the early 1800s. After each passage, I have included the complete reference should readers wish to check them in their own Bibles.

Pacing Wolf's encounter with "a voice" is modified from an actual event that happened to a trusted individual quite close to my heart.

Writing books is far easier for me than making readers aware they exist, so please consider leaving an honest review on Goodreads or the site where you purchased Light Bird's Song. I am deeply grateful for any help, and reviews make a huge difference.

Lastly, you have been getting to know me (nothing could more accurately reflect my heart than this series); I would enjoy getting to know you. If this idea appeals to you or if you would like to know more about walking in I-Am-Savior's steps, please drop by my Facebook author page. I have made many new and dear friends this way!

Meet the Author

Sydney Tooman Betts and her protagonist-inspiring husband currently reside in the Shenandoah Valley near the extensive cavern system that inspired the setting for several early chapters of this book.

While single, Ms. Betts (B.S. Bible/Missiology, M.Ed.) was involved in a variety of cross-cultural adventures in North and Central America. After marrying, she and her husband lived in Europe and the Middle East where he served in various mission-support capacities. Her teaching experiences span preschool to guest lecturing at the graduate level and serving as the Sunday School Superintendent, Children's Church Director, or Women's Ministries facilitator in several evangelical denominations.

Before penning her first novel, *A River too Deep,* she ghost-wrote several stories for an adult literacy program.

Made in the USA
Middletown, DE
18 November 2021